DIVEMASTERS

COMPLETE SERIES

GOING DOWN

GOING DEEP

GOING HARD

JAYNE RYLON

Copyright © 2016 by Jayne Rylon

All rights reserved. No part of this book may be used or reproduced in any manner whatsoever without written permission from the author, except in the case of brief quotations used in reviews.

This book is a work of fiction. The names, characters, places, and incidents are products of the writer's imagination or have been used fictitiously and are not to be construed as real. Any resemblance to persons, living or dead, actual events, locale or organizations is entirely coincidental.

eBook ISBN: 978-1-941785-19-5
Print ISBN: 978-1-941785-99-7

Edited By Mackenzie Walton
Cover Art By Jayne Rylon
Interior Print Book Design By Jayne Rylon

OTHER BOOKS BY JAYNE RYLON

DIVEMASTERS
Going Down
Going Deep
Going Hard

MEN IN BLUE
Night is Darkest
Razor's Edge
Mistress's Master
Spread Your Wings
Wounded Hearts
Bound For You

POWERTOOLS
Kate's Crew
Morgan's Surprise
Kayla's Gift
Devon's Pair
Nailed to the Wall
Hammer it Home
More The Merrier

HOTRODS
King Cobra
Mustang Sally
Super Nova
Rebel on the Run
Swinger Style
Barracuda's Heart
Touch of Amber
Long Time Coming

Compass Brothers

Northern Exposure
Southern Comfort
Eastern Ambitions
Western Ties

Compass Girls

Winter's Thaw
Hope Springs
Summer Fling
Falling Softly

Play Doctor

Dream Machine
Healing Touch

4-Ever

4-Ever Theirs
4-Ever Mine

Standalones

Nice & Naughty
Where There's Smoke
Middleman
Report For Booty

Racing For Love

Driven
Shifting Gears

Red Light

Through My Window
Star

Can't Buy Love
Free For All

Paranormals
Picture Perfect
Reborn

Pick Your Pleasures
Pick Your Pleasure
Pick Your Pleasure 2

CONTENTS

JAYNE RYLON
NEW YORK TIMES BESTSELLING AUTHOR
"Jayne can melt the words off your ereader!"
~Guilty Pleasures Reviews
GOING DOWN
DIVEMASTERS #1

DEDICATION

For Mr. Rylon, who has sacrificed by traveling to each gorgeous setting in the Divemasters books even though he's afraid of flying, then explored them along with me to be sure my research was as thorough as possible. I know that was a tough job for you. ☺

You're the best SCUBA buddy a girl could ask for (except for that time you were sure my dive computer had gotten stolen when it was actually in your BCD pocket for the whole week of diving). I hope you enjoy the character I made you in this series...not that you read my books! But just in case, someday, you peek inside this one.

ONE

Archer Banks's ringing cell trampled the tropical night symphony composed of lulling waves, chirping bugs, and rustling palms. He would have fumbled around on the nightstand to silence the racket if an armful of bronzed, slender woman hadn't stopped him. After rolling the beach bunny off his chest, he settled her gently on the edge of his double bed. Refusing to be distracted by her wild, sun-bleached mane, or the way the moonlight streaming in the window highlighted her damn-near-perfect ass, he forced his dick's attention from the adorable snuffle she surrendered as she burrowed into his lumpy pillow.

Archer turned his back on all that natural beauty. He rebelled against everything in his soul by lunging instead for one of the only remnants of offensive technology he allowed to intrude in his life. He didn't have a choice, really, since the hunk of plastic threatened the integrity of his eardrums by refusing to shut the fuck up.

Only one contact in the entire world had been programmed with the specific God-awful racket that now blared from his phone. The man who was instructed to interrupt Archer's solitude only in a life-or-death emergency.

Fuck. Fuck. Fuck.

Phone in hand, halfway unlocked, he launched himself from the freshly laundered sheets, which smelled of sunshine and ocean spray. He growled to the caller, "Don't expect me to rush to that bastard's side for some kind of deathbed confessional."

Archer figured he maybe should have said hello first. His bitterness had rushed out like pus from a festering wound before he could manage anything else. Odd, since he would have sworn these old injuries were scarred over by now.

"No need. He's gone." The familiar voice on the other end of the line, thousands of miles away, made Archer more homesick than the news of his own loss. "It was fast. Painless. Though probably traumatizing for the young ladies your father was attempting to have sex with when the stroke hit."

"Jesus." Archer stumbled across the room. He slipped out the sliding glass door that led to a half-rotten deck barely big enough for a pair of plastic chairs, then down the three steps to the beach. Naked, he sank onto his knees in the sand. He glanced over his shoulder toward the woman whose name wasn't nearly as memorable as the way she'd sucked him off before getting him hard again, then riding him with thighs powerful enough to cling to a breaching humpback.

Brittany! That was it. He was *almost* sure.

Was he turning into everything he'd spent his entire adult life trying to distance himself from? Had his father remembered the names associated with the assassin pussies that had finally managed to take the bastard out?

Archer's stomach churned at the thought. Acid seared his esophagus. Just like it had before he'd left that world he'd never belonged in. He hadn't looked back since. Not even for a glimpse of the girl he'd abandoned, who wouldn't welcome his attention after what had happened.

This was definitely going to be the second worst night of Archer's life.

"Sir?"

He shook his head when the question came softly—kindly, even—from his family's butler, who'd been more like a true relative than any Archer shared filthy blue blood with. It was the reason he'd borrowed the guy's name when he'd fled and remade himself. "Come on, Banks. You changed my shitty diapers plenty of times. Don't you think formality is uncalled for? I've never been that person. Much to my father's disappointment—"

"Archer." A soft chuckle warmed Banks's tone this time. "That might have been true once. But not always. Over time, I think he might have envied your escape. Admired it, though he was too proud to admit such things. Or maybe he respected you too much to go against your wishes and contact you to let you know."

"I highly doubt that." Archer swallowed hard against the feelings he'd thought he'd buried deeper than a pirate's treasure. He might be a thirty-one-year-old man, but some small part of him would always regret that he hadn't been able to be the son his father wanted.

"Well, this is for certain. He didn't truly disown you. You were never cut out of his will. In fact, despite your wishes, he left you everything."

"Shit! *Everything*?"

"His entire holdings. All of it, down to the last cent." Banks delivered the most devastating news of the night.

Everything Archer had never wanted had finally caught up with him. Golden chains ensnared his wrists and ankles, keeping him from imagining he could ever move freely again. He'd seen firsthand what it took to run an empire.

As quickly as a barracuda snaps up its unsuspecting dinner, Archer had gone from beach bum to billionaire.

Fuck him, life as he knew it—and *loved* it—was over.

He scrubbed his hands through his hair and caught sight of the woman he'd left in his bed dressing hurriedly by the light of the wall-mounted gooseneck lamp before blowing him a kiss and heading for the door.

At least he'd gone out with one hell of a bang.

Literally.

"It's not exactly a death sentence, sir."

"Banks," he growled.

"I mean...*Archie*."

The shock of hearing that long-lost nickname, right now, had Archer blinking fiercely. Somehow he didn't think there was enough salt in the air to blame his reaction on that. "It feels like it. I'm proud of who I am these days. I don't want the money. I don't want to be like him. I can't afford to lose myself."

He scrunched his eyes closed. It was as if he were a recovering alcoholic who'd been offered an entire chain of distilleries. Archer knew unimaginable wealth could corrupt him. It hadn't been easy to sacrifice everything once, but he'd quit superfluous material possessions cold turkey and had never been happier than he was here, with next to nothing.

Good friends, a job he loved, willing women, and time to enjoy life. Those things were priceless.

"So we'll give it away. Form an umbrella foundation that supports any number of charities, funds, and projects for worthwhile causes. A lot of problems can be solved with seven billion dollars, give or take." Banks's solution seemed genius. Simple yet complicated at the same time.

"Perfect. Will you help me? And by help me, I mean run it. Make the day-to-day decisions. I don't need to know the details. Use your judgment."

"Of course. If that's still what you want, after you've really thought about it some," Banks promised. "I am the estate's executor. It will take some time to settle things. Let me see to the legalities, and you start dreaming about who you'd like to help. This fortune could change the world."

"I...uh... Okay, thanks." Archer couldn't believe this was happening. "Name it after yourself. Call it the Banks Foundation."

He had to make sure his father's name wasn't included. No glory for that fucker.

"I suppose that's naming it after *us*, isn't it?" Banks sounded pleased with that. At least he didn't mind that Archer had appropriated his name in his attempt to go incognito.

"Make sure you pay yourself, too. A shit-ton. Ten times whatever you think is an outrageous salary. You deserve a hazard bonus for the decades you've put up with my family's shit. God knows I couldn't do it. As if that wasn't obvious when I bailed."

"I will." Banks laughed, then said warmly, "For the record, I'm proud of you, too. Dream big, Archie."

Only slightly after the ass crack of dawn, Archer blocked the past several sleepless hours from his mind. He verified the headcount of their boatload of guests for the morning's two-tank SCUBA dive. Then he began double-checking the equipment. Sticking to routine ensured he never missed anything vital. After all, it was his job to guarantee no one interrupted the fun-and-sun portion of their vacation by dying on his watch.

As he worked, he surreptitiously observed each of the three buddy pairs he'd be going down with. How they set up their gear was a decent indication of how they would dive. At least, he'd found that to be true in the past.

One couple, a husband and wife team, had stacked their gear neatly so that the first thing they'd need was on top and the last at the bottom. They spoke quietly as they worked seamlessly, assisting each other with their wet suits before unhurriedly progressing through their own personal buddy checklists. As he watched, they verified today's plans against their dive computers to ensure they wouldn't exceed their no-decompression limits given the nitrogen load they'd taken on in their shore dives the day before.

Of course, Archer had already done the same thing before they'd left the shop. Still, he was glad they were independent divers and didn't rely on his word for it.

They'd be fine.

Two brothers made up the second pair. They'd come to the dive shop yesterday afternoon asking plenty of questions about the boat, the tour size, the dive location, the depth of the sites they'd be visiting, typical currents in the area, notable marine life to look out for, and recent weather patterns. They had shared their religiously completed logbooks, which detailed over a hundred dives each, with the shop manager, too.

Archer wasn't worried about them either.

The third set of guests... He shook his head. There were a couple like them in every bunch.

True, the diving here in Bonaire—a fairly dinky desert island off the coast of Venezuela in the Southern Caribbean, next door to Aruba and Curaçao—was some of the easiest and most beautiful in the world. It made it a great spot for newbies to put some experience under their weight-belts. He didn't have any problem teaching the tadpoles good habits or helping them gain confidence in their emerging skills.

Unfortunately, this duo had enough experience to know better than some of the shit they were pulling already. They bickered, sniping at each other for losing this thing or that thing—extraneous, flashy doodads they probably didn't know how to use anyway. Their jumbled gear spilled across the modest thirty-six-foot boat's deck, causing Archer's fellow divemaster, Tosin, to have to dodge it as he helped his own half-dozen divers on the other side of the vessel. The problem children had already dunked their boots in the camera-and-regulator-only rinse tank before anyone could stop them.

Archer could also tell by the bulges of lead stuffing the pockets of their buoyancy control devices relative to their average builds that they were about to go overboard with far too much weight. Some was necessary to keep divers down. That much could be dangerous. He mentally prepared himself to grab for them if they overcompensated for their inevitable negative buoyancy at depth by puffing up their BCD's with an entire blimp's worth of air, which would expand on the ascent, rocketing them toward the surface as if they were helium balloons slipping free from a toddler's grasp.

Spending the day filling out incident reports and loading Mr. and Mrs. Yelly McYellington into a hyperbaric chamber after their lungs popped or they gave themselves the bends would not improve his pissy mood.

He kept trying to pretend today was exactly like the past 4,380 other days—give or take some—he'd done pretty much the same thing as this. Pencil lead snapped when he pressed too hard against his ratty clipboard mid check-off.

"Rough night?" Miguel winked as he took his place at the boat's helm and curled his fingers around the wheel. Though he was the third divemaster onboard this morning, it was his turn to drive. He'd stay on the surface, assist any divers who aborted early for mechanical, health, or safety concerns, and make sure nobody surfside bothered their stuff.

Things could be worse, Archer acknowledged. At least he'd get to dive today.

He grunted. "You have no idea."

Nor would they any time soon. Discussing serious personal matters in front of their clients was a no-no. Besides, he had to find the right time to come clean to his best friends about his sordid past.

They pushed off the dock and headed through the muted peach-and-rose post-dawn for Klein Bonaire, an *exceptionally* dinky uninhabited blob of land less than a mile offshore from the main island. Protected by the curvature of Bonaire, it held plenty of opportunities for excursions. Most of the guests went shore diving on their own when unguided. The guys preferred to take them somewhere they couldn't reach in the rusty white mini pick-up trucks that came standard with their condo rentals.

"She did look like a wild catch, you lucky bastard," Tosin joked from where he meticulously verified everyone's equipment set-up. Another set of eyes. He had their backs.

Just like Archer and Miguel would have his. Focused, he thankfully didn't read too much into Archer's lack of a response. He turned on tanks, checked air pressure gauges, and helped a few people with rental gear clip their neon-yellow secondary regulators to the proper place for easy access in case anything went haywire with their primary.

Considering the three of them also serviced the equipment at the shop they currently worked for, Archer didn't think that was likely. Never hurt to have a spare, though. Especially when you were more than a breath's worth of a swim from the surface and counted on it to deliver your air supply.

Twelve guests, two divemasters, and one captain.

Archer, Tosin, and Miguel had worked for operations that ran much bigger ratios of clients to guides, but they preferred not to. This way they could make sure everyone had a safe, personalized experience.

Today, Archer's group would be staying shallower than Tosin's. That meant he had the less experienced people. Or in the case of his married couple, ones who preferred nicer light for capturing the best underwater photos and videos. The brothers had chosen a depth that would allow them to stay under the longest. Another smart choice, Archer thought.

If he only had a few days a year or every couple of years to dive while on vacation, he'd milk every one of them, too. Sounded like hell to him.

Different priorities for different folks. Everyone had their own reasons for the decisions they made. No different than him. At least that's what he promised himself to assuage his guilt for not being honest with his two best friends about his life before they'd started exploring paradises together nearly a dozen years earlier. Twice for not telling them about how everything had changed overnight.

He'd confess...eventually. When he could convince himself that it didn't matter and wouldn't impact the partnership they'd built. Part of him screamed that wouldn't be possible, not when he told them about the worst of it. About the unforgivable thing he'd done to *her*.

Archer couldn't help himself. A vision of a young woman with hair fanned out around her and gorgeous eyes looking up at him as he made love to her flashed into his mind. It simultaneously turned him on and made him feel sick.

So he ignored any further ribbing from Miguel and Tosin. Let them think what they would. Sure, his date had wrung a few solid orgasms from him, but he'd already practically forgotten about that. God knew he could use a few more to relax him now.

What would he do if this whole existence disappeared? If he had to go back, he'd bleach out and die off like coral in ever-warming ocean waters. He wouldn't be able to survive in those conditions.

Archer gripped the edge of the cabin and stuck his face into the wind, closing his eyes as he savored the strengthening sunrays and the salt spray pelting his cheeks. He wasn't ready to let go.

Not now.

Not ever.

Miguel interrupted his wandering thoughts with a low warning. "Archer, behind you."

He snapped around, searching for the problem.

Married couple had finished getting ready. Without distractions, people sometimes had too much time on their hands. It seemed that was the case today, as they skimmed across the surface of the water toward their destination.

Another common occurrence.

"Need help?" He forced himself to smile as he approached the pair. Crouching down, he held on to the rinse tank at the center of the boat to keep his balance on the moving vessel.

"Sorry, I get nervous. Every time." The wife swiped at a stray lock, putting it right back where it had started for only a millisecond before a gust slapped it over her eyes once more. Glamour had no place in diving. Skin-tight suits, wind-blown hair, an odd assortment of UV protection—hats, oversized sunglasses, rash guards—and mismatched towels. That's what he considered their uniform.

Functional. Not too pretty. Definitely informal. Exactly the way he liked things.

Archer wondered if Banks would work some magic and keep him from having to wear an entirely different kind of suit for the first time in a decade. Or, God forbid, a tux. Could the man really pull off the legal and financial shit without dragging Archer back to the States in person?

Lost in thought, he hesitated too long in reassuring his charge. She'd progressed to biting her lip as her husband squeezed her knee. His friends had him covered as usual, though.

Tosin piped up. "No worries. If you don't do this every day, it's easy to get rusty. But you'll be diving with the best. I guarantee when you put your mask in the water and take a peek at the reef below you, your nerves will disappear. Besides, Archer is willing to hold your hand the whole way if you need some extra reassurance."

Great, he didn't need his ass kicked by a jealous husband today. Usually they saved that line for the single ladies. And meant it. Diving with a woman was probably the most intimate experience he'd ever had with one. Fortunately, this husband chuckled, confident in his bond with his wife and seemingly grateful for the divemasters putting her at ease.

Archer wondered what it would be like to have that sort of relationship.

He, Tosin, and Miguel had never stayed in one place long enough to try. Being pinned down like that sounded like torture, except for one or two things—like, say, decent home cooking—they might be missing out on. It had seemed like an easy sacrifice before.

Suddenly, he was second-guessing everything.

Damn his father.

Even from the grave, the bastard had the power to fuck with Archer's head.

Tosin gave him a kick in the ass.

Nervous lady. Right. Archer shook his head, probably making his dark hair stick up worse than it already had been. He didn't give a shit about that. "Tosin's right. You're prepared. I watched you set up. Why don't we go over the dive plan as a group?"

Head in the game once more, he gathered his six charges around and spoke loudly enough to be heard over the engine. "This is going to be a nice and easy dive at one of our favorite sites, Knife. The boat will be moored in about fifteen feet of water. Sandy bottom. We're going to head out over the ridge of the reef, where the sea floor begins to slope down. I'll drop to about fifty feet or so and judge the current. It's usually going east from here, so we'll likely turn right, keeping the reef on that side of us. Stay with your buddies, wherever you're comfortable. I'll be using a very conservative profile. As long as you let me be the deepest person on the dive and the farthest ahead, you'll be all set, even if you aren't confident in reading your computers or the battery goes out or whatever."

He'd added that last part for his problematic pair.

"Whoever hits eighteen-hundred PSI first will signal to me using the half-tank sign." As a reminder, Archer demonstrated, putting one hand up and the other across the top so that it made something like a T. "At that point, the whole group will turn around. We'll ascend—*slowly.*"

Extra pointed stare at the disaster duo there.

Unfortunately, they were digging around in their pockets, not paying attention.

"Stay around twenty to thirty feet deep and put the reef on your left for the return swim. The current will be in our favor, helping us back to the boat with less exertion in a shorter amount of time. Plus, the decreased pressure at the shallower depth will ensure we make it there with plenty of air left. Feel free to use it to explore the area beneath the boat. Tosin and Miguel spotted a seahorse and a frogfish in that exact location last week. We may get lucky. I'll be sure to point out anything of interest so you can take pictures or come in for a closer look.

"When you're down to about eight hundred pounds of air, I'll send you up to the base of the boat's mooring line to do your safety stop. Stay for three minutes at fifteen feet. Your computer will count it down for you. Then ascend nice and easy to the boat. Miguel will be waiting to help you out. As always, please remember this is a protected marine reserve. Do not touch anything. Keep your distance from the reef, especially the soft corals. Don't harass the animals. And definitely leave only bubbles behind."

With a plan in place, his nervous diver seemed more relaxed. Good thing, since they'd reached the mooring pin. A buoy connected by a line to a concrete slab carefully placed on the sea floor allowed the boat to stay in one place without dropping an anchor that could tear up the reef.

Miguel and Tosin were securing a rope to the mooring pin. Archer checked his tank one last time, ducked into his BCD, snapped himself in, tightened the straps, and headed for the platform at the back of the boat. His gear seemed heavier than usual. Or maybe he was simply off balance. He hated to admit, even to himself, that he might be reeling from the news Banks had given him.

He slipped on his fins and mask then waited for the all clear from Miguel. When his friend flashed the sign, Archer turned to his group and said, "I'll be waiting in the water when you're ready. Miguel will help you if you need anything prior to entry."

Tosin's group of more advanced divers were already giant striding into the ocean and bobbing behind the boat, talking excitedly about how clear the water was and what they might see. A few were hoping to catch a lionfish for dinner. The species wasn't indigenous to the Caribbean and had been devouring juvenile fish on the reef, so it was open hunting season. Malicious and delicious, as the locals liked to describe them.

With a final glance over his shoulder and a nod from Miguel, Archer put one hand on his mask, the other over his regulator, then took a single step out into the ocean.

A curtain of bubbles rose around him as he plummeted a few feet below the cerulean surface. He loved the moment he became part of the sea again. The puff of air he'd added to his BCD before entering lifted him enough that his head stuck out of the water, though, as he waited for his guests to join him.

One by one, they splooshed into the water.

When all six of his charges were huddled around, peeking at the hidden world below their dangling flippers, he asked, "Who's ready to go down?"

He flashed the thumbs-down. In return, he received an okay gesture from most of his divers. Of course, the sixth one—part of his trouble couple—shot back a thumbs-up. In diving language that meant "ascend", not "awesome". He shook his head and the diver corrected himself, changing to an okay instead.

With that, Archer popped his regulator back in, held his deflator hose up with his left hand, dumped the air from his BCD, and began to descend. Water filled his ears and closed over his head as he entered the magical universe beneath the surface. At least for an hour or so, he could forget his worries.

Had to, in order to do his job right.

These folks trusted him with their lives. He'd never lost a diver yet, and didn't plan to start today. Sure, they were only fifty-three feet below the surface of the Caribbean Sea.

Still plenty deep enough to drown.

That wouldn't be happening on his watch. If nothing else, he was certain of one thing.

He was a damn fine divemaster.

∽ THREE ∾

month later, Archer did a lazy frog kick, propelling himself through the warm, blue ocean. Tosin was a few feet to his right and Miguel a bit ahead of them as he peered at the shoal of squids that hovered in the shallows nearby. Their fins fluttered along the length of their bodies like a girl's skirt ruffling in the wind. They changed colors and textures as their tentacles waved, flashing some sort of mesmerizing message the humans in their midst couldn't decipher.

Though they'd seen these animals or ones like them many times before, the cephalopods still fascinated Archer. His friends, too.

Sure, it was their day off. That didn't keep them out of the water.

Instead, they got to enjoy their time below the surface instead of worrying about anyone else. Miguel and Tosin were plenty capable of taking care of themselves. So was he. They glided offshore from Windsock, a dive site they visited often. It got its name from the device at the end of the island's runway, which was right across the street from the beach where they'd made their shore entry for today's excursion.

Though they normally set an easy pace on their guided dives so that the tourists who'd hired them could keep up while gawking at the marine life surrounding them, today they progressed even more slowly. Deep, measured respiration maximized their bottom time. It also forced Archer to chill out for a while—a skill he seemed to have lost any time he wasn't underwater lately.

Despite the fact that they'd already been down more than an hour, they hadn't covered nearly as much ground as they did when they were escorting passing visitors through as much of the aquatic landscape as possible.

Keen eyes, trained, could pick out any number of curiosities less experienced divers would zip right past, none the wiser. Like the lobster hiding beneath a vase sponge at depth, or the seahorse clinging to a swaying soft coral a few hundred feet back, or the teeny Pederson cleaner shrimp nestled in an anemone. They went about their business less than three feet from his face right then.

Each thing he saw awed him, as if it were his first time witnessing the splendor of this environment. Down here, Archer's troubles couldn't eclipse his wonder.

The only other time he experienced a rush this intense followed by contentment this profound was during an epic fuck. Just like then, no matter how hard he tried, he couldn't make it last forever. Too soon, regret rushed in. When compared to the single night he'd spent with the girl whose name he couldn't bear to think—even to himself—every other experience paled, even if it made him a sick fuck to admit it.

Tosin clinked a carabiner against his tank a couple times. When he had their attention, he flashed his low-air signal. Together, the three of them turned toward the shore and made their way to the outcropping of fire coral they used as their safety stop marker when they dove here.

Those final 180 seconds ticked by in a flash. Literally, as Archer watched the lacey reflections of the powerful sun dancing across the sea floor. They lit up the electric blue spots and fluorescent yellow tail on the juvenile damselfishes peeking out from between the blades below him.

How many of them would survive long enough to thrive on the reef? Despite their best attempts at hiding, the majority would be gobbled up by something higher on the food chain before they could fully mature.

He wondered if his odds were even half as good as the ones dealt to the fingerlings, who darted into some hidden nook when Archer's shadow passed over them.

After their countdown completed, they followed each other single-file through a channel in the coral, over a bed of rubble. Archer's computer marked each foot they rose, from fifteen to five. Before he was ready to rejoin the realm of land-lovers, his head crested the surface.

"Did you see how that thing almost ran into me?" Miguel was pumped over his close encounter with the squid.

"It was awesome. I could see the surface of its skin changing colors and my own reflection in its eyeball. Lucky it didn't hypnotize me or some shit!" Tosin joined in.

Usually, the first moments above water bubbled over with excited chatter as everything they'd been thinking rushed out once they regained the ability to speak. Sure, they had perfected their own version of sign language, and carried slates to write notes to each other when that wouldn't suffice, but nothing beat talking about their discoveries.

Today, Archer had nothing to contribute.

The whole world had flipped upside down. Dropping his regulator and taking his first breath of air from the atmosphere, he suddenly felt like he was drowning.

He sighed as he braced himself against the waves in thigh-deep water, then tugged on the spring straps of his fins, completing his transformation from merman to stealth billionaire. A guy he wasn't sure he wanted to be anymore.

With one final glance over his shoulder, he ducked his head and trailed behind his friends.

They trundled through the gentle surf toward the beach. Salt water sluiced off him, making his footprints in the sand turn dark and clumpy. He relished the burn in his calves and thighs as he hauled himself and his sixty-plus pounds of equipment up the unstable incline, over rocks and past cacti, until they reached their truck, parked at the side of the road.

No need for a gym membership when this was part of their daily regime. Sometimes they did as many as five dives in a day. Often they followed it up with some midnight cardio that worked entirely different sets of muscles. Exhausting, but he'd never gotten sick of it.

Miguel rested his tank on the tailgate as he slipped off his mask, then unsnapped from his BCD. "If you guys will break down my stuff, I'll go get in line at the street-meat stand."

Fish from a roadside tin can? Guaranteed food poisoning, right?

Archer had been skeptical once, too.

Now he knew better than to listen to his inner snob.

The place served the freshest fish, caught daily, and had become a staple of their diet since they'd landed on the tarmac not too far from where he stood. Hard to believe that had only been a few short months ago.

If their patterns held true, it wouldn't be too much longer before one of them got a tip on another destination looking for help. Someone who'd be downright giddy to take on a trio of divemasters with their credentials. Off they'd go again.

Who knew where they'd end up next?

Well, he actually had some idea. But would the guys be onboard? Would they come onboard?

Archer screwed the dust cap onto his regulator and finished neatly arranging their gear so they could dunk it in the freshwater bins back at the resort before retiring to the tiny cabanas provided for each of the staff members in an attempt to justify their ridiculously low wages.

Honestly, he wasn't in any hurry to return. He hadn't been able to sleep much recently. Every time he closed his eyes, dreams of her turned into a nightmare replay of the situation that had driven him to leave it all behind. Another night of staring at the bamboo ceiling might push him over the edge of his sanity. Tosin and Miguel went out a lot of nights, or were otherwise occupied, so he'd spent a lot of time alone lately.

He snagged their pile of blankets then headed back to the beach. Lizards scattered in front of him, and a kickass blue whiptail sunned itself on the yellow-and-black painted rock that marked the location of the dive site along the way. More than sixty of those helpful stones dotted the shores of Bonaire, which was truly one of the most SCUBA-friendly places they'd ever lived and worked.

Had they visited every single site on the island yet? He'd have to check the marine park map tucked into his logbook tonight, and speed up the process if they hadn't. They couldn't have much time left. A week at most, he figured.

Maybe the impending shakeup made him clingy, since Archer found himself nostalgic for once. Curious, since they'd been places so lush and green they almost hurt to look at. Somehow, he'd fallen in love with the deserts of Bonaire, the donkeys that wandered into the road and blocked traffic, and the one-way roads on the north side of the island that forced you to do a tour of the lake just to get back to town. He couldn't get enough of watching the world-class kite surfers on Lac Bay, kayaking through the mangroves, exploring the caves complete with ancient paintings, or hanging out in the blustery gusts on the wild east side...next stop, Africa. Even the salt fields where the locals pumped water onto the land—no good for anything else, certainly not growing anything edible—to evaporate it and sell the sea salt left behind seemed charming when they were dotted with grazing flamingos. And the salt pier where the goods were put on giant ships was one of the coolest places to dive under and around, always teeming with tarpon, groupers, and schools of barracudas.

People in Bonaire made the best of everything they'd been given. Like he, Tosin, and Miguel had done.

He remembered the adventures they'd had together so far instead of looking forward to whatever came next. If things worked out like Banks kept assuring him it would, maybe they could return someday. Here or to any of the other places they'd discovered on their journey around the world.

Tosin dropped a cooler full of beer onto the sand between the blankets Archer had only barely finished spreading over the crushed coral. He rubbed his bare abs above the shorts he'd tugged on to conceal his European-style trunks. "I'm starving."

"Nothing new there." Archer snorted.

"Hey, all that swimming makes a man hungry." Tosin practically drooled. "Besides, I burned off a ton of calories last night with the gorgeous Asian woman we met in the market a couple days ago."

"Aki?" Archer prided himself on recalling her name along with the lilac bikini that hadn't concealed her outstanding rack.

"Sounds right. Why? You didn't already do her and forget to mention it, did you?" Tosin squinted at Archer. He glanced away, pretending to stare at the waves kissing the shore. His friend misinterpreted his awkwardness. "Wait, you didn't call dibs and I forgot—?"

They may have been players, but even they had their own code between them. *No poaching* being one of the cardinal rules that had kept them from having a major falling out these past twelve years.

"Nah, nothing like that. Just...an unusual name. Pretty."

"I guess. Not as pretty as some other things about her, though." Tosin shrugged. "Anyway, it was her last night in town. She showed up at my door, so I helped her make some sexy memories for her scrapbook."

Lucky for the hungry horndog, Miguel was heading back, his arms piled with takeout containers.

Archer promised himself he'd put away every morsel of his. Not only because he could see the chalkboard bolted to the side of the truck. Lionfish—his favorite—was the special of the day.

It seemed a month of freaking out every moment he wasn't underwater had started to take its toll. He'd mooned an entire boatload of divers the day before when his trunks had refused to hug his hips no matter how hard he yanked on the tie that cinched the waist. The straps on his BCD couldn't get any tighter either.

He rubbed the back of his neck.

"Still not sleeping well?" Tosin asked.

"There are probably better mattresses in prison than my bunkhouse. Or maybe I'm getting old. Creaky. Probably should make an appointment for a massage or something." That was no lie. He practically got a cramp in his knotted shoulder muscles as he tried to shrug off his friend's concern before Miguel could wander into hearing range and start hounding him again.

Too late.

"What you need is to get your dick sucked," Miguel ribbed Archer as he passed out orders, slinging his shaggy hair out of his eyes with a whip of his head.

"You offering?" He kicked some sand in the asshole's direction, knowing that wasn't his intention.

"Hell no." Miguel snorted. "That new brunette working the fryer wrote her number on a napkin and asked me to give it to you, though. I'm pretty sure you could pretend I forgot your fork and have that food cart rocking before I finish my salad. Be careful you don't set any important bits on fire while you're at it, though."

"Not interested." Archer shook his head. Now, if she'd had black hair and blue eyes, maybe he could have pretended it meant something long enough for his dick to get hard.

Tosin and Miguel exchanged stares for a little too long.

"What?" he asked.

"Look, I don't want to get up in your business, but...what the hell is going on?" Tosin demanded as he tore into a mountain of garlic shrimp. "She's your type. Tall, athletic, tan. Natural. Down to fuck. If she doesn't do it for you, no one will. And you haven't taken a woman home in weeks."

A month, Archer mentally corrected.

Miguel jumped in when Tosin ran out of steam. Or needed another bite of his dinner. Priorities, people. "I can't remember you ever having a dry spell like this before. Did you break your dick? Catch something? What? Come on, we won't laugh...much. Tell us."

Archer grimaced. "You're idiots. Both of you."

"*You're* dodging. Is he right, then? You're clearing up a case of the clap or something?" Tosin's eyes narrowed as he thought back, as if trying to figure out when Archer might have snuck off to the botika for a shot of antibiotics in the ass.

"Jesus, no." He groaned. "My junk is fine, okay? It's just that I've been thinking a lot lately."

About mistakes he'd made, and how he might fix them going forward. About her. About holding out for someone who might make him feel like she used to or, at least, something close.

"*Thinking*! What the fuck you doing that for, bro?" Miguel chided with a smirk as he inhaled another piece of grilled barracuda from between his fingers.

Tosin agreed, "Dumb idea."

"Tell me about it." A grimace crossed Archer's face. He had to give them something or they'd keep hounding him. Besides, maybe it was time to dip a toe in and see how they might react. "I guess I'm starting to wonder if there should be more to life."

"More than great sex, diving, and hanging out at the beach with your friends?" Tosin spread his arms, still clutching some shrimp between his thumb and forefinger.

Archer picked at his lionfish nuggets, which suddenly seemed like a mountain of a meal. "Yeah."

"You're worse off than if you *had* caught some crotch funk." Miguel stopped and stared. "This has been our goal for the past dozen years. Doing exactly what we love until we get bored and move to the next gorgeous place where we can start exploring all over again. Haven't we always said we're the luckiest bastards in the world?"

He nodded. "We *are*. We totally are. We've travelled around the globe, seen incredible things—"

"Given lady tourists the vacation fling of a lifetime," Miguel added with an exaggerated jab or two of a French fry topped with Dutch mayo sauce.

Archer probably would have laughed if what he wanted to say wasn't so serious. "What if we're capable of something equally awesome and more meaningful?"

"Hey, it may not be brain surgery or ending hunger, but I think showing people the time of their lives underwater or in my bed is a valuable contribution to society. And I also happen to enjoy it. Thoroughly." Tosin pounded himself on the chest.

He did have a reputation for pleasing his partners. Hell, each of them did.

"You're right." Archer choked down another tasteless bite of what was usually his favorite meal. Then he slammed the rest of his beer, as if that would soothe his parched throat.

"Don't bail on us now, Archer." Miguel frowned. "We're a team. This is what we do, who we are. Divemasters. That's always been good enough before."

"It still is," he was quick to reassure them. "Always will be. Forget I said anything."

"Sure." Tosin nodded so fast he might have given himself whiplash. On their previous day off, he'd leapt from the cliffs at Boca Slagbaai without thinking twice. He probably found that a million times less daunting than this heartfelt discussion they were stumbling through.

Before things could deteriorate into some sloppy show of their devotion to their best friends, Miguel lightened the mood. Right when Archer went to wipe his hands on his napkin, his friend dove forward, snatching it from his grasp. Then he crashed into the sand, holding the scrap of recycled paper aloft in his fist.

"Waste not, want not. Since you're not interested..."

"Go for it." Archer laughed. The hottie—he'd learn her name tomorrow, he promised himself—*had* caught his eye. Beautiful and carefree, she might have tempted him if he hadn't decided that sex should involve something more than a temporary endorphin rush from now on. It would be another way to distinguish himself from his father. Besides, he knew from experience that as great as casual sex was, it had nothing on sleeping with someone whose top three attributes were something greater than her tits, her ass, and her willingness to give him a blowjob.

Although that last one might be a keeper, the other two should probably be shit like shared interests or a similar sense of humor.

Archer hadn't allowed himself to believe he'd have another shot at a genuine connection like that in his lifetime. Or maybe he'd been too scared to find it, only to fuck it up royally. Again.

Miguel returned from getting seconds he didn't really need just to chat some more with the cute young kite surfer slash food truck worker. He splayed on the sand like a beached whale and let out a world-class belch. "I'm never eating again."

"Yeah, sure." Tosin laughed. "You know you say that like twice a week, right?"

"I mean it. At least until breakfast." He grinned. "But I don't plan to move from this spot for a while."

"Fine by me." Archer could listen to the waves for hours as he watched iguanas scamper through the dusty soil or up the divi divi trees surrounding their oasis. Soon the sun would set. Then maybe they'd start a fire and hang out under the stars as they had plenty of other times.

Close to Kralendijk, the largest town on Bonaire, they had a great view of the comings and goings from the island's main harbor. A departing cruise ship shrank on the horizon as her thousands of passengers prepared to invade and overwhelm the port at their next destination.

Focused on the pair of tugboats returning to their stations after helping the ship out to sea, Archer didn't realize there was another large vessel on the horizon at first.

"Wow. Check that out." Miguel practically purred as he drew Archer and Tosin's attention to the incoming megayacht.

Archer's stomach churned. He slapped the lid of his takeout box closed. So much for that.

He swallowed hard as he studied the sleek profile of the ship, more impressive than he remembered. This was it. His time had run out.

Please, let him have done the right thing.

Tosin stood, shielding his eyes against the lowering sun for a better view. "It's gotta be over two-hundred feet. We might not be the luckiest bastards in the world after all. Imagine the guy who can afford something like that. Damn."

Archer didn't have to. "She's actually 273 feet long. Has room for a crew of sixteen plus twenty-five guests comfortably. Specialized dive platforms, two rigid-hull inflatable boats, and gear areas. A pool, medical center, fitness and rec room, three sun decks, pretty much anything you can think of."

"You know that boat?" Miguel squinted, as if he could read the name freshly painted on the bow. It wouldn't have mattered. This vessel wasn't one they'd seen in a past port they'd visited.

"Yep. She's mine," Archer admitted, then prayed he wasn't about to destroy the best thing he'd ever had.

Their friendship.

~ FOUR ~

Miguel and Tosin cracked up. Tosin shoved Archer's shoulder, toppling him into the sand beside the blanket. "You own a megayacht. Right. You had me going for a minute there, asshole."

Archer shrugged, dusted himself off, then figured he might as well start playing his cards. If he wasn't about to crap his trunks, it might even be kind of fun to see their reactions once they realized he wasn't fucking with them after all.

"What if it was true, though?" Archer pressed on. "Imagine that instead of jamming our stuff into a beat-up old duffle bag and taking off from here, we never had to pack again. We'd each have our own cabin onboard. A permanent home that moves with us. One a hell of a lot nicer than the places we've stayed before, too."

Archer wasn't referring to the marble and teak finishes the staterooms boasted. He meant the plush beds, world-class diving facilities, and the gorgeous natural light that would pour through the large cabin windows. The ability to go anywhere, anytime they felt like it. Those luxuries he

26

could get behind, though Miguel and Tosin might not reject opulence for the sake of it like he did.

The guys started to get in on it then, making Archer's jaw unclench just a little. Miguel leaned back, knitted his fingers together, and let his hands rest on his washboard abs, still flat despite how much he'd gorged. "Hell yeah. We could run charters and escort rich people around the world. Show them the places we've discovered. Make a killing while we're at it."

"We could." Archer cleared his throat. "Or...since, you know, we'd have to be rich enough to take golden dumps to own a yacht like that, we could let people come along for free. Figure out some way to invite remarkable and deserving guests to join us on an all-expenses-paid trip of a lifetime. Use our matching private jet to shuttle them to wherever we're docked and go from there. Make people's dreams come true. Only fair since we'd get to live ours."

"I like that way better." Tosin nodded. "Like some kind of seafaring Willy Wonka."

Archer snorted. Only his dumbass friend would put it like that. Except, now that he had... "Yeah! We'd send out golden tickets or some shit, maybe sometimes auction off spots then donate the money to charities. Even better would be if there was a club on board so we could socialize. A place where people could unwind at night and make sure we're never lonely out on the open ocean. Not that different from what we do today, just at a whole different level."

"Now you're talking." Miguel grunted. "Make it a sex club—a hedonistic one like the places we went to in the Philippines—while you're at it. I'll sign up right now."

"Seriously?" Archer held his breath.

"Yeah, I mean, do I look dumb?" He whipped his head around to stare at Archer. "Saying no to a gig like that would be as idiotic as you turning down prime pussy. Oh, wait...fucking moron."

Unable to drag things out anymore, Archer asked, "Want to drive into town and watch her dock up close?"

"Sure. Maybe we can offer our services for a day or two if they're staying until Wednesday," Tosin suggested, referring to their next day off. "Hell, I'd volunteer just to score a tour. I bet that thing is ridiculous inside."

It was.

"We'd better hurry. She's fast. Must have a lot of horsepower below deck." Tosin had already climbed to his feet, scooped up his blanket, and lifted the cooler to his shoulder. Miguel and Archer were right behind.

It only took them a few minutes to navigate the roundabout and the narrow, cluttered streets of Kralendijk. They parked island-style, halfway on the brick sidewalk near the market, which was rapidly emptying of vendors now that the cruise ship had departed.

"Come on," Archer called to his friends as he unbuckled himself and headed for the dock. His anticipation grew, muffling some of his anxiety. The yacht was truly gorgeous. Sleek and modern. Not normally what attracted him. This time, he knew what that exterior held, though. He couldn't wait to catch a glimpse of the hardwood decks or the elaborate diving setups he'd instructed Banks to arrange. Not to mention seeing the man himself.

Archer admitted he'd missed the guy, especially after working covertly with him the past several weeks to approve the establishment of the Banks Foundation and start outlining some of the programs it would support, like the one he was about to pitch to his friends. Banks had been the person Archer had always chosen to go to when he was growing up—for help, to confide in, for approval. His younger self's judgment had been bang on. Banks was one of the good ones.

He'd made good time. The weather must not have been as bad as expected for their Atlantic crossing. Banks had cleaned house, hiring a brand-new crew that was aligned with Archer's mission for the *Divemaster.* Then he'd overseen renovations and transporting the yacht from where it had been docked in the Mediterranean for years, hardly ever used by Archer's father, who'd only commissioned one of the biggest ships in the world because he could, and because he couldn't stand for his associates or competitors to have something he didn't.

That's not at all what this was about for Archer.

"You coming?" he asked when Miguel put his arm up along the back of the seat and stared wistfully out the window.

"Our gear is in the back." Miguel sighed. "I'll stay with the truck. You two can check it out."

Archer shook his head. Hell, let someone take their stuff. He'd already arranged for upgraded equipment—the top-of-the-line products each guy had drooled over in catalogs—to be onboard. "I'll cover it up. It'll be okay for a minute or two. We can see the lot from there."

Archer rearranged the blankets to obscure their things.

"Not smart, but screw it. Let's do it." Tosin could never resist an adventure. Even unwise ones.

Maybe this was going to work out like Banks kept promising it would.

Miguel rounded the bed of the truck, joining them on the sidewalk. He pointed at the ship's hull as they jogged down the dock. "Hey, cool! She's called the *Divemaster*."

"Then I guess they probably won't be needing us." Tosin damn near pouted, as if someone had just broken the news to him that he'd missed something rare on a dive, like the enormous whale shark Archer and Miguel had glimpsed on their final shift in Útila.

"Don't rule it out yet," Archer mumbled as they closed in.

They arrived at the end of the pier around the same time a deckhand maneuvered a motorized gangway into place. Archer didn't bother to take a seat on the heavy-duty chain strung between two pilings like his friends did. Instead, he stood near the metal railing and waved at the man waiting at the other end of the bridge between Archer's past and his future.

"Good afternoon, Archie." Banks smiled and extended his hand as he glided down the gangway, as sophisticated as ever.

Archer skipped formality and used the grip to pull Banks in for a hug, earning a surprised grunt from the guy. It didn't take long before Banks reciprocated with a tender pat on Archer's shoulder blade. When they separated, Archer realized Banks had a hell of a lot more silver in his hair than the last time Archer had seen him, over a decade ago.

What differences would Banks notice about him? Pretty much everything, he figured. A ton more than a couple of grays.

He found it impossible to know what to say. If Banks was shocked, he masked it well.

Tosin and Miguel, however, were exchanging bug-eyed glances while Tosin mouthed, *Archie? What the fuck?*

Banks to the rescue again. Social niceties were his business. "This must be Mr. Torres and Mr. Ellis. I've heard so many wonderful things about you both."

Too dumbstruck to respond, first Miguel then Tosin took Banks's hand and shook woodenly before Tosin turned to Miguel and asked, "Is someone punking us right now?"

In sync, they looked around as if a camera crew would pop out from behind a rock to deliver the punch line of this joke.

For the first time in a month, Archer laughed. Once he started, he couldn't stop. He grabbed his middle then doubled over, relief and terror mingling, threatening to drive him mad.

"Why don't you invite your friends onboard, Archie?" Banks nudged him when he gasped to catch his breath. "There's a lot to discuss still, yes?"

That sobered him pretty quick. He nodded.

"I've set up a table for you in the bar, unless you'd prefer one of the decks or a meeting room instead." Banks had thought of everything Archer found overwhelming. As usual.

Tosin hadn't moved. "I think maybe you'd better introduce us first, *Archie*."

"Ah, shit. Sorry. I never was good at manners." He shook his head ruefully. Other than stating his name, there was no way to explain who this man was to Archer. Confidant, surrogate dad, business manager—he played a lot of roles. So he stuck with simplicity. "This is Banks."

"Wait. What?" Miguel tipped his head. Not surprising since that was Archer's alias and he now shared it with the other guy he so obviously knew. "I thought you didn't have any family."

"Technically, we're not related, sir," Banks replied for him.

"Sir!" Tosin snorted, recovering some of his easygoing nature, or maybe he attempted to counterbalance Miguel's growing agitation. "That's a first. Even better than Archie!"

"These guys are my friends, Banks. They're not going to respond to civility any better than I do." Archer looked away from Miguel when he realized the man had, consciously or not, balled his fists. It was entirely possible Archer would get his ass kicked today. And deserve it, too.

"Very well, then." Banks smiled and turned his back. "Get your asses onboard if you want to find out what the hell your friend is up to. Please leave your shoes in the bin at the top of the gangway."

Tosin whooped and raced onto the ship, excited to check it out despite the mysterious circumstances.

"I'd better not." Miguel frowned. "Our gear is in the truck, unattended. And I'm starting to think I'm the only one here who hasn't lost his damn mind."

Before he could come up with another valid reason to disappear, maybe forever, Banks dispatched a crew member toward the vehicle they'd left haphazardly on the curb nearby. "Your belongings will be safe. I promise."

"Holy shit. You've got to see this pool, Miguel. Come on!" Tosin shouted from the main sundeck.

Miguel grunted, then grudgingly followed, glancing over his shoulder periodically at Archer, who brought up the rear.

At least he was going to give Archer a chance to explain.

That was as much as he had dared to hope for.

Archer pinched the bridge of his nose, hoping he hadn't initiated a countdown sequence that led to the implosion of their friendship.

◌ **FIVE** ◌

Banks graciously asked the men, "Would you like a tour of the ship?"

"Hell yeah." Tosin practically vibrated as he looked around.

Archer hoped he'd be equally excited when he learned that the *Divemaster* could be his new home.

"Hang on. No." Miguel glared directly at Archer, as if he had blinders on—or didn't want to be softened up by their surroundings. "Not until we know what the fuck is going on here."

He was smart.

Archer didn't blame him at all. He gave a curt nod then said to Banks, "Show us to the bar, please."

"The papers you requested are at your place," Banks murmured as he guided them through a fiberglass door.

Even Archer was impressed when he took in the wide polished-wood hallway with calm, neutral-toned accents. He suspected Banks had done more than change out the crew onboard and make minor updates. Everything suited his tastes to perfection. Masculine, earthy, and understated elegance. Not a single garish embellishment lingered to remind him of his father.

Quietly, he asked Banks, "How'd you manage to redecorate so quickly?"

"Everything is possible with enough money, Archie." He winked.

They didn't have time to argue about that before they'd reached their destination near the bow of the ship. Floor-to-ceiling windows, contoured to the ship's silhouette, lined every edge of the room, giving them an unobstructed view of the harbor and northward along the western shore of the island. Klein Bonaire looked close enough to swim to from here.

It took Archer's breath away. Far more than the things inside that had caught Tosin's attention. The privilege of being able to witness something so spectacular and the potential to do it every day for the rest of his life was far more valuable to him than the yacht they stood on. Though he had to admit that, as a vehicle for bringing his dreams to life, this one was pretty damn impressive.

Even Miguel seemed to thaw a bit. He ran his fingers over the glossy live-edge tabletops before sinking onto one of the stools arranged around it. It wasn't hard to tell which place was his since his favorite top-shelf liquor was set out, ready and waiting for him.

Tosin's and Archer's, too.

Miguel grabbed the shot of Macallan whiskey and downed it in a single gulp before slamming the glass onto the table with a resounding clunk. He hadn't had time to swallow before a well-dressed crew member appeared, seemingly from nowhere, with a refill.

When the man had disappeared once more, Archer sat too, his fingers picking at the edges of the folder Banks had left there for him. Where the hell did they start?

Miguel helped him out.

"So you fucking lied to us? You're loaded? This whole time, were you looking down your nose at us? Laughing at how pitiful we were?" He crossed his arms, looking toward the exit as if he might dart out of there faster than a rainbow runner, leaving Archer blinking at the vanishing back of his friend.

His worst fears began to come true. He would be rejected, judged undeserving of his companions' respect. Fucked over by his inheritance. If the only thing these two guys could see was his net worth, then no one else in the universe would do differently. They knew him better than anyone else.

Pain stabbed his chest. He rubbed the ache, but it didn't fade.

The worst thing he could imagine was dying as alone as his father had been, accompanied only by bought sycophants.

"Hey, don't be like that." Tosin punched Miguel in the biceps. "He's lived with us for twelve years. Roughing it. Having fun even when we didn't have a lot else. Why don't you let him tell us why? I would like to hear that."

Fair enough. Archer nodded and swallowed hard.

When Miguel faced him again, curiosity in his gaze, Archer confessed, "I hated who I was. The lifestyle, the obligations, and the political maneuvering that left innocent victims in its wake."

He scrunched his eyes closed as a particular face appeared in his mind. Raven hair down to her perfect ass, porcelain skin, and eyes as blue as the spots on the juvenile damselfish he'd stared at not very long ago.

His biggest regret.

The final straw that had sent him packing. "So I opted out of it all. Left. Became someone else entirely."

"You're saying you're not an orphan like you told us forever ago. That's why you never said a peep about home or your family. You're a runaway." Miguel wasn't cutting Archer a lot of slack. The way he sneered *runaway* made it sound sort of like *chicken shit*. Or *quitter*. Two things they definitely didn't respect and never had allowed themselves to be before.

Archer reminded himself that as much of a shock to his system it had been these past few weeks—imagining his life proceeding in an entirely different direction from what he'd planned—for these two, hearing these things would be the equivalent of taking a polar bear plunge into the Arctic after a decade of tropical swims.

They probably had no idea some people really lived like this.

Until you'd seen it yourself, it was impossible to really visualize.

At least that's what he'd been told by Banks.

"It wasn't exactly a lie. My father was dead to me. Or maybe I was reborn. I walked away when I was nineteen and never looked back. My father said he would disown me the instant I crossed his threshold. I thought he had. I didn't care. About a month ago, he kicked the bucket and left me everything. So, now it is true. I *am* the last of my family. Before I'd only wished that was the case."

"How can you say something so cold?" Miguel—who had lost his parents in an accident when he was eight and grown up in a group home in South America—glared at Archer as if he was more disgusting than the sludge that sometimes accumulated in the corners of their dive boat. "I don't know who you are anymore. Maybe I never did."

He stood in a rush, making his stool tilt precariously, then turned toward the door.

Until Tosin asked quietly, "What did your dad do to you to make you hate him? You don't have a temper and I've never known you to hold a grudge."

"He..." Archer cleared his throat and broke eye contact, staring out the window at the desert paradise he'd come to adore so much when the memories threatened to overwhelm him.

Sitting on his couch, not able to hear the knock on the door right away...staggering to the front door to find it was her. She'd come to him.

If only he hadn't been so intoxicated, he might have noticed something was wrong.

If he'd been sober—and his father hadn't been meddling in their lives—he might not have made such a grave and horrible mistake.

Despite the fact that his father deserved his rage, Archer hadn't forgiven himself. Not for his failures as a son. And *definitely* not for falling for his father's twisted scheme. He should have realized what was happening. Should have stopped before she got hurt.

"Fuck this. He's never going to be straight with us. I'm out of here." Miguel turned and strode toward the exit.

"Fine. Wait!" Archer couldn't let him leave. Except the truth might make him run instead of walk. "He set me up. Conned me into raping someone."

The words seared his windpipe as though they'd been made of stonefish venom.

There. He'd admitted it out loud for the first time. Ever.

Maybe that was the first step toward acceptance. Forgiveness would be too generous. He'd never grant himself that kind of absolution from his own self-recriminations.

"Say *what*?" Miguel turned around then, his head cocked. His bright eyes, such a contrast to his olive complexion and midnight hair, bored into Archer. "That doesn't even make sense, dude. How can you accidentally rape someone? This isn't even funny anymore. Did I hit my head underwater or something?"

Archer tried to explain. Nothing would come out through his raw throat. It was his turn to slam his drink and relish the fire it lit within him. He deserved the punishment. "He made me a monster. Just like him. A pawn in his power plays. I realized I couldn't stay. What I'd done was bad enough. If I didn't leave, I was going to become just like him someday. If it wasn't too late already."

He planted his elbows on the table then dropped his head into his hands, trying to ward off the revulsion his ex-best-friends would likely feel toward him now. He wouldn't blame them.

"This is getting sicker and more twisted by the second," Miguel snarled. "How can you still be sitting there, Tosin? Let's go."

Their joint friend looked from one guy to the other. Who would he side with?

Archer braced himself for them both to walk out.

"Calm down a second and think, Miguel." Tosin urged the man to wait. "Don't you remember the night we spent in that skanky Mexican jail for brawling?"

That had him pausing. Consciously or not, he edged a couple steps closer. "Yeah, because this moron got us tangled up in some domestic dispute."

"Right. Does a real rapist stand up for a stranger who's fighting off a dude, who clearly is not taking no for an answer, in a bar bathroom? Does he snap and beat the man to a pulp?"

Archer clearly recalled the flash of fury that had overtaken him in that instant.

"Maybe they do if they feel guilty about what they've done," Miguel answered, his voice a lot softer now.

"I do. I regret what happened. Every day. Every hour. The woman I hurt... She's spectacular. Special."

"Why don't you tell us the full story?" Tosin asked.

"I—can't." Archer shook his head. "The details don't matter anyway. They would sound like excuses. I did it. I accept responsibility for it. But I wasn't about to hang around and let anyone put me in those kinds of situations again."

"I'm going to have to disagree on that point. I feel like you owe us the rest." Tosin ruffled Archer's hair briefly before polishing off his own liquor. "Someday soon. A less crazy day than today, tell us. I have a feeling we might see it differently. Seems like you could use a sounding board on this one."

Archer dreaded that conversation, though he knew they'd have to have it.

Wait.

"Does that mean you're planning on sticking around, then?" He could hardly breathe.

Tosin nodded, a faint smile curving his lips. "For over ten years, we've done everything together. Trusted each other. I know you, Archer. You're not the person you obviously think you are. *Right*, Miguel?"

Archer risked a glance at his partner. The guy seemed unsure. With one foot out the door, he studied Archer's face. Hopefully he could read the genuine remorse there. A lifetime of regret wouldn't be enough to change what had happened that night, but he desperately wished it could.

Sometimes even a Scrooge McDuck-sized fortune couldn't buy your way out of a problem.

Some things weren't for sale.

Like forgiveness.

Or a time machine.

Or the faith of your two best friends.

Living with mistakes as awful as Archer's could cost a man his soul.

"Shit!" Miguel ran his hands through his hair, then pivoted. Step by step, he returned. He fell onto the barstool, looking as deflated as Archer felt. "I'm gonna need another drink."

No sooner had he said it than his wish came true.

The three guys glanced between each other, weirded out and enjoying the indulgence simultaneously.

"So basically, you came into a crap ton of money and decided to buy a megayacht and live out the rest of your life in luxury?" Tosin hummed. "Not a bad plan, really."

"That's not exactly what I had in mind." Archer shrugged before opening the folder in front of him. "I had Banks draw up some contracts. I'd like you to read them. It should make everything clear."

Already he sounded like the tool his father had always hoped he'd become. When stakes were this high, he supposed some formalities couldn't be avoided. He handed each of his friends a copy of the agreement he hoped they'd sign.

Tosin skimmed his before asking, "You're offering us a job? All that stuff we were joking around about on the beach. That's what you actually intend to do, isn't it?"

Archer nodded. "Yes. I've appointed Banks to be the executive director of the Banks Foundation. The sole purpose of the organization is to take my money and put it to good use. He asked me a ton of questions about things that are important to me, like women's rights, abuse hotlines, transitional shelters, domestic violence awareness, those kinds of things. But also stuff like conservation, renewable energy sources, and clean drinking water initiatives. He's figuring out how to address as many of those global issues as we can by creating charities dedicated to them and funding research by the world's leading scientists in relevant fields."

"What does that have to do with a megayacht? Is this the headquarters of the Banks Foundation or something?" Miguel asked, sounding truly interested for the first time.

"Not quite." Archer shook his head. "Though Banks will be living onboard and he's the head of the foundation, so...maybe. This is one of the Banks Foundation projects. Banks actually came up with it and talked me into getting personally involved. We're calling it the Divemaster Project, for obvious reasons."

"What exactly is the Divemaster Project supposed to do?" Miguel wondered.

"It'll be just like we talked about earlier. A pretty cushy arm of the Banks Foundation. Deserving passengers will join us for a while at sea. We'll foot the bill and try to tip the karma scales in their favor a little. Reward them for whatever it is they've done to not be assholes like some humans. Banks is taking care of the administrative shit. He'll be sourcing the guests for us. Making all the arrangements for them. Managing the staff. We'd be mostly business as usual with a few extra perks. We'd live here and act as the divemasters on the *Divemaster*."

"So we'd work for you?" Tosin's brows drew together, causing some fine wrinkles to show on his forehead. "Not that I think you'd be a bad boss—"

"No. Stop, please." Archer didn't bother to let him finish. "Nothing changes between us. I want you to be my partners like always."

Miguel, who paid the best attention to detail of the three of them, scanned the paper he'd accepted from Archer. He mumbled, "'...eligible to purchase a one-third share of the *Divemaster* for the price of a single US penny.'"

Tosin's jaw dropped.

Miguel continued, "'With the stipulation that should you decide to terminate your stay onboard permanently, you'll offer your share to the Banks Foundation for full market value before listing it for sale publicly.'"

"Archer, that's nuts." Arms flung wide, Tosin interrupted. "A third of this thing has to be at least—"

"Eighty-five million dollars, give or take. Probably more in a few years." He shrugged. "I know what it's like to be trapped by this lifestyle. That's not what I want for either of you. If there comes a day you're ready to get out, you'll still be able to enjoy the things you'll become accustomed to while staying here. Worst case would be if you hung around longer than you wanted to and came to resent me because of something as unimportant as money. You're free to stay here forever...or go. At any time. I'd never lock you in."

"Can I ask something rude?" Miguel leaned forward. He didn't wait for permission before shooting out his questions. "Just how motherfucking loaded are you? And why does Banks have your name if you're not related?"

Tosin didn't blink as he waited for Archer to respond. He must have been wondering, too.

"Actually, *I've* got *his* name. He was our butler, although that doesn't really convey everything he handled. You know, like raising me and shit. I borrowed it when I went incognito, hiding from my father. Every day, Banks showed me the kind of person I wanted to be like when I got the chance to make myself."

He'd held himself to that standard. Except for violating that girl... He couldn't let himself think of her now, though. That's what nightmares were for.

"I should have realized that conniving bastard knew where I was all along. Anyway, on my birth certificate, my last name is Quartermane."

"Like the software company?"

"Yeah. That's where my father made most of his money. But I sold everything and put it in some kind of trust. Well, actually, Banks did it for me. I tried not to listen when he told me about it. All I care about is that this obscene amount of cash makes a positive impact. I don't want anything else to do with it."

Tosin looked like he'd gulped down a few lungfuls of seawater. "So, what you're saying is…you're a goddamned multi-billionaire?"

"More or less." Archer shrugged. "If it was all sitting in my bank account it'd probably be five, six, maybe seven, billion depending on the day and the stock markets. I don't plan to touch a cent other than what we've got in the yacht and her expenses. Banks assured me the essentials are more than taken care of by the interest on several long-term investments dedicated to the holding company that technically purchased the yacht, which we will also jointly own. Blah blah blah, whatever. Long story short, we can do this. Forever, if you guys don't get sick of it. And if you do, you're welcome to go try whatever else makes you happy instead."

Tosin reached into the pocket of his cargo shorts. He slapped his hand onto the table, leaving a penny on top of Archer's now-empty folder. "Reporting for duty."

Together, Tosin and Archer looked at Miguel.

"I've just got one more question," he sighed.

"What the hell could matter after all that?" Veins popped out in Tosin's neck as he practically had a coronary. "Pull your head out of your ass and sign on the dotted line, fuckface. Do it now, or so help me I will come over there and do it for you."

"Hear him out." Archer put his hand on Tosin's shoulder and pressed steadily yet firmly. "It's okay. What else do you want to know, Miguel?"

"Will you lend me a penny? I spent the last of my cash on that second helping back at the street-meat wagon." For dramatic effect, he paused before adding, "I'm good for it. I swear."

Laughter burst from Archer's chest. It was either that or surrender to the burn behind his eyes. "For real? You're coming, too?"

"You're not going anywhere without me, bro." Miguel held his fist out over the center of their table.

Tosin and Archer took turns bumping it before doing the same to each other.

They stared around, dazed, until Miguel said, "I can't believe that really happened."

"I'm still in shock myself." Though the oily grime finally seemed to be dissipating from Archer's guts some.

Eyes narrowed, Miguel growled, "When, exactly, did your dad pass away?"

"My guess, a month ago." Tosin's features regained some of his storminess. "This is what the fuck has been wrong with you. You've been freaking out. And you didn't say a damn word."

"I think that pisses me off more than you forgetting to mention you were a billionaire." Disappointment cast a shadow on Miguel's acceptance.

"I'm sorry." It felt good for Archer to finally give them the apology they hadn't known they'd deserved before. "I swear, from now on, no more secrets."

Quick to anger, but faster to forgive, Miguel nodded. "So now what the fuck do we do?"

Tosin stood. "Yo, Banks, you out there somewhere?"

A few seconds later, he rejoined them in the bar with a flute of champagne in his hand. "Celebrations are in order, yes?"

"Yes," Archer practically roared with relief.

"To the divemasters." Banks drained his glass as well.

The three guys cheered for him.

"First order of business, I want that tour you promised, Banks." Tosin slapped the older guy on the back, knocking him forward a little.

"I would recommend you boys go quit your jobs first." The guy probably had a schedule etched into his brain. He would keep them organized. Thank God.

Archer would have felt bad about leaving their shop in a lurch with such short notice if Banks hadn't already arranged for a dozen candidates, who would be flown in—or maybe had been already—for their shop manager to interview.

Confirming Archer's suspicions, Banks continued, "If you don't leave now, your replacements might arrive at the shop before you give notice. That could be a kind of awkward, don't you think?"

"The dude seriously thinks of everything, doesn't he?" Miguel stared at Banks in awe.

"It's my job, *sir.*"

Miguel squirmed like Archer did when Banks *sir*ed him. Somehow that was way funnier when it was happening to his friend.

"Okay, fine," Tosin amended. "First we quit. Then we get our tour. And after that, I think we should throw one hell of a going away party onboard."

Miguel stiffened.

A wince crossed Tosin's face. "I mean, if that's okay with you, Archer."

"Guys, let's get one thing straight right now." He stared at both of his best friends. "We're in this as equals. You have every right to make decisions. In fact, let's sign those contracts and make it official. The last thing I'd want is for this to fuck up our friendship. Things should be the same..."

"But hella better!" Miguel held out his hand in a silent promise and Archer clasped it. The other guy drew him in for a man-hug, clapping him on his back a few times hard enough to rattle his organs around. "I don't know what to say."

"*I* say, here's to new adventures." Archer swallowed against the lump in his throat as he caught Banks's wink from behind Miguel. They'd done it.

For once, he was starting to believe it might be okay to enjoy this opportunity his father had left him.

"And *I* say...party time, boys!" Tosin jogged down the hall, burst out the door, and shouted loud enough over the rail to the bystanders gathered below that Archer, Miguel, and Banks had no trouble hearing him despite the soundproofing. "Who's ready for a wild time?"

Archer was.

∽ SIX ∾

"**A**rchie! Yo, Arrrrchiiiieeeeee." Shitfaced and amped up, the guys had decided they liked Banks's nickname for him a little too much. It was going to be hell getting them to stop calling him that.

He winced then pitched his voice over the music, which pumped across the deck they were partying on. "Over here, Miguel."

"I brought you a going away present." He tugged a gorgeous woman in an ultra-feminine sarong dress behind him as he cut through the crowd. Long, tan legs peeked from thigh-high gaps in the sides as she walked. A fresh hibiscus adorned the clip holding her wavy hair back from her face. When she looked up, Archer recognized her despite the subtle touches of makeup—something she didn't ordinarily wear—highlighting her already striking features.

The kite-surfing street-meat dealer.

"Hey." For the first time in weeks, his cock perked up at the sight of a very willing woman.

It wasn't permanently broken! Hallelujah!

Mistaking his enormous grin as an invitation, she plastered herself to his side and gave him a hug as big as if she were an octopus wrapping all eight tentacles around him simultaneously. He found himself reflexively returning the gesture. Who was he to squash a woman's hopes?

Sure, he'd promised himself he wouldn't fool around for the hell of it anymore, but tonight had turned out to be one of the best of his life.

He deserved to celebrate. Besides, she'd tried to get with him before she'd known he was rich, so he already preferred her to the dozens of circling sharks who smelled cash in the water.

Bonaire wasn't a very big island. Rumors had spread from one end to the other before he, Tosin, and Miguel had even packed up their cabanas. He swore half the population had crammed themselves onboard tonight, suddenly acting as if they were long-lost relatives.

Archer much preferred the genuine bond he had with his partners, and women like this one.

"Hi." She backed off just far enough to extend her hand. "I'm Savannah. Nice to officially meet you, finally."

"Likewise." He brought her hand to his mouth and kissed her knuckles. Afterward he didn't let go, entwining their fingers instead. "Would you prefer to go somewhere quieter, so we can talk? Or were you looking forward to dancing?"

"Whatever you want."

Ugh. No. There'd be time for that later, once he had her splayed out across his bed. He liked his partners to have a strong will so that when they chose to surrender to him, he knew he'd won something truly precious. Something he'd thought he'd earned from *her*. "Lady's choice."

"Dancing." She smiled up at him, kind of shyly. Yet still seductive, full of promise.

The evening was about to get even better.

"Thanks." He nodded to Miguel as he passed. "I owe you one."

"I think you've covered it already." His friend slapped him on the ass.

They both laughed at that. It didn't feel like he'd done much of anything. With Banks's guidance, he had changed their lives forever, he supposed. Selfishly, Archer had mostly considered that he didn't want to leave his best friends behind when he embarked on the next phase of his life. If that made him an asshole, so be it. In the end, each of them had benefitted.

When they'd made it to the center of the floor, people parting to let him pass, Archer spun Savannah around then swallowed her up with his arms and tugged her close. He let his hips grind against hers, giving her a calculated preview of what the rest of the evening could have in store for them.

It only took a few songs for her to ride his thigh and begin pressing her chest, including her pebbled nipples, into the patch of tan skin his partially opened dress shirt exposed. She stared up at him with a blend of heat and desire that he was not about to waste.

"I think I'd like to see that quieter place now, if you don't mind," she said just loud enough to be heard despite the pulsating beats.

Soon enough she'd shatter the calm of whatever nook he hauled her off to by crying out his name as she came. She'd triggered his instincts with her sweet request, and he was about to exceed her expectations. Some people might consider him egotistical, but he preferred to think of himself as frank about his skill level as a lover.

Archer excelled at seduction.

With a hand in the small of Savannah's back, he guided her through the throng, angling his shoulders to protect her from being jostled by frenzied revelers.

There was one place he hadn't checked out on the ship yet.

Time to rectify that oversight.

Archer didn't feel like stopping to gawk at the yacht's interior. Instead, he scooped Savannah into his arms and allowed her to think of it as a romantic gesture. Her heartbeat tripped beneath the fingers he curled around her ribs.

Without speaking, she rested her head on his shoulder, and he knew he'd won. She was his for the taking. And he would give all of himself in return. For a little while.

When he reached his destination, he cradled her with one arm, and used a palm scanner to unlock a smoky black glass door. Then he brought Savannah inside, waiting for her telltale gasp.

She didn't disappoint, making his cock twitch in his khaki shorts. "What *is* this place?"

Now *that* was a good question. During their many discussions about the *Divemaster*, Archer had told Banks he thought it would be a good idea to have a place the guys could relax discreetly with any personal guests they might choose to entertain. One that didn't require inviting them to their private space. It seemed the guy had used his imagination and taken things over the top. Maybe Archer's father wasn't the only one who'd kept tabs on him. Could the divemasters' penchant for visiting sex clubs have been notated in some report?

He bet it had been.

Tosin and Miguel were going to lose their minds, or come in their pants, when they realized the extent of the facilities onboard. Looked like the *Divemaster* still had some secrets to uncover. He wasn't surprised—the more they'd explored, the more they realized how huge it was. There hadn't been much time between when they'd gotten back from the dive shop and guests started arriving, either.

"Looks like it's our private playroom."

"I like to play," she purred. Then, without hesitation, she began to strip. First her dress, then her matching lace bra and boy-short panties. When she stood naked before him, she sank to her knees, reaching for the waistband of his shorts.

Just like *she* had, making him feel like she craved him as he had her.

Too bad he could have been anyone with a cock, and she would have reacted the same way.

Archer shook his head and concentrated on Savannah.

She wasn't subtle or tentative as she unbuttoned then unzipped his shorts. That was fine with him. He didn't need her to be.

Archer whipped his shirt over his head and dropped it beside her clothes. Then he shoved his shorts and briefs to the ground, stepping out of them. Since he was already barefoot, there weren't any shoes to deal with. Handy.

When Savannah licked her lips, staring at his erection, he shot her a wicked grin.

Archer grasped her face between his palms and held her in place while he bent down to steal a kiss. She moaned and responded, opening to his demanding tongue.

After he'd taken his fill, he speared his fingers into her hair and directed her to his aching balls. She licked them, in no way hesitant as she nuzzled his groin, sucking gently while she bathed them with the flat of her tongue.

"Yes, that's it." He encouraged her like a teacher with a student. There wasn't anything tender about it. That's not what either of them was here for. "Just for that amazing job you're doing down there, I promise to give you plenty of orgasms before the night is through."

It seemed she appreciated his dirty talk as much as most women did.

Would *she* have? He hadn't tried it since he'd only had affectionate things to say to *her*.

Savannah redoubled her efforts, lavishing her attention on his cock as well.

He didn't bother to hide how well she played his body. Instead, when she took him to the back of her throat, he rewarded her enthusiastic sucking by limiting the time she needed to spend on her knees.

Archer tugged her hair, pinning her close to his abdomen, then came down her throat in a rush complete with a series of heartfelt groans. She swallowed around him eagerly, drawing out his pleasure.

When he withdrew, leaving a sheen on her lush lips, he reached down and lifted her to her feet.

"Thank you," he rasped before sealing his mouth over hers and making sure she knew he meant it. Savannah might not be *her*, but he appreciated her generosity in sharing herself nonetheless. Damn, he'd needed that fast, hard release to take the edge off.

Now there'd be plenty of time to recover before demonstrating he had better stamina than a horny teenager. Though he'd done well—too well—with *her*. They'd screwed for hours before he realized what was going on.

Savannah reminded him to stay in the present. The party below decks was just getting started.

"You're welcome." She smiled up at him, glancing around the floor as if preparing to make a grab for her dress.

"Oh, hell no." He stopped her with his curt command. "That's not how I roll. Get your sexy ass over to that...whatever the fuck that thing is."

Archer pointed at a contraption that seemed like the world's craziest dentist chair. Black leather, straps everywhere, segmented and fully adjustable seat sections. Oh yeah, that would do.

If he wasn't mistaken, she whimpered then shivered before practically dashing to the equipment.

"That's better," he growled as he stalked to her, arranging her to suit his intentions before buckling her in for one hell of a wild ride.

Archer crouched between her spread thighs, feasting on her for so long his mind blissed out and all his worries faded away. Including the ones about how disastrously this could end up in the morning.

No matter how bad it was, it couldn't possibly be his worst morning after.

Trying to shove those thoughts away, he applied himself to maximizing Savannah's pleasure as if it was some kind of penance. He'd stopped counting the number of climaxes he gave her as he steadily jerked himself back to full hardness. By the time she went limp, her thighs quivering against his shoulders, he was ready to fuck.

It was right about then that the door opened.

Archer rose, blocking as much of his partner from prying eyes as he could.

He shouldn't have worried. It was only Miguel with a lady, or three, of his own. Kind of hard to count precisely since his entourage merged with Tosin's, who followed right behind.

The space was big enough for them to keep out of each other's way. Or not, if that's how they rolled. He didn't give a shit if they saw him plowing into Savannah's pretty pussy, as he planned to do in a just a few more seconds. But how would she feel about it?

"I need to be fucked, Archer. Let them watch what you do to me." She surprised him with her steady plea. "I don't care about anything except having your cock in me. Now."

He couldn't agree more. Like diving, fucking was one of the few things that could turn off his obsession with the past. It was hard not to compare every partner to *her*, but he tried. It wasn't fair. They would never measure up to perfection. Or at least what he'd thought was total compatibility.

Though he heard his two best friends cheering on the action as they got into some fun of their own, Archer's attention didn't drift from his temporary partner unless it was because of rogue thoughts. Of *her*. Always *her*.

Plucking a condom from a bowl on a table nearby, he tore open the package and sheathed himself. Without torturing either of them longer than he already had, he set the tip of his cock at the opening to Savannah's pussy and bored inside.

The slick channel, prepped by his feasting, admitted him easily.

At least when coaxed by his unrelenting forward pressure.

He let his head drop back so he could savor the fisting of her flesh around his. Once he bottomed out, he began to retreat.

Archer took it slow until they'd both adjusted to the sensations, then began to drill into Savannah with a steady and fluid motion that shattered her around him a couple of times within the first few minutes. The squeeze and ripple of her muscles against his cock was enough to have him gritting his teeth while he rubbed light circles around her clit, keeping her aroused.

Still not as tight as *she* had been. Virginal, until he'd ruined her.

As he really dug in, he leaned forward. The graceful arch of Savannah's neck tempted the animal within him. He wrapped his fingers around it lightly, careful not to come close to hurting her. It might make him a savage, but there was no denying he loved this feeling.

Being in control.

Granting them both pleasure by revealing his inner beast.

It might make him hate himself later. Confuse the hell out of him. But he'd worry about that some other time.

One of his friends' companions edged nearer for a close-up view of the action. Archer fucked harder, faster, fulfilling each of Savannah's moaned pleas, which encouraged him to intensify their experience.

And when she seemed to stall, on the very edge of one final epic release, the female bystander graciously helped him out. He hoped Miguel or Tosin would treat her especially well for her generosity.

Because when she leaned in and captured Savannah's mouth in a gentle kiss he would have been utterly incapable of bestowing to anyone but *her*, she shuddered and clenched on his shaft, threatening to fracture his cock.

Archer roared then poured jet after jet of come into the condom he wore.

He half expected to see that he'd ripped a hole in it with the force of the blasts when he withdrew from Savannah's still-twitching pussy. Thankfully, he hadn't.

Dripping sweat and high on endorphins, he released her as quickly as possible, rubbing her wrists and ankles to return full circulation.

The entire time, she made out with their new arrival. It should have been every man's fantasy come to life. Except now that he was utterly spent, fucked dry, Archer found himself wishing he hadn't done it at all.

It had only reminded him that no one could replace *her*. Was he doomed to be unsatisfied with even fantastic sex for the rest of his life? It would serve him right, he supposed.

The only problem was he'd utterly exhausted this free-spirited woman, and he refused to walk away and leave her in such a vulnerable state. Even though he knew Miguel and Tosin would tend to her properly, it wasn't their responsibility.

For tonight only, it was his.

And he'd sworn he would never let another woman down. Like he had *her*.

The guys had obviously been inspired by his show. They didn't bother to say goodnight when he gathered Savannah to his chest and passed by them as the group of ladies spoiled his friends rotten. Good for them all, if that's what made them happy.

Archer ignored his better judgment and took Savannah to his room, both of them completely naked. If he encouraged her to stay over, maybe he could pretend that what they'd shared meant more than simple physical relief.

It didn't work.

He should have been sated. Instead, he felt hollow.

And she...well, she was knocked out by the time he'd made it down the hall.

All through the night, Archer kept Savannah close, watching over her. No matter what, he appreciated the raw passion she'd shared with him and did his best to meet her needs beyond sticking his dick in her.

As if he might float away or cease to exist if he let his eyes close, he blinked up at the night sky visible through the domed glass ceiling.

Despite everything around him, or maybe because of it, he felt insignificant. Incomplete.

His eyelids never drooped. Propped against pillows and the headboard, he ran his fingers through Savannah's hair, happy to give her what she craved for the few hours they had left together. Wishing someone other than *she* could do that for him. Even while dreaming, she curled closer to his touch.

Maybe someday he'd find another person who could inspire that kind of reaction in him. He'd be the richest man in the universe if, when he did, the woman capable of taming him felt the same in return.

He would do anything to deserve her love. Because all the money in the world couldn't keep him from drowning in loneliness, which made it impossible to sleep.

Hours later, early morning sunlight gilded Archer's cabin, which was a grossly understated label for these quarters. He'd have to figure out where the controls for the automatic blinds were before he actually attempted to sleep in here. It was dazzling, and kind of blinding, to watch the sunrise from his new home. The entire ceiling of his suite was constructed of aqua-tinted glass. It was almost as if he had camped outside.

If camping meant sleeping on a cloud in climate-controlled air while staring at the stars.

Though he knew they were on a boat, the size of the ship and the insignificance of the chop in Bonaire's sheltered port had made it as steady as a rock. He couldn't possibly have been more comfortable.

Unless he'd shared his bed with someone he cared for.

Idiot. From now on, he would stick to his plan.

Savannah began to rouse beside him, stretching and yawning into her fist. She was beautiful mussed, but he immediately began to think of ways to avoid a round of morning sex he simply wasn't into. It wouldn't be fair to mislead her.

Banks to the rescue again.

A non-intrusive tone chimed from beside the bed. It was subtle enough that Archer didn't register it as an incoming phone call until the third ring. He reached over to the side table to answer. "Yes?"

"Morning, Archie. Our final crew member is onboard. When you and the other divemasters are recovered from last night, I'd like to hold a staff meeting. We should get introductions out of the way and talk about some ground rules before the first set of guests begin arriving this afternoon. Does that work for you?"

"Of course, I'll be right out." Truthfully, he couldn't be more glad that Banks had spared him an awkward goodbye. "I'll stop and get the guys on my way. Otherwise, they'll never make it."

"Probably wise. They seemed to be enjoying themselves last night." Banks pitched his voice lower. "I left Ms. Ridley's garments outside your door and there's a breakfast buffet waiting. You're welcome."

Then he hung up.

Archer rolled out of bed and collected their belongings. He left them on the bed while he used the restroom and yanked on some clothes. When he returned, Savannah shimmied into her discarded dress. She hadn't made any demands, for which he was grateful. Still, he felt familiar disappointment tainting the pleasure they'd brought each other the night before.

If he'd felt something for her—even a faint echo of the something he'd felt for his long-ago girl—he could have justified bringing Savannah along on their journey. Unfortunately, their sexual chemistry seemed to be the extent of their connection. Just like it had been with all the women he'd enjoyed.

Except one.

The one he couldn't have.

The one he'd caused irreparable harm.

Archer opened the door and Savannah stepped into the hallway. She smiled up at him.

"I hope you'll stop by for lunch again someday...when you're good and *hungry*." The way she practically purred the last part made it clear what kind of appetite she hoped to slake.

He might have made an empty promise then, if he hadn't seen a ghost out of the corner of his eye. Had he summoned it by thinking about *her*?

What the—?

A uniformed crew member darted past, head down, as if embarrassed to have interrupted his obvious morning-after farewell. It must have been a trick of the light, or maybe his guilty conscience for breaking his promise to keep his dick in his pants until he'd made a meaningful match with someone, because he could have sworn it was *her.*

Or someone who looked like she might now—grown, gorgeous, strong.

He was going to have to find out who that actually was so he could stay far, far away.

Fortunately, he was about to enter a staff meeting and learn her name. Some part of him couldn't deny the morning's job requirements had just gotten a lot less onerous.

"Let me walk you out," he said to Savannah.

She smiled wistfully, then shook her head. "No need. Thanks for an unforgettable evening. I'm glad we got a chance to do that before you left. It was everything I hoped it would be."

Archer kissed her cheek. He wished he could feel more for her than he did.

Without looking back, Savannah swayed down the hall, off the boat, and out of his life.

He couldn't do this again. He swore he was going to hold out for someone who meant something to him. Someone he couldn't live without. Otherwise, disappointment might crush him.

It hurt too much to think he was the kind of man who found it this easy to turn away affection.

What kind of coldhearted bastard did that make him?

One just like his father.

Fuck.

∽ SEVEN ∾

Lieutenant Commander Waverly Adams squared her shoulders, assuming her military-grade posture. She strode down the hall from her assigned bunk, where she'd dropped off her midnight blue camo duffle. It was hard to believe that as part of the crew she had a room, however cramped, to herself. Hell, it even had a porthole to let in natural light and give her a glimpse of paradise outside the ship.

After a dozen years of living in barracks, she would so take that.

If she stayed.

Waverly headed toward the stairs that led to the upper deck, where their staff meeting would be held. Her heart pounded in her chest. It felt odd to have her hair down, brushing her butt. Even braided, it seemed wild compared to twisting, wrapping, and pinning her mane into a bun that conformed to the Navy's strict grooming standards.

Something had urged her to shed a couple of those uptight habits. Maybe so her old acquaintance would have some hint of the kid she'd been to jog his memory.

Would Archer Quartermane—her first and everlasting crush—even remember her?

She thought so, but feared that he might not.

What if, like so many other people who'd faded from her life, he'd meant much more to her than she had to him? Sure, they'd gone to different schools. Hers a private, all-girls preparatory academy. His even more exclusive. But he'd hung out with her sporadically for years at pretty much every event they'd found each other at, when both of their fathers had been required to attend.

It had gotten to the point where the first thing she'd do when she could break away from shaking hands and looking pretty by her father's side was beg the doorman to check the guest list for Archer's father. Even the most boring events had been tolerable when he had been there to help her pass the time.

As they got older, their haphazard run-ins had turned into flirt fests.

One evening in particular had occupied a disproportionate amount of her teenaged daydreams. They'd been out exploring a hedge maze on the grounds of some socialite's mansion, laughing and chasing each other around the fountain at the center, when she'd tripped on her gown and crashed into him.

To keep her from bashing her brains out on a cherub statue, which pissed into the basin—how the fuck was that supposed to be classy anyway?—he'd caught her against his chest. It had started making the transition from scrawny to the broad torso of a grown man. His sheer size, the flex of his muscles, and his general...hardness...had amazed her. He must have liked what he'd felt, too. Because, as he steadied her on her feet, he leaned in.

Waverly had held her breath, afraid to hope that she might share her first kiss ever with Archer.

He'd made her unspoken wish come true.

The rest of that summer they'd skipped the chasing and gone straight to making out whenever they could find a shadowy corner, an abandoned boathouse, or an intricate garden.

Even now, the memory of his lips on hers and the remembered comfort his protective arms around her had the power to make her swoon. The warrior in her hated to admit it since the woman she'd grown into was nothing like the naïve, entitled brat she'd been before he'd taken off without warning—right around the time her fairy tale upbringing had officially gone to shit.

Waverly figured she'd had to crash and burn to truly appreciate life.

After all, starting over from scratch had allowed her to rebuild herself from the ground up, into the fierce, independent, competent person she was proud to be today. According to Banks, that would be another thing she had in common with her new boss. Something sure to earn his respect.

It had been a long time since she'd felt this vulnerable or sought someone's approval.

This was either the best or worst idea she'd ever had.

They were about to find out which it was.

Lost in thought, she jogged up the staff staircase that dumped out into the main hallway two floors above. She hadn't gone more than ten paces when the door immediately in front of her opened. Out stepped Archer along with a lovely—if rumpled—woman who'd clearly spent the night in his bed.

Whoa.

Waverly hadn't prepared herself for the pang of jealousy that threatened to unsheathe her formidable claws. Worse, attraction flared inside her as she caught a whiff of Archer's clean, masculine scent along with a peek at his melted-chocolate eyes.

Gorgeous and untouchable as ever.

She ducked her head and practically dashed along the immaculate hardwood past the couple. Her bare feet slapped some as she hustled in the direction of the lounge where Banks had instructed her to join their upcoming gathering.

When she turned the corner, she paused to regain her balance, safely out of sight.

It wasn't the ship tilting. It was her.

As if it wasn't weird enough being here—in circumstances so different than all those years before yet no less awkward—coming face-to-face with Archer and his latest lover didn't do much for her attempts to loosen up. Especially when a fraction of a second in his presence made it clear he was out of her league in every way that mattered.

Rich. Yup.

Suave. Yup.

Handsome. Yup.

A lover, not a fighter. Yup.

Capable of enjoying a casual hookup. Yup.

Archer had exactly zero things in common with the safe, boring men she accepted dinner invitations from on occasion.

Waverly drew in a deep breath, concentrating on settling down. She'd need to rely on her training to get her job here done despite being in constant close quarters with the only man who'd ever made her systems go haywire. And apparently still did.

It had been years since she'd wrestled with her confidence like this. That could be why she had come. It required proving to herself that she could handle things now that had been insurmountable obstacles before. A new challenge.

Except she might have gotten in over her head. The onslaught of memories, none of them as precious as the ones Archer had made with her, threatened to suffocate her. It had all been downhill from there. She just hadn't known it yet.

Cool, controlled, and skilled, she'd flown rescue missions the military wouldn't entrust to anyone else. Why did it feel like this time she might be the one who needed some saving?

Waverly stared at her hot pink pedicure. A bold, feminine display since she traipsed around barefoot. In the Navy, she had kept her girly selections hidden in her boots. Another dirty little secret. She should have realized that everything about this job would be different than what she'd grown used to. The drastic shift—not to mention the rekindling of her inappropriate attraction—left her raw and exposed.

On the *Divemaster*, there was nowhere to hide.

"Everything all right?" Banks asked, startling her.

She snapped to attention. "Yes, sir."

"It seems we're both going to have to work on cutting that out." The butler turned executive-agent-of-Archer's-life slung an arm around her shoulder. Grateful for his warmth and support, she leaned into the affectionate gesture just a bit. "Archie gets cranky if you *sir* him."

"Good to know." She definitely didn't want to piss him off.

Banks tugged on her braid. "And I am a simple servant. I don't deserve the title."

She slapped his gut with the back of her hand, making him *oomph*. "Bullshit."

"See, you're much tougher than I am." He murmured, "Stronger than you think, I bet."

If Waverly hadn't sworn off crying for good, she might have been tempted to give in to the sting behind her eyes right then. "Thank you."

"Anytime." He gave her one last squeeze then released her. "Come on. Let's feed you some breakfast and introduce you to the rest of the crew."

She nodded, afraid of what her voice might sound like if she attempted to speak.

Within the lounge, she discovered a situation that was at least sort of familiar. A group of high-performing individuals gathered around bulk-prepped food, exchanging banter before things got serious. When she entered, many surreptitious yet appraising glances were aimed in her direction.

Nothing new there.

Their combined scrutiny didn't impact her like the thought of a single glance from Archer did.

She hadn't even made it all the way into the room when a man—slightly less than six feet tall, she guessed—set down his plate and made his way to her. He had brown hair dark enough that she might have thought it was black if the sun hadn't shone through the windows onto it. Of course, it was also peppered with some gray that gave him a distinguished air. Gray eyes evaluated her from behind squared-off glasses that were both somewhat nerdy and very flattering. His goatee and mustache, an indulgence he wouldn't have been permitted in the military, were close-cropped and neat. The unmistakable black stripe adorned with an anchor above four gold stripes made it perfectly clear who he was even before Banks completed pleasantries.

"Captain Alex, I'd like you to meet Lieutenant Commander Waverly Adams."

She returned his firm handshake. "Nice to meet you, sir."

He didn't object to her formality. Banks had filled her in earlier so she knew he was a fellow veteran. No amount of cajoling would convince her to treat him differently.

"I'm glad to have you onboard. You came highly recommended by an old friend of mine—Commander Smith."

As soon as he mentioned one of her mentors, they were off exchanging stories. She had no idea how long they'd stood there while Archer probably finished saying goodbye to his overnight guest, or untangled the other two divemasters—the only other missing staff members—from similar situations.

Long enough for her to polish off a ham, egg, and cheese croissant and forget about her nerves, though. She was chuckling at some antics Captain Alex related when everyone else went quiet.

Her laughter rang out in the silence, drawing the attention of her new bosses.

Waverly froze.

So did Archer.

Their gazes locked. She wondered for a moment if he might actually be Superman with a laser-beam stare. It nearly set her blood boiling.

Until the two guys dragging ass behind him crashed into his back, shoving him forward and severing their link.

She figured it was best to act as if she were on the first day of any normal job. One where she hadn't repeatedly sucked face with the boss in another lifetime or fantasized about him far more often than was healthy ever since.

Waverly straightened her spine, assumed her best resting bitch face, and tucked herself into the corner of the room, behind a few other crew members. That seemed to work.

Archer glanced away to address the room in general. "I apologize for making you wait. Tosin isn't exactly a morning person."

The sleepy—and sort of hung-over—looking guy rolled his eyes, drawing an exasperated sigh from one of his partners. Clearly they were also best friends. They could practically finish each others' sentences.

"Oh, I'm a *hell* of a morning guy. As I was about to demonstrate…"

Banks stepped in before they could deteriorate too much of the professional atmosphere he'd created for the staff. At least not on the very first day of the Divemaster Project. "Okay, everyone, today is show time. Our first batch of guests will arrive in just a few hours. The two dozen passengers have one thing in common. They are all family members of children who passed away unexpectedly. They chose to donate their loved ones' organs and saved countless lives despite their own personal losses. Each person was nominated by the family of a transplant recipient who felt they deserved the vacation of a lifetime. For many of these people, significant stress is a constant part of their daily existence. I see it as our mission to help them forget their personal tragedies for a little while. Or if we can't do that, at least give them some space to reflect in peace and quiet away from their obligations."

Well, that sobered things up real quick.

Damn.

For the first time, Waverly realized another massive benefit of this position. It was one she'd loved about her time as a sailor as well. She'd be doing something to enrich people's lives. Maybe make a small difference, like she wished someone had done for her in her time of need.

With that in mind, she swore to iron out any lingering weirdness with Archer and do the best she could for the beneficiaries of his organization. It would help if he didn't keep ogling her, though.

When she caught him doing it again, he looked away.

Yet every few seconds he repeated the performance.

Was he trying to figure out who she was? Or was he hoping she'd take a hint and leave? Maybe he didn't want to remember where they'd come from any more than she did.

One thing was for sure—he wasn't leveling any smoldering, seductive stares in her direction. Intense, yes. Googly eyes, not so much.

Too bad. That might have been the *only* thing she missed about her old life.

Banks continued his briefing. "We've arranged vacation time and everything imaginable so that this group of guests can stay with us for the next three weeks. During that time we'll visit each of the ABC islands, starting here with Bonaire, then moving to Curaçao and on to Aruba before venturing farther out to sea. There is a chain of uninhabited islands Archer, Tosin, and Miguel have visited briefly in the past that they'd like to explore. Depending on how that goes, we could also make a side trip over to Venezuela. We'll adjust the schedule as needed to accommodate weather or other situations that arise. If there are no questions, I'd like to go around the room and have each of you tell us what you do here, your name, and anything else you'd like to share with our newcomers."

The majority of the crew had worked on this ship for weeks as everything was prepared for their inaugural run. Nearly everyone had experience doing the same work on other vessels before that, each experts in their duties. The *Divemaster* hadn't had a helicopter before the renovations, so Waverly was one of the handful of newbies here today. A masseuse, Vanessa, had introduced herself earlier and stood nearby, along with Maria, an addition to the kitchen staff.

This was the first time the rest of the crew was meeting Archer, Tosin, and Miguel as well. That sort of took precedence, deflecting a lot of the pressure from her.

Waverly listened attentively, though she could feel the blast of Archer's stare from time to time. She ignored him, or tried desperately to, memorizing the names and roles of each person on the team.

Staff was organized into a few main groups—officers, deck crew, engineering, and interior. She didn't really fit anywhere. Along with the ship's medic, massage therapist, and of course the divemasters, Waverly was lumped in with the other specialists. Since she'd been the last to arrive and was standing near the end of the line, she was the final person to run through her spiel.

"Good morning, everyone. I'm the ship's helicopter pilot. I spent the last eleven years training with and flying Seahawks for the Navy." If she wasn't mistaken, Archer seemed to relax visibly as she spoke, so she tossed in a joke. "I promise I won't fly like I have on some of my missions. Easy does it. Unless you ask for a wild ride."

She risked a peek at Archer then, only to find his nostrils flaring.

What had she said...?

Oh, oops, she hadn't meant it like *that*. Shit.

She would have tried to smooth over her gaffe if Tosin Ellis hadn't shot his hand in the air, his eyes growing huge. He shouldn't have bothered since he spoke before anyone could give him permission. "Hold up a second. If she's a super sexy, badass helicopter pilot...does that mean we have a helicopter for her to pilot?"

"Yes, sir." Banks nodded solemnly as a few other staff members attempted to disguise their snorts behind napkins.

"Hells yeah! I call first ride in the chopper, suckers!" Miguel fist pumped as he looked between Tosin and Archer.

The guys laughed along with their counterpart, but choked when Banks interjected, "Seems only fair then that Tosin and Archie take the maiden voyage in the supercars we have on board for shore excursions. I assume a Lamborghini and a Bentley will suffice?"

"Are you shitting us right now?" Miguel clasped his chest over his heart. "You wouldn't joke about something like that, would you?"

"I shit you not, sir," Banks replied with the perfect dose of feigned snootiness.

Waverly tried not to let a smile crack her stolid mask. It was impossible. They were so fun to be around. She felt herself wanting to belong already. A dangerous proposition.

Archer shushed Miguel as best he could. Then he nearly melted her insides when he turned his full attention directly on her. "Sorry, with this dumbass losing his mind over here, I didn't catch your name."

So he didn't recognize her after all.

Her smile dulled, becoming forced.

Banks nodded at her, so she drew herself up and led with the bit she was most proud of even if technically she was retired. "I'm Lieutenant Commander Waverly Adams."

Archer gripped his mouth then wiped his hand down his chin. The motion didn't disguise the fact that his jaw had dropped. Flabbergasted, he practically gasped, "Holy fucking shit. It *is* you."

Not in a *Well, how about that! My long lost puppy love. What the hell have you been up to this past decade? So great to see you again!* sort of way, either.

Color leached from his face. His mouth opened and closed a few times. Then color rushed back into his cheeks. This time it was an unhealthy shade of lava red instead of tan, though.

"Banks. I need to see you out in the hall. Immediately." He marched off without another glance—steamy, intense, or otherwise—in her direction.

So...that hadn't gone well.

Of course not. Since she'd just decided she hoped to stick around.

With everyone gawking at her in utter disbelief, she didn't know what to say.

Or what to do.

After a couple tense minutes and muffled shouts, she had had enough.

"If I don't come back, send a search party, would you please, sir?" she asked Captain Alex.

"I'm more worried about that idiot," she thought she heard the man mutter as she stormed out the door, simultaneously humiliated and crushed.

And pissed off because of it.

EIGHT

Archer pivoted, swinging around to face Banks, trying not to bellow.

He failed miserably. "Why the *hell* is she here?"

"Because the lieutenant commander is highly qualified for the position. Overly so, in fact. I only hired the best for you, Archie." Placid expression in place, Banks merely stared back, hands folded in front of his uniform. His ensemble consisted of khaki shorts and a navy polo instead of the full tux required by Archer's asshole father. Somehow the cotton had been pressed and was perfectly crisp.

He clearly took this role no less seriously than he had his estate manager duties.

It was also painfully obvious that he'd endured far worse temper tantrums from Archer's father. Though Banks didn't flinch in the face of Archer's ire—and, to be honest, pure terror—he did seem surprised by the uncharacteristic outburst.

Shit. This wasn't the kind of guy Archer aimed to be. But...*Waverly!*

Seeing her had just about knocked him on his ass. Thinking about her sharing opulent, yet still limited quarters with him...

No. That wouldn't work.

Because one look at her had him forgetting the promises he'd made to himself the night before. As she always had, she turned him on in a heartbeat. It must be some crazy compatible pheromone thing they had going between them. What else could explain this instant and insatiable lust?

It was even more inappropriate now than it had been back then.

When he was sixteen, he'd thought his guaranteed boner in her presence was...well, due to being sixteen and horny every minute of the day. When he was nineteen, he'd thought it was because she might be *the one* for him.

Though they'd never gotten a chance to find out before that possibility had been ruined.

Now that he was thirty-one, he had matured enough to be positive his attraction was driven by something a hell of a lot more potent. And more treacherous. Addictive, too.

Even now, like some creeper, he wished he could spy on her in the other room. See the thick braid of onyx hair that would make the perfect tether as he mounted her from behind and rode...

Damn it.

No!

Not after what he'd done to her. She'd *never* be down for that. And he did not blame her.

Disgusted with himself, he hung his head and tried to think.

Why would she sign on to the *Divemaster*?

Wasn't seeing him as painful for her as seeing her was for him?

And...seriously? She was a kickass helicopter pilot?

Confusion battered him from a dozen directions at once. What the hell was going on here?

He'd never have assumed she'd have to work at all, let alone conquer something as daring and non-traditional as that. If he'd ranked every single job in the world he thought Waverly Adams might have in her lifetime, helicopter pilot would likely have fallen below fire breather in a traveling circus or rattlesnake venom milker or pet food taste-tester.

Had he been responsible for the complete annihilation of the playful, fuzzy bunny she'd been before *that* night?

If so, did it make him even sicker that this ferocious version of her turned him on even more than the softer side had?

How had she convinced her ultra-conservative, elitist father to allow her to enlist in the military?

She was obviously stronger willed than he'd given her credit for.

Add another black mark to his record with her.

Uncounted questions swirled around his brain, paralyzing him.

"If you'd like me to release her and find someone else, I will." Banks tipped his head almost imperceptibly. For him, that was as blatant a dissent as if he'd screamed. "I assure you, though, this wasn't some nepotistic hire. She's ranked at the top of her field. Has several commendations in her file. Besides, Archie, I remember how well you two used to get along. You asked me to keep an eye on her when you left. So I thought—"

"You couldn't have known. But you thought wrong. Get her out of here. Please." For the first time, Archer wished he'd done as Banks had requested and reviewed the staff applications. He'd have crumpled Waverly's and thrown it in the trash.

Or maybe even burned that fucker.

Anything to keep her safe from him.

Because even now, he didn't want her to go.

What kind of insanity was this?

"Excuse me?" Anything but contrite, Waverly stood a few feet away, her brows arched, her hands on her lush hips and her toes tapping against the teak.

Even pissed, she looked amazing.

Pure temptation.

Archer could hardly catch his breath, never mind think straight. Had she come here to demand an apology? If so, he would gladly grovel. It was just that he didn't think acts of contrition would suffice. Words couldn't take back what he'd done.

Or did she plan to haunt him?

His mind scrambled, trying to analyze the problem from every angle, starting with her perspective. The one that mattered most.

What if this wasn't about him at all?

So far she hadn't made it seem as if it was. Hell, she hadn't even mentioned his sins when she could have outed him to a roomful of people.

If that was true, and she was here to prove something to herself, then he owed her anything she desired. If this position was it, he'd have to find a way to bury his attraction to her. Demonstrate that he had preserved some shred of a gentleman in him somewhere, despite his inherited evil streak.

Except he wasn't sure he had.

Even now, he was finding it hard to pry his attention off her breasts and the way they filled out the Banks Foundation shirt she wore. Some part of him roared in satisfaction, seeing his name on her body.

Could putting up with his lechery really be worth it to her?

"Why the hell do you want this job?" he barked at her.

She didn't retreat despite the things she knew he was capable of. The military had hardened her.

Or maybe he had.

"Because I've earned a cushy gig after risking my life for my country this past decade?" She didn't sound a hundred percent convincing when she said it, but he was willing to let it slide.

"Just tell me one thing." He stared at her fingers as he asked. He'd seen her rubbing the hem of her polo between her thumb and forefinger earlier. Right when she'd revealed herself. A classic Waverly tell. He'd know if she lied.

"What?"

"Are you doing this only for the money?" He swallowed hard, downing some of his pride to make as many amends as he could. "You know I'd have Banks write a check right now from the Foundation with as many zeroes as you tell him to add if that's what you're after. It's yours. Anything you need. Or hell, even if it's just what you want from me. No reason to make us both suffer."

The only thing her fingers did was curl into a fist at that last bit. He was liable to end this conversation with a well-deserved shiner if he wasn't careful.

"I think you've lost your mind. Yeah, I took a job for money. That's how most people do things. But...that stuff, about the kids. That means more. I would have liked to have been part of something generous, compassionate, and consequential. Whatever's happening here, though, it's not worth it. You know what? Fuck this. And fuck you." She turned as if to leave.

Archer reached out without thinking. His fingers wrapped around her upper arm to stop her. To turn her to face him. Something.

No matter what his intentions were, they were asinine.

He would have to learn to suppress his instincts around her if she stayed.

He had no right to touch her. Ever again.

So why did electricity arc between them when he did? And why didn't she shrink from the contact?

Archer could no longer figure out if he wanted her to stay—or wanted her to go.

Then he realized he was screwing up again. If she was okay with this, who was he to punish her further by denying her a pretty damn sweet job?

He owed her.

If this was what she called her debt in for, he would make it happen, even if it meant he would be driven insane with remorse and guilt before their first tour was complete. It wouldn't come close to paying for what he'd done.

At least she didn't seem afraid of him. If she had shrunk away, or whimpered, it would have killed him.

Hopefully he could convince her that he would never hurt her again.

Never would have the first time either, if he'd realized what was happening.

Not that it was any excuse.

He was a man now. One intent on doing the right thing, no matter how hard the universe seemed to try making that for him.

"Take your hand off me," she snarled.

Why was he still holding on to her? Part of him was scared she'd storm away and he'd never have the chance to set things to rights. This could be his shot at redemption.

Archer released her. His fingers splayed, palms perpendicular to the floor as he backed away step by step. "I'm sorry, Waverly. It won't happen again."

He hoped she realized he was talking about more than that single stolen touch.

She dusted herself off as if he'd given her cooties then stood straight, defiant, and committed.

Banks stepped between them then, breaking their line of sight and whatever insanity seemed to have overtaken them both. "I have to admit, I've got no idea what's going on here."

"That makes two of us." Waverly threw her hands up.

"Three," Archer growled.

"So why don't we try this? The guests will be here shortly. Call a truce. Go to separate corners of the ship for a while. Tomorrow you can hash things out like adults." The steady calm with which Banks outlined his plan had Archer unwinding slightly. Enough to see the wisdom in his suggestions. "If either of you decide then that I've royally screwed something up, there will be plenty of flights back to the States from Curaçao. For Waverly, or me, or both."

"No one's getting fired." Archer wanted to bang his head on the wall. "But if you want out, either of you…"

"I never intended to upset you. Or Waverly. But I clearly have stepped in it this time." Banks frowned. "There should be repercussions for poor judgment."

"I couldn't agree more," Archer said, thinking this might be payback for his own errors.

Anything he added would take them right back into their argument.

So they left it at that.

For now.

∾ NINE ∾

Waverly slid her dark sunglasses into place as she wound her way to the bottom level of the yacht and into the divemasters' realm. Not only because it was as if someone had taken the sunlight from Charleston, where she'd been stationed the past eighteen months, and cranked it up about a hundred notches. But also because she needed shielding from Archer's piercing gaze, if yesterday was any indication.

It was sort of like barging into some sea monster's lair. She was determined to plow ahead, though. Shrinking from her fears was not something she believed in doing anymore.

Her fingers trailed along the curved chrome handrail as she descended the final gorgeous staircase that led to the enormous staging area and dive platform. Though she'd never been on a boat this size intended solely for recreation, she was fairly certain these facilities were over the top and custom designed.

Wet suit racks and lockers lined the back wall near the entrance to the interior of the ship. Benches with tank holders and individually assigned milk crate bins tucked beneath each place to keep everyone organized. In the center of the wide-open area, a high counter held camera equipment. There were even a couple of tables being used as desks next to a whiteboard. Tosin appeared to be teaching a handful of guests, who either weren't already certified or were maybe taking an advanced course toward earning a specialty.

Miguel was over by the compressors, refilling tanks. They must have taken a group out far too early for her this morning. Sleeping in was a rare treat. So she'd indulged. Who knew what today would bring? Might as well make the most of what time she had here.

Waverly kept searching, only one person on her mind at the moment.

When she spotted him, bending over in a damn near scandalous pair of white swim briefs that revealed almost all of his fine form, she was even gladder for her cover. Daaaaaaamn!

On display, his ass looked entirely too grab-able. Powerful thighs, and his back—lean and muscled—made her pray he would turn around soon so she could catalog the rest of his killer features.

There wasn't a spare ounce of fat on him anywhere.

"Ahem." Miguel cleared his throat, winking at her as he gave his friend a head's up that she was standing here watching the Archer Show.

When he caught sight of her, he didn't bolt upright. Nope. He finished what he was doing, then gracefully unfolded himself, dropping a dozen or so snorkels and masks into the rinse tanks. The view from the front somehow managed to rival his spectacular buns.

Archer's hair stuck up, wet from his earlier plunge. In sexy disarray, it made her palms tingle with the urge to finger comb it. Then again, she might be distracted by touching the scruff of his light beard—which he definitely hadn't had the last time she'd kissed him—or following the smattering of dark fur over his chest and tight abs down to that skimpy suit hugging his hips.

Thankfully, the rinse tank kept her from eye-fucking his package.

That might have gotten embarrassing. Sunglasses to the rescue.

Especially since she was fairly sure she looked like an owl with her eyes about to pop out of her skull.

Tosin paused his class for a moment, peeking between her and Archer. Great, an audience. Just what she didn't need if things went to hell like they had the day before. She swallowed hard and mentally measured the distance between herself and the staircase. Still, she refused to run.

"Good morning," Waverly said quietly as she approached Archer.

"Morning." No *good* from him.

At least he didn't seem like he was about to explode again.

"Want some help with those?" She picked up the gallon jug of dish detergent he was about to disinfect the gear with, poured some onto one of the rags nearby, and began to scrub before he'd agreed.

"What are you doing, Waverly?" He gazed at her, pitching his voice low when he asked, clearly inquiring about a lot more than her scrub job.

She followed his lead, keeping their discussion as private as could be given the people surrounding them. "Do you think we could start over? Just pretend yesterday—hell, our whole lives before right now—never happened?"

It would simplify things, she figured.

"Can you really do that? I think it would be harder for you than for me." He scrubbed his face. "Even if you can, should you? I don't expect you to let me off easy."

She thought she'd called him on his shit pretty thoroughly yesterday. What else did he expect her to do in retaliation for losing his temper? Cane him?

An entire career spent in the midst of mostly men had conditioned her to dealing with their methods of communication or the avoidance thereof. "Um, sure. Everyone screws up. I'm not the kind of person to harp on it once amends are made."

Nor did she want to get mired down in a rehash of yesterday's bewildering argument. She didn't think she'd understand what had set him off even if he tried to explain. When she'd thought over it as she tried to fall asleep, all she could come up with for sure was that the two of them still had the capacity to affect each other deeply.

That didn't seem like a horrible thing to her.

Eventually, Archer caved. "You said *make amends*. What can I do to make it up to you?"

"Let me tag along with your snorkel group. It's been a while since I swam in tropical water like this." She'd even put on the modest one-piece suit Banks had issued as part of the uniform beneath her shorts and polo, just in case.

"Sure, I guess that's a start, though I'm certain the punishment doesn't fit the crime in this case. I thought about it a ton last night and I realized it would be even more of a dick move for me to dictate how you should feel about it." He seemed far too serious when he stared down at her. "So, I'm not joking here—whatever you want, you get."

Waverly found it odd that he kept treating her with such kid gloves. After yesterday, she didn't want to rock the boat, though. Since she wasn't pissed anymore, and he seemed to have gotten over whatever had swum up his ass, she didn't see any reason to prolong their discord.

Their arms brushed up against each other as they worked, distracting her for a moment. She stuck out her sudsy hand and said, "Truce?"

Archer swallowed hard, as if she'd given him something much more valuable than simple forgiveness. "I don't deserve that. But, yeah. Truce. Thank you."

For a while they worked together in silence, except for the squeak of their fingers on clean plastic. It wasn't awkward or strained, though. Waverly spared a few moments to take in the surroundings. They'd cruised overnight to their next destination. The beautiful beaches of Curaçao stretched out before her. Anchored a ways offshore today, they had stayed closer to prime diving locations.

Some of the guests had taken tenders to shore to explore the island. No one had plans to use the chopper. Except maybe Miguel, if he requested his ride later.

"Of all the crew, I have the fewest responsibilities." She thought about spending some quality time catching up on her reading and tanning. That would probably rock for a while, but sitting idle didn't suit her much. "I can help you out when I'm not flying. With this kind of stuff. Diving, too. Another set of eyes never hurts when you're down there."

"You're certified?"

"Want me to run down to my cabin and bring you my PADI card and logbook?" She smirked. "Of course. I traveled to a lot of excellent destinations and used leave to explore where I could. Egypt was probably my favorite. Took the Navy courses for non-diver personnel, too. Which means I'm qualified to assist dive teams or aid in search operations, though let's hope we never need one of those. Could probably blow some shit up down there in a pinch if necessary."

He blasted out a laugh. "It's so weird to me, thinking of you like that. I'll keep it in mind if we ever find ourselves in need of an explosives expert."

Waverly beamed up at him, glad that although he hadn't thought of her that way before, it didn't seem to make him like her any less. If anything, his smile and head shake led her to believe he was kind of awed. Or maybe even impressed.

By the time they'd finished the batch of gear, people had begun to wander into the staging area to prepare for their snorkel tour. Some had obviously never tried it before. So she busied herself calming those who exhibited nerves by demonstrating techniques and promising to stick close by until they got the hang of it.

Archer and Miguel were outfitting everyone with fins, masks, and snorkels, plus pool noodles or cameras or inflatable rafts, whatever they needed to feel safe and have fun. A couple of the more experienced passengers were staring longingly at the sea, getting antsy, when someone shouted, "Look, dolphins!"

Waverly rushed to the edge to ooh and ahh along with the rest of the folks gathered nearby. Sure enough, they were darting around near the ship.

"Mind if I get in? Take anyone who's ready with me before the dolphins swim off?" Waverly asked Archer, a little louder than she'd intended as excitement coursed through her.

He seemed unsure at first. "If you're comfortable..."

"I am." Would he trust her?

"Okay, go ahead. Holler if you need help."

She grinned as she stripped off her shirt and shorts then dashed over to the neat stack of equipment she'd prepared for herself. Right about then, she realized he was appraising her just like she'd done to him earlier. Hopefully he liked what he saw as much as she had.

Except when their gazes caught, he looked away, guiltily, whereas she'd only stared longer.

Then thoughts of Archer and the havoc he was wreaking on her libido vanished.

Waverly slipped on her gear and leapt into the ocean. She told the rest of the guests, "Whenever you're ready, join me."

It was a rush being in the water with animals as intelligent, agile, and predatory as dolphins. They weren't the cute cartoons most people envisioned. She was mindful of that and kept her distance, absolutely transfixed when one of the undomesticated creatures buzzed past her, whistling and clicking to its friends.

A couple of snorkelers made it in with her, chattering excitedly as they observed the pod passing by. Waverly divided her attention, making sure each of the swimmers seemed at ease with their apparatus. The salt water made it easy to stay afloat even without clutching the pool noodles some of them leaned on. Still, sometimes it could be intimidating to jump off a perfectly good boat into endless water. She remembered the first open water swim she'd participated in on an aircraft carrier. Talk about isolation. Nothing but empty horizon in every direction she had looked.

And yet the entire ocean was their swimming pool.

Neat and terrifying at once.

Someone coughed. Waverly spun around until she identified the struggling guest. She put her face in the water and swam, cutting through the baby waves with an efficient breaststroke.

Archer must have heard the sputtering, too. Without hesitating, he executed a perfect dive off the platform and headed toward her target. The woman wasn't really in any danger. Still, instincts could sometimes trigger panic when water unexpectedly splashed you in the face or you got a swallow of it down the wrong pipe.

And *that* could kill you.

Panic, that is.

Waverly wrapped her arm around the thrashing snorkeler. "Hey. You're all right. I've got you."

She grabbed the foam pool noodle that had slipped from the woman's grasp and returned it to her. The guest clung as if it were a lifesaver.

"Tilt your face up a little, out of the chop, and take a nice deep breath," Waverly coaxed the woman.

By the time Archer emerged and shook the water from his eyes, she had the situation well under control.

He didn't try to overrule what was obviously working. Instead he floated nearby, ready to assist if needed, and let her do her job. Well, actually, he let her do *his* job. Somehow that was even more satisfying.

"I missed the dolphins." The woman sighed, then put her snorkel in her mouth, cleared it properly, and leaned forward, peeking through her mask once more.

"They may come back." Archer said, trying to cheer her up. "Besides, there are lots of other cool things to see."

He raised his hand and called the rest of their charges over to him now that the excitement was over. "We're going to split into two groups. If you just want to stick around the boat and take it easy, you'll be with Miguel. If you want to check out the reef and are up for a little swim, grab a noodle and come with me."

Waverly floundered, debating what she should do.

"Would you mind joining me?" he asked her. Then he repeated what she'd said before. "Never hurts to have another pair of eyes. Or another very capable guide."

She smiled at the compliment, then agreed.

∽ TEN ∾

Floating beside each other, kicking lazily, the pack of snorkelers skimmed over the reef. Archer noticed things she never would have seen from this far away, making sure to draw everyone's attention to the highlights.

Waverly couldn't wait for her next opportunity to dive. Once she'd experienced SCUBA, snorkeling didn't cut it. Not when you wanted an up-close, full-immersion experience. It was fun, just not the same.

With her eyes glued to the reef, she noticed a dark green splotch start to move in a direction contrary to the ebb and sway of the soft corals. She lifted her head high enough that she could take her snorkel out of her mouth and call, "Turtle!"

Then she held out her arm, pointing toward the creature that ascended in their general direction for a breath of air.

"Please remember not to touch it or spook it if it comes near you," Archer educated their guests. "Turtles need oxygen. We don't ever want to risk trapping it beneath the surface if it needs to breathe."

The snorkelers made room for the turtle. Their lack of threatening gestures convinced the little guy that it was okay to come closer and they all ended up scoring a better view. After their new friend had wandered off in search of his next meal, Archer steered the group back toward the *Divemaster.*

"It's funny how the turtle hardly moves its fins and yet it's still faster than me," Waverly bitched, wishing she was half as graceful in the water.

"You seem like you're doing just fine to me. Made it to that woman in a flash earlier." Warmth and pride colored his comment in return, making her stomach flutter as if she'd swallowed one of those small, schooling fish whole. "If we didn't have the group with us, I'd race you back to the boat."

"Next time." Waverly had developed her competitive side in the Navy.

When they reached the *Divemaster,* Miguel climbed aboard and began to assist people as they grew tired and exited the water. Waverly and Archer remained.

For her, she simply didn't want to leave the relaxing water any time soon.

For him, he kept an eye on every last person, making sure they got their fill of the activity safely.

Eventually, it was just the two of them, floating near the swim line that trailed behind the boat. It was ingenious. The rope had plastic bubbles spaced periodically along its length. Each end of the line was attached to one of the back corners of the boat and the slack drifted out forming a semi-circle. It acted as a corral, keeping their pool noodles, inflatable rafts, and other toys from escaping to the open ocean.

They took off their gear and piled it on the ship's platform so they could enjoy a simple swim unhindered, then collected anything else left behind by the guests as it floated within the swim line. When they were finished, he turned toward the ladder that dipped into the water off the back of the ship.

"Mind if we stay just five minutes more?" she asked him—begging, really, since swimming in the ocean alone was definitely not allowed.

"You sound like me. Nah, I could do this all day." He grinned then put his arms up on the swim line, his body rising to the surface, ankles crossed, as he stared up at the clouds overhead. Completely relaxed.

In his element.

Waverly licked her lips.

"Pretty woman. Sunshine. Ocean breeze. Have Miguel toss me a beer and I'm good for the next week or two," he elaborated.

"So, you still think I'm pretty, even though I'm not so feminine anymore?" She hated herself for asking, but the question had slipped out before she could stop it. "Can't remember the last time I wore a fancy dress or had a manicure."

He looked at her like she was crazy then. "I didn't like you for your wardrobe."

Waverly thought back on their encounters. He'd always been the aggressor. Showing her just how much he wanted her.

Now, though, he was clearly not about to budge.

Conveniently, she'd gotten a hell of a lot bolder since then.

She swam close enough that she could see the droplets sparkling like diamonds on his eyelashes. Still, he only stared back at her. His hands never moved from that damn rope.

Why? Could it be he wasn't interested anymore?

"Would you like me if *I* kissed *you* right now?" she whispered.

"You're calling all the shots here." Archer reclined, letting the buoys do their job and keep him afloat as he lazily treaded water.

Maybe it was his thing these days to let women come to him. She had no problem with that.

"Am I?" She drifted closer still.

The wake of a passing boat finished the job, shoving her into him. Her hands landed on his bare chest. He hissed as if she'd scorched him.

Waverly peered up at him, full of mischief, and wondered if her eyes reminded him of the ocean he loved so much. He seemed like he couldn't stop looking into them. Hell, he didn't even blink. "In that case…I think I'd like to forget the past twelve years—especially yesterday—ever happened and say hello to you properly."

She wound her arms around his neck and levered against his shoulders to lift herself out of the water enough that his mouth was within reach. Gently, she pressed her lips to his and began to kiss him.

Far more patient now that he was grown, he didn't devour her in response.

Admitting that disappointed her just a little, she took it upon herself to taunt him into surrendering some of his newfound control. Waverly missed the unabashed passion he'd shared with her in those never-forgotten kisses.

She wanted this one to be every bit as memorable for them both.

When she paused, peering up to see his reaction, she didn't necessarily like what she saw. So she separated them a tiny bit.

"Isn't this weird for you?" He stared at her, worried.

"It wasn't until you asked that." She lost some of her enthusiasm. "Now it kind of is."

Still, she tried one more time to recapture their spark.

Waverly wrapped her legs around Archer's trim hips, hugging him so she didn't drown when she lost herself in the taste of salt and his mouth. His hand came up, cupping her ass to keep them steady when he returned her kiss and deepened it.

Finally!

She sucked on his tongue, teasing him into dipping inside her mouth. Hints emerged of the Archer she had known and—

Known and *wanted to fuck*, she substituted mentally.

Kiss by kiss, he grew bolder until she felt his cock start to make its presence known against the softness of her belly. There was no hiding when two thin layers of Lycra were all that separated them.

Waverly moaned—twice when he bit her bottom lip.

"You getting out, *Archie*?" Tosin called from above. When he peeked over the edge and realized why they'd suddenly gotten so quiet, he said, "Oops. Don't mind me! I didn't see anything. Much."

Backpedaling, he disappeared from view.

But the spell had been broken.

"I can't do this." Archer broke away, breathing hard.

Was it because his friend had busted them sucking face like the teenagers they'd once been?

"I'm sorry. Until we've really talked, in private, and I can apologize properly..." That again? Ugh. She'd thought they'd gotten past that, but he kept bringing it up. Killing her buzz. "Maybe not even then, Waverly. It just doesn't feel right."

Funny, it had felt perfect to her.

"Okay." She let go and swam for the ladder, hoping he hadn't glimpsed the disappointment carved on her face. The last thing she wanted was his pity.

"Wait. Don't go. Have lunch with me?" Archer asked as he climbed up behind her, probably not even taking the opportunity to check out her ass.

Silent as she swiped salt water from her legs, she debated declining. Had pretty much decided that it would be for the best if all he was going to do was knot her up inside and send her mixed signals. That would make this job hell.

"Hey," he said softly, drawing her attention back to him. "I'm sorry, okay? Just...this one time can we put it all out on the table? Then we never have to mention it again. I swear. Deal?"

Fine. "Let's get this over with."

Archer nodded. Then he used a nearby intercom to request lunch for two be served on the private sundeck off his quarters. At least they agreed about something. Interruptions would be unwelcome.

Unfortunately, she suspected they believed it for entirely different reasons.

⚬ **ELEVEN** ⚬

Waverly tried to act like it was no big deal when Archer admitted her into his personal space. Not because they were *finally* adults who could do whatever they damn well felt like. Or because they were alone in what was essentially his bedroom. But because even for former rich kids like them, this place was spec-tac-u-lar.

She twirled around in the center of the cabin, which was more like some fancy conservatory than sleeping chambers with the glass everywhere. Cover blown, probably.

He chuckled at her delight. "You haven't even seen the best part yet."

Archer waved her over to the accordion doors that essentially removed the entire wall, opening the cabin onto his own personal sundeck, complete with a double-wide lounge bed thingy, a table for two, and a jetted hot tub. She might never leave.

Wow.

"Not going to lie, it *is* pretty awesome, huh?" His smile was crooked, one corner of his lips lifting higher than the other, accenting his hawkish nose and jaw line. She thought he could pass for a slightly paler version of an Arabian prince.

"Uh huh." She nodded then sank onto one of the chairs at the table.

None too soon, either. Someone knocked.

Archer called to grant them permission to serve lunch. Maybe he was better off than that prince after all, she thought with a laugh.

"What's so funny?" he wondered aloud as their server, Maria, presented plates of cheese, meats, hardboiled eggs, and fruit. Freshly baked bread, too.

Her stomach gurgled happily at the smells wafting from the tray to her nose. She waited until they'd thanked Maria, and the woman left, before answering.

"This whole situation, really." She shrugged. "How did we go from riches to rags and back to riches? Well, I mean, not that I'm loaded, but working here is plenty good enough."

Archer sat next to her. He plucked some grapes from the assortment, popping them into his mouth. "What do you mean by that? Yeah, I walked away from my dad's fortune. But...you...how'd you end up in the military? Did your dad disapprove when you told him you wanted to join the Navy? Is that why you went rags? I have to admit, that surprised the shit out of me."

"I could tell." She remembered the utter disbelief on his face when she'd told him her name the day before. "I have no idea if my dad approves of what I do. Or if he's proud of me. Things turned out as well as they could have, I guess. But it started out with pure desperation. I mean, in a single day my dad got locked up, my mom took the easy way out with all those pills she swallowed, and the feds seized everything we had. I'd just turned eighteen a couple of days before, so they considered me an adult. I was out on the street. On my own. I was never really close with any of the girls at school, remember? And after so many scandals, well, you know how it is. I was the drama llama. Unwelcome. Didn't have many options, to be honest."

"Time out." Archer was shaking his head. He dropped his fork and scrubbed his hands over his face. "Nothing you're saying makes sense to me. I have about twelve more questions now. Your dad did what? Your mom committed *suicide*? Jesus, Waverly! And the feds? What the fuck?"

"Oh." She tried to remember the details of the timing. With so much shit raining down on her at once, it had been kind of hard to keep up. And she hadn't even told him the worst of it yet.

That's right—he'd left soon before her life had imploded. She knew for sure because a day or two or three after someone had obviously tasted blood in the water and attacked her, knowing no one would give a fuck, she'd taken a taxi straight to Archer after being discharged, looking for help or maybe simply solace. She wasn't sure anymore.

Probably hadn't been very clear on the matter then either, given the fog that had lingered in her brain for more than a week afterward. She couldn't honestly remember much of anything. Including who had found her and taken her to the hospital in the first place. She did know it had been touch and go there for a while, so she definitely owed her life to whoever had looked out for her.

When she'd knocked on the door to the guesthouse behind Archer's father's mansion, where Archer had been staying since he'd graduated high school the year before, the door had swung open. Things were strewn about and his luggage was missing.

He'd already vanished.

That discovery had been traumatic, which was likely why she remembered the stabbing pain she'd felt then so vividly given the haziness of everything before and after it.

How she'd wished she could have gone with him wherever he'd vanished to. Hopefully somewhere a million miles away. Maybe that was what had pushed her to enlist. Or to accept the position on his ship now. It felt like coming full circle.

Archer was staring at her, waiting for her to explain.

Easy stuff first. "Turns out my dad is a sack of dog crap."

"I know the feeling," he commiserated.

"Well, mine is also a criminal. He's rotting in jail. Got busted for scamming your dad and a bunch of their friends out of millions of dollars. Everything we had became evidence in his trial and was eventually used to repay a fraction of what his victims had lost." She sighed then, finally realizing one thing that had gotten her hackles up wasn't a concern. "I guess I wondered if you freaked when you realized it was me on your team yesterday because you thought I might be untrustworthy like him."

"What?" Archer's brow scrunched. He scratched his cheek, then looked out to sea as if it was too hard to meet her stare. "No. I've only ever thought the best of you. Don't judge me by my old man. This seed fell far from that fucked-up tree. So did yours, obviously."

"I'm glad you feel that way," she admitted softly. "When I realized you had left without saying goodbye back then, I was kind of surprised myself. I thought we had something going, you know?"

"I didn't figure you'd want to see me. Or anybody, really."

Because her mother had killed herself? Or because she was mortified by her father's actions? She was growing more perplexed. He'd just admitted he hadn't known about any of that.

If he had, he would have damn well been sure she had needed a friend. Him.

That only left one other thing.

Could he know about *that*? He must. Nothing else made sense.

But how? And had her assault made him think less of her? She shoved that thought away. It had taken a long time—and a lot of counseling—to wrangle those types of insidious self-judgments and beat them into submission. She did her best. Every once in a while, her old insecurities and scars showed themselves.

She must have been quiet too long.

"I am *so* sorry, Waverly."

Oh yeah, he definitely knew. Was *that* why he'd kept his hands to himself before?

How had he found out about her attack but not her father's fuck-ups or her mother's death? Why hadn't he reached out to see if she was okay? She hadn't been. He could have made an enormous difference. Instead of allowing anger or sadness to well up, she remembered that she'd taken care of herself and put it behind her. "It was a long time ago."

"No amount of time can erase something like that."

She shrugged. "I've accepted it. Moved on as best as I can. The hardest part was not knowing—who or why, I mean. Never being able to bring my attacker to justice or simply stare him in the eye and ask how he could have been such a coward as to drug and rape a barely legal girl."

What?

Archer blinked. Suddenly it all made sense—why Waverly had come here, how she could stand to be around him.

She had no fucking clue.

Son of a bitch!

He might not have done the right thing back then, but he wasn't about to make the same mistake twice. No matter the consequences. He deserved her loathing and any other repercussions for telling the truth.

"Waverly," he croaked as bile eroded his esophagus. "I can fix that for you at least."

"What do you mean?" She tipped her head, nibbling on her lower lip.

"The man who did such a horrible thing to you...who hurt you so bad..." He drew a shaking breath, nearly crushing the tabletop in his hands, which gripped the edge as if he were clinging for dear life lest he be washed overboard in the storm brewing around them. "It was me. I'm so, *so* sorry."

Her head whipped back as if he'd sucker punched her. Then she flew from the table, knocking the chair over in her haste to escape. He wanted nothing more than to go to her, to keep her from falling as he had once in a place far, far away, but he wouldn't dare advance on her or make any moves that could be interpreted as threatening.

No wonder she'd accepted his apology so readily this morning. She hadn't even known what he'd been begging forgiveness for.

Trembling all over, pale as an albino fish's belly, she staggered away from him.

The only thing she said before she disappeared inside was, "I quit."

"I understand." Archer felt as though he'd gotten sucked into the ship's propellers where blades chopped him to bits. Nothing in him remained untouched, unscathed, or unbroken. His heart and soul were minced. Yet the only thing he cared about was Waverly.

He slapped his hand on the intercom. "Banks!"

"Archie? What's wrong?"

"It's Waverly. Find her. Help her. Whatever she needs. Tell her to take the chopper if she wants, but make damn sure she's sound to fly before you let her take off." He couldn't bear the thought of something happening to her because of him.

Again.

"Are *you* okay, Archie?"

"No." He didn't elaborate. "But Banks, anything she tells you, believe it. It's true. All of it."

He groaned as he imagined the extent of the man's shock and disappointment in him. "If you would like to go with her, I don't blame you. I'm sorry."

"Archie!"

With a vile curse, he took his hand off the intercom button. Then he locked the doors to his cabin. He wasn't fit company for anyone.

And might never be again.

∽ TWELVE ∽

A week later, Archer sat on the dive platform, dangling his legs in the ocean as he stared at the waves rolling by. He couldn't remember the last time he'd eaten, or slept, or taken a shower for that matter. Even finding the energy to dive was impossible.

He leaned forward, wondering how much farther he'd have to tilt before he slipped into the warm water and let it close over his head. It would be peaceful, he bet.

"Archie," Banks called softly.

He didn't bother to turn around or reply, annoyed that the promise of solace had been stolen from him. For now.

"We need to talk to you." Tosin this time.

"Enough is enough, man." Miguel was here, too.

Great. This was officially some sort of intervention.

He didn't bother to acknowledge them. It would never be *enough*.

They hadn't seen the devastation in Waverly's gorgeous eyes. Like the ocean on a bright day overtaken by a violent summer storm. He'd done that to her. And more.

No telling what damage he'd done by letting her kiss him. He'd been totally insane to believe she could want him after he'd abused her trust so totally.

"Tell us what happened?" Banks asked, though Archer knew it was actually a demand disguised by politeness.

He still didn't speak.

"You know, when the two of you vanished within days of each other, I actually thought she might have run off to be with you," Banks confessed. "There was something between you, wasn't there?"

"There might have been, eventually." Archer shrugged.

Shit, he hadn't meant to say that out loud.

Now that he had, though, he kept going. "I kissed her a few times. Followed her around, waiting for her to turn eighteen. Wanted to do a lot more."

Had done a whole lot more, when she'd been unable to consent.

"Ah, but you never got the chance," Banks said softly.

Archer let him think that.

"Anyway, her position here was the final one I had to fill. When her resume popped up in an online search of the top one hundred helicopter pilots in the world, I thought it was destiny. I knew she flew. I had kept tabs on her like you asked. Was aware she was making a life for herself. I just hadn't realized how good she was until I started digging in."

Archer nodded, completely unsurprised she was *that* successful at what she'd elected to do with her life. "You couldn't have known. I'm certain my father went to great lengths to keep our relationship a secret. For various reasons."

"Would you tell us more about whatever happened?" Tosin wondered as he sat next to Archer.

Miguel took the spot on his other side, then said, "We're guessing it has something to do with that crap you were spouting. About why you hated your father."

Banks sighed wearily as he sank into a deck chair. Glad he didn't have to face the man as he confessed, Archer nodded. "It does."

Maybe it would help to finally say it out loud to people who would actually listen. The one time he'd come clean, it hadn't gotten him anywhere. This would be a different kind of confession, one more about saving his soul than requesting justice be served.

No need to pretty it up.

Archer blurted out the truth: "I raped Waverly."

He dropped his face in his hands, too mortified to face his friends and the man who was more of a father to him than the one who'd knocked up his mother. If he had any tears left, he probably would have bawled. As it was, sickness gnawed at his guts.

Instead of condemning him, Banks came closer. He must have crouched behind Archer because his palm landed on Archer's back, lending him strength. "Archie, I have known you since you were three years old. There is no way you're capable of something that vile."

"Not intentionally. That doesn't mean that I didn't do it, though." He had to make them understand. "She showed up at my door one night. I knew she'd just celebrated her birthday. Hell, I'd had the date circled on my calendar for months. Was trying to decide how to approach her. She hadn't returned any of my calls or acknowledged the roses I sent her that day. So I figured she wasn't interested. I didn't know that she was occupied by her life falling apart."

"And then she came to you." Tosin smiled weakly. "I can picture her barging in with those brass balls of hers and taking what she wanted."

"Waverly wasn't really like that back then," Banks corrected him. "She was sheltered. Timid. Never encouraged by her family to explore that side of herself."

"A damn shame." Miguel cursed. "You two are starting to make me think I was better off having no parents at all than people who held me back."

He had no idea.

"Exactly, Banks." Archer turned then to meet the man's gaze briefly. "So I should have known something was up when she did exactly that."

He remembered her tearing her clothes off before she'd even made it through his foyer. Feverish and refusing to wait even until they could make it upstairs to his bedroom, she'd jumped him.

"I'm not saying this excuses my actions, but when I think back on it—as I have over and over and over—it had to have been why I didn't realize something was wrong. Remember James Trudhart?"

"Now, *that* kid was trouble," Banks muttered. "I tried to keep him away from you. He was the son your father never had, that one."

"Yeah, well, that night he'd brought over a bottle of some nasty liquor he'd stolen from his father's bar. We put away a solid amount, considering neither of us were legal yet and had never drank more than a half a glass of wine at a time during some dinner party. After he'd barfed in the flowerbeds around the pool a few times, he gave up trying to polish it off with me and staggered home. I was still pretty hammered when Waverly practically kicked my door down."

Now that he'd finally began to spill his guts, the guys let him keep going.

"Hell, I slept with her thinking she *really* was into me. That I was a sex god at nineteen, turning this virgin into the best kind of nymphomaniac. It was pretty much the highlight of my life—until way later, when I realized she hadn't just fallen into a post-sex slumber. She was unresponsive. That's when I sobered up the rest of the way. And figured out what had happened. *Who* was responsible."

"Oh God," Banks rasped. "Your father was involved, wasn't he?"

"Yep, dear old dad drugged her. Or, more likely, had someone else do it for him. He told me all about the chemical later. It was fresh on the market, the early stages of something he wanted to *invest* in. They were calling it Sex Offender. Cute, huh?" Archer held his hands up, then let them drop to his thighs.

Useless.

"Why?" Tosin, who rarely lost his temper, sounded like he might punch something.

"For years, I wasn't sure. I thought maybe he was setting me up. Getting dirt on me to keep me close and force me to do as he told. He wanted me to take over his business. I knew that wasn't the path for me. We'd fought over it. A lot."

"A *lot*," Banks confirmed.

"So after I took Waverly to the hospital and made sure she was going to pull through, I thought I'd give him the biggest fucking middle finger of all time by rejecting everything he was. His money. To me it was dirty. I didn't want any part of that. Instead, I thought I'd bring as much shame as possible to our family. I went to the police. Turned myself in." Rage filled Archer as he realized how gullible he'd been about how the world really worked.

What's right wasn't what ruled.

Greed won. Every time. Even if it was corrupt as fuck.

"Archie, no." Banks had worked for the man long enough to know where this was going.

"Yep, the officer I *confessed* to was on my dad's payroll. He didn't take a word of it onto the record and instead delivered me straight home, to my father." Here's where Archer started to get angry all over again. "And even after *all of that*, I was still stupid enough to fall for his fast-talking diversions. I was so wrapped up in what I'd done and how much I hated him that I missed the bigger picture."

"What do you mean by that?" Miguel asked for clarification.

"I thought he'd fucked me over to get me to settle down and be his bitch." He huffed, his blood pressure skyrocketing until it was a miracle he didn't keel over from a stroke right then and there. "After what Waverly told me the other day, about how her dad conned mine out of millions, I'm sure I know the truth now."

"I think you're right, son." Banks sounded as miserable as Archer felt. Even from the grave, that demon had the power to destroy things. Hurt people.

"It wasn't some kind of blackmail fodder. Or a diamond-studded leash. It was punishment." Archer groaned. "He used me to hurt Waverly. And through me, her father. An agonizing blow for any dad who actually gave a shit about his kid. Hit 'im where he's most vulnerable. How many times had he given me that bit of advice?"

"I gotta say, I was thinking you were kind of harsh with that hate business back at Windsock." Miguel spit into the sea. "Now I see you weren't ruthless enough. I hate the fuckwad, too. And everything he's done to you. This is so messed up."

"If it mattered anymore, I'd have the authorities reopen Waverly's mother's case, too. My guess is he did the same or worse to her." Banks practically vibrated with fury. "Archie, I want you to try to see this my way, okay?"

He shrugged.

"What happened was a damn tragedy. Lots of innocent people got caught in the crossfire. Yourself included."

"I'm not—"

"Be quiet until I'm finished." Banks put some steel in his tone then, making Archer, Tosin, and Miguel whip around to look at him in unison. It might have been funny if things hadn't been so damn serious. "Your father was ruthless. I admit, at first I stayed because he paid me well. Then I stayed because I loved you, and I thought I could be your advocate. In the end, I only stayed there as long as I did because I was helping the authorities build a case against him."

"You were what?" Archer almost did go overboard then. "Do you have any idea how dangerous that was?"

Banks nodded. "It was worth every risk."

"Damn, Banks. You're the man." Tosin said what Archer was thinking, and that was even before he processed the part where the guy had said he'd loved him.

Archer had to clear his throat before he could say, "Thank you."

They stared at each other for a while.

Until Miguel asked, "Why didn't the authorities crack down on Archer's dad if he was as horrible as I suspect?"

"Every time we'd get close to nailing him for some shady thing or another, he'd weasel out of it. I couldn't prove anything, but that doesn't mean I didn't know what he was up to." Banks sighed. "I would bet everything I have that he was responsible for Waverly's mother's death. And I don't doubt for a single second that his intention was not only to have Waverly's innocence stolen. How bad was she when you got to the hospital?"

"Her heart stopped three times." Archer did choke up then.

"Don't you see? You saved her life, man," Tosin grabbed him by the back of the neck and shook him as if trying to knock some sense into him.

Miguel agreed. "If it wasn't for you, she wouldn't have gone on to be a badass helicopter pilot. You gave her a second chance. A better life where she got to become the person she should have been all along. I'm not trying to say it wasn't horrible. And completely wrong. What happened to you *both*. But…you're not thinking straight about this. About her."

"You've got to go to her, Archer," Banks encouraged while Tosin and Miguel nodded. "She should hear all of this from you. Besides, she's holed up in some dump in Caracas and won't let anyone near her. She hasn't gone out for food or anything in days. I'm worried."

Shit! He couldn't let her suffer more because of him. Of course the bomb he'd dropped had shocked her, probably ripped off scabs and left her bleeding out.

Alone. In a foreign country. One that wasn't especially safe.

Considering that he'd abandoned her while wounded once, he didn't intend to fuck up like that again.

Archer climbed to his feet. "What's the fastest way to get there?"

"We had the chopper flown back onboard with a temporary replacement pilot. Give me five minutes and you can be on your way." Banks's best efforts couldn't squelch the panic bubbling up inside of Archer, now that he knew she might be in danger. "Captain Alex sent one of his officers to tail her. Not because we think she needs a babysitter or anything, but because she was upset—not thinking rationally—when she left. He can lead you to her when you get close."

"Fine. Let's go." Archer spun on his bare heel and headed for the stairs to the main deck.

"Yo, *Archie!*" Miguel called.

"Yeah?" He was tempted to spring back and hug the guys but was afraid he might lose his shit when he had something important to focus on.

"Make sure you bring our pilot back. I never did get that ride," he finished with a smirk.

"Shithead," Archer muttered, though he smiled the barest bit.

"We lurve you, too!" Tosin professed in a shout half the Caribbean had to have heard.

Waverly paced the dingy hotel room she'd been hiding in for a week. It wasn't a very satisfying circuit since her room was half the size of her cabin onboard the *Divemaster* and nowhere near as clean. In fact, she tried really hard not to speculate about what had caused each of the mysterious stains on the worn avocado-green rug. Her imagination was far too good for that game. Blech.

Hey, it wasn't like she had paused to consult TripAdvisor when she'd fled from Archer.

If she had been thinking rationally, things would have gone down differently. Any sort of logic had been impossible to muster in the face of the overwhelming reaction his claim had triggered. It had been emotional and primitive.

Unbearably painful.

Archer had achieved the impossible when he'd broken her heart all over again. She hadn't realized there was that much left to smash. Apparently, some kernel of her puppy love had been hiding down deep in her chest. Maybe he was right. No amount of time would heal her entirely. Especially now.

That didn't mean she planned to let this latest development shoot her down permanently.

Sure, she'd spent a solid day or two bawling her eyes out in between cursing him for making her break her no-tears edict. Then another few had been dedicated to nursing the mother of all headaches as she stared listlessly out the window at Caracas's barrios. Today, though, she'd decided enough was enough.

She had to move forward.

Get the hell out of this shithole.

If only she could decide where it was that she should go.

Waverly shushed the totally whacked part of her brain that reminded her about how the *Divemaster* wasn't so far away and that she had Banks's direct number in her phone. As betrayed as she'd felt when those unthinkable words had passed Archer's lips and blown up her world, something kept niggling her consciousness.

It could be the crazy recurring dream she'd been having. One that seemed too real to be entirely a product of her imagination. The fantasy confused her, though, because it didn't mesh with what she now knew had happened. In the vision, she and Archer were young again and making love. Frantic, reckless sex. But definitely something mutually enjoyable. *Very* enjoyable.

How could her mind romanticize her own attacker?

Maybe she knew where to go after all, straight to her therapist's waiting room.

Because trying to puzzle out how her subconscious could still so desperately want Archer that it manufactured pleasurable memories to cover up the awful ones...it made her feel like her own mind was violating her.

Or was it?

What if her dreams were actually rooted in memories she hadn't been able to recall?

What if Archer had misrepresented what had happened?

Had she really understood what he'd said to her or why he would have bothered to rape her when she would have gladly slept with him of her own volition?

No.

Something wasn't making sense, but she couldn't work it out on her own.

As it had since the sun rose through her dirty window this morning, her brain attempted to reengage. She couldn't quite force her thoughts to coalesce into whatever epiphany she felt brewing, but maybe that was because she hadn't had a decent meal in a while.

Or even a cup of tea to jumpstart herself.

Mmm, tea.

Promising her rumbling stomach she would do a better job of taking care of it today, she hoisted her suitcase onto the bed and began to gather her belongings.

She'd gotten about halfway there—she didn't have much—when someone pounded on the door. *"Privacidad, por favor."* She requested to be left alone, as she had every other time the maid came by to do what she could with the place.

"I have no idea what you just said. Open the door, would you?"

Archer! What the fuck was he doing here?

She stood staring incredulously at the entrance to the room when he started banging again. "Come on, Waverly. Please. I need to talk to you."

Should she? Shouldn't she?

While she debated, he thumped his fist on the flimsy barrier one time too many. The door ripped off one of its hinges and hung so she could see him through a wedge-shaped gap. His hand hovered in the air, mid-knock.

The shock on his face and the utter absurdity of the situation pushed her over the edge. She couldn't take her eyes off his horrified expression while he glanced repeatedly between her and the busted door.

Then, together, they burst out laughing.

"Going somewhere?" he asked, eyeing her open suitcase and the fistful of dirty laundry she'd been about to stuff into the front pocket to segregate it from the few remaining clean items she had left.

Just like that, her amusement evaporated. "Not your business."

"I feel like an idiot out here." He tried to pry the door open from the outside. It only cracked more. "Would you please let me in? If you don't feel safe alone with me, then maybe could I have a few minutes of your time somewhere public? It's just that...I think you'd rather not have anyone overhear what I'd like to tell you."

Waverly dropped her clothes and picked up one of the other items inside her suitcase instead. Without warning or hesitation, she spread her legs, raised her arms, and aimed her pistol slightly off from his face. Enough to scare him, but not actually on target. Besides, he didn't have to know it was unloaded at the moment. "I can take care of myself these days. Why don't you start talking?"

"Jesus Christ!" He ducked behind the ruined door, as if that would stop a bullet when it hadn't been able to handle the impact of his fist. "Waverly, chill out. I'll stay in the hall. I just thought you deserved to know what happened that night, okay?"

That made her pause.

It had eaten at her, not knowing all those years.

And he didn't *have* to enlighten her. Hell, he hadn't had to confess to being her attacker either.

There it was. The thing that had been bugging her all morning.

Why *had* he done that?

Guilty conscience? Maybe, but if so, spilling his guts obviously hadn't worked because here he was, looking as distraught as he had when he'd confessed to her.

"Waverly?" he asked again, probably expecting her to turn him into Swiss cheese any second.

Instead, she crossed the room, straightened the door as best she could, then yanked the handle.

It was a teensy bit fun to see him jerk in surprise. Evil, yet satisfying.

"You're responsible for getting this fixed. It's not going on my bill." She shook her head at him as she wandered back to the rumpled bed and plopped down, placing the gun within easy reach on the nightstand. It might not have any ammo in it, but she could always hit him with it, if it came to that.

"I'm good for it." He shrugged. "I told Banks to give my money to charities, but he keeps finding ways to squirrel away emergency funds here or there for me and forgetting to mention it until later."

"He's a good man."

"The best." He nodded.

Since you've officially lost the crown, she added mentally.

"So...you want to kick me out of a chopper at five thousand feet above shark-infested waters or something?" He cursed then. "I don't blame you, honestly. But you should know that I hate myself enough for both of us because of what I did to you."

"Nah. The US military doesn't condone torture, Archer. I'd take you out quickly."

"Are you actually cracking a joke right now?" He groaned, "Waverly—"

"Stop. Get to what you came here to say. I don't have a lot of patience left." She rubbed her shirt between her fingers, nervous as fuck that he might be about to impart knowledge more deadly than her pistol.

He closed his eyes for a couple of seconds. When he opened them again, he went straight to the point. "My father drugged you with some designer libido-enhancing substance. I didn't know. You showed up at my door and morphed into a fantasy come to life. Telling me you wanted to get with me, and that you were legal now. All I could think was how beautiful you were, how untamed under all your shyness. I was kind of drunk, though I'm not saying I shouldn't have realized something was off. I—"

He swallowed hard, his eyes turning glassy.

A flash of memory blazed to the front of her mind. She grabbed her skull and folded in half, putting her head between her knees. Her dreams. They weren't dreams at all.

It *had* happened like that.

"Waverly!" he shouted then ran to her, dropping to his knees at her feet. His hands reached for her, but he stopped before making contact.

Would he be so considerate of her boundaries if he was some kind of sexual predator?

She might have wondered more about that if his explanation hadn't unlocked something subliminal. It was like trying to watch TV when the signal was nearly non-existent. All she could make out was the faintest of images through the static. "We fucked on your entryway floor."

"Yeah. Then the stairs. And a few other places as I tried to get us to my bedroom." He rested his forehead on her knee then.

Automatically, her fingers sank into his hair, soothing him, though the gesture also brought her comfort.

He kept going, describing the whole night, in detail, painting a picture of everything she'd missed that matched the glimpses she'd gotten while sleeping. She hadn't said a peep about them, so there was no way he could have lied and yet described everything she had recalled—not knowing that's what she'd done.

Things were finally beginning to make sense.

When he got to the end of his story, he cringed. "I didn't know what I was doing to you, that you weren't yourself. Until you slipped into unconsciousness."

"*You* took me to the hospital."

"Of course! You almost died in my arms!" He lifted his face toward hers then, his eyes bloodshot.

This time her heart found an entirely new way to break.

For them both.

Because it was painfully obvious what had happened. Like a lightning strike, the pieces of the puzzle he'd given her aligned, lighting up her world in an instant. "Archer, your father used you. To hurt my father. It was ruthless revenge.

You and I, we were both pawns. Well, maybe *weapons* is a better way to put it."

"I know. I realized that after you told me about what had happened between them." He groaned. "All that time, I had no clue."

"That means, Archer, that you were violated as surely as I was."

He froze. "Huh?"

"They made you do something against your will. Worse, something that violated the core of who you are. I've had years of counseling to help me cope with what happened. You haven't been able to come to terms with it at all, have you?" When he didn't respond, she reached out and cupped his cheek, brushing away the single drop of moisture trailing down the strong bones. "I can't imagine what that's done to you. Or how you've survived."

"You...you don't hate me?"

"I hate your father. And mine."

"That makes two of us," he snarled.

"It's going to take me a while to think all of this through. Rewrite history again in my mind. But how could I blame you, Archer? I can't. Not after what you've shared, the tiny bits I can remember, and what my gut is telling me. You know what's pissing me off more than anything right now?"

"Hopefully, not me for once." He smiled faintly at her.

"No. Well, not really." She shook her head and he frowned. "I mean, it's that not only did they use us, but they also stole my memories of my first time. Something I'd looked forward to sharing with you for a really long time. Was it awesome?"

"Right up until I realized you were in some kind of coma, barely breathing." He looked like he might break more shit then.

"But before that..."

"It was incredible. *You* were incredible." Archer brushed his thumb over her lower lip and she couldn't help but suck it into her mouth and nip the pad before he withdrew.

"That fucker made me believe some fiend took my virginity, when I'd hoped to give it to you all along. They erased the knowledge that it was you I shared that night with and replaced it with horror. Bone-deep terror. That I might have been exposed to diseases. Violated by someone I'd never consent to a relationship with. They spoiled my joy and made me afraid of something that probably was magnificent. *That's* what's making me furious." Waverly's hands shook and she got more fired up by the second. "I hate what they did to you. And that they ruined any chance the two of us had of getting together."

Archer changed before her eyes. His grief took on a bitter edge. Then pure fury hardened his features. "You're right. They robbed us of that, too. All these years we spent apart, it hasn't changed the chemistry between us. We might have been happy together. Had a family. Made a life. And now we'll never know if we could have."

Another thing she would mourn forever.

Waverly put her hands on his shoulders, then skimmed down his arms until she clasped his hands in hers. He squeezed in return, giving her the courage to say, "We can't go back. But maybe sometime you'll give me an instant replay of what I missed?"

"You'd want that?" Undiluted sexiness. That's the only way she could think of to describe the look he shot her then. His eyes blazed and his lips parted. His pupils dilated as he leaned closer.

"Uh huh." She nodded.

"I need to hear you say it. Clearly, Waverly. No mix-ups this time."

"I would love to finally know what it feels like to have you inside me, Archer. Where you've always belonged." Well, there was no going back from a statement like that.

Except he didn't say anything. Didn't even seem to breathe.

The stress of the week hit her then, sapping the last of her strength and energy. She thought longingly of the *Divemaster* and his circular bed, surrounded by all those windows. A place of light, and beauty, and safety.

And food.

Courses and courses of gourmet chow.

She cleared her throat, but he was still staring at her with that powerful gaze, processing her statement.

"Can we go now?" The sooner they left here, the sooner they'd be back there.

They could stay locked up there for the next week, fooling around, sleeping, making up for lost time, and gorging on desserts prepared by the pastry chef she'd been standing next to at their staff meeting, which seemed like a lifetime ago.

It sounded like heaven to her right then.

"Nope. We're staying a little while longer." He launched to his feet, then crossed to the door in two long strides. Without straining, he grabbed the dresser next to the entrance and heaved it in front of the broken wood, propping it into place while barricading them inside.

Then he strode back toward her, whipping his T-shirt over his head as he did.

Waverly's heart somersaulted in her chest. "Does that mean you'll show me what I missed? Give me that, at least."

"Hmm…" He wiggled his brows. "Yes. I think I will. *If* you'll agree to come back to your job as soon as we're finished with this demonstration."

"Done." She shoved out her hand.

He shook it, but didn't let go.

The warmth of his palm on hers had her melting already.

Archer used their connection to tug her up and into his arms, nuzzling the side of her face as he whispered, "I hope you know I'm only teasing if you decide you don't want the position anymore. I'd do anything to make this up to you. To set it right, as best I can. Making love to you would be an honor. One I don't deserve. Except I'm not a good enough man to turn you down."

"Then let's do this."

Waverly wasn't about to wait for Archer to change his mind.

Or for her to lose her nerve.

She wrapped her arms around him, stroking the exposed skin of his back as if she were petting some powerful animal. It probably would bum him out if she admitted she was imagining something along the lines of the jaguars prowling through the jungles surrounding them rather than one of his beloved sea creatures.

Although he did seem to have something in common with a swordfish at the moment. Maybe she'd share her nickname with him some other time. One not so incredibly crucial for them both. Laughing now would probably bruise his ego. The fact that she could even loosen up enough to have thoughts like those amazed her.

And reinforced her belief that this was absolutely the right thing to do.

The two of them had always meshed. Had fun together. Been attracted to each other from the first moment she'd been capable of experiencing those feelings for another human being. It had been him she measured other men against. And they'd always disappointed. Not their fault. He was just...special.

Archer surprised her, seeming to be caught in the same current she was. Instead of ridding her of her clothes immediately, he cradled her against his chest for a minute, swaying in time to some slow music only he could hear while he stroked her hair, and then kissed the top of her head. She felt cherished and protected.

Two things that only turned her on more.

"Kiss me," she murmured against his collarbone. "Like you used to."

"How about if I do it better than back then?"

"I'd like to see you try." She grinned, or would have if he hadn't curled an index finger below her chin, tipped her face toward his, then descended, fusing his mouth to hers.

Softly at first, with tiny sips that left her room to suck in breath between them. Quickly, though, their tenderness morphed into something more urgent. He cupped the back of her neck and held her in place so that he could situate his mouth to allow it to fit tighter to hers. His tongue fluttered over the seam of her lips and she opened to him.

One of his hands dropped to her ass, pulling her flat against his body so she couldn't ignore how turned on he truly was. His cock impressed her—thick and long between them.

"Is that okay?" he paused to ask.

"No," she gasped.

He froze.

"More," she demanded, tired of waiting for the real thing. "Take your time later. Right now I want it like you said it was. Wild. Frantic. Desperate."

Because that's how she felt knowing she was about to have something she'd dreamed of for as long as she could remember.

"I'm not normally a slow-and-steady-missionary kind of lover. Though sweet sex doesn't sound half bad when I'm thinking of doing it with you." He balked. "Are you sure it's a good idea for all of me to come out and play right now?"

"Absolutely." She smiled then went onto her tiptoes for one final sweet taste of him. "I want you for who you are, Archer. Not for who you think I need you to be."

He nodded at her as he evaluated her sincerity close up.

Then he walked until the backs of her knees hit the bed. He kept advancing, pressing her backward until she bounced onto the mattress and he followed her down.

That's when clothes started flying—his shorts, her shirt. Archer toed off his sneakers, letting them drop to the floor, followed by his socks. Finally, she wormed out of her pajama pants.

Good thing she hadn't bothered to put on a bra or panties yet today.

Saved time.

"You're even more beautiful now," he rasped before he sampled her exposed body. First a lick on her collarbone, then a suck on one breast, followed by a pet between her legs. It was as if he didn't know where to start first.

She could understand. Because while he lit up nerve endings all over her body with his random introductory touches, she was studying his body.

Yes, she'd seen nearly all of it the other day.

But it was different to observe him in motion, hovering over her, about to devour her.

Of all the things it made her feel to watch his power, grace, and strength, *frightened* was not one of them. Not even close.

Waverly returned the favor, groping every inch of him she could reach, wanting to catalog it in case she never got this lucky again. It was frenetic. Fevered. And honest.

When Archer rose, she took the opportunity to surge forward and crash their mouths together for another round of making out. This was no clandestine peck, though. Nothing like the innocent kisses they'd shared as teenagers.

It seared her from the inside out.

He groaned into her mouth and dropped lower, squashing her in the best of ways. She spread her thighs so his hips could rest between them. The rest was magic.

His erection aligned with her center.

A swing of his hips had the tip of his cock prodding her entrance. It was as if he was knocking so she would admit him.

"Son of a bitch!" he shouted, his head tipping back to expose the tendons in his neck. She couldn't resist taking a love bite out of one. Until she registered his regret and the slight shift of his lower body.

Away from hers.

Fuck that.

She arched up to maintain contact, though it wasn't as steady a pressure as she needed.

"Waverly. Wait," he commanded between gritted teeth. "I don't have protection. Definitely didn't expect our conversation to go like *this*."

Oh. Well, at least he'd thought of it. All her common sense had flown out the window around the time he took his shirt off. There was no way she was stopping short of the goal here. "Banks made each of the crew members get a full physical workup. I'm clean. And on birth control."

"I'm clean, too."

She nodded. "Then why are we wasting time talking?"

"Seriously, you trust me?"

"Would I be letting you fuck me in the first place if I didn't?" She gave him a pass since there was some serious diversion of blood flow from his brain to his cock at the moment.

He gave her a curt nod. "Right."

Then he didn't waste another moment. He took his erection in hand and rubbed it over her mound, making her moan and writhe. Especially when he used the fat head to separate her pussy lips and rode the furrow up until he prodded her clit a few times for good measure.

He went one step beyond when he grasped his shaft then slapped his dick on her pussy, the vibrations making her mewl and forget about attempting to say anything coherent. Even more thrilling was the way it made her feel...owned.

"Inside. Now." She planted her hands on his hips, loving the flex of his ass beneath her fingers, which rested on the upper swells of his tight muscles. Using her grip on his slim waist, she drew him closer, taking initiative in driving his cock within her the barest bit.

It had been a while since she'd indulged in sex with a real live partner. He had her vibrator beat both in length and girth. So when he wedged inside her, it took some adjusting to make him fit.

"Shh." He held her still as he worked into her pussy bit by bit. "I'm gonna give you all of me, don't you worry about that. Just let me take care of you. My way."

When she relaxed, he slipped another few inches deeper within her.

They both groaned.

"That's right. Take me."

She did.

So he kept giving.

Each time she thought they couldn't possibly be connected any tighter, he showed her that they could. With every push and retreat, he simultaneously stoked her lust and delivered additional pleasure.

And that was before he even really began to thrust.

Archer smothered her with kisses. He supported himself on his forearms, which were braced somewhere near her shoulders. His fingertips caressed her cheeks while he rippled his body above her, making contact with her breasts, belly, and pelvis.

Then he did it faster.

Harder.

With a wicked twist that pressed his abdomen against her clit in the most delicious way possible. It was at that precise moment that Waverly realized exactly how badly she'd underestimated him and his abilities as a lover.

"How the hell can I not remember this?" She moaned and hugged him tighter, probably scratching the shit out of his back in the process. He didn't seem to mind.

"While *you* blew my mind, I probably wasn't this great in bed back then. I've learned a few tricks in the past decade." Unapologetically sexy, he demonstrated one or two then, sucking on her neck somewhere below her ear as he ground his pelvis against *exactly* the right place to make her spasm around him.

"Not sure I caught that one. Better show me again," she panted.

He did.

Repeatedly.

"Oh, fuck!" she screamed. "Archer!"

"Am I hurting you?" His stride hitched then, making his cock slip from her pussy. "*Scaring* you?"

"Only because you stopped. Now I'm afraid you might leave me hanging. Get back in there and finish the job."

"I'm not used to taking orders when I'm fucking, Waverly." Something in his stare made her shivery at the revelation.

It wasn't threatening when he admitted it. It was exhilarating.

"Then I guess you'd better do something to shut me up. You know, like fuck me some more. Harder." She didn't know where these suggestions were coming from. They weren't like her either.

Though he plunged back inside her body and rode her furiously, her plan backfired.

Instead of keeping her quiet, his jackhammering hips only made her more vocal.

Waverly put one arm over her head, palming the headboard to keep him from shoving her into the wall with his frenzied fucking. She cried his name over and over.

Pleaded for him to get her off.

For all she knew, she might have begged him to marry her if it meant he'd do this with her every day of their lives. There was no telling what he drew out of her during those impossibly long minutes. One thing was certain, though—it was something that no one else had ever evoked.

The next time he kissed her, she knew she was going to shatter.

She tightened around his stroking shaft, trying to keep him as deep within her as possible. Sweat slicked his chest, making him glide over her.

And when she felt the first flutters of orgasm, she called to him.

"Yes, that's it. Come for me, Waverly," he grunted. "I'm right there with you. Going to fill you so full. Fuck."

Who knew dirty talk did it for her?

Archer did, now.

She drummed her heels on the bed as she flew apart, afraid that she might never recover from bliss this complete. Her heart nearly exploded in her chest when he began to shoot deep in her pussy, branding her with the rush of his come.

Feeling him share this ecstasy with her set her off again. She wrung him dry.

Archer collapsed onto his back, making the entire bed shake as if there had been an earthquake. Then he patted his heaving chest, calling her to him. She gladly went, cuddling into the crook of his arm. Her head rested perfectly on his shoulder and she slung a thigh over his. He kissed her forehead then lay still, recovering.

It took a few minutes before she could even think straight again. What they'd shared hadn't been perfect, or careful, or planned. It had been authentic. An outpouring of relief and passion that had been stored up for years.

Of course, it was also exhausting.

When she became aware of their surroundings, she wanted nothing more than to pack up and leave so they could do this all over again. Somewhere not so creepy.

"I have to admit. I never pictured my first time—actually, second, I guess—with you going down in a place like this." Waverly chuckled as she glanced around at the yellowed wallpaper, which peeled up at the corners.

"Try not to look. Next time we do it in a hotel, I'll make the reservations." He put his hand over her eyes and drew her closer still.

"Yeah, right. You'll ask Banks for help."

"Even better idea."

Waverly snuggled against him, sighing in bone-deep contentment.

She stayed there, utterly relaxed, until her body refused to listen to her brain's demands any longer.

"Archer?" she mumbled on a groan, hating to ruin the moment.

"Hmm?" He sounded half-asleep. Content and relaxed in a way she never remembered seeing him before, unless it had been for a split second when he reclined on the swim line after their snorkel last week.

Her stomach protested. Loudly. "I'm *starving*."

"I don't suppose this place has edible room service?" he sighed.

"Negative." She shook her head, sending her hair flying.

He ran his fingers through the messy waves and smiled softly at her. "You're so fine. Leave your hair down from now on. Loose, like this. It suits you."

"Thanks." She shoved him off the edge of the bed. "Now get up. Before you give me any ideas. Because I'm seriously going to pass out if you don't feed me soon."

Archer growled. "Oh, I'll feed you all right. Once we're back on the ship."

Though she realized he wasn't talking about lunch, she couldn't help but ask, "How long is that going to take? Can I swing by McDonald's or whatever the equivalent is here on our way to the airport?" Honestly, she didn't recall from her harried trip here. Her mind had blanked.

"I'll buy you a whole damn restaurant chain of your own if you get it to go." He eyed her with an entirely different sort of hunger. "I'm going to be hard again before we even make it there. I don't suppose road head is an option when you're the pilot, huh?"

"Sky head," she corrected as they yanked their clothes on nearly as fast as they'd shed them. "And sorry, no."

"That's all right. I'll entertain myself by watching you handle the stick and being jealous." He grinned.

Just then, Waverly heard voices outside the broken door. Maybe someone on staff had noticed the damage. Oops.

Except they weren't speaking Spanish.

Archer noticed that, too. He put his finger over his lips and stepped between her and the door.

Without wasting a second, Waverly grabbed the gun off the nightstand and unpacked her bullets. She had not found Archer again, and begun to make things right, just to get jumped by some street thugs who might do more than steal their wallets.

Archer was wealthy. That made him a target wherever he went.

Confirming her suspicions, the dresser rocked. They were trying to get in.

"You need anything else out of there?" Archer pointed to her suitcase.

"No."

"Then I think we're going to have to go out the back way." He lifted his chin toward the rickety fire escape outside the window. At least it had that.

She nodded.

They hadn't made it there before the door splintered and two guys toppled in over the tipped furniture.

"Get the window open!" he shouted. No use for subtlety now. "I'll take care of them."

She thought that was an odd call given that she was holding a gun, but there wasn't any time to sit there and bicker. So she yanked on the window.

Painted shut, of course.

Waverly wrapped one of her discarded shirts around her fist and the pistol, then smashed the window as she'd been taught. She knocked out the remaining glass as best she could, then turned back to Archer. He had a mean right hook, she noted, as if this were just another training maneuver.

Shaking off shards of glass and the shirt covering her weapon, she leveled it at the intruders.

"Stop!" she shouted. "Or I *will* shoot."

They hesitated long enough for Archer to sprint to the window and dive out, testing the rusty fire escape. Fortunately, it held. He stuck his hand through the opening a moment later and helped her climb through with only minor scratches.

When they hit the street level, they ran around to the front of the hotel, screaming for Captain Alex's officer to get his ass in gear. To his credit, he didn't ask questions, simply kept up as they made their way to the rental car Archer had left in the lot across the street.

He drove. She sat shotgun, her pistol ready yet held out of sight as they tore down the street toward the airport.

"Guys?" The officer tried a few times to buckle his seatbelt then gave up as Archer flew around corners like he was driving that Lamborghini Banks had promised him.

"Did you see two men come inside just now? One about my height, the other six inches shorter? Both on the bruiser side of the spectrum?"

"Uh...maybe?" the officer, Ted, stammered.

What was up with that?

Was he in on whatever had almost happened? Or had he been sleeping on the job?

Archer looked at her, shooting her a look that clearly said *stay alert*.

Yep. No problem there.

She probably had enough adrenaline in her system between the orgasms he'd given her and the scare the bad guys had given her to keep her awake for a week. Her fingers drummed on her knee.

After ten miles, winding through dense city streets, Archer slowed. There hadn't been a single sign of the guys from the hotel or any other pursuit, so they started to relax. At least she calmed down from, say, a nine-point-five on the Oh Shit scale to a solid seven.

Bad luck? Could be. Nothing to completely freak out about. Right?

Waverly laughed internally at that. How fucked up did your life have to be that after having your afterglow snuffed out by muggers you thought hey, that wasn't so awful?

"What's funny about this?" Archer threw up one hand while the other guided the car proficiently through traffic. He was a great driver.

That had her squirming in her seat.

He peered at her weapon, shaking his head.

"Are you intimated by the size of my gun, Archer?" She spared a glance at him, lifting one brow dramatically.

"Only when you aim it at me." Now he was laughing, too. "You know this is not normal right? You're not supposed to enjoy yourself when you're being chased by thugs."

"Eh. I've lived through worse."

He slid his free hand to her and squeezed her thigh before returning it to the wheel. Then he addressed the bewildered and slightly green officer in the backseat. "Hey, Ted. Get Banks on the phone. Tell him you're going to need a ride home in a second chopper since ours is a two-seater. You'll have to take it to Aruba, and we'll send a tender in for you, since Waverly will be on our pad. Make sure he has something ready for her to eat as soon as we land. Also, I need him to settle up Waverly's hotel bill and pay for some damage."

The guy nodded and took care of the details.

Waverly almost mentioned that she could make two trips to transport Archer and then Ted, but she figured it was for the best if she didn't. Obviously that was where Archer was going with this, too.

But was he concerned for her or did he want her to himself when they got back?

She figured she knew the answer to that when he only stopped long enough to clean out the mini bags of peanuts from a vending machine in the crew lounge at the private airport before hustling her out onto the launch pad. "Let's get you the hell away from here."

When they were safely tucked into his helicopter, she paused to toss back a few handfuls of the snack he'd given her. With her mouth full of nuts, she said, "Mmm, salty.

Probably not the kind you imagined me eating when you asked about sky head, huh?"

Though he laughed, he was still tense, so she tried again.

"Feel free to show me how you handle your stick while I play with this one." She winked at him as she fired up the engines.

It might have sounded flippant, but if she didn't joke, she might freak out. What the hell was happening? Who would have thought active duty would have been less dramatic than retirement?

"Definitely no distractions today. Take us home, please, Waverly."

Once they were airborne, she took a moment to appreciate the view. It never failed to amaze her. Archer had the sea. *This* was her world, and she loved it every bit as much.

"How mad is Miguel going to be that you got to fly with me before he did?" she asked over the headset as they picked up speed, flying directly toward the ever-changing coordinates sent to her by the *Divemaster's* systems.

Landing on a moving target was always an exciting challenge. One she was more than capable of executing even in her current condition.

"He'll probably get over it by the time we turn fifty." Archer didn't seem too disturbed.

Miles of gorgeous blue water streaked beneath them as they raced back to the *Divemaster*. Lost in the familiar rhythm of flying and the gorgeous landscape they zipped through, Waverly felt like their trip had just begun when her instruments told her the *Divemaster* would be in sight any moment.

Archer finally broke the silence. "I've never seen something up top come close to being as beautiful as what I see underwater." When she glanced over, he wasn't looking at the spectacular scenery or the megayacht where he did good while having fun.

He was staring at her.

"Do you still need me to fly you somewhere this afternoon?" Waverly asked the next day as she emerged from their over-the-top bathroom, which could easily have passed for a high-end spa. Funny, he didn't think of it as his quarters anymore. Overnight, she'd changed his perspective on everything.

It felt right when she shared his space. Less lonesome and wasteful.

For the first time, he found himself actually enjoying the deluxe appointments, proud he could ensure her comfort and pamper her as she deserved.

Naked, she tipped her upper body to one side so to blot water from the long length of her hair with a thick towel. The motion put her perfect-handful breasts and the soft dip of her waist on display. She didn't resemble models he'd seen in either fashion or jack-off mags. Not overly voluptuous or stick-thin, either.

That didn't matter. To him, she was the ideal woman. Her fit and healthy proportions had him regretting his decision not to shower with her. Except he'd had to finish arranging some final details before they left.

"Yeah, if you don't mind." He made sure she couldn't see his face when he replied. Didn't want to give any of his plans away. Unlike most people, she knew him well enough to recognize when he wasn't being entirely upfront.

She laughed. "You're the boss, Archer. Literally."

"Should I fire you?" he asked, in all seriousness. It had been weighing on his mind as the connection between them strengthened, turning into something precious that he was afraid to sever with bullshit like this. "I mean, I don't want you to think of me as your employer. We're equals, Waverly. In our relationship, and in what we do here on the *Divemaster*."

"It's up to you." She strolled over to him then, probably intending to use her nudity to her advantage, though he didn't mind. It was a highly effective strategy. After placing a quick kiss on his cheek, she said. "Let me put it this way...you know how even if you never got paid for it, you'd keep diving?"

He nodded, reaching for her hip.

She slapped his fingers away then abandoned him in favor of rummaging through the dresser, which also meant her ass was on display for him to ogle. Banks had waved his fairy godfather wand or something, sending one of the housekeeping staff on a shopping spree at his request. They'd stocked her wardrobe with sundresses, bikinis, and killer underwear so she had selections beyond her Banks Foundation uniform.

"Archer?"

He had to think back for a moment as he watched her shimmy into a skimpy pair of panties. He was going to order Banks to give himself a giant Christmas bonus this year. "Yes? Of course, I love diving. Doing it for a living was really just a way to survive while I did what I wanted anyway."

"Flying is the same for me. Except I need an aircraft to pilot. So as long as you supply that, I'll gladly schlep you anywhere you want to go. Because it means I get to do what I love most." She smiled slowly at him then as she finished clasping the bra he already couldn't wait to peel off her later. "Make that *second* most."

It was going to be harder than he had thought to keep his hands to himself until they arrived at their destination.

"Okay. If you're going to do the work regardless, you deserve to be paid for it. But I need you to understand that I don't see you as hired help. In fact…" An idea came to him then.

"Yes?"

"How about you ditch that uniform? I feel kind of sleazy lusting after you when you're wearing it." He wouldn't tell her about his true stroke of genius until he'd already made it official. That way, she couldn't argue. Or refuse.

"I bet you wouldn't complain if I found a French maid outfit in here, though."

Archer thought of her in seamed stockings. He'd bend her over, flip up her skirt, and… "Banks didn't really put one in there, did he?"

"No!" She slapped her hand over her mouth. "But I bet one of the housekeeping staff has a feather duster I could borrow when we get back."

If they had enough energy for roleplaying tonight, it would probably mean his plan had been an epic failure. "We'll see."

"Where's your sense of adventure?" she asked him as she ducked into a short, silky dress that looked like an oversized handkerchief. It left her sexy legs—and a good amount of her cleavage—exposed. Fine by him.

Hell, he'd have no problem with her walking around naked all the time.

Maybe he'd have to talk to Banks about filling one of their tours with nudists.

"Ready?" he asked, eager to be on their way.

She plucked her sunglasses and a big floppy hat from a table near the door, then said, "Yep. Where am I taking you anyway?"

"There's a small group of people subsistence living not too far from here. One of the other arms of the Banks Foundation will be supporting indigenous people who would rather continue their traditions than modernize. Since we're in the area anyway, we're going to take some supplies and medical aid over to them."

"Sounds good to me. Not that different than what I used to do in the Navy sometimes." Waverly shot him a stare so full of warmth he felt it heat his entire body. This time it wasn't the lusty sort either. Or not only that. It was something more profound.

"What?" he asked as he opened the door and ushered her out.

"Think of how many people in the world are going to be impacted positively because of you." She linked her arm with his as they wound their way through the yacht on their path to the helipad.

He shrugged, kind of uncomfortable with that assessment. "It's not because of *me*. It's because of my father's money. Considering how many people probably suffered or were fucked over so he could amass that pile of cash, it seems only right."

"Even so, we both know that just because something *should* happen doesn't mean it *will* happen." She turned him toward her, then pulled him down for a long, lingering kiss. "You're really doing it, Archer. Making this happen."

"All I did was sign a bunch of papers. Banks is the hero, not me."

She whispered up at him then, thinking about how he'd saved her more than a decade ago even if she hadn't known it then. "You'll always be my hero."

"I'll do my best for you, Waverly."

With a pat on his cheek, she turned and they continued walking in no hurry, pausing in several of the common areas to talk to passengers who'd gone diving with him over the past few weeks and waved hello to others they were also coming to know from shared meals or simply living on the *Divemaster* together for a while.

As a freelance divemaster, Archer's clients usually hadn't stuck around more than a week or two at most. Though some came back year after year to the same resorts, he, Tosin, and Miguel hadn't been there the next time they returned.

This was different. He was learning about each of the people temporarily living onboard and coming to care, especially when they shared some of the heartbreaking details of their loved ones' health crises.

It made them more real to him. More than tourists passing through.

He was starting to feel like his nomad days were over. Sure, the *Divemaster* moved for him. But he could no longer imagine himself leaving her behind for another place he couldn't grow some roots.

It would be kind of sad when the passengers who'd taken this maiden voyage with them switched out with the next group of guests. Then again, it was wonderful to see how much they'd relaxed in the time they'd been onboard. How many more smiles were exchanged than when they'd first arrived.

Some of the passengers had taken it upon themselves, with help from Banks, to organize their own support group meetings in the evenings and had plans to start up a virtual edition on social media so they could keep in touch after they went home. One good deed expanded and grew, picking up momentum as it went.

Archer thought they might actually be making a difference, however small, in these people's lives, and he couldn't wait to see who Banks would bring in next and what they could do to help them.

Caught in an introspective mood, he soon found himself relaxing in the passenger seat of the helicopter as Waverly did her thing. He didn't feel the need to scrutinize her or ask if she felt everything was okay. He was like the blissfully ignorant subset of clients who'd relied on him to lead their dives.

He trusted her, absolutely, with his life.

So he didn't bug her before or during takeoff, limiting his glances in her direction to the ones he needed to keep his stiffening dick happy.

"I wonder if I'm going to have a hard-on every time I fly with you. So far we're two for two." He might have caught her off guard with that statement, but though she risked a glimpse at the tent in his shorts, she didn't so much as bobble the stick. "It's sexy, watching you like this. Confident, competent, totally badass. Miguel was right about that."

"Thanks, Archer." She flashed him one of her dazzling smiles as they began to accelerate toward their target. "That might be the sweetest thing anyone's ever said to me."

He was saved from responding when a charcoal wedge appeared on the horizon. It grew bigger as they flew in that direction.

"Is that someone from the *Divemaster*?" She pointed at what turned out to be a Zodiac—an inflatable motorboat—which bounced along the waves, hauling ass in the opposite direction from where they were headed.

Considering they were out in the middle of nowhere, relatively, he figured it wouldn't make any sense to deny it. He grunted, thinking they'd cut things close. "Yeah. I think it's Tosin and Miguel. They said something about going fishing earlier."

"I wonder why they didn't cast off the yacht." She shrugged.

Because they hadn't really been fishing. Archer crossed his fingers and hoped she wouldn't be pissed at him when she realized that he'd fibbed.

"Mind if I have a little fun now that you're pretty sure I'm not going to kill us?" she asked. "We have plenty of extra fuel for this run."

"Does that mean you're going to show me what this thing can really do?" Archer teased. "I wasn't going to point out that you drive like a grandma..."

That might have been the wrong thing to say.

Waverly screeched, then muttered, "I'll show you a granny."

She did a pretty good job of making sure he'd never malign her again with a daring swoop that brought them low over the waves as they circled back. Soon they buzzed Tosin and Miguel.

It got even better when Miguel stumbled at their unexpected nearness, and fell overboard with a splash. They zipped around like a gnat, crisscrossing the air over the guys until they were sure Miguel had climbed in safe and sound—if soaked—once more.

Only when he offered them a double-fingered salute did they fly off again, laughing.

Waverly hadn't finished with her freestyling, though.

She swerved her way from island to island on the general course to their destination. Lush foliage and even a waterfall they spotted along the way made for an amazing tour of the area.

If Archer didn't have a stomach of steel and immunity to motion sickness after years of working on a boat, he might have ruined their afternoon. Instead, he whooped and cheered as she took him for the ride of his life.

Even if he did clutch the seat in a death grip a time or two.

The highlight of the trip came when they passed over a marshy inlet on one of the bigger landmasses. An entire flock of flamingos launched themselves into the air, not high enough to be a concern. Looking down on a sight he'd seen numerous times from the ground in Bonaire gave him a new viewpoint.

Just like Waverly kept doing to him in other aspects of his life.

For one, he hadn't felt so aggressive with her, didn't always need to be in control like he had with other partners. Though, there went his cock again...the thought held some appeal. Maybe someday, after their unfortunate start was further in the shadows of the past, he could ask her to explore the clubroom with him.

For now, playing in the sunlight with her was everything he could hope for.

His restlessness, and most of his bitterness, had vanished, too.

He felt weightless. As if he could fly without the chopper, though he didn't plan to put that to the test.

"Are you sure you gave me the right coordinates?" She glanced at him then, looking a little nervous as she punched buttons on her various monitors. "I don't see any outposts for the supply run."

"Don't worry, Waverly." He smiled. "We're in the right place for what I had in mind. There's a clearing right over there that you can put us down in, if that works for you."

Given that she often landed helicopters on postage-stamp-sized pads that were essentially moving targets, he had figured it would be a cakewalk for her.

The guys had scoped it out for him and taken pictures that he'd reviewed with Captain Alex, who also had an extensive knowledge of aviation from his own time in the Navy. The guy had given Archer the thumbs-up on his selection. Just in case, they had plenty of gas to make it back if she didn't feel comfortable for whatever reason.

"Archer?" she asked. "Is this *really* a business thing we're doing?"

"Nope." He grinned then, knowing the jig was up. "It's a very, very personal thing. A romantic-as-fuck date thing."

"Seriously?" She raised her brows but kept her eyes forward as she descended, landing dead-center in the clearing.

"Yes. This whole helicopter pilot business is awfully convenient. I loved my life before all this, Waverly. I swear I did. But some of these perks..."

"I totally know what you mean." She finished shutting down, hopped from the helicopter, then waited for him near the edge of the palm trees. "I mean, in my old job, I never got to make out with my boss."

They kissed for a while, forgetting where they were or that the rest of the world even existed outside of this slice of heaven. Eventually, he entwined their fingers and led her toward the beach on the south side of the islet.

When the path opened up and he could see what his friends had prepared, he realized why they had taken so damn long. They'd gone overboard for him today. Twice, he thought with a chuckle. Knowing they cared enough to help him score points with Waverly only made the day that much more meaningful.

"Oh, Archer." She dropped her shoes and jogged the rest of the way toward the set up, her hair and dress blowing in the breeze as if she were a sea goddess. He'd never seen someone more elegant and gorgeous than her right then.

He wished he were a painter so that he could capture the moment forever.

When she looked back at him, the undiluted bliss on her face—rosy cheeks, sparkling eyes, and captivating smile—made the mountain of suffering they'd done before finding each other again worth it. If he could spend a day like this with her even every once in a while, he'd die happy.

In the midst of hundreds of currently unlit pillar candles that dotted the beach, she spun around, her arms out.

At their very center was a humongous heart drawn in the sand. Of course his smartass friends hadn't been able to resist and had also written *Archie + Waverly 4Ever*. He felt less guilty about Miguel's impromptu dip after that, though Waverly seemed to love it.

She took out her phone and snapped pictures of the setup from every angle, as if she never wanted to forget a thing about it.

Two upside down, squared off U's constructed of driftwood at least as tall as him had been pounded into the sand and draped with a long panel of sheer fabric, which fluttered in the wind. It provided shelter from the afternoon sun for the blanket spread and staked beneath it. A dozen or more oversized pillows made the space seem comforting and inviting.

Nearby, a table for two was set, and an ice chest waited for them to unpack it.

A handful of tiki torches scattered around completed the masterpiece.

Everything they needed for an exclusive, romantic retreat...they had it.

Most importantly, they had each other.

After the double drama of the day before—their emotional turmoil and the near-mugging, which the local authorities weren't interested in investigating—they could use a day away from the rest of the world.

He planned to give her that.

Hopefully complete with lots of bone-melting sex.

What better way to relax was there than that?

Archer thought for a change of pace he would try drawing things out instead of pouncing on Waverly immediately. Each time they'd fucked the night before he'd had intentions of going slowly, taking her impossibly gently, but never seemed to make it past a few kisses before he lost every shred of restraint he possessed. Just like he had in the hotel in Caracas. Or hell, even the night she'd come to him the first time.

She didn't help his cause, though, when she asked, "We're alone here, right?"

"Completely," he confirmed.

It was only a three syllable word, but by the time he got to the end of it, she'd grabbed the hem of her dress and whisked it over her head. Her bra and panties followed soon after as she made a beeline for the shore.

He started to jog toward her, leaving his own clothes in a trail on the sand as he ran to catch up with her. When he did, he growled, "Damn, you are something."

"Something good, I hope." She peeked up at him, still a tiny bit shy at her very core, giving him a glimpse of the girl he used to know.

"Magnificent." He wrapped his arms around her bare shoulders and drew her to him for a kiss that felt more sensual to him than fucking had with other partners in the past. He savored the coconut and lime flavor of her lip gloss as he attempted to seduce her mouth with his own.

Her hands ran down his sides to his ass, kneading the muscles there even as she attempted to yank him closer to her. He resisted, not wanting to get carried away too soon.

Breaking their kiss, he said, "Come on."

Their fingers automatically found their way to each other again, knitting together as they headed for the surf. It broke gently on the pristine white beach. When they reached it, Waverly kicked, splashing and laughing as if neither of them had a care in the world.

Did they have worries anymore? It didn't seem like it when they were together.

Right now the only thing on his mind was making this a perfect afternoon and evening for her.

For them both.

He led her deeper, first up to their knees and then a little more. His hips were below the surge. Taller than her by a half a foot or so, he was steadier at that depth. So he braced her by putting his arms around her in another tender embrace.

The guys would never let him hear the end of it if he admitted that this—staring into her eyes, laughing together, and simply enjoying life—would be enough to satisfy him. Even if he didn't know they were about to rival the intensity of the sun with their lovemaking, he would have been content just to hold her.

"You know, before you came back into my life, I'd sworn off meaningless affairs," he told her then.

"Whatever." She rolled her eyes. "I saw that woman leaving your cabin less than an hour before we were reintroduced, remember?"

"Yeah, that was a moment of weakness. One that made it clear I was over that kind of hook up." He grinned. "But thanks for making my vow of celibacy a short-lived one."

She laughed.

He tucked a strand of hair behind her ear even though it only blew loose again immediately, wild and free, just like her. "I knew as soon as I saw you again that it hadn't felt right because I wasn't with the right person. I've only barely gotten you back, so this probably sounds crazy, but you've always been the one for me, Waverly. I know that now. It doesn't feel like this with anyone else."

"For me either." She burrowed into his chest before continuing, "I dated. Slept with a handful of guys who were nice enough. Polite enough. Successful enough. But none of them ever made me desperate to be with them, like you do."

"Does it scare you?" he asked.

"A little. After I left home, I swore I'd never depend on anyone again. But I'm starting to feel like if I don't have you, I can't be happy now that I see what it's like already and the potential for what we could become to each other. It's hard to give up control of my own destiny like that. And I have a feeling it's only going to get more intense."

He nodded, understanding perfectly. "Then at least I have company. I'm terrified, Waverly. Of fucking this up, of not deserving you, of not being able to be what you need."

Silently, he thought of the clubroom on the *Divemaster* and what it would be like to tuck that facet of his sexuality away for good. It wasn't as if Waverly was a submissive woman. He would miss it, but he thought he could make compromises, if it meant keeping her in his bed.

And his life.

"Don't worry, Archer. You tick all my boxes. Everything I've ever wanted—everything I looked for in a man—was someone like you." As she said it, she hopped, wrapping her legs around his hips.

He caught her, groaning as the heat of her pussy seared his bobbing erection, which had been chilled by the sea a moment earlier. "I'm falling for you, Waverly. All over again. Twice as hard, for this new and improved version of you."

Her tight little nipples scored his chest as she rubbed against him.

"I've been obsessed with you since I was sixteen. I don't see that changing any time soon. Especially not if you keep rocking my world in bed...or on the beach. It's better every time. More than I could have imagined possible."

Neither one of them dropped the L-word. He was okay with that. It was too quick for her to really mean it, considering how wary they'd both been forced to become about their surroundings and the people closest to them. When she said it to him, he wanted to believe it completely.

He'd work on earning it. Forever if he had to.

Starting right then.

When she was ready to hear it from him, he was prepared to say it.

"I can't give you back your first time—*our* first time. But I can try to make every time even more special than the last." Archer palmed her ass, making her squirm. The motion only aligned them better, his cock nudging her pussy. He kissed her again then, spending an inordinate amount of time exploring the textures and tastes of her mouth with his tongue, teeth, and lips.

When neither of them could stand to be teased any longer—by the warm water washing over them, the heat they generated, or the intimacy of the moment—he carried her up onto the beach.

He didn't go far.

Couldn't, honestly.

So he sank to his knees right where the waves kissed the shore and laid her out before him. Her spread hair floated and moved each time the water came up to swirl lightly around them, making her look like a siren. Especially as she beckoned him nearer by spreading her legs.

When she cupped her own breasts as she stared up at him stroking himself a few times to the sight of her, he buckled.

Archer leaned down and took her nipple into his mouth, lapping and tugging until she cried out his name. He left it with a kiss then did the same to her other side, balancing his attentions. Meanwhile, his hand traveled along her softly rounded stomach to her mound and began to rub gentle circles around her clit as he devoured her breasts.

"Please, Archer. Fuck me," she begged when she finally cracked.

His cock pulsed at the thought of her welcoming heat and slickness. But no, not yet.

"Not until you've come on my face a few times. Feed me your pleasure, Waverly. I want to learn what it tastes like. Get my fill so I can never forget." He slithered down her body until he could blow lightly over her pussy.

She moaned and arched as if she might come from that alone.

He sank a couple fingers into her, loving the way she hugged him tight, just before he applied his open mouth to her outer lips. He let her adjust before easing closer to her center. When his tongue licked her clit for the first time, she shattered, surprising them both.

Waverly's orgasms were sweet.

To watch, and to taste. He wanted more of them.

To be the cause of them.

Archer eased up until she'd recovered, then started the process over again, bringing her up and letting her crest a few times. His cock leaked, dripping pearly fluid into the water where it swirled before disappearing into the ocean.

But he still didn't take her or the release her body would so easily grant him. Not yet.

He gathered Waverly into his arms and stood when he noticed she shivered slightly. In the sun, blanketed by his full form, she'd warm right up.

She curled into him, utterly relaxed, trusting, and docile as he transported her to their makeshift cabana. Her complete surrender transfixed him. The strongest woman he had ever known was putting herself in his hands. It made him wonder if someday she might be up for testing deeper waters with him after all.

Was this her true self? The one at the core of the tough-talking, fiercely independent warrior he adored? If so, he knew he had to be delicate with her now because she wouldn't often expose this vulnerable part of herself.

Archer deposited her as gently as possible on the soft blanket and propped her hips up with a pillow. He wanted this to be perfect for her.

"Please, Archer." She drew his attention to her wide eyes, which blinked slowly up at him despite the sunshine illuminating the world around them. "I need you."

"I need you, too." He'd never spoken a truer vow than that.

Except he wasn't only talking about her body.

He needed all of her. For keeps.

It seemed only a fair exchange since he'd given her all of himself and never wanted it back.

Surrendering to primal desire, Archer gathered her wrists in one hand and pinned them to the blanket. The force of his hold made a divot in the sand below, helping him keep her securely in place. With the other, he strangled the bottom of his shaft, certain he'd never been this hard in his entire life before.

There was nothing left to say. Instead, he stared into her eyes, which were a reflection of the bluest skies and the deepest oceans, as he fed her his cock inch by inch.

Agonizingly slowly, he penetrated her, giving her everything he had.

And when they'd locked together, as tightly fused as possible, he began to move.

With subtle rocks of his hips, he pressed into her again and again, never retreating very far. It was a whole new kind of fucking for him but it felt right, so he kept doing it. Slow, steady, rhythmic pressure. Whatever it was, it seemed to be working.

Waverly's eyes had turned glassy and dazed as she took what he gave her and loved every second. Her channel clenched around him, threatening to milk him dry far too soon.

He bent down to kiss her, craving connection at every possible pleasure point.

And when he slipped his tongue into her mouth, she screamed, vocalizing her climax. How he didn't break then and pour himself inside her, he didn't know.

He could tell she had more left in her.

Stopping before she was fully satisfied wasn't an option.

Archer sat up a little, kneeling between her legs to gain leverage so he could fuck the old-fashioned way.

They both groaned as he took those first ultra-deep lunges within her.

Soon he was sliding his cock in her as far as he could reach, then withdrawing until he would have slipped free if it wasn't for the perfectly timed flex of her muscles, which locked around the head of his cock and held him within her. His balls got in on the action, slapping up against her ass when he really dug in.

The soft impact was another stimulant. There were too many to resist now. It wasn't a matter of if he was going to come, but when.

Waverly made the decision for him when, on a particularly vigorous thrust, she rose up. Strung tight, she shattered. She yelled out his name over and over, begging him to join her in rapture.

It was an unnecessary request. A blaze of pleasure at the base of his cock was followed by the pumping of every bit of his come directly from his balls into her pussy. He came so hard and so long that he overflowed her.

Waverly levered up onto her elbows to watch the spot where they were joined. Both of them witnessed his seed spilling out of her and trickling toward her ass.

The sight had him mesmerized.

He hoped she realized that with this act, he'd staked a claim, one he never intended to forgo.

Waverly crashed then, a slave to her ecstasy and the endorphins pumping through her bloodstream. So he tended to her, using some of the washcloths and supplies the guys had left on the sidelines to clean her up and make her comfortable.

He adjusted the material covering their shelter to make sure she was shaded properly, got her a bottle of ice water to sip, and brought her a few chocolate-covered strawberries to snack on.

Only then did he settle in beside her, giving her the last thing she required.

Him.

It amazed Archer that he could be part of that equation.

Neither of them interrupted the rush of the waves in the background or the call of the birds in the trees behind them with unnecessary words. They'd said everything before they'd come together.

Archer couldn't believe how satisfied he was. All this time, he'd been doing it wrong.

As he'd suspected, sex with someone who meant more than a good time or simple relief was next level shit. Nothing else would do ever again.

Eventually, he dozed, still wrapped around Waverly, protecting her as best he could even while unconscious.

When he woke, the sun rode low on the horizon. Waverly had already gotten up and was putting the finishing touches on their picnic dinner. Okay, so that was the understatement of the century. It was a fancy-ass meal that he was sure to enjoy because it had been prepared for them by people who cared, and would be shared with the love of his life.

Shhh, he thought, afraid to even think it in case she could read his mind. She wasn't ready to hear it yet, but that didn't make it any less true. He stretched, then realized the sand looked like it was moving.

He scrubbed his eyes and looked again.

She'd been busy, lighting the candles. The flames danced all over the beach.

When the sun fell below the horizon, it was going to be gorgeous.

A little while later, they were humming and sighing over the delicacies they devoured when Waverly said, "So that whole indigenous people aid story..."

"Actually, that was true." He smiled. "But we didn't want to freak them out by sending the chopper the first time we made contact. Tosin and Miguel brought the stuff over by boat. When we saw them earlier, they were coming back from the run. They also gave the locals a head's up that we would be dropping by the neighborhood so that they didn't think we were stranded over here. Wouldn't want anyone to barge in looking for survivors in need of help."

"Good thinking." She winked at him. "Because I wasn't about to stop, no matter who came wandering by."

"Seriously?" His cock perked up at the thought, surprising even him. Damn, he thought he'd be good until they climbed into their bed tonight at least. But riding a woman while his friends watched, witnessing what he was capable of doing for his partner, was actually one of his favorite lecherous activities.

"Hell yeah." She laughed. "For a show like that, we could probably have charged admission."

He knew she was teasing. Still, he found himself adoring her just a tiny bit more. He held his hand out to her and she took it.

Archer kissed the back of her fingers.

"You've still got it, you know," she said breathily. "That Prince Charming thing. It's in there somewhere, way down deep."

"Do you like that?" he wondered. "I enjoyed life as a simple man, but maybe there's a middle ground."

"I do. I like all the parts of you, Archer."

"Good, because I'm thinking I'd like to eat my dessert off of you before showing you just how much my parts like you back." So much for waiting until later.

He grabbed their chocolate cake and barked, "Strip."

"Yes, sir."

He shuddered.

They didn't have a lot of time left here, and when she artlessly said things like that, she mashed his buttons. While she obliged his command, he did the same.

"Well, hello. There's my sexy swordfish," she sing-songed as she blatantly stared at his erection.

Archer choked. "Never let Miguel and Tosin hear you say that. *Please.*"

She flopped to her back in their nest of cushions and laughed as loud as she pleased, knowing he was the only one around to witness her amusement and total abandon. It didn't take long, though, before neither of them was giggling.

Grunts and moans filled the evening when he placed her on her hands and knees in front of him. She lowered her face to the blanket and put her ass up, with her arms folded above her head. She was the picture of perfection.

Archer fucked her then, more savagely than he intended.

Her breasts swayed as he clamped his hands on her hips and used his grip to impale her on his stiff shaft. She didn't seem to mind, coming all over his cock just before he pulled out and decorated her ass with shot after shot of his seed.

After a quick dip to clean off, they finished feeding each other their dessert with fingers coated in chocolate.

As daylight faded into night, and the candles illuminated their sanctuary, he leaned over to his pile of clothes to check his watch again. Only a few more minutes to go…

"Got a hot date or something?" Waverly asked when she caught him, though she flashed him a wicked grin when she said it.

"As a matter of fact, I do." He tugged her into his lap, spellbound by how perfect she felt in his arms, curled against his body. Like it was where she belonged. Because it was.

And then, there in the brilliant sunset, a familiar ship was silhouetted.

"It's the *Divemaster*!" Waverly actually clapped.

"Yeah, Miguel and Tosin have one more surprise for you."

She buried her face in his neck for a second, though he wished she would have stayed that way longer. "Oh, man. I feel really bad about my stunts this morning."

"I wouldn't. It's not going to be long before they're pulling some prank on you. They're just giving you a head start."

"I'm glad we'll have a really short flight back." Waverly kissed him then.

"Yeah, I didn't want you to have to fly in the dark after a whole day of exhausting ourselves on this excursion."

"I meant because I might not make it through another flight where you're sporting wood within reach. Two of my favorite things at once. It's overload." She sighed. "You're not the only one who gets riled up on those trips."

"I would normally say it's not going to be a problem, after a day like this, but with you...I can't help myself." He grinned.

"Only fair since it seems like the more I have of you, the more I want," she whispered.

"I'm not going to complain about that."

She sighed. "Thank you for today, Archer. For everything."

They kissed then, with heat and promise. His hand cupped the side of her neck.

In the background, the sky turned gold and red as fireworks exploded then trickled down toward the ocean. Waverly paused and glanced out to sea without breaking their connection.

They made out as the show continued, the explosions of light and sound complementing the impact they had on each other.

EIGHTEEN

A week and a half or so later, Waverly reclined on an obscenely comfortable lounge chair. It was strategically positioned near the railing on a lower deck so she could see Archer doing his thing down below.

The damn chaise kept tempting her to drift off into a nap to make up for some of the rest she'd happily sacrificed while "sleeping" with Archer instead. That probably wouldn't be recommended for a few reasons.

First, because the skimpy bikini she had worn to drive Archer nuts left a whole lot of her exposed, and sunscreen only cut it for so long. Risking a massive burn on her ass or thighs or boobs or any of Archer's other favorite places to manhandle might keep her sidelined from rasping against the sheets as he made love to her. No thanks.

That was a risk she wasn't willing to take.

More importantly, though, she'd chosen this spot to work on her tan so she could keep her eye on her man, who was doing who-knew-what as he puttered around on the dive deck. Whatever it was, it seemed to be satisfying him. He smiled often, whistling while he worked.

It was gratifying to see him embracing his new life.

One that miraculously included her.

Together, they were living the *Divemaster* dream.

Rather than risk falling asleep, she decided to wander down there for a close-up view of the action. As she did, she looked around at their surroundings. They hadn't seen another boat in forever. Wherever they were, it felt really remote.

Waverly wouldn't have minded if they never went back to the real world.

"Hey there, can I help you, miss?" Archer came up behind her, kissing her neck as he looped his arms around her waist.

She leaned into his touch. "Just came to say hi. I missed you."

"I agree. It's been far too long since we've been together." He groaned, rubbing his semi on her ass.

Waverly laughed. "It's been less than an hour. You're insatiable."

"When it comes to you? Yes, I am." He squeezed her and they stood together, admiring the view.

"Where are we anyway?" she asked.

"It's kind of dumb. Don't laugh. We got hired to work this charter once and ended up diving somewhere in this vicinity. We were on our way back in and Miguel *swore* he saw something down in the sand."

"What did you see?" Waverly turned to the other guy, who was sitting nearby, and asked him directly.

"I don't give a fuck if they want to harass me for it." He crossed his arms, making her think he wasn't being exactly honest about that. "I saw jewels. Treasure. I'm sure of it."

She leaned forward, imagining how it would sparkle under the water while fish swam lazily above it. "So why didn't you investigate?"

"We'd been diving a lot on that trip. It was my fifth one of the day and I was going to require decompression if I went back down." He cursed in Spanish.

Archer grimaced then. "What he's being too nice to say is that I talked him out of making it an issue with the captain."

"*We* did," Tosin sighed. "We figured there'd be plenty of time to poke around on our dives the next day."

"Except that night a huge storm took a freak twist and headed straight for us. We had to pull up anchor and dodge the weather." Miguel groaned as if it still pained him. "The charter had no choice but to go back into port. On our next day off, we took a prop plane flight as close as we could get, rented a boat, and checked it out. Though we have a pretty good idea of where we were, it was impossible to tell *precisely* where we'd been anchored. The sand in the area had been totally redistributed by the storm, erasing some landmarks we'd used. Hell, maybe it's something about the topography there that causes those freak cells to strike. That could explain what doomed the ship in the first place."

The way he talked about it wasn't like the sunken treasure was a possibility. It was a certainty.

Miguel believed it.

And they believed him.

Waverly felt a tiny pang of jealousy over their bond, except she realized that their friendship extended to her through Archer.

"We haven't told anyone. Nobody except the three of us knows about this," Archer said, giving her some warm tingly goodness. They trusted her, too.

"Now's the perfect chance to poke around a little. Maybe the sand has shifted again. We could get lucky." Miguel seemed even more eager than usual to get in the water.

"Not that we need the money anymore, but...who doesn't want to find a long-lost pirate's booty?" Tosin's eyes probably gleamed as much as the jewels they hoped to find.

"So you're going down to look for it. Cool. Can I come?" she asked. She didn't dive as often as they did. Still, she loved joining Archer in the place he loved so much on occasion. Even without the possibility of riches, she would enjoy her time with them.

"I was hoping you'd want to." He held her tighter, hugging her to his chest. In her ear he whispered, "Maybe someday you'll help me live out *my* underwater fantasies."

Unlike Miguel's, she figured his involved sex. How would that work exactly?

Determined to find out, she waited until Archer had gone to retrieve her gear from their private locker on the other side of the dive deck.

"Psst. Hey, Miguel, can I ask you something?" She blushed.

"I don't fool around with my friends' girls, but thanks." He grinned, obviously picking up on her naughty vibe.

She smacked him on the ass, hard.

"Damn, babe." He rubbed his butt. "You ever hear the phrase 'swing like a girl'?"

"Hard, you mean?" She dared him to say something stupid then.

"Right. So, anyway…"

She leaned in and whispered so none of the guests lounging around could overhear. "Is it possible to do it underwater?"

"Your man is seriously the luckiest son of a bitch in the universe." Miguel pretended to pout.

She was afraid Archer would finish whatever he was doing and she'd lose her chance to mine information. "Come on, tell me. Maybe nothing too crazy the first time we try it. But, like, what are the odds that Archer's going to drown if I give him a hand job during our safety stop?"

Manslaughtering your boyfriend during sex would probably be traumatizing, she figured.

"I should tell you it's too dangerous, just to fuck with him. But…yeah, go for it. He can handle it." Miguel chuckled. "You've only got one obstacle to a stealth jerk that I can see."

"What?" She hoped she didn't sound too disappointed.

"Wetsuit." He pointed to where his was pulled up his legs and bunched around his waist. unzipped on the top. "Sure, he can doff his BCD and tank and all that shit underwater but it's not really fun. Let me see if I can talk him out of wearing it. Sometimes on our days off we like to dive bare. Skin on ocean. Feels different to have the water pressing all along your body with nothing in between."

Whoa. Miguel really loved the ocean. He talked about it like he would a lover. Sort of like Archer had when they'd decided not to use condoms. She must have looked at him oddly then as she suppressed the urge to blurt *that's what she said*.

He wagged his finger at her. "I didn't even mean it like that. Anyway, it's warm enough here, and we're not going that deep. He doesn't need it."

Then he rummaged in the weight bins, selecting a pair of two pounders. "I'll add these to your back pockets for this dive so you don't have to worry about your buoyancy if you're thrashing around down there. Just remember you'll probably add additional air at depth with these along for the ride, so make sure you let it out on the way up. More than you usually would, okay?"

She nodded. No problem.

"And once you've got him...distracted, it's probably best if you keep an eye on his regulator. If it slips out of his mouth while he's, um, in the middle of something, you might want to grab it and hand it back. He can do a reg retrieve in his sleep, but I'm not sure he's ever tried while he's busting a nut before."

What had she gotten herself into? Waverly put her hand on her flaming face. "Okay, thanks for the advice."

They both laughed kind of awkwardly.

"You're good for him, Waverly," Miguel said as he finished prepping his own stuff. "Good thing, since he'll probably ask you to marry him as soon as you hit the surface."

Her tummy did flip-flops, even though she knew he was joking.

It was way too soon for her to be having thoughts like that about Archer. That didn't mean she wasn't, though.

"Almost ready?" Archer called to them as he finished hooking up her tank and setting out her mask, fins, and snorkel.

Waverly hoped she didn't give away too much with her wicked smile. "Oh, yeah. I'm ready."

Miguel shimmied out of his wetsuit, looking mighty fine as he did. Damn, the man had a lot of muscles. "It's nice out. I'm going without this today."

"Sounds like a plan." Tosin followed his lead, ditching his wetsuit as well.

"Want to try it?" Archer asked her. "It's kind of fun. You don't get cold easily, do you?"

"Never when I'm with you," she sealed the deal.

Waverly did a covert happy dance when Archer bent to tug his wetsuit down his legs while Miguel hid a laugh behind a faux cough.

❧ NINETEEN ☙

Waverly held Archer's hand as they stepped off the back of the *Divemaster* and took a plunge into the unknown. She wasn't nervous going down. Not with him by her side.

No matter what they found, or didn't, they'd handle it together.

The first thing she realized about bikini-only SCUBA was that the giant stride was positively wedgie-inducing. Miguel looked over at her with laughter in his eyes as she plucked the fabric out of her crack. She figured that was payback for the helicopter stunt the other day, so she gave him a quasi-friendly finger.

He wrote something on his slate then turned it so she could see. A giant smiley face with HA HA HA coming out of its mouth. Tosin snagged it out of his hand, added "x 2", then showed it to her again. She peeked over at Archer only to find him struggling not to laugh. So she shoved his shoulder. He took her hand, brought it toward him, and slipped his regulator out of his mouth long enough to kiss her knuckles before putting it back in.

If she had been out in the atmosphere, she would have sighed.

He presented a thumbs-down and she nodded.

When they'd descended forty-seven feet to the bottom of the shallow shelf not far from the *Divemaster*, Miguel, Tosin, and Archer began flashing each other hand gestures that made absolutely no sense to her. It was fascinating to watch how they communicated, working together seamlessly.

After about thirty seconds, Miguel and Tosin peeled off and headed over a ridge. They swam as fluidly as the fish around them. She started to follow. Archer squeezed her hand and shook his head. He pressed his fingers and the thumb of his right hand together until it formed a flat blade. Then—arm extended—he gestured with it, in the opposite direction.

Oh. They were splitting up into pairs to cover more ground.

Made sense.

Plus, Miguel might have been doing her a favor, granting them some privacy and giving them the easier assignment so they could fool around without undue risk. She was shocked at how close to the surface the reef was here, and how it seemed to slope upward as it got farther out to sea. In some places, it seemed like it might poke through the waves into the air depending on the tide.

If there really was a shipwreck somewhere around here, she wouldn't be surprised. That would be a bitch to run up on unexpectedly, especially in bad weather like the guys had described.

Ordinarily, or at least on other dives she'd done with Archer lately, they crept along, investigating the reef in a direct path. Today he did something different. Something she recognized after a moment or two. He pointed to an unusually large sea fan.

She thought it was beautiful, too, with its lacey panels.

Until she realized he wasn't sightseeing. He was using it as a marker. Of where they started. Then they spiraled outward in a standard search pattern, making sure not to overlap or leave gaps in their trail. He used a compass and took a lot of notes on his slate to keep track of where they'd been. When something unusual caught his eye, he aimed a torch at it, though none of the leads turned out to be anything other than the usual rocks covered with algae or coral.

Unlike other times, they didn't dally. Instead, they swam at a pretty steady clip while they scanned back and forth. They didn't follow the reef at all, focusing on the sandy patches in between the coral mounds more heavily.

After forty-five minutes, she wondered if Miguel and Tosin were having any better luck. She hadn't seen anything except the pristine natural beauty one would expect this far from the normal tourist destinations. She eyed her dive watch to check their bottom time, then peeked at her air gauge. Although she had more than nine hundred pounds remaining, she shook the little metal cylinder Archer had hooked to her BCD with a carabiner earlier.

A ball bearing rattled around inside, making a distinct noise—similar to a ringing bell—that got his attention in a hurry.

He whipped his head around to face her.

His eyes locked on hers through their masks as if asking, *What's wrong?*

Even from there, their coffee color distracted her with their richness. He shrugged at her.

Oh. Oops. She pointed to her air gauge and then to the line that led from the ship's anchor upward. Good thing she'd only planned to attempt a hand job. She'd have to wait until they visited someplace with a shore entry and a shallow, beach-y stretch to execute any more complicated maneuvers.

Hanging on the line during their safety stop would mean she only had one hand available.

Still, she felt comfortable enough to move ahead to stage two of her wicked plan.

Side-by-side, they ascended. She made sure to dump all the air from her BCD like Miguel had instructed her. She noticed the pull of the extra weights, but it wasn't difficult to kick lightly toward the surface to counteract them. They'd come in handy if she got distracted in a minute.

It was easier to swim up than it was to slow your ascent if you got out of control.

Waverly had no desire to experience the bends. That would probably ruin Archer's good time, too. After everything he'd done for her—from saving her life, to giving her a dream job, to providing a place to live on the *Divemaster*, to the grand romantic gesture of their beach date, and all the everyday things he did to show her that he cared—she wanted to do this for him.

Show time.

Archer grabbed hold of the line when they were exactly fifteen feet deep. She hoped they weren't clearly visible to the people on the *Divemaster*. Because right then she made her move.

Instead of gripping the rope beside his hand, she put her palms on his shoulders and clung to him. His eyes sparkled with joy, even through his mask. When he took his regulator out, she did the same, remembering to blow tiny bubbles the entire time it wasn't in her mouth as she'd been trained.

Quickly, they came together, sharing a brief but powerful kiss.

Then he was nudging her hand, putting her regulator between her lips and tapping the button on the front to clear the water from it. Smart, since the maneuver had definitely stolen some of her concentration and all of her breath.

He pointed to the rope, indicating she should hang on.

She glanced at her dive computer, steadily ticking off the 170 seconds to go before they could surface safely. So she shook her head no and scooted her hands down his torso, until her face was level with his crotch. Using his hips as her handholds she was steady, only kicking every once in a while as the extra weight Miguel had added to her BCD did its job, keeping her under.

Waverly peeked up at Archer, who had gone stock-still.

He was staring at her.

So she didn't disappoint. She shoved his suit down to the tops of his thighs, just low enough to expose his cock. It was half-hard by the time she wrapped her fingers around it and began to pump. He made a gurgling noise, so she looked up to make sure he was okay.

Oh, he was fine.

Looking like an ancient god of the sea as he hovered above her, he leveled a commanding glare at her. In her mind, she could imagine him growling, "Don't stop."

So she didn't.

Waverly ran her fingers up and down his length, cupping his balls every once in a while. When his hips began to rock, thrusting his hard-on through the ring of her fingers, she knew he was enjoying himself. Dangling off the anchor line, submerged in the ocean he loved so much, he took the pleasure she gave him.

Both of them knew it wouldn't last long.

She pumped harder, as fast as she could given the resistance of the water.

His breathing became erratic, sending gushes of bubbles to the surface. Quickly, she peeked at his air gauge. Insanely efficient with his breathing most times, he still had five-hundred pounds more than she did. He'd be fine even if he sucked down some extra puffs.

Waverly began to tease him then, sliding the pad of her thumb across the underside of his shaft and onto the head as she added a twist of her wrist to her jacking. Muscles rippled along the entire length of his body as he gave himself fully to the experience.

A few seconds more and his free hand squeezed her shoulder. She understood what he was trying to tell her. He was about to come. So she took a deep breath, popped her regulator out, then finished him off. With her mouth.

It was an odd sensation. Though she fit her lips around the tip of his shaft before sliding down it, a trickle of salty water got in her mouth along with the release he pumped down her throat immediately upon her first contact. He came so hard, she couldn't quite get it all before she had to pull off and reclaim her air source.

She cleared her regulator, coughing a few times as she got settled. Archer watched her the whole time, making sure she was safe.

In the meantime, she examined him as he wrapped his hand around his cock and stroked himself through the remainder of his orgasm. Silky strands of his come rippled in the current like ribbons as they floated away.

Waverly double-checked to make sure he was breathing okay when his chest expanded with an enormous breath followed by an equally huge exhalation. His regulator was still in place. Check and check.

Then his entire body sagged, deadweight on the end of his arm. His hand still instinctively clung to the rope.

That's when she noticed the look in his eyes. It was nearly enough to make her spontaneously combust, if by combust you meant come on the spot. He reached for her then, with the hand not still clutching the line for dear life.

So she swam up to him.

Again, they shared a brief underwater kiss. She thought they'd have to practice this skill a lot more often. It made her feel like he was the center of her universe. Because in that moment, he was.

When he motioned for her to put her regulator back in one last time, his bonelessness evaporated with a jerk. Then his eyes got *humongous.*

What? Was Jaws about to make a meal out of her?

She whipped around, but there was nothing behind her.

When she looked back she realized it wasn't her he'd been gawking at. He must have felt something slipping. Because now, as they dangled there on the rope together, she followed his stare far below their flippers to where his bathing suit was sinking into oblivion.

Now *that* was funny!

Waverly laughed so hard she choked a little. He was right there, making sure she was okay. She pointed at her dive computer, which said their safety stop was complete. Time to get out.

He shook his head no vigorously, then gestured to his junk.

She shrugged. It wasn't like he had anything to be embarrassed about. He was hung.

Archer rubbed his forehead, looked down again wistfully in the direction of his long-gone trunks, then released a huge cloud of bubbles she could only assume was an exasperated sigh.

He gave her a thumbs-up.

They slowly ascended the rest of the way to the surface.

Waverly was surprised to see Miguel and Tosin on the dive platform. How had they made it out so quickly? Sure, they'd gone deeper than her and Archer, which meant they couldn't stay under as long, but they were practically marine mammals and could make their air last forever. Whereas she'd called their dive early so she could fool around.

Of course, Archer did not take this as good news. She heard him mutter, "Fuck."

A laugh escaped her.

Miguel must have heard. He looked down at them. "Getting out?"

"Could someone toss me a towel?" Archer asked.

"It's traditional to use those once you've left the ocean. They're not very effective for drying off if you get them soaked," the other guy teased, but he looked to Waverly as if asking how things had gone. She winked then headed for the ladder.

"Waverly!" Archer begged.

"Remember when you laughed at my unfortunate wedgie incident? Toodle-oo." She gave him a finger wave over her shoulder then hauled herself and her bazillion pounds of equipment onto the ship.

Tosin joined them, peering overboard. "What's taking so long? Hustle, would you? We have something to show you."

Waverly couldn't help but turn around and stare when the two divemasters began to crack up. Whistles and catcalls cut through the afternoon, drawing the attention of the guests. Even Captain Alex, who must have been making rounds.

The captain surprised everyone when he called Archer out on the tan lines left by the tiny triangle his suit usually covered. From a few decks above them it was easy to hear him shout, "Put some pants on, kid. You're blinding us up here."

Archer shuffled across the dive deck, his fins held in front of him to preserve some of his modesty. A shame, really.

By the time she made her way to her slot at the bench, dropped her tank in the holder, and got her gear off, Archer was back. He wore a pair of cotton shorts that he usually pulled on over his swim trunks. They rode low on his hips, showing off his washboard abs and the V that pointed straight to her favorite new toy. He flipped off Miguel and Tosin as he came to help her break down her set-up.

"Not pissed?" she asked as she chuckled.

"After what you did down there, it would take a hell of a lot more than that to put me in a bad mood." He leaned in and kissed her solidly, making her hope they were headed back to their cabin for a mid-afternoon quickie. "That was fucking incredible. Thank you."

"Maybe next time we can swap places." She thought of the possibilities and hummed.

"Archie!" Miguel called from the table in the center of the dive deck. "You two can bask in the afterglow later. Get over here already."

He held his hand out to her and she took it. Together they approached the other two divemasters.

"What the hell is so important?" Archer glared at them. "I was thinking I might need to be kind of busy for the next hour or two or ten."

"Well, my friend." Tosin positively beamed. "I may not have joined the Going Down club today, but I think this makes a nice consolation prize."

He lifted the edge of the towel on the table to give them a peek at what was beneath.

It was blood red, the size of a golf ball.

"It coordinates well with this, I think." Miguel was grinning then too as he revealed the fistfuls of gold coins he'd retrieved.

Holy shit.

They'd found it.

"It was right where I remembered." Miguel hummed. "Just waiting for us to come back and do this right. Now we actually have the resources to retrieve what's down there. Maybe sometimes things really do happen for a reason."

Archer whooped. He tugged Waverly into his arms and spun her around. The whole time, he stared into her eyes. "You know, I think they're right about that."

"So do I."

⌇⌇ TWENTY ⌇⌇

Later that night Archer sat in a private nook on one of the upper decks with Tosin, Miguel, and Banks. They huddled around a table with tons of documents scattered across it. Who could have known it would require this much paperwork to set his plans in motion?

A bunch of empty beer bottles made perfect paperweights, warding off the breezes that kept getting stronger the longer they hung out. He did his part to help by draining another one then plunking it on top of the contract he'd just signed.

Away from city lights, the night sky sparkled as if it were littered with the diamonds they hoped to find when they could explore the shipwreck further. They'd spent the afternoon taking pictures and documenting the exact coordinates of the visible portions. Then they'd agreed it was best to take off, heading back to Bonaire for the end of their guests' stay.

The last thing they wanted to do was tip anyone off about what was waiting beneath the waves. If they weren't careful, treasure hunters would swarm the site, compromising the integrity of the find and cherry-picking valuable items.

They would have to keep the secret safe for the few weeks it would take to have the Banks Foundation file a claim, get any necessary permits, and organize an official salvage operation as one of its divisions. Now that most of their business was wrapped up, Archer couldn't wait for Waverly to finish the massage he'd convinced her to get so that he could talk to the guys alone about their future.

Five more minutes, then he'd go search her out.

"I have one last thing I want to ask you all." Archer scanned the face of each man around the table. "We're joint owners here, so I don't have the authority to give our shit away, but with my portion of the treasure proceeds, I'd like to buy our helicopter from the Divemaster Project."

It wasn't too hard to figure out what he might intend to do with one of those.

"Wow, that's a hell of a Valentine's Day gift. Are you in loooooove, Archie?" Tosin teased him as he had known the guy wouldn't be able to resist doing.

"I—" Of course he loved Waverly. Loving someone and being in love with them were two different things, though. And he hadn't said those words out loud to anyone yet. Not even himself.

Banks smiled at him.

"Yeah. Have been since I was eighteen, I think." He rubbed the back of his neck. "Here's the thing. The same way I didn't want you guys to feel stuck here, I'm having the same issue with her."

"She doesn't like working for her boyfriend?" Miguel asked. "I guess I can understand that."

"Waverly doesn't have a problem with it so much as I do." He cleared his throat. "I was hoping I could give her the helicopter, then we could hire her as an independent company to run it. Fair market value on the contract."

"You know, she could decide to take off." Miguel pointed out the obvious. It didn't make Archer's leg stop jittering, either.

"Uh huh. But I'm hoping she won't." He shrugged.

Banks came to his rescue. "I'd say that's a safe bet, Archie."

"I haven't said anything to her about it yet. So can we keep it on the down low until I find the right time?" He rubbed his hand over his mouth and chin. "She can be kind of stubborn about stuff like that sometimes."

The guys laughed at his understatement.

"You know we're happy for you, seriously." Tosin slammed the rest of his beer, then said, "I just want you to be sure, Archer. This is a lot all at once. Our lives have completely changed and—"

"Thanks, but I'm positive."

"If it's the real thing, taking some more time to think things over isn't going to change the outcome," Miguel added.

Archer found himself grinding his teeth. He knew they meant well, but, what the hell? "She's the perfect woman for me. The perfect *partner*. In every way."

Okay, so that might have been a low blow. Both Miguel and Tosin winced.

Could they be jealous of Waverly and the extraordinary amount time he'd been spending with her lately?

"Boys, let it go for tonight," Banks advised them. "Or someone's going to end up with a black eye, and I'm fairly sure the doctor has already turned in for the night. Would hate to wake her up for an ice pack and some x-rays."

"Is someone hurt?" Waverly asked then, making each of them jump. Even Banks.

Whew, that had been close.

In the background, Banks gathered the heap of paperwork and tucked it into an accordion folder that he placed discreetly beside his seat.

"No, Banks is just busting our balls," Miguel answered for them.

"I don't recommend that. I hear it's painful." Waverly smiled as she strolled to Archer and kissed him on the cheek. "Miss me?"

"Tons," he admitted.

If the guys rolled their eyes, he chose to ignore it.

"You were right. That was heavenly. Vanessa is amazing with her hands." Waverly sighed. "I didn't realize how sore I was."

If it wasn't so dark out, he probably could have seen her blush. It wasn't any secret that he'd contributed to her aches by using her so well, so often, lately. Hell, he could have benefited from a rubdown himself. It was a lot of work pleasing her. And he enjoyed every minute of it.

Archer grabbed her around the waist and tugged her into his lap.

"Oh, nice." She squirmed, getting comfortable and putting him in danger of popping a boner at the same time. That's what he got for enjoying her mild embarrassment. "My favorite seat in the house."

"Be careful or he'll put you over those knees next time you're in the clubroom. Bet you won't like that as much," Miguel teased her.

"Huh? What's the clubroom?" she asked, chuckling kind of uncomfortably as if she'd missed the punch line.

Oh, shit.

When she finally noticed the serious stares on the guys' faces, she realized—for once—they weren't joking. "Guys? What'd I miss?"

Miguel clammed up. He looked to Archer as if asking for help out of whatever hole he'd managed to dig for them both. Even Banks raised his brows, which was about as shocked as Archer had ever seen the guy before. Was it that big of a deal that he hadn't felt the need to play in there with her?

Well...maybe.

"Archer?" She looked at him then.

"You've seriously never taken her there?" Tosin asked, making the whole thing worse. "What's up with that? And your little speech earlier... It made it sound like she met *all* your needs. Are you sure, Archie?"

How dare they imply he was changing who he was to suit her? It just hadn't come up yet. Plus, they'd had a lot to work through, given their past. Could *that* be why he had toned down that side of himself around her? Because he still felt guilty? Or like he had to hide those parts of himself?

Could the guys be right?

Damn it. He'd rather believe they were butthurt because he hadn't participated in any late-night private parties, taking that aspect of their bond with him.

"Archer?" Waverly's pitch went up and her volume increased as she repeated herself. She sprang up from his lap and propped her hand on her hip.

They might have had to excuse themselves then to have a very private discussion, and maybe their first serious fight since getting back together, except right then someone screamed.

The animalistic sound left no doubt that something was fucked to hell.

Archer and the rest of the guys shot to their feet, trying to figure out where the noise had come from. A few seconds later, a more controlled shout followed. It didn't ease his anxiety in the least.

"Help! Someone please, help! Oh God, I think she's dead!"

Archer sprinted toward the hysterical guest, who begged for help.

By the time he arrived, a few other crewmembers and guests had gathered around. The head stewardess, Maria, a married couple from Denver, and one of the ship's officers—Ted—were alternating between trying to calm the screaming person and staring at the pool.

Floating on the surface, face down, in a spreading maroon cloud, was the ship's masseuse.

He skidded to a stop and tried to prevent Waverly from seeing the woman once he realized who it was.

Miguel didn't bother. Though it was unlikely they could help the woman, he dove into the pool and checked for a pulse. He shook his head. No.

When he lifted her face out of the water, he grimaced then set her down gently before heading for the edge. He drew himself up and out, dripping bloody water onto the deck. "She's gone."

"Is that Vanessa?" Waverly flailed at Archer's back. "Oh my God, how can that be? I was just with her a few minutes ago."

Everyone turned to stare at her then.

"She was…not like this. Alive. Very alive." Waverly paled.

Captain Alex began barking orders over his radio. "I need all hands on Deck Two. Bring any weapons you have. Be on the lookout for suspicious persons heading away from the pool area."

He looked to his officer then. "Ted, grab the log book from the office. I want to verify every gun we have onboard against it. Immediately. Check each one to see if it's been fired since last cleaning."

They had several, for safety in sometimes dangerous parts of the world.

"While you're in there, download the camera feeds for the past fifteen minutes. Put them in the officers' shared folder and be prepared to forward them to the authorities when I have more information."

"Yes, sir," Ted answered before running toward the interior of the ship.

"Archer?" Waverly seemed dazed.

He faced her then, pressing her to his chest so she couldn't keep staring at the dead body.

Tosin assigned himself to crowd control, corralling the guests away from the area while keeping them together for their safety. It also prevented anyone from leaving before they could be questioned.

Captain Alex approached the pool and knelt, carefully retrieving a two-liter bottle from its surface with gloved hands and setting it aside. "Whoever did this knew what they were doing. They silenced the shot with this."

"Explains why we didn't hear anything." Banks grimaced. "We were right up there, though it is quite windy tonight."

Archer thought back to how they'd had to pin down their papers.

"There's a storm coming. I'm going to call this in." Captain Alex frowned. "Closest port is Kralendijk. They'll probably have us dock as planned so they can conduct an investigation."

"Who would do this? Why?" Waverly trembled in Archer's hold.

Those were very good questions. He wondered if she was also thinking about the fact that they were trapped onboard with a killer. No matter how much he rubbed her arms in an attempt to warm them, she shivered harder. Banks appeared with a blanket. Together they wrapped her up.

Miguel stood nearby, not saying anything. Quietly, he observed everything and everyone around them.

It wasn't long before Ted returned carrying a binder. He set it on a nearby table, grabbed one of the four thousand tabs on the side, and opened it. Crew members lined up to present their weapons. He swabbed the inside of each one with a Q-tip before confirming it was clean and checking it off the list.

When everyone had made it through the line, he slapped his hand flat on the table. "Damn it. That's all of them."

"Well, it wasn't a ghost that put a hole in that woman's head." Captain Alex turned an unhealthy shade of purple.

Archer thought he might only be a couple of hues behind.

"Excuse me...sir?" Ted seemed almost afraid. "I know of another weapon onboard. Not listed here."

"Whose is it?" Captain Alex demanded.

Ted pointed. Directly at Waverly. "She had it in Caracas. When we ran from those thugs. And she damn well knew how to use it, too."

Archer growled. Waverly flinched in his grip. "Of course she does. She's a Navy veteran. Waverly had *nothing* to do with this!"

"It's fine, Archer. Sorry, I should have thought of it myself." She separated from him then and turned to the captain. "Yes, I have my weapon. It was cleared by Banks that I bring one."

"Where is it?" the captain asked, not unkindly.

Good, Archer thought. *I won't have to fire his ass.* Ted, however, was on thin ice.

"He's just doing his job." Waverly patted Archer's chest when she realized what he was fuming at. "The gun is in the safe in our room. It's unloaded. Should I go get it?"

"Why don't you stay here?" Miguel said both too quickly, and a little too loudly. "I'll do it. Archer told me the combination earlier because that's where we put...*stuff*."

He'd almost mentioned their treasure.

Waverly nodded. "Thanks."

Unfortunately, Archer didn't think his friend was motivated entirely by kindness. He'd better knock that shit off fast.

"While we're waiting, let's pull up the camera feeds, Ted," Captain Alex boomed.

The guy looked miserable. Like he'd rather have anything else to say other than, "When I went to download the footage, they weren't running. Looks like they were shut off about an hour ago. Sorry, sir."

"Fuck!" Archer couldn't stand how everything was spiraling out of his control.

Little did he know, it was about to get a whole lot worse.

Miguel stomped back onto the deck. He shouted, "It's gone!"

"My gun?" Waverly put her hand on her chest. Archer cupped her elbow, keeping her upright.

"That too." He kicked a chair over, making a clatter that drew the attention of everyone in sight.

"Oh, shit." Tosin put his head in his hands over where he sat with the guests.

"Does someone want to fill me in on what's going on?" Captain Alex spoke quietly. It was so much more intimidating than if he'd yelled.

Banks shuffled close and spoke low enough that no one else could hear. The captain's eyes grew wide. Then he released a string of curses that impressed Archer with its creativity and pure vileness.

His thoughts exactly.

"I didn't do this!" Waverly wrestled with the blanket, shoving it off. "Swab my hands. Please."

"No. You don't have to do that." Archer's hackles rose.

"She does. We shouldn't assume she's innocent just because you're fucking her," Miguel spat.

Archer's hands balled into fists and he advanced.

Banks stopped him in his tracks. "Let her do it. It will go a long way in clearing her name. We both know there's nothing there."

At least one of them was thinking straight.

Waverly held out her hands. He couldn't help but notice they shook.

Ted zoomed in and used a bunch of the cotton swabs, then put them in a plastic bag and sealed it. At a loss for words, or what to try next, most everyone milled around. Captain Alex pulled Vanessa's emergency contact sheet and passed it to Banks. Waverly groaned when she realized the phone call he'd have to make soon.

Captain Alex gave more orders. "We're going to conduct a room search. Top to bottom of this boat. We're looking for a handgun, or anything else out of place."

Still, Miguel wasn't satisfied. Against everyone's cautioning, he edged nearer. He lowered his voice so only Archer, Banks, and Waverly could hear. "I'm worried for you, bro. You went from believing you raped this girl to chasing her like a puppy dog. She had you wrapped around her ring finger in a matter of days. It looks bad. Let them do this the right way so you don't get any blowback. I know she'd have to be like the world's greatest actress—a master manipulator—to have fooled us all, but..."

He stopped short of mentioning that it might run in her family.

Even that seed of doubt felt like a complete betrayal to Archer. How could his best friend be this disloyal? "She had *nothing* to do with this."

Waverly stared blankly at the two men. She seemed overwhelmed and unable or unwilling to defend herself. So not like her. It infuriated him.

"How can you be so sure? Is this going to be like the time you forgot to mention you were Daddy Warbucks?"

Miguel ripped out of Banks's restraining grip on his biceps. "Are you telling us everything you know?"

"Shit! Yes. Guys, I swear. I don't know what's going on, but Waverly isn't to blame." Archer stood tall, wondering if they'd make it past their first destination before their entire future went to hell.

"I'm starting to feel like I don't know who you are anymore," Miguel sneered. "I hope you're not being used. Blind faith doesn't cut it for me. You're already changing who you are for her, staying out of the clubroom. That'll never last. The two of you won't make it if you can't be honest about who you are and what you like."

The sound Waverly made then threatened to rip Archer's heart out of his chest.

She tapped out. "That's it. I'm done. I'll be in our cabin if anyone wants to arrest me. Or make me walk the fucking plank for that matter."

Then she took off. For her to show even a hint of weakness meant they'd really hurt her.

Archer roared, then lunged at Miguel. "Fuck you! She's innocent!"

Before Miguel could take it back or say something to make it worse, Archer shut him up with a punch to the face. Tosin scrambled to Miguel's side and helped him sit up, shaking him from his daze.

Archer and Miguel stared each other down like two groupers defending their territory.

"Enough!" Banks shouted as he smacked his palm on Archer's chest, keeping him from pressing ahead. "What he said about Waverly was out of line. That girl isn't capable of hurting anyone. I know it, same as you. So why don't you go help her instead of making things worse? Captain Alex and I will handle this. In fact, everyone return to your rooms for the night. No one is to be wandering about until I say otherwise. We'll assemble a small team to conduct the searches. Cooperate with all staff instructions. Use your intercoms if you need anything or see something suspicious."

Archer blinked then, thinking about how he'd let Waverly go when there was still a murderer on the loose. He wanted nothing more than to take her into her arms and promise everything was going to be okay.

He spun on his heel. As he strode away, he heard Banks scolding Miguel, "What did I tell you about earning that black eye, huh?"

It might have been funny some other time.

Not with a corpse onboard, though.

Or his woman, falsely accused, nursing some stab wounds in the back.

He jogged the rest of the way to their cabin, ignoring the worried looks everyone shot at him as he passed. Only one person mattered at the moment. Banks and Captain Alex could handle the rest.

When Archer arrived, he found the door unlocked, which only pissed him off more. She should be taking better precautions. Someone had been here. Invaded their personal space once already. His anger transformed into something more desperate when he stood outside the door to the bathroom and heard the sound of weeping, nearly—though not entirely—disguised by the running shower.

It wasn't like Waverly, though she'd softened some since she'd returned to the *Divemaster*. He was sure she would hate for him to see it. So he paced, waiting for her to emerge on her own terms.

He'd be there when she was ready for his open arms.

But it wasn't easy.

In fact, it was one of the hardest things he'd ever done.

For her, he would manage.

⌒ TWENTY-TWO ⌒

"**Y**ou can't blame them for their suspicions, Archer. They're right. This looks bad." Waverly chewed on her fingernail as she stood at the glass accordion doors that led out onto Archer's stateroom balcony. The ocean looked mean and kind of angry as the wind picked up and waves crashed, a storm rolling in. Just when she'd started to feel like she belonged, the world reminded her that anything could be lost in an instant.

She tugged the thin silk robe she'd thrown on after her shower more tightly around her.

Maybe she'd been deluding herself to think this could be her forever. She wasn't a partner in the Divemaster Project. Hell, she wasn't even an owner-operator of her aircraft. Waverly was a simple pilot, working a job, and she'd let herself forget for a while that she could be banished from her new haven as quickly as she had been admitted.

They could fire her over this. Worse, have her thrown in a foreign jail for a murder she didn't commit.

She might not survive losing everything again if it meant Archer went with it.

"I don't give a fuck what it looks like. I've learned my lesson about that shit—believing what people lead you to think. I *know* you had nothing to do with killing that woman and nothing will ever convince me otherwise."

His unwavering faith changed her. Altered everything she felt and opened new doors.

If he was strong enough to have confidence in her after the damage his father had wrought on his impressionable young psyche, she should be able to do the same for him. "Take me to the clubroom. The one the guys were talking about."

"What?" He tipped his chin. "Now? This isn't the time—"

"It is." She put her hand out, waiting for him to take it. "You trust me. And I trust you, too. I know it must be hard to let go of your unnecessary remorse after years of thinking you'd taken advantage of me. I'm guessing *that's* why you didn't tell me about the clubroom. Like Miguel said, if you can't get past that, we'll never last. So we might as well test it out and see before either of us is too invested."

"He's an idiot. He was freaked out and pissed off and not thinking straight."

"That doesn't mean he wasn't right about some of it. Besides, I need this tonight. You. Anything goes. Hell, from now on, that's how it should be. You've given me everything I need and believe in me completely. Allow me the opportunity to do the same for you."

"Waverly..."

"This is *my* choice. I don't want there to be boundaries between us. Limits on our relationship." She drew a deep, somewhat shaky breath. "I can't stand the thought of losing you. You should have told me this is something you need."

"I'm not going anywhere." Archer cursed. "*You* are what I need. I'm sorry the guys questioned you. They'll come around. They're—"

"They're just looking out for you. Totally understandable." Though it had stung, still did, she appreciated their loyalty. "Still, if I'm going to be out of control when it comes to the awful shit in my life, you might as well show me the upside of freefalling."

"What do you mean, Waverly?" He nudged her shoulder until she rotated, facing him. "Look at me when you explain."

He wanted to read the truth in her eyes? Fine by her.

"Ever since…what happened to us all that time ago, I've protected myself by staying in charge. Of myself. Of situations. Of lovers. Not with you, though. I can't do it with you. Don't care to. So take me all the way. Show me what it feels like to give up power. Completely."

There, she'd said it.

"You're sure?" He rubbed her upper arm with the palm of his hand, slowly, comforting.

"Yes. Especially tonight, I don't want to have to think. I just want to feel and experience what you do to me. My brain hurts, my heart hurts. Take all of that away. Fix me. That's what you're into, right?" Could he hear the plea in her voice? She needed this. Needed *him*.

"No, Waverly. I told you, I'm into *you*." Without another word, Archer scooped her into his arms and marched down the hallway to the black glass door she'd wondered about once or twice.

So *that's* what they were hiding in there.

His jaw clenched and unclenched, making his bearded cheeks bulge. Was he second-guessing himself?

"Don't." She stroked the side of his face. "This is what I want."

He lowered her feet to the ground, steadying her before he let go. He used his palm to scan the door open then stepped inside. "If you come in here, it has to be of your own volition."

She stepped across the threshold without hesitation. Going one step further, she unbelted her robe and let the silk slip off her shoulders. It landed in a pile at her feet, leaving her entirely naked.

"Will you wish you hadn't done this tomorrow, after tonight's insanity dies down?" he murmured as he surveyed every inch of her body.

She shook her head, shivering at the feel of her own hair brushing her back. Sensual and liberating, it confirmed his assessment that she should leave it down most times.

"You promised you trust me. So trust me to know my own mind." Waverly tipped her face up and waited for him to accept the invitation.

Archer didn't make her wait long. He laid his lips on hers and slowly ate at her mouth. Her knees went weak and she relied on him to support her, which he did. They stayed that way for a long time, soothing each other with the caress of their lips and tongues.

From far away, Waverly heard a beep. Then another. And a third.

The door rattled as someone tried the handle.

Was one of the other divemasters trying to bring a date to the clubhouse? She hadn't heard of them fooling around with any of the guests, but maybe they were capable of more discretion than she imagined. Or maybe they also needed release after the stress of the evening.

Archer cursed. He settled her on the floor when it was clear she couldn't stand on her own right then. He positioned her so that she was kneeling, sitting on her heels, her hands clasped on her thighs. "Stay right here."

He strode to the door and unlocked it before opening it a crack. Could whoever it was see her? Maybe. Why didn't that bother her as much as it should? In fact, she shifted a little, trying to ease the ache in her core at the thought.

She didn't lift her stare off the ground to find out for sure either way.

"What?" Archer snarled with a venom he'd never aimed at her before. Hopefully, never would. "I'm occupied."

"We wanted to apologize." It was Miguel.

Waverly's earlier stomachache returned.

"You can tell me how stupid you are tomorrow. When I'm not in the middle of something important. Like repairing the damage you caused." Archer didn't add *you idiot*, but his tone said it for him.

There was a pause, and then Tosin said, "We want to apologize to *her*, not you. Let us do it our way. So she knows we're serious and that we do care for her. Anyone this important to you is important to us."

"We fucked up," Miguel admitted to Archer. "Me especially."

At that, Waverly felt something unravel inside her. Her breath caught and a sob escaped before she could clamp her throat down around it. She hugged herself then, rocking to alleviate the sharp stab of pain caused by the sudden snap of tension, which had wound her tight.

They didn't really believe she was a monster like her father. Or Archer's.

"Waverly!" Archer forgot about their visitors and dashed to her side. He crouched by her and wrapped her in his arms. "I've got you. You're okay."

It turned out power exchanges played with her emotions instead of only her body. Who knew?

She was glad she did now, as she experienced a whole new level of intimacy with Archer. "I moved."

"I'll punish you for it later." He smiled as he said it, making her sure she wouldn't find his penalty tortuous in the least. "You heard what they said? That they're dumbasses who should never have doubted you? Not even for the blink of an eye?"

Well, he'd taken some creative license in his paraphrasing, but she didn't argue. Waverly nodded.

"Remember what you said before, about trusting me absolutely?" He drew a long, slow breath.

She nodded again.

"We're about to find out if you meant it." He leaned down to kiss her nose then turned toward the door. "Miguel. Tosin. Get in here and lock that behind you."

If she had said no right then, Archer would have kicked them out in an instant. Knowing that made her comfortable enough not to do it. Even though she was naked and they were not as they eyed her with the same hunger they reserved for the Sunday brunch buffet. Their favorite.

Archer lifted her as if she were a doll. He didn't go far. Just a few strides of his long legs took him to a leather-and-chain contraption that hung from the ceiling. Some sort of sex swing.

She whimpered when he set her down on her back. It moved beneath her, making her prepare for impact with the floor. Waverly wrapped her legs around his waist as if that would save her.

Miguel was there, taking her hand. "We won't let you fall."

He kissed her wrist, testing the waters.

She shivered. So he continued distracting her while Archer strapped a wide belt around her middle. He shook the swing. Chains rattled. Truly secure, she didn't budge.

Meanwhile, Miguel increased his contact, leaving a trail of soft, wet kisses along the inside of her forearm as Archer petted her hip, silently promising it was okay for her to enjoy his friend's attention.

It felt odd to be touched in so many places at once. Even more so when Tosin caressed her leg before prying it off Archer and shackling her ankles to the dangling stirrups. The device was much more comfortable than she would have guessed. It conformed to her, moved with her.

It was surreal, to be the center of attention, surrounded by three smoking-hot men. Especially when they began to strip, letting her watch.

She wasn't about to complain.

"I want you to know," Archer said to her then, "I'm not going to let them fuck you."

She flinched at the thought while his friends groaned their disappointment.

No, she belonged to Archer alone.

"You're mine. But for what they did to you earlier, I'll let them bring you pleasure to replace the pain. I'll let them watch as I do the same so that no one can deny how much you mean to me or how well-matched we are." Archer reached out and inserted two fingers into her soaked pussy.

Going from nothing to something that quickly shocked her system.

If she thought that felt good, it was nothing compared to the arousal that lit up every nerve ending in her body when he withdrew the digits and held them out to Miguel.

Without question, he sucked her flavor off his best friend's hand.

"Shit, she's delicious. Let me taste her while you fuck." She'd never heard Miguel's voice sound so gravelly before. Sexy and rough. He would be most women's fantasy come to life. A passionate Latin lover, committed to pleasing his partner. Thoroughly.

Waverly no longer had the ability to respond. Instead, she watched as Archer directed his friends, and all three of the men worked as a team to shower her with ecstasy.

"Wait until I'm fully buried inside her, then you can play with her clit," Archer told Miguel. "She's extremely responsive and multi-orgasmic. So if you don't have her coming on my cock every couple of minutes, you're not doing a good enough job."

Miguel looked at her reverently. It glued some of the cracks he'd caused in her heart earlier. She'd say their plan was working, because there was no way she could deny their admiration and respect when they treated her like this. Like she was special. Prized. Meant to be worshiped.

Tosin joined the action then when he said to Archer, "Put me in, coach."

Miguel snorted.

"Get to work on her tits. She likes medium-firm pressure. Lots of tongue. Not so much teeth."

It shocked her that he already knew how to play her body that well. She figured it shouldn't since they'd spent a lot of time in bed together these past few weeks, but to hear how finely he'd catalogued her reactions made her glow.

Tosin smiled at her. He brushed his thumb over her lower lip before leaning in. Without making her beg, he plumped her breasts in his hands then took the tip of one into his mouth. He suckled her differently than Archer would have but quickly adapted his style based on the moans and sighs he drew from her with the flickering of his tongue and the suction he applied.

Her eyes kept trying to flutter closed. She fought the temptation so she could burn the image of the three men standing around her into her memory. Though the trio was present, only one directed their union.

Archer.

He was staring down at her as he fisted his cock, preparing it for the fuck of a lifetime.

When their gazes collided, he moved forward, poking her with the tip.

She arched as much as she could in the swing, trying to embed him within her.

A stinging slap landed on her thigh, surprising a shriek out of her. The tingling burn that followed made her wish he'd done it again. Until Archer grabbed the chains holding her legs up and open for him then advanced the last step necessary to slide the fat head of his cock inside her pussy.

At the same time, Tosin switched his skilled handling to her other breast, making her quake.

Archer's well-defined arm muscles bulged, pulling her toward him so that he used her to fuck himself. He hadn't gotten more than the tip of his erection inside her when he stopped, either to let her adjust or to keep himself from getting too fired up too quickly. Could have been both.

"Archer," Miguel warned. "Condom."

"We don't use them." It was another sign of their commitment, she thought.

A declaration of monogamy and confidence. Or foolishness.

She'd certainly never let any other guy fuck her without one.

"Damn," Tosin lifted his mouth from her chest momentarily to groan. "Bareback? I can't wait to see her pussy dripping with your come."

Waverly's muscles clenched at the thought, causing a chain reaction. Archer sank inside her farther. Tosin clung to her nipple even as she rocked, adding more pressure than he had before. And Miguel, refusing to be left out of the mix, bent over so that he could lap her clit while Archer continued to fit himself into her body.

Watching the three men, so close to each other, focused on delivering as much ecstasy as possible, had her poised on the edge of orgasm before they'd even gotten started. As if that wasn't enough to obliterate any remaining self-control she had, someone shocked her by pressing a lube-slicked finger to her ass.

She didn't even know who it belonged to. It didn't matter. It was an extension of Archer.

"Shh, let it in," he coached her, obviously more aware of their surroundings than she was. "You'll like it. I promise. They know what they're doing."

Filled in front and back, with a pair of tongues lashing her most sensitive parts while Archer rode her, it didn't take long for Waverly to reach her breaking point.

"You're going to come for me already?" Archer didn't sound like he was upset about that. "Show them how lucky I am to have you. Go ahead."

Six hands now stroked her, from her arms, which had gotten attached to either side of the leather pillow her head rested on, to her ribs to her calves and everywhere in between. Tongues licked, mouths sucked, and Archer's dick fucked.

And fucked.

And fucked.

Sometime after her fourth or fifth orgasm, Tosin spared her breasts and diverted his attention, at least for a little while. He whispered, "We're sorry, Waverly."

Then he kissed her. Lightly, in contrast to the escalating thrusts of Archer's shaft within her.

In the midst of the passionate tsunami that threatened to wipe her out with a mammoth wall of pleasure, she had an epiphany.

Waverly met Archer's stare as he rammed into her. Sweat poured down his face and chest. She'd never seen him so frantic, or so honest. Was it because his friends were there to make sure he didn't go too far? Or because, for the first time, he planned on ravishing her without stopping short?

Given their history, she figured it was the former.

She realized then that up until this moment he had still been cowering. Running from the negative aspects of his legacy. Too afraid he would become his father—though two men couldn't possibly be more dissimilar—to embrace his wealth, his power, or his dominant streak.

This man unleashed, fully revealed to her for the first time—*this* was Archer.

And she couldn't possibly love him more.

Too bad every cell in her body was focused on complying with his demands or she would have told him so.

Waverly looked at Miguel, then Tosin, hoping they knew how much their apology had meant to her. That went double for the affection they lavished on her. For Archer's friends to so obviously approve of her as his mate, it mattered.

To them all.

"She's getting close again," Miguel warned Archer and Tosin, though she was fairly sure there was no way Archer could miss that fact considering how tightly she gripped his shuttling cock. For that matter, her ass clamped down on the finger buried inside it, too.

Her entire being gathered, compressed like a black hole about to explode in a big bang. She was afraid to surrender to the overwhelming feelings that were inspiring her in case she flew apart and could never pull herself back together again.

"Do it," Miguel urged her. "Let go of it all. Give him everything. It will be okay. We won't let anything happen to you. We're sorry we let you down, Waverly. It won't happen again."

Archer stared at her, unblinking as he pummeled her in a frantic pace.

When she realized that by holding out, she was prolonging his torture, she listened to Miguel.

She surrendered.

The rapture that overtook her then made the whole world seem brighter for an instant. Energy pulsed between her and the three guys who bonded with her. Most of all, with Archer.

She threw her head back, discovering that the ceiling was mirrored.

Waverly studied their reflection as she absorbed the sensations given to her by one man, though he used two additional people to make his gift. The image that came back to her like the hottest porn she'd ever watched multiplied her pleasure.

With one final massive thrust, Archer shattered her.

Waverly came and came and came as she felt him do the same.

The guys got their wish as they watched up close while Archer blasted her with his come, painting her pussy from the inside out. He coated her in his epic release, making Miguel and Tosin curse then shout.

Had they been jerking off? She couldn't see since they knelt beside the swing, their lower bodies out of view. Were they coming too?

She no longer cared, though the thought that witnessing her and Archer's joining could impact them too only made her more shivery inside. She flew, riding the rush that accompanied the best orgasm of her life. When it was over, the three men around her helped her glide back to earth with soft pets and kind words.

Eventually Tosin and Miguel stood to go. They each kissed one of her cheeks before Miguel murmured, "Welcome to the club."

She drifted off then, barely able to stay awake as exhaustion washed over her.

The last thing she remembered was Archer praising her as he collected her and took her back to their room. He tended to her, sitting with her in the hot tub on the balcony for a few minutes so the jets could massage her sore muscles. Then he dried her off and tucked her into their bed. He spooned her as he held tight, refusing to let her go.

If only they could stay that way forever.

Archer must have sensed her slight tensing. He stroked her belly, taking it away again, helping her stay relaxed after the enormous relief he'd granted her. "We'll worry about tomorrow, tomorrow. For now, sleep. I'm with you," he promised before placing an achingly tender kiss on her cheekbone.

Trusting him, as she had promised she did, she sank into his sheltering arms and yielded to unconsciousness.

⌒ TWENTY-THREE ⌒

Trouble came looking for them before tomorrow could fully become tomorrow.

A triple bang on the door to the owner's suite had Archer sitting upright then rolling from bed in an instant. He hadn't slept long, but he'd slept hard. The best sex of a man's life would do that to him, even if there was trouble as massive as theirs looming.

A glance at the bedside clock confirmed it was two in the morning.

For a split second he thought, *please don't let there be another body*, followed by, *if there is, at least I can be Waverly's alibi this time*. It was an awful thing to think, and made his stomach roil.

When he opened the door, no one was there.

Or at least, not at eye level.

A groan drew his attention to Ted, slumped on the ground. Blood poured from between his fingers, which clutched his abdomen. "Son of a bitch! Waverly, get the doctor!"

Archer whipped off his shirt and pressed it to the gash in the young guy's torso.

In the background he heard Waverly calling for help.

It wasn't long before people rushed them from both sides of the hall. Miguel, Tosin, Banks, Captain Alex, and the doctor huddled around. It only took a look or two for the doctor to say, "I can get him stable, but we don't have blood onboard for a transfusion. He needs to be flown out of here. As quickly as possible."

"Let me get dressed." Waverly ducked back inside long enough to throw on her uniform.

"Is the weather too bad for flying?" Archer asked. "I don't like this."

"I'm not going to let another person die if I can help it." She dared anyone to stop her.

Miguel spoke up. "Hey, don't feel the need to prove something just because I was an idiot before. No one thinks you had anything to do with Vanessa's murder. If this isn't wise, you shouldn't do it."

Ted groaned again, drawing their attention. He seemed less alert.

Captain Alex kept asking him who'd attacked him. He wasn't responding.

"It's the right thing to do," she insisted. "I can fly in this. It's not that long of a flight and I'll be heading away from the storm. The sooner we take off, the better."

Archer wrapped her in a bear hug. "Be safe."

"I promise."

"Come back quick. I've got more things to show you in the clubroom." He kissed her then, branding her with his passion. Or at least he hoped he had.

Then there was less time for talking as people did their jobs. Tosin helped the doctor get Ted situated and into the chopper. Banks called ahead to the hospital and let them know there was a patient en route. Captain Alex spoke with the authorities.

Archer watched as his girlfriend climbed into a helicopter to save someone's life.

She was amazing.

He held his breath as she lifted off and watched until she blended into the darkness. His chest ached when he could no longer make out the blinking lights on the helicopter.

"Let's go to the bridge. That way you can still talk to her until she gets there safe," Miguel offered, nudging Archer inside.

They got there just in time to hear Ted command Waverly, "Turn off the radio."

Archer's spine went ramrod straight. Why would he say that? And why didn't he sound as out of it as he had been a few minutes ago? His condition should deteriorate as he lost more blood, not improve.

A couple of clicks came over the air before Waverly said, "Okay, it's off. What's up?"

Captain Alex acted quickly, mashing a few buttons on his own control panel. "I've muted our end so he thinks she really did it."

If Ted believed that, he would be the stupidest guy on the planet. Then again, there was no faking how much he'd bled. Maybe he was afraid or wanted to make a deathbed confession, just in case. "Good, thanks. We're not going to the hospital. Not to any island, either. Take me back to Caracas. Or someplace else in South America we can reach easily. Anywhere I can rent a car and be on my way. You're the pilot, use your imagination."

Every person on the bridge went quiet. Dead quiet.

"Why should I do that, Ted?"

Archer wondered if he was the only person who could hear the barest hint of fear in Waverly's voice. For her, that was a lot. There was a whole heap of *fuck you* in her tone, too. That scared him to the bone.

"Because I'll split the profits from selling these with you." A rustle, and then a pause.

"Where did you get a giant ruby and a bunch of gold coins?" Waverly asked, clearly letting them know what was happening.

"NO!" Archer shouted as he swiped his arm across the table. He sent papers, glasses, instruments, and who knew what else crashing to the floor. This couldn't be happening.

His nostrils flared. He had to do…something, anything, but there was no way to reach Waverly. He couldn't intervene or assist. Helpless, all he could do was listen.

"Let's call it a parting gift from your boyfriend. I found them in his safe after I overheard him telling Miguel the combination this morning. Saved me a step. I was going for the gun so I could take you hostage and maybe get some ransom money out of him. I mean, I know that didn't exactly work out the first time I tried it, back in Caracas, but first I didn't think he gave a shit about you. And then when they said he was on his way, those assholes took forever showing up. How did I know your boyfriend was going to get there so damn quick? He must really like you. Which is great for getting top dollar. But this…this is way easier." He laughed then, and it was clear he might be a couple rubies short of a necklace himself.

"So what's in it for me?"

"I'll give you a cut. How's thirty percent?"

"Why shouldn't I haul you back to the *Divemaster* and collect a reward the honest way?" she asked.

"Don't antagonize the wackadoodle, Waverly!" Banks shouted, though he knew she couldn't hear him.

Ted didn't say anything to that.

But Waverly did. "Oh. Well, I guess that answers the question about where my gun went."

Archer couldn't breathe, couldn't see. Miguel and Tosin were there, holding him steady.

"If I'm crazy enough to stab myself to get airlifted to South America, I'm crazy enough to use this." No one would argue with him about that. "If Vanessa hadn't seen me coming out of your room and ran off to tattle, I wouldn't have had to shoot her. Then I could have waited until tomorrow and taken off before anyone knew this stuff was missing. The room searches were getting closer. I couldn't take any more chances. I've never done anything like this before. I don't particularly like it either. Couldn't stand it on that ship, being ordered around, nowhere to go to get away and no other skills to earn a living. What good is a ship's officer who doesn't want to live on ships? It was driving me nuts. I need a way out. This is it. Sometimes you do what you have to in order to survive, right?"

"Right. I know exactly what you mean," she said.

Captain Alex muttered something about background checks. There hadn't been any dirt to find. Archer didn't blame him, or Banks, or anyone except Ted himself for this disaster.

"I'd like my gun back now, Ted." Waverly sounded calm and almost friendly, though Archer knew she was seething inside.

"Um, how about no?" the punk answered.

"We both know that as soon as I land this helicopter, I'm of no use to you. What's to keep you from shooting me then?" she asked.

Archer was wondering the same thing, and he couldn't imagine this ending well.

In the background he heard Captain Alex calling in an update to the authorities. Why bother? There was nothing they could do either. Waverly was the only one who had even a bit of control over her future right now.

And he didn't like her odds.

Ted didn't answer again.

"Look…" Waverly tried another tactic. "You're bleeding really heavily still. You're going to need help to get fixed up. Give me the gun, and I'll take it as a good faith gesture that you'll keep your word on splitting the cash from the treasure. I'll help you hide from Archer and back you up when the doctors ask where you got that gash."

It said something that no one in the bridge reacted to her faux-bargain. Not a single person believed she would actually do that to him. Archer especially.

"Just fly, bitch."

"If that's the way you want it." Waverly sighed. Then whispered, "I love you, Archer."

"That's sweet. But your boyfriend isn't here to save you."

"That's okay. I've got this," she said.

Right before a gunshot rang out and the communications with the chopper failed for real.

Archer didn't care who heard—he howled, the sound tearing out of him like someone had ripped his soul from his chest. He crashed to his knees, unable to stand.

Everyone else in the room was still as statues, frozen by shock at what they'd just heard.

Not Archer. He went ballistic. "We've got to find her! What are her coordinates?"

Someone called out the final reading before everything had gone dark.

"It'll take a few hours for the ship to get over there given the tides and this current, if we can even make it with the weather escalating and nighttime to contend with. We could run aground. I don't advise attempting it before dawn, if at all." Captain Alex closed his eyes briefly. "In fact, I *can't* do it. There are other people's lives at stake on this ship. They're my responsibility. I'm sorry."

Miguel stepped up then. "Come on, Archie. We'll take the Zodiac."

"Is that prudent?" Banks asked, utter devastation twisting his features into an unrecognizable mask.

Captain Alex said, "No."

At the same time, Archer, Tosin, and Miguel said, "Yes."

"Wait." Banks tried again. "Let's think. Another senseless death, or three, isn't going to bring her back."

"Don't talk like that! Like she's gone!" It couldn't be. Archer continued, "I'll drop dead of a heart attack anyway if I have to sit on my hands for hours to find out what's happened to her. She could be hurt. Without help, she might...no. I can't take that chance. I wouldn't be able to live with myself."

"I said it wasn't smart. But I won't stop you." Captain Alex admitted, "It's what I would do if she was my girlfriend."

So it was decided.

"Be careful, boys." Banks did something Archer had never seen him do in all his life. He sank to his knees and began to pray.

The three divemasters slammed out the door and into the pouring rain. They prepped the boat without bothering to shout above the wind. Then they strapped themselves into life jackets. Just before they climbed in, the thing bucking so hard they clipped themselves to it with lines and carabiners, Archer turned to them. "This is crazy. I should go alone."

"No way," Miguel said immediately. "You can handle the navigation and the driving solo, but you can't reach the spotlights from back there. Without those, you won't make it more than a quarter mile before you're lost or hit something on the surface and put a hole in this thing."

"You're wasting time," Tosin agreed. "We're doing this together.

With that, they launched the boat and took off, leaving the relatively safety and ultimate comfort of the *Divemaster* behind them, possibly for the last time.

Archer had never been so scared in his life.

Not because of the waves, or the storm…

But because he didn't know what he would find when they reached Waverly's final transmitted coordinates.

It was the longest thirty-five minutes of his life.

The rough ocean tossed the guys around like a rubber ducky in a whirlpool.

They'd circled the area Waverly had last radioed from at least a dozen times and didn't see her anywhere. He wasn't sure what he'd expected but was starting to feel foolish. It was entirely possible that his rash decision could get them all killed.

He refused to think about the possibility that Waverly was already waiting for them below the surface.

Every bit of him hurt.

"Archer, I hate to say this," Miguel shouted from up front. "But…I think we've got to call it for the night. It's getting rougher. We're in trouble. I don't even think we should try to make it back."

Tosin didn't say anything. Instead, he nodded, looking green.

"Fuck!" Archer yelled, then admitted defeat. "You're right. Find someplace to beach this thing and ride the storm out. We can start searching again as soon as it's clear."

In his mind, he apologized to Waverly for giving up. *I'm sorry. We tried our best. Hang on. Please, don't you quit, too.*

~ TWENTY-FOUR ~

"It's okay. I've got this." Waverly hoped her bravado eased the agony Archer was likely suffering while listening in on this conversation.

If she was going to have any hope of surviving this, shit was about to get even more fucked up than it already was. Before giving Ted too much time to consider what she might be up to, she lashed out with her right hand, grabbing for the gun.

BANG!

Waverly had never been shot before.

It hurt like a motherfucker.

Nothing like in the movies. Adrenaline didn't do shit to numb the blinding pain. Fortunately, it appeared that the bullet had hit her upper left arm. She didn't need that to clobber Ted, who seemed stunned by the reverberations of the deafening blast in such a small space.

More good news, she wasn't dead.

Waverly lashed out, fueled by pure rage and indignation. She punched him where it would hurt most—in the stab wound he'd given himself. Judging by the amount of blood on the bandage, he might have done a better job of that than he'd intended.

Which might have been why he didn't react fast enough to stop her.

With an *oomph*, he dropped the gun.

Waverly didn't pause to think about what she was doing. Survival instincts and her military training kicked in. She snatched the gun, put her finger on the trigger, pointed it straight between Ted's eyes, and squeezed. Twice.

To be honest, she didn't even feel bad about his brains splattered on the window.

If it was her or him, she knew which one she would pick. All day long.

Unfortunately, the gunshots had damaged more than her flesh.

When she tried to radio the *Divemaster* to let Archer know she was okay and about to come home, the damn thing wouldn't work. In the next few seconds, instruments started going dark. Fuck. One of their bullets, or maybe bits of all three, had clipped some important shit.

If it wasn't for the storm, which seemed to have intensified, she might have tried to find her way to the *Divemaster* without some of those tools. Over open ocean, with nowhere to put down quickly, and—oh, yeah—blood slicking her arm, there was no way she was risking it.

Waverly groaned as the pain intensified. She scrunched her eyes closed a few times, trying to see better. In range, a blip of an island with a wide, flat beach beckoned her. It was going to have to do.

It was her worst landing ever.

Later, she couldn't even recall most of it. Though she wasn't really a religious person, she might have believed she had a guardian angel helping out.

But when she turned off the engine, she was down in mostly one piece.

For a while she just sat there and stared. Thanked every power in the universe for helping her save herself. Then she prepared to rough it for a while. No one was going to be able to reach her tonight.

She debated sleeping in the helicopter, but it was pretty exposed on the beach and if it toppled, or sank into the sand as the tides changed, she could be trapped and drown. Given the state of her arm, she couldn't wrestle Ted's body out anyway. The thought of sharing the space with him all night long...

So much nope. Not happening.

Waverly tried to get the radio going one more time without success. So she grabbed the first aid kit and her backpack, then jumped out of the pilot's seat.

She trudged up the beach far enough to huddle at the base of a thick copse of trees. First she treated herself as best she could, using strips of bandages and thick gauze pads—thank you, Ted—to put pressure on her wound without going full-on tourniquet. Her military days had made her aware that she could do permanent damage if she left one of those on for longer than two hours, and it was going to be several times that before help arrived.

They couldn't reach her, never mind find her, in these conditions.

She didn't think her arm was bleeding enough to be life-threatening. Then again, if she passed out and couldn't make a tourniquet once it turned for the worse, saving her arm wouldn't really matter, now would it?

Hard decisions.

After she'd patched it up as best she could and applied the most pressure she felt comfortable with leaving on long-term, she took the Mylar thermal survival blanket out of the first aid kit and wrapped it around herself. A fire was out of the question given the rain and wind, but it wasn't particularly cold out. This would do.

Comfortable? Not especially.

Survivable? Hell yes.

To keep herself from throwing a pity party, she used her teeth to tear open a pack of dried fruit then chugged an entire bottle of water, hoping her body got busy replacing some of her lost blood pretty damn quick.

She estimated she'd been out there less than an hour when she wondered how she would survive an entire night without going bonkers.

Waverly used her good arm to collect the fallen palm fronds she could reach without jostling her injury too much and began to stack them up. She wasn't cold, but it made her feel more secure to have some barrier, however flimsy, between herself and the storm.

When she'd run out of resources, she rested up against the tree trunk that formed one support for her lean-to shelter and wondered how she'd pass the rest of the time. Maybe she could write Archer love letters in the sand. Or draw pictures of positions she wanted to try fucking in once she had healed.

Before she could, a light glinted in her eyes.

Something painfully bright after the deep midnight she had gotten used to.

It was only there for a second, then gone.

Then it came back. And stuck.

Could it be a searchlight?

Holy shit!

Waverly stood up, using the Mylar around her as a reflector. She ran toward the surf then, making it about halfway before a familiar gray rigid hull inflatable boat beached itself on the sand with a landing nearly as poor as hers had been in the helicopter.

She gave it a four out of ten, at best. It was the most wonderful thing she'd ever seen.

Until Archer came flying over the side, tearing up the beach toward her.

Then *that* was the most wonderful thing she'd ever seen.

She supposed they could have cried, flung themselves at each other, or any other number of things. Instead, they stood there, about a foot apart, wind whipping their clothes and hair, grinning like fools.

"Imagine meeting you here," Archer said before his face darkened. "Ted?"

She shook her head. "Dead."

Then he closed the gap between them and crushed her to him.

"I've never been so relieved in my entire life to see someone," he said. "It might be best if I never let you go again."

She was good with that, too. Except just then his arm knocked into hers, right over her bullet wound.

Waverly cried out, wishing she could take it back when worry rushed back to his face. "Arm. Ouchy."

She tried to smile as she winced, probably looking totally weird.

"Is it broken?" he asked. In the meantime, he checked out the helicopter. It perched on the beach, a little wonky, but obviously not crashed.

She knew he was estimating the likelihood she had internal injuries. "No. Shot."

"What?" he yelled.

"Shot."

"And you're *just now* mentioning it?" He tore the thermal blanket off her as if he was making sure she didn't have any other new holes. "Jesus, woman."

There was more blood there than she'd realized. Yikes.

Miguel and Tosin hauled the boat toward them, out of reach of the waves and wind. Exhausted, and stumbling, they began to set it down, even as they told her over and over how glad they were to see her. Tosin used his shoulder and upper arm to wipe moisture from his face. Probably just spray from the ocean. That had to have been an uncomfortable ride.

"I have a camp started over there." She pointed with her good arm, so they angled toward her spot. Archer wasn't having any of that. He plucked her from the beach and carried her. Resting her head on his shoulder, she admitted to herself that she was grateful for the lift.

As they neared the tree line and the wind and rain subsided, she shouted over the crashing waves, "I can't believe you got in that thing with the ocean looking like that! Are you fucking crazy?"

"Well, I had something to say to you that couldn't wait until morning."

"What's that?" She blinked up at him.

"I love you, too, Waverly."

And *that* was the thing that broke her. Tears rolled down her cheeks as he set her on the ground between his best friends. He kissed her with the barest brushes of his lips while Miguel and Tosin propped the boat up on its side, using the wind itself to hold it in place, making a very effective wall against the storm.

With that done, Miguel started pulling things from inside it.

He combined their first aid kits, taking a needle and thread, some topical anesthetic, and a packet of antibiotics from inside. Tosin handed Archer the waterproof radio. "Why don't you do the honors?"

The four of them huddled around the communications device.

"Banks!" Archer shouted.

"Archie! Are you okay?" he asked.

"Yes. We've got her. Waverly's here. She's alive! We've got her!" He beamed at her as if he couldn't believe how lucky they'd gotten.

A riot of claps, whistles, and cheers came over the radio, making Waverly shed a few more fat tears before dashing them away with the back of her hand. To know that she'd gone from being absolutely alone in the world to having this incredible group of people who loved her...

It was everything.

With these guys, she wasn't afraid to let her feelings loose either. They wouldn't judge her or take advantage of her temporary weakness.

Tosin piped up then, his sandy hair looking crazier than she'd ever seen it. "No, she's not just alive. She's sitting here under a palm frond shelter living it up while we all worried about her. Might as well have happened upon her sipping a piña colada."

"Is she wounded?" Captain Alex asked.

"Yup," Miguel confirmed. "Took a bullet to the arm. No biggie, according to her. Honestly, it does look like a flesh wound. We're about to see if I can stitch it up without passing out."

It was crazy how a few near death experiences made these things seem inconsequential. Except... "Guys. Someone else is shot, and this time I *did* do it. I killed Ted."

"You protected yourself," Archer corrected her.

Nobody contradicted him.

She sighed.

"We'll be there as soon as we can get the ship closer or dispatch another helicopter from somewhere," Captain Alex assured them. "The worst of the storm should be past now. Will you be okay until morning?"

"Absolutely," Waverly answered.

"As long as I have her, I'm good." Archer didn't care if it made him sound like a pussy. It was true.

⌒ TWENTY-FIVE ⌒

Waverly stood at the rail of the main deck of the *Divemaster* as Captain Alex and the harbor pilot navigated them safely out of Kralendijk. They'd dropped off the guests, who would take the Banks Foundation's private jets back to their regularly scheduled lives. Despite the events of the past few days, the passengers had assured them the initial run of the program had been a success.

Part of her was still raw, and probably would be for a while. Her new family here onboard the ship was doing their best to help her forget and move forward. In time, she would.

"I really do love this place," Archer sighed from beside her as he said goodbye to the island that had been his home for a little while.

"At least this time goodbye doesn't have to be forever." Miguel put his hand on Archer's shoulder and squeezed. "We can always come back."

Waverly thought about how she'd returned to Archer and couldn't agree more.

Banks nodded at the guys from where he stood on Waverly's other side. "If there are any special requests, just let me know and I'll adjust the schedule."

"Where are we heading next, anyway?" Tosin wondered. It didn't matter much to them so long as they were together and doing what they loved.

"Eventually, we'll sail to the Panama Canal and out to the Pacific for a while. The season is right over there for great diving," Banks said. "But first we're going to take a detour up to the US Virgin Islands, where the planes will meet us with our next round of passengers in a week or so. It'll be a nice break for the crew. I think everyone could use a few days off."

They all seconded that.

"Am I the only one who's never been before? I've heard it's beautiful." Waverly smiled at Archer, excited to investigate a new place with him. Hopefully one that didn't involve almost getting killed. But did involve lots and lots more of the mind-blowing sex they'd been having since he'd introduced her to the clubroom. Or underwater sex. Or ultra-romantic sex.

Or just plain sex in general.

He'd officially turned her into a sex fiend.

"It is," Archer assured her. "Sorry, though, I need you to do some boring business stuff with me when we get there. After that's done, I'll take you on a sightseeing tour if you want before we have to start the next trip."

"What kind of business stuff?" Something about the way he'd said it tipped her off.

Banks encouraged Archer to continue when he paused. "Go ahead, tell her."

"As partners in the Banks Foundation's Divemaster Project, we've agreed. You deserve a reward for how you handled the situation last week. So Banks helped me buy a new helicopter. An upgrade. A six-seater Eurocopter EC 155."

"Oh my God." Waverly thought that might be better than sex. "I've always wanted to fly one of those."

Archer spilled the beans. "We're picking her up at the Henry E. Rohlsen Airport on St. Croix. And...she's yours."

"What?" Waverly might have jerked away if he hadn't had his arms around her.

"You're free." He smiled softly. "To be honest, from the beginning it didn't sit right that you were tethered here, to me, by the thing that allows you to do what you love most. If you stay—and God, I hope you will—I want it to be because this is where you belong. Where you *choose* to be."

"I..." She couldn't believe what he was saying, or that he might think she felt obligated to remain in his presence. A helicopter, especially one like that, was a ridiculous thing to just give someone. With the chopper itself, she could open a charter business, using the income to cover the operating costs and still make a healthy living. "I don't have anything to give you that could compare to that. Except—"

"I don't need anything in return." He stole a quick kiss, trying to shush her attempts at fairness. "Your happiness is all I ask for."

"What if I want to give you my heart?" Waverly swallowed hard but continued. There was no going back now. "Hell, Archer. You've had it all along. I hope that's enough."

"It's everything," he whispered, his hand trembling where it rested on her neck. "I love you, Waverly."

"I love you, too." It felt so good to say it out loud. She had nearly worn out the words since he'd appeared on that beach to save her ass. She intended to keep being obnoxious about it, too.

"So you'll stay? Let us hire you as an independent contractor. Will you keep traveling the world and hanging out with these crazy shitheads, too?" He waved at his friends and Banks, who were grinning like fools.

"Hell yes!" she shrieked as she flung herself into his arms.

They kissed and kissed while the divemasters cheered them on, until Banks cleared his throat.

"Oh. Hi, Banks. Are you still here? Sorry." Waverly blinked as she returned to reality, hopefully only for as long as it would take Archer to lug her off to their cabin.

"There's one other thing I need you four to do while we're there. The lawyer has contracts for another arm of the Banks Foundation that's been recently established. It will be responsible for the salvage and protection of artifacts from shipwrecks. The organization's first order of business is to retrieve the treasure you discovered. So it's only fitting that you be joint owners of the venture. Early estimates based on the data we sent in say this wreck alone could be worth eight hundred million dollars, give or take. I'd recommend refinancing the next excursion with the profits then splitting the rest between you equally. There will be plenty to go around. Operating expenses for a chopper can be astronomical."

Waverly knew the kind older man was looking out for her, more than her blood relatives ever had. He loved Archer like his own son. And since it seemed that *Archie* was really into her, she had no doubt Banks was finding ways to make her feel like an equal in his company.

An asset instead of a freeloader.

The last of her anxieties eased. She would be forever grateful.

"Thank you," she murmured, then squirmed from Archer's hold to kiss Banks on the cheek.

"You are so very welcome." He hugged her then. Maybe it was possible that after all this time they had managed to shake off the lingering effects of their shady beginnings, and triumph.

Every bit of good the Banks Foundation wrought blasted shadows from the world one by one. She was proud and thrilled to be part of bringing sunshine to people living in the darkness any way possible, seeing as she'd once been a night dweller herself.

Waverly couldn't wait to see where life would take them next, or in ten years. The only thing she knew for sure was that wherever it might be, Archer would be with her.

"I love you," he whispered again while he hugged her tight, as if she might forget.

Sailing off into the sunset with him was as magnificent as she'd always dreamed it would be.

Only, she had never imagined that would be the start of their adventure, not the end of it.

JAYNE RYLON
NEW YORK TIMES BESTSELLING AUTHOR
GOING DEEP
DIVEMASTERS #2
"Want alpha men, gripping storylines, and hot sex scenes? Read Jayne Rylon!"
~New York Times Bestselling Author Lorelei James

DEDICATION

To Jayne from Mr. Rylon, keep up the good work.
(Also, don't leave your laptop open and unlocked!)

Sabine Reynolds bounced in her laboratory's ergonomic desk chair as she waited for the video chat to connect on her laptop's screen. It had been nearly a month since she'd spoken live with her mentor, Heinrich—better known as the illustrious Dr. Geld. Emails didn't really cut it, especially when he was being so uncharacteristically secretive in his messages lately.

Sure, the time difference was a bitch, especially with her wrapping up a project for the Monterey Bay Institute in California and him still teaching at the Fischer Center for Marine Research in Germany, where she'd recently graduated from the doctoral program he chaired. They usually found ways to touch base more often than they had lately, though.

Heinrich had been obsessed with his current studies, to an even greater extent than usual. He'd missed a few of their regularly scheduled chats and hadn't responded to her messages for days, even though he was the sort of guy who typically replied in an instant. Marta, Heinrich's wife, had laughed it off when he'd completely forgotten their thirty-seventh anniversary the week before. Only because it was the first time since they'd been married and she was a much kinder, more patient woman than Sabine.

An absentminded professor type?

That wasn't the Heinrich they knew and loved at all.

Sabine grudgingly admitted to herself that she was curious, and maybe a tiny bit jealous that he was having so damn much fun without her. The urgent yet furtive tone of the series of texts he'd sent her in the middle of the night—which had practically ordered her to take his call first thing this morning—made her wonder if he'd had a breakthrough.

It had been worth dragging her ass to the lab at the crack of dawn to find out a few more details. Besides, she couldn't wait to geek out with the man who'd literally taught her everything she knew about marine biology and chemistry. A minor finding wouldn't cause a scientist as experienced as Heinrich to go bonkers like this. He was in the midst of a major discovery. Sabine was sure of it.

After downing a gulp of her coffee, she checked her watch. Not yet six o'clock and she was already at her desk. Meanwhile, Heinrich would be finishing up his afternoon lecture.

When the incoming call icon appeared on her laptop, she clicked it faster than a mantis shrimp nails its prey.

"Good morning, Dr. Reynolds!" Heinrich beamed when he saw her. He leaned so far forward she could map every wrinkle around his eyes and mouth, a testament to a lifetime of laughter.

It still gave her a thrill to be called by her relatively new title. She'd earned that son of a bitch less than a year ago. The sound of it was glorious to her ears. The result of a hell of a lot of hard work. A compromise with the sides of herself that had warred between roaming the far reaches of the world and doing something meaningful with her life.

Staying in one place for six years had gone against her nature. If it hadn't been for Heinrich and Marta's encouragement, she never would have seen it through and reached her goal.

That was probably why Heinrich—who'd become a surrogate father to her—always greeted her in the same way, as proud of her accomplishments as if she was truly the daughter he and Marta had never had. Which was the only thing that could have convinced her not to respond with his title. Respect he'd earned. Still, it made him grin when she used his first name. It was the easiest way she knew to communicate that he'd come to mean more to her than a simple professor or colleague. "Same to you, Heinrich. Er...afternoon, I suppose."

That's when she noticed that the German precision with which Heinrich usually trimmed his beard and combed his hair had also slipped some. Tousled looked good on him. But weird.

"Careful...a few more missed haircuts, notes scribbled across your whiteboard, or goofy grins, and you're going to cross into mad scientist territory." She smiled at him, certain he knew she kidded out of love. It was amazing to see him so ecstatic.

"Now you sound like Marta." He waved away her thinly veiled concern.

"She's a smart woman."

"It's true." He nodded before barreling on, skipping their usual chitchat. His pen tapped against his desk furiously. "I have something important to ask."

"Anything."

He squeezed his eyes shut for a moment then blurted, "Come home? Work with me on this."

"What?" It shocked her to hear him refer to Germany as *home*, though she supposed it had become that because of him and Marta and the six years she'd spent under their roof after they'd taken her in.

Sabine considered herself a gypsy of sorts. She'd moved on more often than she'd stayed put in her life. Her parents had been in the military together. She'd traveled across the globe both with them and on her own after they'd been killed in a freak training mission gone wrong when she was seventeen.

Without clear direction, it had taken her a few years longer than the average student to decide what it was she wanted to do with her future, but when she'd met Dr.

Heinrich Geld while he'd been on an expedition and she was working in a marina in the Solomon Islands, her fate had been sealed.

She tried to limit her relationships to superficial ones, given her history and her tendency to say goodbye often. With Heinrich, that had not been possible.

He and Marta had wormed their way into her heart despite her reflexive defenses.

"Sabine, please." This time he wasn't joking. "I *need* you. You'll get full credit. Co-researcher. I—"

"Hang on, Heinrich." She rubbed her temples, not quite awake enough yet to process what he was saying. "I'm not reluctant or worried about glory or some shit. It's that I don't even know what *this* is, really. You've been so cagey. Vague. Something with coral enzymes and their potential use in treating cancer."

"Shhhh." He motioned for her to keep her voice down.

"There's no one in the lab this early, don't worry," she promised, though his level of concern seemed like it was in the realm of tinfoil hats. Most people wouldn't understand their science-speak even if they tried. The rest would be bored to tears after thirty seconds.

"Okay, then." He spoke so quietly she had to rely on reading his lips to confirm she heard him correctly. "Yes. I believe we've isolated a substance that destroys cancer cells without attacking healthy systems. Or maybe it's reprogramming the rogue cells, resetting them to normal. I can't quite figure out why it's happening yet. I just know it is. I've never seen anything like this. Nothing even close. It could be...*revolutionary*."

Heinrich wasn't one for dramatics. If he was this worked up, it had to be promising. And concrete. Something beyond a theory decades away from practical application.

"Wow." She didn't quite know what to say. Or feel. Amazement, joy, and flattery didn't even scratch the surface. "Of course. If it's that monumental, I would love to be involved, do whatever I can to make this a reality. Shit, you know I'd be in regardless since you want me back that bad. All you had to do was ask."

Who wouldn't want to be part of changing the world so incredibly?

Renown or not, that didn't matter to her. Being present for someone important in her life, maybe repaying a fraction of what he'd given her...*that* mattered.

"Seriously?" He sagged in relief. "I'm afraid if I don't isolate what's happening, it could slip away. We need to protect these findings. They're powerful. In the wrong hands..."

Sabine couldn't imagine what he meant by that. Regardless, her mind was made up. "Sure. Don't worry, Heinrich. I'll be there. Can you give me the two weeks I have left on my grant here to wrap things up the right way?"

"Of course. I wouldn't expect any less of you." He winked. "After all, my partner should have the best reputation in the industry."

She gave a whoop as she considered things in those terms.

He clapped as she did a chair-bound version of a happy dance. Only then did she realize how stressed he had been lately. It wasn't exclusively excitement causing him to lose his grip on mundane things. The weight of his project was taking its toll. "With you onboard, we'll have this reaction understood, documented, and published in no time so that a cure can go into production as quickly as possible."

"Production?" Could he have already made a successful trial version? Be that far along?

No fucking wonder he was going nuts.

"Yes," Heinrich whispered conspiratorially as he came impossibly closer to his camera. It was sort of creepy and really funny because all she could see was his eyeball, giant-sized.

Which made it insanely easy to detect his biological response to the explosion that sent a shockwave through his laboratory, and her life.

BOOOOOOOOOOOOOOOOOOOM!

His pupil dilated. He stopped blinking.

Heinrich's face covered almost the entire screen. In the far periphery, Sabine thought she saw a masked man pass through the frame. Or had it been a shadow? Smoke? Because flames were definitely flickering up the walls. In the background an alarm began shrieking louder than a howler monkey.

Shouts were followed by crashes. "We've got it all. Let's go!"

Were first responders on the scene already?

"Help! Someone help!" she bellowed because Heinrich couldn't.

And the whole time, he remained still.

Dead still.

"Heinrich!" Sabine didn't care who was listening in now. She had to rouse him. Black clouds had begun to billow across every inch not blocked by his permanently stunned expression. "Please. Get up. Heinrich, please."

Fortunately, the heat of encroaching flames melted his laptop, keeping her from witnessing any more gruesome fuel for the nightmares she would certainly have for the rest of her life.

"Heinrich! No!" she screamed.

He couldn't hear her.

Clutching her middle with one hand to try and hold herself together, Sabine dialed 911 with the other even though she knew it was too late. It took forever to explain to the operator that an emergency was occurring on the other side of the world. Silent tears poured down her cheeks as if she were right there in the cloud of acrid smoke with Heinrich's body.

He was gone.

Her mentor, her friend, her second father.

His discoveries—the priceless contributions he had been about to make to science and society as a whole—had gone up in flames with him.

Through silent tears, Sabine vowed to honor his memory in the best way she could. She resolved then and there to continue his work and ensure his legacy remained strong by any means necessary. And if this turned out to have been more than an accident, she would make sure those responsible paid dearly.

～ TWO ～

Miguel Torres bobbed on the surface of the ocean, twenty feet or so behind the *Divemaster*. Water churned beside him, looking like a patch of boiling water as first Tosin, then Archer emerged from the sea following their early morning SCUBA dive.

Turtle Town on the southwest side of Maui had lived up to its name. Dozens of the friendly reptiles were swimming below their flippers or slept nestled in the stone arches on the sea floor. A spotted eagle ray had even floated past, flapping lazily as it went about its business. The morning had started off right. They explored the pass-throughs and mapped out a dive plan for the guests they would escort through the Five Graves site in the coming weeks.

None of them hurried to exit the ocean. So he studied the palm trees lining the shore of one of Hawaii's main islands not too far away. They grew on the hillside that rose upward to the summit of Haleakala, which pierced the clouds in the distance.

Even after six months of living the life, there were moments like this one when he still had to convince himself it was real. A gorgeous, nearly three-hundred-foot megayacht, which was a third his by some miracle, welcomed them home.

He'd finally found the happy medium between his wanderlust and feeling like a vagabond, destined to belong nowhere.

From the dive platform on their ship, Waverly smiled warmly at Archer. The love of a woman as strong, sexy, and wild in bed as her might be the only thing Miguel needed to make this scenario absolutely perfect.

The odds of finding a Waverly of his own on the *Divemaster* weren't the best. The boat was big, but not *that* big.

One thing hadn't changed. No matter how much they lingered, enjoying the sights and adventure of a place they visited, eventually they moved on. Leaving lovers and the possibility of building lasting relationships in their wake.

Miguel had indulged in a fling or two with their guests. They were fun while they lasted, which was never very long. He wasn't a greedy man, though. This was plenty to keep him satisfied.

Variety had its perks.

He sure as hell was never bored. Especially not when they had the clubroom onboard to pursue their darker pleasures in. Yeah, he truly was a lucky bastard. He must have been a goddamned saint in a past life to deserve this. Through Archer and Tosin, he'd found a lifelong friendship, a partnership, a home, and a family of sorts. Things he'd never dreamed possible.

So maybe he could get blessed by good fortune one more time.

"Hey, Miguel, are you listening to me?" Tosin asked, rapping on Miguel's tank with the hilt of his dive knife. The racket roused him from his thoughts.

"Ah, negative." He blinked behind his mask as he peered around. That's when he realized Banks, their business manager and so much more, had joined Archer's girlfriend. Together, they waited patiently for the trio of divemasters to swim over. Maybe Banks had details for them on the next group they would be hosting through the Divemaster Project.

Archer and Banks's brainchild, the program they ran from the megayacht gifted deserving people with a free trip of a lifetime. It was one of many ways they'd concocted to spend the billions Archer had inherited and bring some light to the rest of the world.

Miguel didn't pay too much attention to the scheduling, but he knew they'd been without guests for at least a week. Banks seemed to give them, and the rest of the crew, a break now and then. Honestly, he didn't really need time off to relax when his job guiding their special visitors was really more like fun than work.

Reluctantly, the three men removed their fins then climbed up the ladder. Miguel slipped off his mask and snorkel, dropped his regulator from his mouth, unsnapped his buoyancy control device, and swung his tank into one of the holders on the bench.

He peeled the top half of his wetsuit down to his waist then ran his fingers through his hair to try to tame it some as he joined the group.

Banks cleared his throat. "I wanted to speak with you boys to see if you'd consider accommodating an unusual request. I'd like to bring someone on for longer than the standard visit."

"Why?" Archer wasn't objecting, merely curious.

Miguel figured he'd let Banks do whatever he wanted. They trusted the guy. Owed him a hell of a lot. If he thought it was a good idea, they'd back him up. Make it happen.

"To conduct scientific research. Something too sensitive for the conservation arm of the Banks Foundation to handle. I'd feel better if we saw to it personally. It may also require us staying longer in the Hawaiian Islands than we'd originally planned. Perhaps for months instead of weeks, depending on how things go. Would that be okay?"

"I'm in no hurry to leave." Tosin sighed as he stared around, looking equally dazed as Miguel had been earlier. He hadn't always been so content. The stability of their new life had already made some big changes in Tosin. For the better. For the first time in the dozen years they'd known each other he seemed...secure. Looked over his shoulder less. Sometime soon, when they'd had the appropriate number of beers, Miguel thought he might ask what was up with that.

"We've got all the time in the world these days, don't we?" Miguel added.

Archer hummed, brushing his thumb over Waverly's knuckles. "As long as we're together, I don't care where we are."

"Besides, it could be cool to check out Maui too. Take a few excursions on land. Spend time with humans other than you knuckleheads." Miguel hoped they wouldn't decipher his code for…find someone to fuck for more than a one-nighter.

From the pointed looks his friends shot him, he figured they'd seen right through him.

Ah well. He shrugged, acting as if it wasn't a big deal. When Archer's father had died, leaving him more money than there was water in the ocean, Archer had started to question their purpose in life. Wondered if they could do something more significant than survive as nomadic beach bums who partied with lonely women on vacation by night, making even their kinkiest fantasies come true.

Miguel had laughed the idea off.

Until he'd seen what life was like for his friend with his soul mate. Maybe it hadn't been such a dumb question after all. Maybe his time here would give him a chance to do a test run at a real connection with a woman, something that went deeper than a night full of orgasms.

Banks cleared his throat. "Actually, Miguel, I was thinking maybe you could help our scientist out. She's going to need a divemaster and possibly an assistant when she's making her collection trips."

"Huh?" That would put a hell of a damper on his plans. He plopped onto the wooden bench seat nearby. "Why not Tosin?"

"Because I think you might have an acquaintance in common with Dr. Reynolds."

He tilted his head, suddenly uncomfortable with where this might be going. Especially since the scientist he'd have to babysit was a Dr. Reynolds, who was probably a gray-haired, spectacle-wearing scientist who would definitely disprove of his filthy missions. "Who do we both know?"

"Dr. Heinrich Geld."

"No kidding?" Miguel perked up at that. "I met him a long time ago. Before I knew Tosin and Archer even. He hired me as support for one of his expeditions."

"I heard." Banks's guarded smile put Miguel's senses on high alert.

"So this woman works for Heinrich?" he asked. "Any chance we could invite him instead? I'd love to catch up with him. I think you'd like him, too. You two kind of remind me of each other in some ways."

It'd be worth skipping out on his pussy hunt for that. He owed the guy a lot and would love to thank him for steering Miguel's life in the right direction.

"Not exactly." Banks sighed. "I'm sorry, Miguel. Dr. Geld was killed in an explosion at his laboratory last week."

"No!" Miguel stood in a rush, jabbing his fingers into his wet hair before gripping the back of his skull. The man had been a freaking genius, and far too young to be done making contributions to the world through his work.

"I'm sorry." Banks put his hand on Miguel's shoulder and squeezed. Waverly did one better and rushed to his side, hugging him despite his soaked suit and damp chest.

"Ah, man. That sucks," Tosin groaned as he and Archer shot Miguel sympathetic looks.

It took him a few minutes of staring at the waves to calm down. No one pressured him. They sat by his side as he got himself together.

"So this lady, she's picking up where he left off?" He'd help out however he could to ensure Heinrich's legacy was fulfilled.

Banks nodded. "Dr. Reynolds was his protégé. Highly respected in their field. I don't know much more than this… He'd somehow found a way to use coral to fight cancer. His notes, and everything related to the project, were destroyed in the blast and subsequent fire."

"Well, shouldn't Dr. Reynolds know what they were up to? She could redo the study, recreate the experiment, right?"

Tosin wondered. "Why does she need to be on a boat for that? Not that I mind."

"It's not that easy apparently." Banks winced. "Dr. Reynolds was actually working on a grant in California. She has some correspondence with Dr. Geld and is piecing together what she can from the ruins of his lab. It doesn't sound like much is salvageable. And apparently he'd been very secretive. Careful. All she knows for sure is the locations he'd been out collecting from before he returned to Germany to study his samples. She may need to retrace his footsteps and start from scratch. The last place he'd gone before returning to Germany ahead of schedule was Hawaii. Specifically, Molokini. So she and Heinrich's wife, Marta, began scouring the area for any vessels that might be able to accommodate her for a while. Assist in her efforts."

"We should do this." Archer crossed his arms, spreading his legs as if prepared to battle for Dr. Reynolds. "I vote yes. Definitely"

Though the *Divemaster* had been part of his inheritance, he never acted like he was their boss, something Miguel appreciated beyond belief. As three dominant men, they'd learned to keep from pissing all over each other's territory to keep their friendship intact. Besides, it wasn't often they disagreed.

In this case they certainly didn't.

"Me too." Tosin nodded.

"Of course I'll help," Miguel responded when they turned to him.

"Good. You can start by picking her up from the airport." Banks grinned then shrugged. "I knew you'd do the right thing."

"Guess I'd better go get the helicopter ready." Waverly didn't bother to act put out when piloting was clearly her second favorite thing—next to fucking Archer—to do.

"I'm coming, too," Archer insisted.

The man might never recover from the time he'd let Waverly fly solo and nearly lost her. Good thing they'd upgraded their chopper to a six-seater. Plenty of room for everyone.

Banks handed Miguel a folder, not unlike the one he'd prepared with contracts the day Archer had invited Miguel and Tosin aboard for the adventure of a lifetime. When he flipped it open, the first thing he noticed was a picture of Dr. Reynolds, who looked *nothing* like he'd imagined.

Whoa.

Far more hippie than nerd. Sabine Reynolds was willowy, natural, and gorgeous.

Sexy as fuck.

Suddenly his assignment was looking up. "Let's go."

He snapped the folder closed and strode off to his quarters for real clothes. If he chose the black shirt that inspired women to stare at his chest and the cargo shorts that hugged his package, emphasizing his best assets, who could blame him?

∾ THREE ∾

Sabine spotted her suitcase on the revolving conveyor and marched over to intercept it. That's what she intended anyway. Her ambitious intentions manifested as more of a swamp-monstery stomp. Only her passion to carry out Heinrich's dream propelled her onward.

She'd flipped her internal clock upside down twice traveling from California to Germany then back through Amsterdam and L.A. to Hawaii. Spent two of the past five days in transit, and the three in between...well, they'd been horrific. Mental, emotional, and physical exhaustion plagued her after one of the worst weeks of her life.

It felt like losing her parents all over again.

More traumatic because she'd witnessed it. Slightly less awful because she'd been able to promise Marta and the rest of Heinrich's loved ones that he hadn't suffered.

Her zombified feet didn't keep up with her mind's directives, and she tripped.

Tucking and rolling to keep from smashing onto the luggage carousel and being dragged through those vinyl flaps separating the passenger terminal from God-knew-what airport underworld turned out to be unnecessary. Good thing, since her reaction time was disgraceful right then.

A strong arm came around her, steadying her. Then a deep voice with a sultry South American rumble asked, "That one with the rainbow stripes is yours?"

All she could do was nod dumbly.

Her savior steadied her then caught up to the bag with three long strides, hefting it from the infinite loop with one hand, even though it contained nearly all of her worldly belongings. *Damn.*

She might be tired, but she'd have to be cryogenically frozen like some of her samples not to obsess over guns like that or how they'd felt, however briefly, around her. Her hormones woke up and took notice.

Sabine subtly, she hoped, checked out the Good Samaritan as he returned with her suitcase in tow. The rest of him lived up to his sculpted biceps.

"Thanks." She offered him a smile, hoping it held at least a hint of pretty beneath the mountain of haggard. The black circles she'd spotted under her eyes in the airport's restroom a couple minutes ago or the gaunt jut of her cheekbones given her inability to eat while upset, made her doubt it.

When she attempted to take the bag from him, he held it out of her reach. "I've got this. Do you have any others?"

Sabine hesitated, unwilling to divulge too much to a stranger. An experienced traveler, she didn't waste a lot of brainpower worrying about the possible nefarious intentions of her fellow human beings. The good, helpful people far outweighed the rest. Still, she was no idiot. It paid for a woman alone to be cautious.

Too bad her entire being screamed that she should cave in to unwise temptations and let a handsome stranger take care of her precisely when she could use his broad shoulder to lean on and his big dick to ride before passing out for a day or two of solid sleep. Well, that middle part was speculation, an informed guess based on the bulge in his shorts. She assumed he wasn't storing extra socks or a taro root in there.

Apparently she'd stood still, staring and debating how to proceed, long enough to cross into the awkward zone.

"Oh, shit. Sorry." He laughed, showing off a great smile—super white against his tan skin—and killer eyes like the turquoise water she'd flown over minutes ago. "I'm Miguel Torres. Your ride, kind of. Banks sent me to pick you up and take you to the *Divemaster*. I'll also be helping you with your project as long as you need me."

Well, *hellllo,* Miguel. She could certainly use him.

Sabine hadn't yet decided if this was fate trying to make up for the pile of shit it had dumped on her or just another trap in a lovely package. A *spectacular* package more like it.

How the fuck was she supposed to concentrate with him hanging around? Miguel. Even his damn name sounded like pure sex when he said it in that sex-on-a-stick accent of his.

Sabine was no prude. She'd been called reckless by some, though she preferred to consider herself daring. Bold in every aspect of her life, she embraced her innate curiosity and was well-studied in animal behavior. Humans included. Sexuality intrigued her. She never hesitated to do some personal experimentation when the chance and chemistry presented itself. But if she'd ever needed to focus in her life, it was now.

Distractions weren't welcome.

Especially not the six-foot-something, ripped, take-charge gentleman variety.

"Are you ready?" he asked when she still didn't respond.

"Uh, yeah. Sorry." She shook her head to clear it, triumphant when she saw his gaze tracking the swoosh of her hair whipping around her upper arms. Misery loved company and all that. "Rough couple of days. I'm running on fumes."

"I can see that." He tugged the straps of her backpack from her shoulders before she could stop him. Somehow she got the feeling he would have scooped her right up along with it if they hadn't met half a second earlier. He was that kind of guy.

The type who took care of his own.

The type she'd never allowed herself to fall for, afraid that she might sacrifice some of her independence in exchange for his pleasure. The type who might consume her if she let him.

As though it had a single loaf of bread in it, he slung her backpack over one shoulder, grabbed her suitcase, and placed his free palm against her lower back, guiding her toward the automatic door. It opened onto tropical heat, which hit her like a shockwave and stole her breath.

Or was that the impact his touch had on her? Uh oh.

"Come on. It's not far to the runway shuttle. Waverly and Archer are waiting for us at the helipad." He matched his pace to hers though she was sure he could easily have had her trotting to keep up with his long, powerful legs.

"Archer Quartermane?" It shocked her that he'd come out to greet her personally. Surely he had better things to do with his time than fetch a lowly scientist from the airport. Hell, she hardly believed he'd agreed to have her onboard, despite rumors of his unimaginable generosity. Then again, Marta had used some personal contacts to get in touch with a man called Banks, who supposedly ran the entire foundation Archer had established, of which the Divemaster Project was only one small part.

"Uh, I guess. He doesn't go by that name anymore, though." Miguel paused for the first time. "We call him Archer Banks. Or just Archie if you prefer. He *loves* that."

Yeah, right. Sabine wouldn't be addressing the billionaire as anything informal until he gave her permission. Probably not even then. He was supplying a golden opportunity to bring Heinrich's life work to fruition. She wouldn't do anything to jeopardize it.

"Banks? Like his executive director?" She didn't find that as weird as others might. "He must really love the guy to have named his charitable foundation, and even himself, in the man's honor."

"Sometimes families are made of the people you choose, not the ones you're born with." Shadows clouded Miguel's striking eyes for the first time as he spoke words she couldn't have agreed with more. She was sorry he'd had experiences similar enough to her own to allow him to relate.

"I understand that." She blinked as she thought of Heinrich. And Marta. Poor Marta. Brokenhearted.

Sabine hoped that by completing the study, Marta's loss might seem more worthwhile in some twisted way. Right now a hollow sort of ache occupied Sabine's gut. It hadn't been long enough for the authorities to finish their investigation into the circumstances behind the explosion. It could have been chemical. A deadly, accidental reaction.

Something completely innocent, though tragic.

Neither Sabine nor Marta believed Heinrich would have been careless like that despite his recent preoccupation. Though law enforcement hadn't found any evidence of outside involvement, she couldn't shake her recollections of those horrible moments. She'd been sure she heard someone shouting in the background. Thought she'd seen a masked man.

Which meant someone had stolen him from them. Intentionally wreaked havoc on their family unit. That realization only steeled her resolve to make sure the people responsible didn't get what they wanted—for Heinrich's results to disappear with him. She wanted revenge for the agony rotting her gut.

It must have also been written on her face as they climbed onto the waiting mini bus.

"I'm very sorry about Dr. Geld," Miguel murmured as he helped her sink into a seat and took the place next to her on the empty shuttle. Without hesitation, the driver headed off. Was this what it was like to be rich? It would be easy to get used to treatment like this, though she'd better not.

When she noticed the sincerity in Miguel's warm eyes, she saw something there that surprised her. Pain that echoed her own. "Thank you. Did you know Heinrich?"

"Not nearly as well as you." He held out his hand, palm up.

Sabine couldn't say what made her do it, but she accepted. Placing her fingers between his, she allowed him to swallow her up in his protective grasp. Simple contact could have a drastic effect on an organism. Pheromones, pulse rate, adrenaline...natural chemistry could work wonders.

This was one of those times.

Grateful, she sagged, letting her head loll on the rest as relief replaced tension.

"Enough to know how inspiring he was. How decent and brilliant," Miguel continued softly. "When I was twelve or so, I bailed from the orphanage I'd spent a few years in. It was safer on the streets of Rio and better still away from the city. So I made my way along the coast to Búzios. I was trying to figure out a way to survive on my own, fishing and catching whatever I could for food. Stealing some, digging through garbage at resorts, and hiding out. Until I realized tourists would pay me decent money to show them my secret places—the best beaches and hidden treasures I'd found while exploring the area on my own. I would swim with them out to exceptional spots on the reefs for some quick cash and sometimes snag a meal while I was out there."

Sabine smiled a bit, imaging the enterprising kid he'd been once. No wonder he'd grown into such an impressive man. She respected self-made people. Those who forged their own paths.

"Anyway, Heinrich saw me hustling for customers in the town square one day. So he hired me, but not to guide him. He took me to a restaurant, ordered heaps of food for us to share, then asked me to tell him about things I'd seen. He had books with tons of pictures and had me point out different species I recognized. He wondered what spots I'd seen them at, how often, and during what parts of the year. At first, I thought he was a sucker for paying me just to talk. I was prepared to fight if he was trying to trick me into lowering my defenses so he could take advantage of me like some guys did."

Sabine subconsciously tightened her grip on his hand and he squeezed in return.

"Instead, he taught me things to make me better, safer, at what I was doing. He helped me identify new fish I'd seen on my dives and learn more about them. Figure out which were good to eat and the best ways to catch them. I never stumped him. Not once. He knew about every living creature. That goes for people, too. He understood lots about them." Miguel made it easy to imagine him as a lost boy when he stared into the distance. "He encouraged me to educate myself even if it wasn't formally in some fancy college. Told me about SCUBA and set me on the path to becoming a divemaster. If it wasn't for him, who knows where I'd be today?"

"You may have gotten there on your own," she offered.

"Doubt it. I wish I'd taken time to track him down and thank him properly. Hell, I didn't even get to say goodbye. The day his research vessel departed, I got held up by a tree that had fallen across the road into town. It took me and my four guests hours to hack it apart with a rusty machete so their van could make it through. Then it was nighttime and the return trip took hours longer than it would have with daylight. By the time I got back...he was gone. At least I'd given him my present, a *very* small token of my appreciation, the night before."

"Hang on, you're *that* Miguel?"

"He remembered me?"

"Of course. He often wondered what became of you." She thought of the stories Heinrich had told her about Miguel's mischievous antics, and decided not to mention his legendary ability to charm lady tourists even as a kid. There was one thing she figured she should divulge, however. Heinrich would have wanted her to pass this along. "You made him a necklace. Of sea glass and acai seeds tinted with vegetable dyes."

Miguel's gaze whipped to hers. "Yeah."

"He never took it off." Sabine's eyes welled for the thousandth time in the past few days. "I think he assumed something terrible had happened to you. Feared the worst. He was going to ask you to go with him, you know? To Germany. But he never got the chance. The next year, when they returned, you were gone."

She often thought that was why Heinrich had invited her to join his program after only knowing her a few weeks. If it hadn't been for Miguel's influence on him, who knew where she would be today either?

It was funny sometimes, the way the universe worked.

"Well, shit." Miguel looked away then, swallowing hard. "Yeah. After he left, I did, too. I'd saved enough that I was able to start taking classes and got certified. Then I moved around constantly, going where there was work and something new to discover. I didn't have a lot, certainly not internet or a computer or anything like that until recently. I wish I could have kept in touch."

Reluctantly Sabine shook free of his hold. She reached across him to grab her backpack. If she took longer than absolutely necessary while leaning over so she could soak in his strength and catalog the hard planes of his taut chest and abdomen in the process, who could blame her?

It didn't take much searching to find what she was looking for. She knew exactly where she'd put it, wrapped in a scarf for safekeeping.

Once she had it, she took the hand he'd recently offered her and unfurled his loose fist. Then she placed the necklace in his palm, marveling at how dainty it looked there. "Marta, Heinrich's wife, told me to take this for good luck. You should have it back."

He stared at it for a few moments, as if trying to decipher the meaning of it all. Then he shook his head, disheveling his thick, inky hair. "She's right. It sounds like you could use it. Besides, this will look prettier on you than me."

Miguel took the ends of the deceptively sturdy strands and wound them around her neck, slipping the shell on one side through the hoop of fibers on the other. His knuckles brushed along her collarbones as he admired his handiwork, which now decorated her skin.

She shivered.

"What I could really use is your help." She laid her hands on his forearms then, curling her fingers around them as far as she could reach, unwilling to let go now that she'd found an ally. If he'd impressed Heinrich at twelve, she had no doubt he would be a major asset to her research and collection efforts.

He rested his forehead on hers and whispered, "You've got it. We'll make this right. For Heinrich."

The tiny flash of the vulnerable child he'd been only endeared him to her more. Heinrich had liked to take in strays. Like her. Like him. Except he'd slipped through the cracks.

This time would be different, she promised herself. She murmured, "Thank you."

Sabine didn't question her instincts. She leaned forward and sealed their promise with a kiss.

FOUR

Miguel couldn't say women surprised him often. However, Sabine had already managed it more than once in the ten minutes he'd known her. Ferociously determined, yet sweet underneath, she appealed to him even more than the thought of diving in Palau, his favorite SCUBA destination.

So he dove into her instead, deepening the kiss she'd given him to seal their deal in the most delicious of ways. He'd barely had time to register the cinnamon flavor of the gum she'd obviously been chewing recently along with the expert press of her lush lips on his before the flicker of her tongue against his mouth urged him to shed his veneer of civility.

Unleashing his animal instincts, which seemed to be her thing if her encouraging moan was any indication, he slid his hand to the nape of her neck and wrapped his fingers around her. Miguel pinned her in place for better access as he accepted the invitation issued by her parted lips and plundered her mouth. He should stop before he scared her off.

He couldn't.

Miguel leaned in closer, pressing her against the seat. Her short, blunt nails dug into his forearms, begging for more, promising she could handle the full force of his desire.

"What's the hold up? Need help with her luggage?" Archer asked as he boarded the bus, which must have stopped some time ago, though Miguel and Sabine had been totally oblivious to their arrival. Waverly followed a step behind.

Sabine jerked away, attempting to disguise the true cause of their delay. Fuck that. She was his for the duration of her stay and it would be best if everyone knew it up front.

Sabine included.

After just a taste, he craved more. And he would have it. Have her.

Miguel stole one final sample of her spiciness before slowly backing off. He allowed a slow grin to spread across his face as he observed her dilated pupils and the color he'd tongue-fucked back into her cheeks. At least he'd been able to do that for her. She'd looked ready to drop when he spotted her in the terminal.

Instead of coddling her as he'd intended, he'd pushed her. Or had he accepted her challenge? Either way, once the thrill of their meeting wore off, she was going to crash. Hard.

Shit. They needed to get going.

"Seriously, dude?" Archer gave them a resounding slow clap for their sexy performance. "That might be a record, even for you."

Miguel shot his friend the finger, mostly because he didn't want Sabine to think their kiss had been anything like his previous seductions. It had been a hell of a long time. Okay, more like *never* since he'd found this kind of immediate connection with someone. Sexual attraction, sure, but also something…deeper. Rather than fuck it up before it got going, he'd like to see where it took them.

Hopefully their journey together began with his bed and ended up in the ship's clubroom.

Saving the day, Waverly greeted their resident scientist as if it was no big deal that she'd been sucking face with him a few moments earlier. "Welcome to paradise. The weather here is steamy, and the men are even hotter."

Sabine laughed and rose, finger-combing her hair as she made her way to the couple to introduce herself.

Thank. You. He owed Waverly big time.

From behind Sabine's back, he blew Waverly a kiss. She winked in return as Archer shook Sabine's hand and reassured her they'd support her mission in any way possible. Waverly didn't stop there. She went in for a full-on hug, offering her condolences. Now there was a sight Miguel could appreciate.

Two gorgeous women, one tall, sophisticated, and dark-haired, the other more of a free-loving earthy type with wavy natural golden hair, dove-gray eyes, and rocking curves. The necklace he'd made close to twenty years ago, tied in a place of honor around her delicate throat, made it seem like her coming here, now, might be some kind of sign or the answer to prayer he didn't realize he'd uttered.

If he believed in shit like that.

He snagged Sabine's backpack and suitcase, impressed that she could travel so light. Anxious to have her settled in, he wandered closer to the doorway. They took the hint, exiting the bus.

"Thanks," he said to the driver before passing over an insane tip. In addition to living on the *Divemaster* without any room or board expenses, Miguel, Tosin, and Archer each collected incredible salaries from the Divemaster Project for entertaining their guests and keeping them safe on their complimentary retreats.

Though they'd argued with Banks that getting paid any more than minimum wage to work a dream job was unnecessary, the guy had refused to give them a pay cut. Of course, Miguel could legally sell his third of the *Divemaster* at any time and become instantly rich as fuck. Why would he, though, when he had far more than he'd ever wanted already?

Less than a year ago, his entire life had become a dream come true.

Now all he needed was someone besides his best friends to share it with. Watching Archer with Waverly had shown him what it could be like to have a companion, a lover, an intimate and lasting relationship. He hated to admit he'd been jealous of one of his partners. Yet he had been.

It might not become a forever thing, but if she was down with it, he planned to dip his toe in the relationship pool for himself with Sabine while she was around. Why not try something different?

The bus driver tipped his hat and grinned. "Have fun. Don't bother behaving yourself."

"I never do, man." Miguel slapped the guy on the shoulder before disembarking.

By the time he'd crossed to the chopper—a serious upgrade from the one they'd had originally—everyone else had climbed inside. So he handed up the suitcase to Archer then joined Sabine in the back bench seat. U-shaped, the buttery leather couch could hold four adults easily. Waverly and Archer had captain-style chairs up front.

Though they'd never used it before, Miguel eyed the smoked glass partition that could be raised between the pilots and the passengers. Possibilities for another day.

He took the spot nearest the windows on the left side of the cabin and rested one arm along the back of the seat. Of course that meant he draped it over Sabine's shoulders, too. At odds with the confidence and competence she exuded even at what had to be a low point in her life, her petite frame fit perfectly in the crook of his elbow. He tucked her against his side so that she could see better out his window. If that meant they snuggled while she did, he'd take one for the team.

Together they admired the scenery as Waverly launched them into the air. They rose above the east coast of Maui. From their bird's eye view, the Hana Highway snaked between waves and cliffs. Occasionally they caught sight of a sandy beach in a range of colors—white, red, and black— nestled into hidden coves before veering off to the west in a drastic arc that tugged at Miguel's guts and made him want to whoop simultaneously.

He held Sabine to him, bracing her against the G-forces. Without so much as blinking, she kept her stare glued to the landscape below. He couldn't blame her.

The island fascinated him with its epic variety of ecosystems. Lush on this side, practically a desert by the time you got to Ka'annapali in the northwest, although it would only take an hour to drive that far. In between, mighty Haleakala rose over ten-thousand feet above sea level, stretching into the clouds.

"Do you think we can see the astrophysical complex from here?" Sabine asked, referring to the mass of ground-based telescopes on the peak of the volcano. Figured she'd geek out about that instead of most every other woman on the planet, who'd be satisfied with pretty colors in the sky during the legendary sunrises or sunsets seen from the peak.

"Nah, we're not high enough, sorry," Waverly called from the front.

"Ah, that's okay." Sabine shrugged and went back to peering around below them.

Would she be bored with Miguel? Though he knew a shit ton about diving and the underwater world, he'd never been accused of being a genius. He'd have to distract her with some of his other skills to make up for his lack of formal education.

With a wolfish grin on his face, he followed the direction of her gaze.

The emerald jungle of the Iao Valley lined the edge of his sight as they swung around the south side of the volcano's crater. If Sabine hadn't just traversed half the globe after losing someone so important to her, Miguel would have put in a request for Waverly to buzz some of the gorgeous waterfalls at its heart.

Below them, ash fields and scorched earth could have convinced him he'd stepped into Mordor. It was beautiful in its own way. Unusual, desolate, and stark. Beside him, Sabine nestled closer for a better view. He smiled and kissed her forehead before returning his attention to the awe-inspiring landscape.

Zipping over Wailea and its mansions, owned by some of the most famous people in the world, they soon approached the ocean on the southwest side of the island. Gorgeous water, in a million hues of blue and green, welcomed them home. No matter where she was anchored, the *Divemaster* would always be that for him. It was a monumental change from their previous nomadic lifestyle. It allowed them some permanence without tying them down.

It didn't take long to spot it.

"Wow. Is *that* your ship, Archer?" Sabine gasped. "It's beautiful. And huge. Absolutely nothing like the research vessels I've worked on before."

"No. It's the ship I own part of, along with Miguel and Tosin," he corrected. "She's where we live and work. Our sanctuary. You're welcome to call it the same for as long as you'd like."

Sabine yanked her stare from the megayacht for a moment to peer up at Miguel with questions in her gaze. They could discuss those later.

He shrugged then gestured with his chin at the ship, which grew larger in their view as they approached. She was a beautiful bitch, that was for certain. Gleaming in the sunlight, her triple teak decks, complete with a pool, called out to him, encouraging him to be lazy. Meanwhile, inside, luxuries abounded, from the wide-open lounges to the state of the art kitchen, and living quarters that would rival any of the estates they'd flown over moments ago.

From here you couldn't even see his absolute favorite part.

The dive center and platforms.

It was everything he could ever have dreamed of, if he'd been wildly outrageous with his fantasies. Truly, the *Divemaster* was so much more than he could have imagined. He didn't believe at first that real people—hell, that *he*—could really live like that.

Sometimes he still felt kind of guilty about it.

The charity work they were doing with the Divemaster Project and the even more unimaginable scope of the Banks Foundation as a whole helped to ease his conscience. What they used was only a drop in the bucket of billions Archer could have hoarded for himself, yet had chosen to share with his friends and the rest of the less fortunate people in the world.

Sabine's research was only one example of the good they were doing. So Miguel figured it was okay to enjoy a "little" something for themselves while they were at it.

He'd never claimed to be a saint.

Quite the opposite, actually.

Waverly lowered them toward the helipad as gracefully as a butterfly settling onto a delicate blossom. He had no idea how she managed to hit a moving target and make it seem so easy.

As they disembarked, Captain Alex was waiting to greet them. "It's a pleasure to have you onboard, Dr. Reynolds."

"Thank you. Though I do wish it was under different circumstances, I'm so grateful for your help. All of you." She sighed, wavering slightly as the gentle motion of the *Divemaster* rocked her. As Miguel had predicted, she was fading. Fast.

"Where's Banks?" Archer wondered.

It wasn't like him not to welcome guests personally, especially one as important as Sabine.

"He's overseeing the retrofit of the space where Dr. Reynolds's laboratory will go. There have been deliveries and installers messing up my decks the whole damn day." Captain Alex liked things tidy on his ship.

Sabine winced. "I'm sorry."

"Not your fault," Miguel reassured her before glaring at Captain Alex.

The man only smiled smugly before staring pointedly at the possessive hand Miguel had laid on Sabine's waist. Had the captain been fucking with Miguel?

Apparently his claim had not gone unnoticed. Perfect.

Captain Alex waved away Sabine's apology. "Don't worry, we'll have it cleaned up before the sun sets. I just like these kids to think I'm a grumpy old bastard sometimes. To keep them in line, you know. I will ask you to take your sneakers off, please. No footwear is allowed to be worn beyond the entries to the ship."

"Oh." Sabine gave what might have been a laugh if she wasn't wiped out. Instead, it sounded more like a huff. She toed off her shoes with a wan smile. "Never did like wearing them much anyway."

"Swimwear is optional as well. Feel free to lose as much of your clothing as you like," Miguel rasped in her ear.

Sabine's shoulders shook a bit. She hardly responded otherwise.

Miguel figured on a good day she'd have handed him his balls for such a brazen suggestion in front of company she intended to impress.

Captain Alex frowned when the extent of her condition became obvious. Then he said to Miguel, "Banks spoke to you about where Dr. Reynolds will be staying, correct? Would you like to show her to her room or should I call for one of the stewardesses?"

"I've got this." He nodded at the gathering, then led Sabine inside toward the glass elevator that ran through the heart of the ship. When he stepped inside it, he intentionally poked the button for his own floor, not hers.

∽ FIVE ∾

"Is this place for real?" Sabine whispered to herself.

Squinting to protect her eyes against the starbursts glinting off every polished surface surrounding them, she gawked as they descended through deck after deck. The décor and furnishings weren't the kind that made her think of museums or Baroque castles, thankfully.

Decadent, yes. Gaudy, no.

The boat's atmosphere felt warm and soothing. Relaxation washed over her, only adding to the weight in her bones. She hoped it wasn't a half-mile walk to her cabin. The thought of a bunk, however hard and narrow, nearly had her weeping.

She was surprised when they stopped on a level above the waterline. Real windows looked out onto the ocean from the lobby. Staff quarters usually consisted of tiny caves on the lowest deck of a ship. She'd consider herself lucky if she wound up with a porthole to peek out of on occasion.

Still, she didn't have the energy to question Miguel as he towed her along a wide polished wood hallway lined with gorgeous photographs of the sea and the occasional blown glass sculpture that made her think of waves inset in well-lit niches.

Everything was cozy and welcoming, with the exception of a single smoked glass door they passed. The modern monolith, complete with keypad entry, starkly contrasted the more traditional finishes. Sometime when her mind wasn't fuzzy with grief and fatigue, she might ask Miguel about it.

"Here we are." He paused in front of a wide door and entered a combination on the keypad. It seemed odd that he knew the code to her door, though she supposed he *did* own part of the ship. Maybe he had a master key code or something.

Except, when he opened it and ushered her inside the largest stateroom she'd ever seen on a ship, there were belongings on the shelves and a polished desk held an open notebook full of furious scribbles.

"Someone already lives here?" She'd shared housing before. Nothing as spacious or grand as this either. Except… She tried peeking around his broad shoulders to be sure. Yep, there was only one bed. A massive one at that.

"Yeah, me." Miguel crossed his arms, practically daring her to object.

Too tired to argue, she reached behind her for the door. One of his massive hands shot out, covering hers on the handle before she could yank it open.

"Banks has quarters prepared for you in the staff area, if you really want them. I think you'll be far more comfortable in my bed, though. Don't you?" Miguel edged closer, causing her to take a step backward and then another, until her shoulders and ass bumped into the wall.

His heat and the enticing smell of ocean air on his skin weakened her objections. "Maybe."

The man didn't fight fair. He pressed his thigh between her legs, letting her ride the muscle there as he braced one forearm above her head, leaning in so their mouths nearly collided again.

Sabine licked her lips.

"That's right," he practically growled as his fingers brushed her hair behind her ear on one side. "Your hard nipples are telling me you want another shot at me as badly as I need to devour you. Why try to fight nature? Stay. Let me watch over you tonight. Tomorrow...we'll see where this goes."

"I should probably at least pretend to be a professional considering how gracious the Banks Foundation is being by sponsoring my research and granting me this opportunity." She didn't bother to deny their attraction. That would be a ridiculous argument.

Hell, it was all she could do to keep from putting her hands up to feel the solid muscles of his chest for herself. Maybe burrow into them and beg him to put his arms around her, sheltering her while she got some much needed rest.

It was a hard thing to admit for a woman who'd always prided herself on her independent streak. Except her whole soul felt bruised at the moment, and Miguel seemed plenty strong enough to take care of them both. Willing, too.

"We're adults. Who you sleep with is your business. If it makes you feel better, we can store your stuff downstairs for appearances, but we both know that'll be a waste of space." His confidence bordered on arrogance, yet somehow it still managed to make her squirm. In a good way. "Dishonest, too. I'm not the kind of man who sneaks around, fucking in the shadows. I'd be proud to have you stay with me, for everyone to know you're mine, if only for a little while. And I'll make damn sure you can say the same."

"Uh." Why couldn't she think of more reasons to turn down his proposal?

It wouldn't be the first spontaneous decision she'd made in her life. Nor the worst. Most likely.

"Besides, my suite has a jetted tub and the standard cabins only have showers. Big ass showers with fancy nozzles and shit, but still. You know you want my...bathtub." He wiggled his brows.

She groaned at the thought of soaking her aching body in steamy water. Five long cross-country and international flights in economy had threatened to permanently disfigure her. Booking her tickets last minute had meant she'd been the sucker jammed into the center seats. "Fine, you win."

"Always do." He nipped her bottom lip before pulling away to kiss her cheek. "Keep that in mind."

He didn't intimidate her.

In fact, part of her wished he hadn't stopped there. With a few quick movements, he could rip open his fly, shove down her jeans and panties, then help her forget anything except the pleasure he could undoubtedly give her. Yet he seemed true to his word. He wasn't going to manhandle her...tonight, anyway.

Sabine didn't want the guy to get too cocky. Plus, she thought she might test his self-control. See if he was as strong as he appeared. Experiments were her thing. So she stared straight at him as she walked the hem of her shirt up her torso. About the time she revealed her bra, which did a nice job of making the most of what she had, a muscle twitched in his jaw.

"If I knew you better, I might spank you for teasing me like that," he warned.

"Is that supposed to scare me?" It didn't. She'd often fantasized about finding a guy to play those kinds of games with. Only she'd never met one she thought could truly inspire her to hand herself over to like that.

Until now.

He had the potential to shake her up. Dangerous, this game she'd started playing.

That was what made it so fun. Where numbness had resided for days, he brought her back to life. It was a relief. Addictive, too.

Sabine dropped her shirt on the floor then shimmied out of her jeans. Her underwear, socks, and bra made a neat pile beside the rest of her clothes. Soon she wore only the necklace he'd put around her neck earlier. While his once-over may have originated with that item, it didn't stop there. She felt the sear of his gaze as it roamed lower and lower, remotely caressing her breasts before it focused on her center.

"You never have to be afraid of me or the things I'll do to you, *lindeza*. I'll make sure you enjoy every moment." If she hadn't been nude already, Miguel might have set her panties on fire with his thickening Brazilian accent. Would he talk to her like that while they fucked?

She shivered.

He admired her openly. "You should prepare yourself. It's going to be intense. I can tell already."

Sabine got the impression he didn't often wait to take what he desired. So she made the most of the anticipation, spinning to put her ass on display as she sashayed to his bathroom and bent over to turn on the hot, steamy water. Though she'd been drained minutes ago, even simple flirting with him invigorated her.

What would the real thing do for her?

"This is going to be the best assignment of my life." He made no apologies for staring at her, though he did intercede to keep her from lifting another finger. Miguel offered her his hand, helping her into the tub. He encouraged her to get comfortable while he brought her some body wash, lit a few candles, and queued up some nature sounds on his iPod to help her unwind. It reminded her of the time she'd spent in the field, her favorite part of her job. "When was the last time you ate?"

"Miguel, I don't even know what day it is right now," she answered honestly. "They gave us a chocolate-covered macadamia nut and some passion fruit juice on the flight in. Before that...couldn't say."

"Right." He grimaced. "I'm going to order some food for us. What would you like?"

There was a choice? And someone would bring it to them?

That impressed her more than the rest of the trappings she'd spied on their way to his private space. Standard fare on ships was whatever the hell the cook made and you were damn well happy to have it. Her hesitation and wide eyes must have been answer enough.

Miguel chuckled. "I know. I'm not quite used to this myself. It takes less time than you might imagine to get spoiled, though."

"I'm not sure how long I'm going to be around. Hopefully I can retrace Heinrich's steps pretty quick, before someone else does." She sank lower into the bubbles and crossed her arms over her nakedness as she tried for the millionth time to replay those seconds and zoom in on the shadow she'd seen in the corner of the screen. Had it been smoke, or the person she'd imagined at first?

"Hey, don't worry about that now. There will be plenty of time for work tomorrow and beyond. The best way you can help yourself prepare is to rest up and be at a hundred percent mentally before you get started, right?" He brushed his thumb over her shoulder. Though she had always felt comfortable in her own skin, she wished he would ditch his clothes, too.

Partially because she felt vulnerable. Mostly because she wanted to feast her eyes on what promised to be a spectacular body.

"Easy with that eye-fucking, tiger shark. Want me to serve myself up on a platter for you?" His smile made her sure room service would have an entirely different meaning if he was the one making the deliveries.

They might have ended up splashing water across the gorgeous marble floors, if her stomach hadn't growled loud enough to be heard over the running water.

"No more distractions, woman." Miguel asked again, "What can I get for you?"

"I'm guessing grilled fish is an option considering where we are, right?" She practically drooled as she considered eating something other than airport fare. "With some vegetables, maybe? It doesn't have to be anything fancy. Honestly, I'm probably not even going to taste it."

She yawned then. What she would really like was to shovel some sustenance into her face, swallow it in one giant gulp, then crash on the admittedly cloudlike bed she'd passed during her strut into the bathroom, which had apparently sapped the last of the charge in her internal batteries.

Though it was barely noon here, she wasn't going to be conscious much longer.

"Anything you don't like or are allergic to?"

"Nah. I'm pretty flexible." She shrugged, sighing as the warm water lapped over her collarbones.

"I think I'm going to like that about you." Miguel squeezed her hand. "I'll be right back."

The soft purr of his instructions to the chef reached her. Though she couldn't make out the words, she guessed his Brazilian accent was going to quickly become her favorite sound in the world. Maybe he would teach her some Portuguese so that she could listen to him speak more often.

As she considered where she'd started the day and how drastically things had changed the instant she'd met Miguel, she tried not to let guilt swamp her. Knowing how much Heinrich had cared for the kid he'd been, she had a sneaky suspicion he'd approve of her finding comfort in the man's arms. Even a temporary safe haven would be welcome at this turning point in her life.

Heinrich had often encouraged her to find a mate. Someone like Marta had been to him.

She closed her eyes at that, blocking out the pain that threatened to well up again as it had hundreds of times in the past week, and would thousands more in the coming years.

Sabine wasn't sure how long she floated there, buffeted by jets of blissful water. Long enough to doze off.

"Hey, not quite yet." Miguel shook her lightly when he returned. "I should have kept a closer eye on you knowing how tired you are. Jesus. Spend my life making sure tourists don't drown and I almost let a woman go under in my fucking tub."

Before she could reassure him she was fine, he had stripped, making it impossible to speak.

Instead, she beheld a living, breathing work of art finer than any she'd spotted during their trek to his cabin, or even had seen in Europe's most famous museums, which she'd loved to visit on weekends with Marta.

No fig leaf was going to cover *allllllll* of that.

Sabine swallowed hard.

Miguel grinned. "You drooling over this dinner or what?"

She splashed him.

"Hey, be nice or I won't show you what Maria whipped up for you." He took a long skinny tray from where he'd leaned it up against the wall, and laid it across the tub. Then he set a covered silver platter in the center. Two wineglasses followed, along with a decanter of something that smelled expensive even from several feet away.

Two glasses?

Yep. Miguel stepped in on the other side of their makeshift table. When his lower half disappeared below the churning water, she aimed her attention at his cut chest and abs instead. Mmm. He looked good enough to eat.

The scent of lemon butter and fresh lobster pried her attention from his form momentarily. "Is that...?"

"Yep." He nodded, then unveiled the treat along with some rice pilaf, asparagus sticks, and a salad. "We caught them when we went spear fishing earlier. Dig in."

Sabine had already lunged for her silverware.

The first bite tasted divine. The warm, delicious food filled her empty belly.

"This is seriously the best thing I've ever put in my mouth." She hummed, then took another nibble.

"It'll only hold that record for another twelve hours or so." Miguel watched her lips, finally breaking his stare to glance down in the general vicinity of his cock, as if he were making the big guy a promise.

Laughter. She couldn't believe it was coming from her. In the midst of a crisis, she'd met a gorgeous, if crazy, man who ate lobster in a bathtub with her and cracked her up. Who was she to question the way life went sometimes?

Instead, they made the most of a shitty-but-not-so-shitty situation. After she'd finished stuffing herself, she had no hope of extending her get-to-know-you session with Miguel, no matter how many more questions she had for the guy.

Her eyelids grew heavy.

Of course he noticed.

With a single graceful motion, he stood, allowing the water to sluice from his magnificent body. He tucked the empty plates and glasses to one side then stepped out, quickly drying himself off before holding out a hand to her.

Sabine took it, stepping over the high side of the tub. She walked into the fluffy towel he held out to wrap her in. She allowed him to take control, ensuring she didn't skip any of even the most basic tasks she was incapable of performing for herself at the moment. It was odd, and sort of comforting, to let him care for her in this way.

A way she'd never allowed another man to do.

And when he lifted her into his arms and carried her to bed, she didn't protest. He placed her near the center of the mattress then climbed in behind her, drawing the covers up and hitting some button on a control panel nearby. Room-darkening shades blocked the lovely ocean view and plunged them into artificial darkness.

The feel of another human being, skin on skin, grounded her. She turned toward him and wrapped herself around every part of him she could reach. He did the same, entwining them thoroughly. His fingertips glided up and down her spine. For a few seconds, she counted the slow, solid beats of his heart from where her ear pressed to his chest. It must have hypnotized her.

That was the only reason she could think of to explain why she blurted, "I should have been there with him."

She'd thought about it over and over non-stop since the moment her world had blown to smithereens.

"*Lindeza*, no. Then you both might have been lost." Miguel hugged her a little tighter. "What good could you have done against an explosion, huh?"

She recalled the masked man she thought she had seen. Ridiculous, right?

Sabine shrugged. "At least he wouldn't have doubted my loyalties. It's just that after I graduated from his program, I needed to fly solo for a couple years. Earn my own way before latching on to his success like some kind of remora feeding off its host shark, you know? I had lots of offers for grants to study pretty much whatever I wanted. Including one from Heinrich. I should have taken it. My ego kept us apart, and now I'll never get to team up with him again."

She bit her lower lip, trying to squish it to keep it from trembling.

"I'm sorry you won't have that chance." Miguel rocked her gently then murmured against her temple, "But you must be pretty fucking smart and great at your job to have institutions begging for you like that. Heinrich must have been so proud of you."

That was all it took.

There was no protecting herself against the onslaught of grief. Sabine clung to Miguel's shoulders as if he was the *Divemaster*'s anchor while the storm of pain raged around them. He'd accidentally mashed one of her most sensitive spots. No matter how often Heinrich had praised her accomplishments, Sabine had tried to work harder to deserve his praise.

In the end, that drive had kept her away from her second father in the final days of his life.

She would never see him again. Never have the chance to tell him how much she loved him.

Sabine bawled. She cried until she could hardly breathe, despite Miguel's soothing litany of calming nonsense. He never once let go.

Miguel held her as she sobbed, told her it was okay. Even if he lied, she appreciated the comfort he bestowed. And when the anguish had finally snuffed itself out, leaving her empty, she sagged against his side.

"Better?" he asked.

She nodded a tiny bit to keep the pounding headache she felt coming on from developing before she could fall asleep. Which she planned to do as soon as she set the record straight.

"Just so you know, I'm not the sort of girl who blubbers over dumb shit." Sabine sniffled as she glared at him from eyes that must be puffy and red. Boner-killer material for sure.

"Cool, because I don't have a lot of experience here." His lips twisted into a wry smile. "I mean, I'm not the kind of guy who women usually come to with a broken heart."

She winced at that. "No, I bet you're the one who does the breaking."

He blinked, seeming to actually consider what she'd said. "I hope not."

Sabine couldn't believe he'd be so oblivious. She didn't intend to be one of his tragedies. A fling with him would be spectacular. A highlight to balance out the poisonous darkness that threatened to seep into the hole Heinrich had left inside her.

It also wouldn't last forever.

She'd finish her job here. Or he'd grow bored. They'd both move on.

At least she knew that going in. Like all good things, including the very best of people in her life, this too would go away.

Sabine hadn't been ready for Heinrich to leave, but she'd make damn sure she was prepared to let go of Miguel when their time ran out. Until then, she snuggled deeper into his hold. "Miguel?"

"Yeah, *lindeza*?"

"Heinrich would have been awfully proud of you, too." She kissed his neck then. "Thank you."

He went still, but didn't respond. His fingers idly traced the line of his necklace around her throat as he considered what she'd said. Hopefully he believed her, because she didn't have even a speck of energy left to reiterate her certainty.

Unconsciousness dragged her deep under.

∽ **SIX** ∾

Sabine stretched, wallowing in the softness that enveloped her. Well, other than that one warm, solid, hunk of...*manmeat?*

Her fingers flexed, unconsciously kneading muscle of some variety.

She blinked. Yep, that was definitely a ripped abdomen pillowing her head. Looking up, the blurry outline of an inky-haired man with eyes as bright as a turquoise sea gradually came into focus. He watched over her from where his merman-worthy shoulders rested against a padded leather headboard. Miguel.

"Hey," she croaked, her mouth dry. How long had she been unconscious? It felt like a while. Sunlight still limned the blinds covering his stateroom windows, though.

"Good morning," he murmured as he stroked her hair with smooth, repetitive motions. It made her wonder if he'd gotten some practice doing it over the past several hours. Knowing he'd guarded her while she'd been dead to the world stirred something inside her.

Gratitude, and more primal emotions along with it.

True, she had just met the man. But they'd already shared experiences more intimate than those she generally indulged in with long-term lovers. Grieving, bathing, sleeping, reminiscing about shared acquaintances, and even the meal they'd eaten together had been so personal it made their connection seem real and deeper than it could possibly be, given that she'd spent less than a day in his company while awake.

Right?

The illusions of security and permanence could be treacherous. Especially when cast by a stranger. Doubly so if she hadn't had a lifetime of experience in temporary relationships—romantic or otherwise. Fortunately, she did. So she allowed herself to see where their instant chemistry might take them.

It was then that his greeting fully sank in.

"Morning?" She glanced around for a clock.

"Yeah. You were really out of it. Have to say that's a first. Women don't usually spend so much time in my bed actually asleep. Or if they do, it's *after* I've fucked them senseless."

"Now that sounds like a cruise activity I could enjoy. Where do I sign up?" Sabine's hand began to wander along the inside of his leg toward his thick, hardening shaft. He made more than a handful while barely roused. This could be a *big* bonus to her time onboard. Something to help her de-stress.

The instant she curled her fingers around him, measuring him, he tugged her upward, thwarting her plans to demonstrate her appreciation for his very warm welcome.

Miguel captured her mouth with his and showed her again that no matter how bold she grew with him, he wouldn't be unsettled. Neither did he let her wrest control from him with the hint of a hand job or find his determination to seduce her wavering due to the proximity of her lips to his dick. It would take a lot more than that to derail his alpha tendencies.

Challenge accepted.

Meeting her kiss for kiss, he palmed her ass and situated her in his lap as he pleased.

Sabine sighed when her thighs spread around his torso and her knees sank into the plush bedding. The silky brush of skin on skin had her rubbing against Miguel like the harbor seals had done to the kelp in Monterey Bay. When he nudged the seam of her smile, she admitted his tongue between her lips.

Subtle upward thrusts of his hips tucked his still firming hard-on against her mound.

When she tried to lift herself a little more, high enough to put his dick where she really wanted it, he gripped her tighter.

He separated their faces long enough to breathe, "Wait, *lindeza*—"

"What does that mean? You called me that yesterday." Inquisitive by nature, she couldn't help but wonder despite the heat of his embrace or the increasing urgency of her arousal.

"Beautiful. You are. Extraordinarily so." The conviction with which he said it melted her insides. It would have melted her panties too, if she'd been wearing any. Appealing to him couldn't be a bad thing. Not when he looked at her with such hungry eyes.

So she rewarded him with another caress of her mouth over his, this time nipping his lower lip. She didn't know where the compulsion to do it came from. It seemed he brought out something new in her that none of her previous partners had. Their unique combination fascinated her.

Miguel groaned, then ratcheted up the intensity of their kisses. She buried her fingers in his thick hair, pawing at his skull while he did the same to her ass. His thumbs hooked around her hip bones kept her from gliding along the length of his cock. Too bad, she probably could have gotten herself off with the friction of his blunt tip prodding her clit alone.

Well, that along with the way her breasts felt as they dragged against his chest, and the decadent things he was doing to her mouth. Her tongue had certainly given guys plenty of pleasure before. Never in her life had it been the source of so much for her. Miguel sucked on it, raked his teeth over it lightly, and swirled his own around it, nearly making her pant into his mouth.

If he could do that with a not-so-simple kiss, what could he do if he engaged the rest of his body?

When she was breathless and nearly dizzy from making out with him, she paused to suck in some much needed oxygen.

Her fingers ached from where she'd unknowingly dug them into his powerful shoulders.

"Sorry," she muttered as she unclamped them, rubbing out the dents she'd left behind. He seemed to enjoy her caresses or at least indulged them. Good thing, since she'd discovered she loved touching him. Smooth, ultra-tan skin wrapped around warm, supple muscles.

It felt so good, she couldn't stop running her hands along his shoulders and upper arms.

Miguel flashed her a lopsided grin. "Got carried away for a second. That's what I wanted to say. It seems like you and I together could get kind of rowdy. Still think this is a good idea now that you've slept on it?"

"It's probably not wise," she acknowledged.

His grip loosened.

She speared her fingers into his hair and angled his face so he could read the truth in her gaze. "That doesn't mean I don't want to do it anyway. Kind of like when you're stuffed but you order dessert because it looks so damn delicious; how could you not?"

Sabine licked her lips, her eyelids drooping at the taste of him lingering there. Yes, scrumptious.

"I've always had a sweet tooth myself." He grinned as he lunged forward, taking her to her back on the bed as he hovered over her on straight-locked arms. "I have a feeling you could finally satisfy me."

Though his bulk and strength made it clear how exposed she was lying beneath him, his admission gave her power. What exactly had he been searching for yet not finding?

Who didn't want to be that elusive thing for a man like him?

She certainly hoped she could be, at least temporarily. It seemed like they'd both be making the best of what time they had together.

Sabine moaned when Miguel kissed along the column of her neck. Instinctively, she stretched her chin up, granting him better access. When the edge of his teeth raked along her pulse, she shivered. She'd never had a man like this—raw and animalistic.

No polite lover here.

Thank God.

By the time Miguel had wandered to her breasts, licking and suckling one while his hand worked its magic on the other, she had stopped thinking rationally and had given herself over completely to feeling. It was rare that she was able to turn off the side of her brain that collected information and facts, cataloging even her own responses during sex.

For the first time in years, she found herself lost in the moment.

Data be damned.

Leaving her worries behind was a pleasure in itself. Relief enhanced her desire.

When Miguel slithered between her thighs, levering them far apart so that his wide shoulders fit between them, he nuzzled her stomach. The stubble peppering his cheeks rasped lightly over her sensitive skin, making her writhe beneath him. He chuckled, then inhaled deeply, as if memorizing her scent before burying his face in her core.

There was nothing delicate about his approach. Nothing tentative or unsure.

He dove right in and started blowing her mind with bold swipes of his tongue that collected the moisture slickening her folds.

"*Yes.*" Sabine threw her head back as one hand flew to his shoulder. Not so she could keep him there against his will—mostly to brace herself during the onslaught of passion. Though part of her was terrified he might stop before she'd finished coming all over his face because that was certainly where this was headed.

It wasn't going to take very long either.

The man deserved an award for pussy-eating.

And when his fingers circled her opening, zeroing in on the best angle for entrance, she cried out his name.

"Mmm," he purred against her flesh, as if he liked the way it sounded bursting from her lips.

Good thing since he had her screaming for him over and over when he inserted first one finger then another, working her open as he continued to flick his tongue across her clit precisely the way she preferred.

"Miguel!" This time it was a warning, with maybe a hint of a plea.

He correctly read the urgency in her shout, spurring her over the finish line with the press of his skilled fingers on some amazing place inside her.

Sabine shattered. She lifted up in an orgasmic crunch so she could watch him revel in her pleasure. It only made her hotter to see how devoted he was to bringing her ecstasy, knowing soon she would do the same for him.

When she crested the wave of rapture and began to fall back to reality, she collapsed on the bed, marveling at the effects of the host of endorphins that flooded her system. Biology and chemistry held true sorcery sometimes. A rush like this could become a habit.

Before she could dip too much from her high, Miguel rejoined her. Face to face, he smiled as he took in her flushed cheeks and dilated pupils. For all the gentleness in his expression, he couldn't mask the furious desire beneath it.

Neither could he hide the heat and weight of his rock-hard cock against her thigh.

"Fuck me," she practically begged.

"I'd like to take the time to do this properly." Miguel sighed. "Somehow I don't think you're going to let me distract you for much longer, though."

Sabine winced at the reminder of her duties and how she wasn't doing them—until he put on a show for her, retrieving a condom from beneath his pillow, tearing it open, then rolling it down his impressive length fast enough that she knew he'd had a lot of practice with the maneuver.

Before she could make some smartass remark, he'd returned and notched his covered head at her opening, a mere twitch of a muscle from joining them for the first of what she hoped would be many times.

"This will have to do for now." He kissed her, blanking out every thought except the pressure of the tip of his cock embedded in her pussy, on the cusp of entering. "Later I'll show you what I'm really capable of and give you what you deserve. As much pleasure as you can handle. I promise, *lindeza.*"

As he rumbled her new favorite word, he advanced, spearing himself a few inches farther into her. He stretched her wide.

Damn, the man had a fat cock. Not that she was complaining.

Relaxing, or trying to, she admitted him deeper within her body each time they rocked together.

"That's good. Let me in." He crooned to her in a mix of English and Portuguese that she didn't have to understand literally to comprehend.

Sexy talk was sexy in any language. Maybe even more so when she relied on his expression and inflection to interpret the sentiment.

Miguel distracted her from the initial discomfort of her body learning to accommodate his with a flurry of kisses and caresses. He rolled his hips in a smooth, rhythmic pattern that guaranteed he would make one hell of a dance partner, too.

For now, his qualifications as a fuck buddy were far more important to her.

Sabine hissed when he surged forward, his trunk meeting hers finally as she held his entire shaft within her. His balls knocked against her, making her want to scream out some primitive victory.

"That's right. Take all of me." He pressed against her, making quite the impression with his dick.

In fact, she couldn't wait for him to pull out some simply so he could reintroduce them, though nothing might ever match the awe of this very first time she found out what it was like to be filled completely by him...or anyone else. No man had ever imprinted himself on her—in her—like this before.

Not only because of his incredible cock. Or even because he knew how to use it so damn well. It was more than that. His need matched hers in a way she couldn't quite analyze at the moment.

Didn't plan to either.

Sabine rocked her hips, first away, then back. He didn't need any more encouragement than that. "So slick. Tight and hot. You're ready for me, huh?"

She didn't bother to answer. Instead, she repeated her motion, groaning when she couldn't make as big of a difference as she would have liked.

"Don't worry, *lindeza*." He kissed her one last time before getting serious about the ride he was about to give her. "I'm gonna do the work for you. All you have to do is hold on. If you can."

She might have thought his cockiness was exclusively bravado if he hadn't made good on his pledge right then. Miguel didn't bother with a gradual ramp up. Instead, he listened to the demands of her body, fucking her exactly as she needed. Hard, fast, and thoroughly. Without restraint.

She took pride in knowing she could handle the full intensity of a man like him.

Hell, that she could match it.

Sabine planted her feet on the mattress, bracing herself to accept the impact of his pelvis against hers. She stared into his eyes as he lunged over her, withdrawing until the ring of muscles at her opening strangled his fat head, before plunging fully within her.

Even when she clamped around him, clasping his shuttling shaft, he maintained his pace.

If anything, he increased the tempo of his thrusts.

"Yes. Like that." He ordered, "Squeeze my cock with that pretty pussy. Come around it. Let me feel how much you love it when I fuck you deep and hard like this. Take me under with you. Do it. Now."

As if she needed any additional incentives, he reached between them to roll her pebbled nipple between his thumb and forefinger. The extra stimulation proved impossible to resist.

Or was it his command that tipped her over the edge?

Either way, she obeyed.

Sabine screamed as the most powerful orgasm of her life overtook her. The shimmer of gathering rapture blazed and spread like a firework inside her, illuminating each of the dark corners she'd been afraid to acknowledge in the past.

Miguel wouldn't allow her to shrink away from her nature.

Instead, he embraced it, and encouraged her to do the same. "Ah. Fuck, yes. You're even more gorgeous when you're coming for me. Shattering around my cock like this."

His praise set off another round of spasms. This time he proved he wasn't immune to her reactions either.

"I'm going to fill this condom for you." He grunted as he slammed into her pussy a few more times, extending her ecstasy. "My balls have never ached so bad in my life."

Sabine hadn't realized how much of a turn on it could be for a man to express his desires so openly and honestly. She gladly accepted each of his wild penetrations, happy to return even a fraction of the bliss he'd given her.

The tensing of his jaw gave him away.

Sabine clenched around him.

He cursed, then shouted her name as he jackhammered into her. With each slap of his flesh against hers, he growled and shuddered, making her certain he was doing exactly as he'd said he would, pouring his lust into the thin latex reservoir between them.

For a wild moment, she wished she could feel the heat of his release marking her deep inside.

Though no one else might know, she was sure she'd feel the brand he'd left with his possession every time she had sex for the rest of her life. How could anything else be as good as this?

When, finally, they finished jerking against each other, he rolled to his back. Cradling her against his chest, he murmured to her in Portuguese until she regained the ability to think anything other than, *Holy shit. Holy shit. Holy shit.*

"Hey there, *lindeza*." He smiled when her eyelids fluttered open and she caught him observing her as they recovered. "Doing okay?"

"Uh huh." She nodded, rubbing her cheek against the slightly damp plane of his chest.

How had he leveled her completely yet hardly broken a sweat?

"Don't look so proud of yourself." She reached up and tweaked his nipple, causing him to laugh and capture her hand. He brought her fingers to his lips and nibbled her knuckles before placing a kiss over the mild sting.

"Truth is, I'm kind of embarrassed." He shook his head. "I don't think I've ever come so quickly. Especially not when I'm trying hard to impress."

"If that's your idea of a premature ejaculation, I can't wait to see what you consider a marathon fuck."

"Give me five minutes and I'll be happy to show you." He brushed the pad of his thumb over her bottom lip. "Less time if you keep looking at me like my dick is your new favorite toy."

"As tempting as that may be, hiding under the covers won't solve my problems or find Heinrich's cure." She winced. How could she have let herself be distracted so easily?

Oh, right, Miguel *did* have a stellar cock and the skill to put it to good use. Not exactly an everyday occurrence when it came to guys. At least she tried to convince herself it was only his equipment that had aroused her so thoroughly. Anything else was too reckless.

"Can't blame a man for trying." He kissed the side of her neck. "I'll be more convincing tonight."

Sabine hoped he held off until then because she could only muster so much willpower when her pussy cheered for a repeat performance.

Damn. She sighed, frowning as she wondered if she'd gotten herself into more trouble than she could handle.

"Hey, I'm mostly teasing." He kissed her lips softly then climbed from bed, flashing his perfect ass on his way into the bathroom. "We can be in your lab and working thirty minutes from now including a stop in the dining room for some breakfast. I'll try to focus on something other than your sweet pussy for a few hours at least."

"Gee, thanks." Okay, so she liked knowing she appealed to a man as fine as Miguel.

"That's going to require an incredible amount of restraint on my part, for the record." When he turned toward her slightly, she could see his rejuvenating cock, already half-hard.

If only she didn't feel the weight of Heinrich's legacy she might have done something about it. After the spectacular way Miguel had gone down on her before giving her the fuck of a lifetime, she figured she owed him some payback.

"Tonight." She nodded.

"Deal. Now get in here and let me jack off to the sight of your soapy tits jiggling in my shower or I won't even make it to lunchtime before stealing you away for another quickie."

She laughed, but he didn't seem to be joking. Not about classifying the best sex of her life as a mere quickie, or about his need to come again so soon either.

The hand stroking his cock was serious as shit.

What the hell had she gotten herself into with him? Something spectacular, and a little scary, if she was being honest. Ah well, there'd be time to worry about that later.

She wondered if he would come faster if she played with herself while under the balmy spray that rained on her from a half-dozen different showerheads.

He wasn't the only one charged up by their unexpected connection.

Though she didn't have a baseline to compare his reactions to, her gut told her that her hypothesis had been correct when neither of them lasted more than a couple minutes before climaxing while on display for the other.

In her case, it was a clear result.

Miguel affected her like no one had before. He made her crave things she couldn't have. Do things she shouldn't.

At a critical time in her life, she couldn't afford a distraction that huge. As they dressed and prepared to head out, uncertainty crept past her receding rapture. Had she fucked this up before she'd even gotten started?

Maybe this afternoon she'd take Banks up on those staff quarters after all. Just in case, she tidied her belongings, tucking them into the single suitcase she'd brought.

How would Miguel take the news?

"Don't even think it." He seemed to read her mind when he took her hand and guided her from the room before she could finish zipping her bag. "There's nowhere to run on this ship even if you wanted to. And we both know you don't. Not really."

Of course, he was right.

⌒ SEVEN ⌒

After wolfing down an assortment of fresh mango, papaya, and pineapple along with a bowl of granola, Sabine drained two glasses of blackberry mint lemonade. Then she toyed with her spoon, itching to go, as Miguel devoured yet another helping of eggs and bacon.

The man could eat.

She was pretty sure she knew how he worked that energy off, too. Between swimming and fucking, he had earned those golden muscles giving his soft cotton T-shirt so much definition.

"You're antsy to get started. I can be done here." He wiped his mouth on his napkin before taking one last gulp of water.

"No, don't rush. Maybe I should go ahead, though. I feel like I wasted a whole day." She stared out the window hardly admiring the gorgeous scenery, wondering how she could have let attraction—even one as strong as the one compelling her toward Miguel—derail her.

He grimaced. "You weren't any good for anything yesterday. You had to recharge your brainiac batteries."

As he was in the middle of being practical and shit, a tall blond man as fit and *nearly* as sexy as Miguel dropped into an empty chair beside them at a long, polished table on one of the upper decks.

"I guess I don't blame you for disappearing yesterday." Their breakfast buddy slapped Miguel on the shoulder. "Well done, stealing her away for yourself before she had a chance to meet *me*."

Sabine laughed, flattered rather than embarrassed given his obvious approval of their affair.

"I'm not an idiot." Miguel threw a croissant at his friend. "Don't you be one either. She's gorgeous and she's *mine*, so make sure that flirting is as far as you dare go if you want to keep your balls attached."

The man nodded subtly at the warning before turning to her with a brilliant smile. He offered his hand. "I'm Tosin, one of the divemasters on the *Divemaster*."

She wiped her hand on her linen napkin before shaking his, awed by how his fingers engulfed hers with a steady yet careful grasp. "One of the owners, you mean? Miguel and Archer's partner, right?"

He shrugged. "I guess so. Still feels kind of weird. I'm a lot simpler than that, really."

"Simple is right," Miguel grumbled when Tosin held on to her palm a little too long for his liking.

Sabine withdrew, her cheeks heating at the effect these guys had on her. What was wrong with her? Or was it them?

Their bond shone through in the way they seemed to know the other's thoughts and how they read each other's body language. Tosin even stole a few bites off Miguel's plate, which his friend didn't seem to mind in the least. Exactly how close were they? How much had they shared?

Illicit fantasies sprang to life. Ones where she found herself sandwiched between them.

She blinked.

Trying to get her mind back to safer ground she asked, "Is your accent Danish?"

"Close." Tosin smiled. "I'm originally from the Netherlands. Haven't been home in ages, though. I heard you studied in Germany."

"Yes." She nodded, trying to ignore the sting in her eyes.

"I'm sorry about your mentor."

Both Miguel and Tosin covered one of her hands then, squeezing lightly. Miguel didn't glare at his friend for offering comfort, so she gladly accepted it.

Sabine swallowed hard, "Thank you."

"I didn't mean to eavesdrop. I did hear you talking when I sat down, though. Don't worry about yesterday. As much as I hate to admit it, Miguel is right for once. You must have been exhausted. Besides, it took most of the day for Banks to wave his fairy godfather wand and turn part of the dive bay into a lab for you." He promised, "You couldn't have gotten started until today anyway. Banks is good, but even he's human. I think. Pretty sure."

"I owe you so much." She looked to Miguel especially then. He'd given her something equally as precious, helped ground her when she needed to be at her best academically. "I don't know how I'll ever repay you."

"I bet he's got a few ideas about that." Tosin broke the heavy atmosphere, causing her to snort.

"Tosin..." Miguel growled.

"Seriously, though, it's part of what we do around here. Thanks to Archer and his inheritance. We're trying to make a difference in the world. What we do is minor. You...well, you have the capability to make an enormous impact. However we can facilitate that, we'd love to be a part of it." Tosin stood then, grabbing one last slice of bacon off Miguel's plate. "So I'll let you get to it. I just wanted to say hello before I set up for the next group of divers."

Sabine had nearly forgotten about the other guests Marta had explained would be onboard, focused on her own mission.

"Thank you. For everything." Sabine went with her gut, reaching up to pull him into a one-armed hug, which he returned with interest.

"No problem. If there's anything I can do to help out let me know. Even if it's kicking this cocksplatter's ass for you when he fucks up. See ya later!" Tosin hustled out then before Miguel could retaliate with anything other than the dual middle fingers he flashed.

She balled up her napkin and put her hands in her lap, trying not to fidget.

"Come on, I'm finished." Miguel stood and scooted her chair away from the table like a proper gentleman. A complete turnabout from the savage he'd proven he could be in bed. Fortunately, both sides of him appealed to her.

He laced their fingers together as he guided her toward the stern of the megayacht then down a set of winding teak stairs. As they curved, she caught sight of a crescent-shaped speck of land jutting from the open ocean. She whipped her head in the opposite direction, spying the southern coast of Maui, then back. "Is that Molokini?"

Miguel didn't even have to look in the direction she lifted her chin toward. There was no mistaking the islet. Especially since nothing but miles and miles of empty Pacific stretched beyond that. "Yep. We were hoping to take the guests snorkeling and diving at a bunch of the sites within the crater, depending on your plans and whether you're ready to begin your research this quickly. It's notorious for its insane visibility and provides a wide range of difficulties that will make it ideal for the groups with various levels of experience already onboard."

"Oh, that will be perfect!" Sabine felt the first flutters of excitement in her belly. This was what she'd trained for. What she'd dreamed of. Though she never would have hoped for these circumstances, the thought of making a breakthrough discovery still thrilled her. "Marta and I were searching for vessels in range of this area. She found you guys and reached out to the Banks Foundation about the possibility of coming onboard because we know this was Heinrich's last stop on his collection trip, which wrapped about three weeks earlier than expected. He'd never done that before. I believe he quit looking when he found whatever it was that had him going bananas. I didn't realize you were already *here*, though. I'm glad I'm not pulling you off course."

"It wouldn't matter. Wherever you need us to go, we'll be there." Miguel squeezed her hand, infusing his strength into their connection.

He ushered her onto the dive platform and she stutter stepped. He was right there to steady her, keeping himself between her and the ocean lapping at the hull. "Wow."

"I know." He chuckled. "I still can't believe we get to work here."

She looked around at the pristine gear, so neatly organized across the spacious bay. It had everything you could wish for, more than she'd ever had the luxury of diving with before on a research vessel. Damn.

When she'd picked her jaw up off the decking, Miguel led her to a nook tucked into the back corner. It looked like it had been an open-air study area that they'd enclosed with tinted aquamarine glass especially for her. The space inside wasn't the largest she'd ever seen, but it was perfect. Whiteboards, centrifuges, microscopes, test tubes, chemical lockers...you name it, they had it. *She* had it at her disposal. Every essential and even a few perks she hadn't had in her Monterey research facility.

Including a man who was turning out to be the most capable assistant on Earth.

"Will this be okay?" Miguel asked her. "Say the word and I'm sure Banks can arrange for anything else you need. Seriously, just let me know and we'll make it happen."

Sabine wiped moisture from the corner of one eye. Who said there weren't good people left in the world?

She turned to him and flung her arms around his neck. When he caught her, she added her legs to the full body hug.

"Wait until Banks gets *his* thank-you kiss," Tosin teased from the doorway where he leaned against the frame. Archer and Waverly laughed softly from behind him. "It'll probably be the highlight of his year."

"It would indeed," Banks said entirely too primly for anyone to keep a straight face.

Sabine unwound herself from Miguel and trotted to Banks. She went onto her tiptoes to buss his cheek noisily, causing him to beam as he patted her back lightly.

"Thank you so much," she whispered.

"You're very welcome, dear." He straightened the black ruffles around the neckline of her crocheted cover-up, which hid a modest one-piece suit beneath. His stare caught on her necklace. "That's beautiful."

"I think so, too." She smiled. "Miguel made it. When he was a boy."

"Really?" Banks shifted his assessing gaze to the man in question, who only shrugged. "It makes you wonder sometimes, doesn't it, if there's truly such a thing as fate."

"I'm a believer," Waverly said, without taking her stare from Archer.

He rested his forehead on hers and smiled softly before murmuring, "Me too."

Some other time, Sabine would have to ask Miguel about their story.

"So where do you want to start?" he asked her, drawing her thoughts back to the present.

She drew a deep breath then let it out as she studied the ceiling of her brand spanking new laboratory. "While I was flying here, I reread every email Heinrich sent me during his collection trip and the follow up experiments at his research center. I'm starting to think he was trying to tell me more than I realized at the time. I should have listened closer."

Miguel tucked one of her unruly curls behind her ear. "Let's focus on going forward. He wouldn't want you to beat yourself up. You didn't have all the information then that you do now. What did you figure out?"

"There was one letter he sent, after they'd been in this area for about two weeks. He'd seemed increasingly frustrated, which wasn't like him at all. Then one day the tone was totally different. He said, 'Sometimes you fail to notice the obvious when you're trying too hard or making things more complex than they need to be. What you're searching for can be right in front of you. Until you change the way you look at things—blind yourself to what you think you know and dig a little deeper—you might never see it.'"

"What the hell do you think that means?" Tosin rubbed his temple.

She took a deep breath. "As best I can figure, he was letting me know that what he found originated from something ordinary. Probably something he or other marine biologists have studied countless times. As counterintuitive as it seems, I think I want to dive here and collect samples from the most common species around. It could be that he processed them differently than usual, or maybe that something about this location makes them slightly dissimilar—enough to have far-reaching implications—from other forms. Maybe no one noticed sooner because they dismissed those possibilities based on previous results, instead of on the facts alone. I need to blind myself to what I think I know, and start from scratch with the basics."

"It's as good a theory as any, I suppose." Banks hummed his approval as Tosin, Archer, and Waverly nodded in agreement.

"Waverly and I can tell you from experience that assuming you know what's going on instead of questioning everything can really steer you wrong," Archer admitted.

"A solid lesson for life as well as this experiment," Miguel agreed. She wondered what parts of himself he was reexamining at the moment. Could their meeting have shaken him up also?

"So you'll go with me? Point out stuff you see all the time around here? Help me collect and tag everything while we're waiting for my tissue samples to arrive? Run tests and track results once they get here?" Sabine asked Miguel. Having him by her side beneath the waves would keep her level. Another pair of hands in the lab would be invaluable, too.

Already she trusted him. If his SCUBA skills were anywhere near as good as his fucking abilities, she had seriously won the assistant lottery.

"Hell yeah. Let's go diving." Miguel grinned. "I can't wait to go down with you."

For the first time since the explosion that had rocked her foundation from across the world, Sabine felt confident that she could do her mentor justice and complete his research. With this kind of unwavering support, how could she not?

Heinrich's death—no, his *life*—had to mean something. If she could give this to the world in his name, it would.

She nodded at Miguel. "I'm ready."

"I know." He kissed her, right there in front of his honorary family. She didn't pull away either.

✂ EIGHT ✂

Two Weeks Later

Sabine had massively underestimated Miguel. Though she considered herself a seasoned diver, he took things to another level. A true expert, he was mesmerizing to watch, or might have been if she wasn't attempting to focus on the job at hand. All three divemasters had complimented her proficiency after joining them beneath the surface at one time or another recently. She had nothing on them.

In addition to his aptitude with the equipment, constant vigilance for safety issues, effortless buoyancy control, and eyes as sharp as a shark's for spotting creatures or coral specimens she'd have zipped right past underwater, Miguel had stamina that would put that guy who had swum across the Adriatic Sea without flippers to shame.

He dove with her every morning, leading two- or three-tank collecting expeditions that crisscrossed the reef inside the horseshoe of the Molokini Crater, leaving no stone or coral head unturned. It didn't matter what the conditions were like, or how tired he might have been from swimming like a fish—a gorgeous, sleek, and powerful fish—assisting her in the lab every afternoon and evening, then fucking her damn near into a coma each night.

Sabine had never been as exhausted, or as sated, as she was right then.

If they had only made even a hint of progress toward locating Heinrich's mysterious cure, she would be in heaven. Instead, guilt corroded her guts when her laptop made the triple-chirp associated with an incoming call on her video chat software.

Only one person used it these days.

And Sabine had been ducking those notifications for a while.

"Want me to answer that for you?" Miguel asked as he spied her gloved hands and the latest concoction she was about to inject into a cancerous tissue specimen. If she introduced any contaminants during the process, she could invalidate her test, assuming that this one would be any more fruitful than the thousands of others she'd prepared over the past two weeks.

"Nah. I'll call her back some other time." She looked at her hands, unable to meet his gaze.

"Is this Heinrich's wife?" He peered at the icon on her screen.

Sabine nodded, unable to speak around the lump in her throat.

"Are you dodging her?" he asked.

She lifted a single shoulder.

That was all it took. Miguel hit connect even as she cried out, "Don't!"

"I knew you were avoiding me." Marta *tsked*, clearly having heard her shout. "Not like you. Especially since you're the only family I have left in the world, girl."

Toss another guilt log on the fire, Sabine thought. Even worse, Banks had peeked into the laboratory, probably because he'd heard her holler, too.

Miguel shocked her by coming to her defense. He disarmed Marta with a wave and one of the blinding full-on smiles he usually reserved for Sabine. "Hello Mrs. Geld. I'm so sorry for your loss. Please understand that *our* girl is hurting, too. Although we both know she shouldn't, she feels like crap because we haven't had any luck with her research yet."

Was it that obvious? She thought she'd given her best to Miguel, genuinely enjoying their time together, and feeling even shittier because of it. How could she find something to be so damn happy about when Marta's world had fallen apart? It wasn't fair, and it wasn't right.

"*Our* girl? *Ich glaub mein Schwein pfeift!* Who is this handsome *boy*, Sabine?" Marta asked with a slightly harsher than normal German accent. The woman was direct, something Sabine usually appreciated. Right now, though, she wished she wasn't such an open book. How could she explain when she didn't know where she and Miguel stood herself?

The sex was great. Like, better than Marta's infamous black forest cake and four birthdays rolled into one. But when her time here was over, that would go away, too. They hadn't made each other any promises. It would be pointless, as they each would go their own way to keep saving the world with the tools they had. Their paths had crossed temporarily. Eventually they would diverge again.

Sabine opened her mouth but closed it again when Miguel responded for her. "My name is Miguel Torres. I'm a divemaster here. Your husband was a great influence on me when I was younger. A friend, and an inspiration."

"I knew it!" Marta softened immediately, her suggestion of a frown perking up into a smile. "I hope you don't mind that I poked around about the co-owners of the ship my Sabine would be spending her time on. I read your bio and the articles that have been circulating about you and your partners since the formation of the Divemaster Project. About where you're from, how you're self-made, and your impressive goals. Your name matched and I could see the resemblance to the photo Heinrich had of the two of you. After all this time, I hoped it might really be you. My husband was a good judge of character, son. He talked about you often. Remembered you fondly."

Afraid the moisture gathering in her eyes might leak out and ruin her work, Sabine finished up what she had been doing, then set the timer. When it went off, she should be able to detect some progress, *if* the solution she'd prepped and infused made any difference whatsoever. She peeled off her gloves then approached her laptop warily, as if it were a stonefish out to stab her with its poisonous spikes.

Having her two worlds collide like this made it all too real.

Miguel wasn't a figment of her imagination, some dream concocted by her subconscious to help her make it through one of the roughest parts of her life. He was real. Here. With her. But he wouldn't always be. Somehow, having Marta meet him—know that he existed—would make the loss more profound once he was no longer part of her life.

Banks edged closer, and Tosin joined them, too. They must have looked ridiculous, crunched together in front of the screen. Marta was magnetic like that, though. She drew people in, and made them listen.

"That means a lot. Thank you." Miguel put his arm around Sabine, tucking her against his heat and strength. Subconsciously, she toyed with his necklace, which became more precious to her every day. Though she should have pulled away, stood on her own, she couldn't bring herself to do it.

Not when she had to admit her failures to the one person who cared the most about what she was supposed to be concentrating on here. Sabine blurted, "I haven't found anything, Marta. I'm sorry. We're almost out of samples, too. I thought I knew what to look for, but…"

She held her hands out, empty palms up, then dropped them to her sides again.

"I wasn't calling for a progress report," Marta told her. "I needed to see how you're doing. That's all. I'm worried about how you're handling everything. And…I miss you."

If she wasn't going to make a discovery here, Sabine should at least have been by Marta's side.

Her stomach ached when she considered how many ways in which she was letting the other woman, and Heinrich, down. He'd have wanted her to look after his wife, wouldn't he?

"Hey, you might not have found the cure *yet*." Tosin's optimism bolstered her spirits a little. "But at least you got a boyfriend out of the deal."

"Oh, really?" Marta leaned closer to the screen, as if she could judge whether Miguel was worthy or not from those extra couple of inches.

Sabine didn't respond and instead glanced away at the lovely wooden deck and her bare toes, which curled against it.

"Ashamed of me, *lindeza*?" Miguel asked softly. He lifted her chin so she had no choice but to meet his piercing stare.

Could she keep making things worse? At least she seemed adept at that. Her fingers flew again to the necklace he'd given her, and she thought of the lost boy still buried deep within him. The one who'd been abandoned and never known how precious he was to those who loved him. "Of course not."

"It's okay to find happiness for yourself, Sabine," Marta assured her. "More than any scientific work, Heinrich would have been glad to see that."

What else was the woman going to say? That didn't make it okay.

Her affair with Miguel was irresponsible at best.

Sabine began to doubt herself. She wondered if she'd missed something because she'd been spending too much time with him instead of burning the midnight oil down here in the laboratory. Worse, maybe she'd screwed something up since some part of her didn't want to find the cure, because then she would have to leave.

Leave the *Divemaster*.

Leave her new friends.

Leave Miguel—the only man who'd ever made her wonder if she could do without him in a pathetically short amount of time.

In the background, Marta was still trying to reassure her, talking about enjoying her stay in Hawaii as much as possible, and how incredible the *Divemaster* had looked in the photos and stories she'd Googled.

"We'd love to have you onboard to see her for yourself sometime," Banks told Marta. Tosin and Miguel grinned simultaneously. They poked Banks out of the viewable range of the camera.

Sabine's eyes grew wide as she looked between Banks and her surrogate mother. It was nearly impossible to conceive of Marta with any man besides Heinrich. Except when she considered it objectively...they were about the same age. Both incredible people, who thrived on supporting those around them.

Maybe, someday, Marta would be ready to share her life with someone else.

A man like Banks would be an excellent choice, really.

And that felt like a betrayal.

Confused and hurting, Sabine couldn't take anymore.

Overwhelmed, she rasped, "Marta, I'm not feeling so good. It's been a long day, would you mind—"

"I'm going now. I just needed to hear your voice. To see you for myself. Let that boy take good care of you, understand?" Marta wagged her finger.

When had Sabine stopped being able to fend for herself? Her independent streak objected, strongly. She needed to be alone for a while. The *Divemaster* was enormous, but it was still a ship. There was nowhere to run. Nowhere to hide.

"I love you," Sabine whispered to Marta, terrified she might bawl if they didn't disconnect soon.

"I love you, too. Call me next time. When you're ready." With that, she was gone.

Staring at the blackened screen, Sabine didn't know which was worse—standing in front of Marta, facing deserved judgment that never came, or the absence of another important person from her life.

When Miguel put his hand on her shoulder and squeezed, she snapped. She shrugged out of his hold and pivoted on her heel, whipping around to face him.

Whatever unwise words were about to launch from her tongue froze when her timer went off.

She dashed to her workstation, scooped up her specimen, and slid it under the microscope.

If anything, the cancerous tissue appeared to be thriving instead of withering.

"Fuck!" She slapped her hands on the solid surface of the counter hard enough to make her wrists ache for days. In her peripheral vision, she saw Tosin and Banks slip from the lab, leaving her alone with Miguel. Probably for the best.

"You're even beautiful when you're throwing a tantrum," he said in an attempt to get her to laugh.

It didn't work.

"How long can we keep doing this?" She slashed a red marker through the latest on the list of eliminated specimens, then threw her notebook against the wall. "It's pointless!"

Sabine cringed as the pages fluttered then crumpled as it dropped to the ground.

"Are you objecting to the failed experiments or me fucking you so well every night that you hope you never find what you're looking for?" Miguel saw more than she gave him credit for sometimes.

"You arrogant bastard!" She wished she hadn't already chucked her pad or she would have flung it at his big head instead.

Instead of responding, he stalked closer, invading her space when all she wanted was to put some distance between them. She wasn't proud of herself, but she reached forward and shoved him, placing her palms flat against his chest as she leaned into the gesture.

Miguel didn't budge.

He smiled wolfishly then trapped her, his long fingers encircling her wrists. "Maybe. I've been holding out on you, though. Because you're twisting me up, too, *lindeza*. Enough is enough. I know what you need."

"To kick you in the balls?" She thrashed, not that it did her any good.

"You might want to watch that mouth of yours." He backed her against the wall then leaned in so all she could see was the compelling blue of his eyes. "It could get you in trouble tonight."

Why did his bullying turn her on? Despite his pseudo-threats, she was certain he was no risk to her. At least not to parts other than her heart, which seemed to forget more and more every day what her purpose onboard the *Divemaster* was supposed to be.

"Fuck this. I know what *we* need." Miguel didn't give her a chance to protest. He plucked her from the laboratory floor and tossed her over his shoulder as easily as if she was one of the tanks he hefted around day in and day out...not that she'd studied his form while he did it. "I have something to show you."

"Put me down." She shoved futilely at his back, her slaps utterly ineffectual.

The crack of his palm landing on her ass startled her more than the zing of sensation that raced from her cheek up her spine. She went dead still, wondering if he'd really just spanked her.

Before she could ask, or freak out, or surrender to the part of her that kind of liked it, he did it again. Then a third time.

"If you want to find out what's behind that black door in the middle of our hallway, you'll keep quiet and stop fighting me." Despite her instincts, which encouraged her to struggle, she went limp in his grasp. Admittedly, it felt better to rest on him than to try to break free.

Curiosity had always been both her biggest asset and her greatest downfall.

"Good girl," Miguel purred. "That's right. Let me make us both feel better."

∽ NINE ∾

Miguel had had enough. The past few days had gotten increasingly difficult, watching Sabine growing distant, smiling less. It had affected him in ways he wouldn't have imagined. After all, he was new at this—giving a shit about a partner's emotions and having responsibilities to her beyond providing a night chock full of orgasms.

Restlessness overtook him for the first time since they'd moved onboard the *Divemaster*. That urge he'd associated with wanderlust in the past—the compulsion that had prodded him to move on to the next place, and new people— maybe that sensation had been dissatisfaction all along. Or a certainty that he couldn't find what he was looking for there, so it was time to try somewhere else.

Except he no longer believed that picking up and moving would solve his problems or fill the void. No, after searching high and low, around the globe, the person who had the ability to quiet that restless part of him had found him instead. What a joke.

Sabine made him feel like Archer and Tosin made him feel. Waverly, too, for that matter. But stronger. Like he was taking his home with him, wherever he went, as long as they were near. Talking with Sabine was easy and entertaining. Sharing meals and work with her had the days flying by.

And the sex...son of a bitch. It was a miracle neither one of them had broken anything yet. Other than that one poor unfortunate chair he'd snapped a leg on when he'd bent her over it and gone a little wild. Shit, she made him feel so incredible he had hardly missed his extracurricular activities in the clubroom these past few weeks.

That was about to change.

He hoped he was making the right decision.

"Do you trust me, *lindeza*?" Miguel was as serious as he'd ever been in that moment. It wasn't a question he asked to boost his ego, or as some sort of foreplay. He had to know before he pushed her like this. Had to be certain he wouldn't frighten her away or do something that wasn't in her best interests.

Deep down, he knew she did. Hearing her breathe, "Yes," even as she hung upside from his rough hold had something in his gut unfurling, stretching, and getting ready to come out and play.

He'd never wanted to top a woman as badly as he did her.

That's why he needed help from someone impartial, who could call him off if he took things too far this first time. Especially after such a long vanilla stretch, who knew what would happen when he unleashed his darker side?

There were only two people he'd trust with that responsibility.

One of them happened to be up ahead, trying to ignore Miguel marching toward him in full caveman mode, Sabine tossed over his shoulder. Her lush ass filled his palm and she probably looked incredible with her wavy hair streaming down his legs. He peeked at their reflection in a window as he passed, shocked at the determination etched into his own features.

Why should he be, though? Their future hung in the balance, waiting to see how tonight turned out. He knew what he was praying for: that she responded to this part of him as well as she did the rest.

"Tosin, open the clubroom," he barked at his friend before Tosin could disappear into his own luxurious cabin.

"What?" The guy stopped mid-stride.

"You heard me." So had Sabine, if her renewed thrashing was any indication.

"Are you sure?" his friend asked. "There won't be any shutting that door again. For either of you, I think. Is this the right time for games?"

"Who's playing?" Miguel wondered. Not in a snarl or a roar, but in calm, collected tone that resonated with his conviction. Years of experience indulging his dominant side with ultra-willing women had taught him to trust his instincts. He knew what to do with Sabine.

Their problem was that he'd held back when he shouldn't have.

He'd let their budding relationship—because it wasn't some kind of experiment to him anymore—persuade him to change his ways. It wasn't going to work like that. And she was becoming too important to risk alienating by withholding part of himself from her.

Either she accepted all of him, fit as perfectly as he suspected she would, or there was no point in drawing out their eventual discord longer than necessary. They could have their fun, then go their separate ways.

A heaviness sank through his guts as if he'd swallowed the ship's main anchor.

Tosin took one look at his expression and nodded curtly. He strode ahead and entered the code only three people on the ship shared. Then he held the door wide, and admitted Miguel *and* Sabine.

"What—?" she gasped as she peeked around his waist. Even upside down there would be no mistaking the intent of the space. Heavy black leather furniture, maroon carpets and paint, and the massive selection of implements and BDSM equipment lit and exhibited like artwork made it pretty obvious how kinky the divemasters actually were.

Surprise.

How would Sabine take it?

"I figure it's a good sign that you're not trying to run away." Miguel lowered Sabine to the ground and slowly released her, hoping she didn't bolt.

She didn't.

Instead, she circumnavigated the clubroom, trailing her fingers along the nailheads on the edges of the bondage table before studying each of the assorted toys on display. He guessed she didn't have experience with them. In true Sabine style, she embraced her inquisitiveness.

"Well, I'm going to go ahead and assume you're not vampires since I've seen you sunning yourself mostly naked before," she said.

Tosin cracked up at that. "It does sort of have that vibe in here, doesn't it?"

"That doesn't mean we're not frightening to someone who doesn't understand what we like." Miguel swallowed hard. The last thing he wanted was to scare her.

"I'm always eager to learn." She turned to him then. "Are you going to teach me a lesson?"

Holy fuck.

She. Was. Perfect.

"Hell yes," he rasped as he practically charged her, scooping her into his arms. When he crushed his mouth to hers this time, he kissed her with everything he had, shielding her from nothing.

Instead of tensing, Sabine relaxed, allowing him to feast on her as he liked.

Why had he waited to bring her here? She was made for this.

For him.

When he feared she might pass out from lack of oxygen, he separated their mouths, giving her a temporary reprieve. Through ragged inhalations, she asked, "Why do we need a chaperone?"

Sabine peered over at Tosin, who'd made himself comfortable. The guy had already sunk into one of the giant wingback chairs, spread his legs wide, and slipped a hand inside the trunks he still wore after playing lifeguard on the ship's evening swim. The other glided over his bare chest as he watched Miguel introduce Sabine to their lifestyle as if it were the most enthralling movie he'd ever seen.

"Because, if you haven't noticed, I sort of lose my shit around you," he admitted. It was the least he could do given how vulnerable she might make herself to him tonight, if he was lucky. "Tosin is experienced. He'll have a clear mind and won't let anything happen to you."

"You're protecting me?"

"Of course," he answered immediately.

"I don't need that kind of insurance." She shook her head.

Maybe he did, though. Just this one time.

It didn't take a shrink analyzing him to figure out that he craved control because of the uncertainty of his childhood. This was how he'd survived. How he'd learned to conquer his insecurity and harness his fears. Turning those negatives into positive energy that had the power to elevate his lovers' experiences thrilled him over and over. With Sabine, though, the compulsion to imprint himself on her drove him to take her beyond the limits of his previous encounters.

Which could be a problem for her, especially during this introduction to power exchanges. It went against every coping mechanism she'd used herself. He tried harder to explain. "I know you've been on your own most of your life. You've had to be in charge and look out for yourself. Never let your guard down."

She peeked up at him then, daring him to deny she'd done a good job of it.

He wouldn't take that from her. No, he respected the strength it had required. But he could give her a break. Lift some of the burden off her shoulders. "Tonight, that's my job. I plan to do it very well. Focus every shred of my attention on that goal. The only thing you have to worry about is enjoying what I give you. Tosin will make sure we're both able to do that fully. Sound good?"

Sabine swallowed hard, then nodded. She asked, "Don't I need some kind of safe word?"

His brows raised. Maybe she wasn't as inexperienced as he'd thought.

"Hey, I read." She shrugged, making him chuckle.

"How about we keep it simple this time? Say stop, and I will. No questions asked. No hard feelings." He couldn't keep from touching her, running the backs of his knuckles over every bit of her exposed skin—her arms, her face, and especially the patch beside the necklace she'd inherited. It had always belonged there.

Banks had been dead right about that.

Sabine shivered, then nodded. Without being told, she pulled her sundress over her head and dropped it to the floor with a single seductive motion. A hissed curse came from Tosin's direction when her plump tits and curvy waist were unveiled. Only a scrap of lace remained, covering her pretty pussy.

Not for long.

⌒ TEN ⌒

"I'm going to choose the place," Miguel informed Sabine as he stalked toward her, closing the gap between them, however insignificant it was.

He pointed to a contraption they'd had specially made. It had been inspired by the hammocks they'd always had hanging around their bunkhouses, except this one had a far smaller chance of dumping someone out of it. Good thing, since a solid floor and not a sandy beach lay below it.

"You'll be bound to the sex net," he told her.

She didn't object.

"You're going to pick some toys you'd like me to use on you while I have you there." He grinned when she immediately looked toward the rack of nipple clamps. "See something you like?"

Sabine nodded.

"It does seem to make you come harder when I pinch them, or bite them." He nuzzled her bare breast, nipping the tip.

She shifted, rubbing her thighs together in response.

So he strode to the display and selected a pair that would make for a mild introduction.

"What else?" he asked, afraid to return to her side before collecting the rest of his gear. Otherwise, he might not find the willpower to abandon her again. He'd end up fucking her straight up, as he had the past several dozen times. At the end of the day, Sabine was enough for him, however she would take him.

She bit her lip.

"Can I make a suggestion?" Tosin asked her.

Sabine blinked a few times as if she'd forgotten he was there. Then she nodded, suddenly shy.

"Go for the rabbit fur flogger." He pointed to one of the instruments Miguel would have steered her to himself.

She nodded again. It thrilled Miguel that she trusted his friends nearly as much as she trusted him. That was critical if she was going to stay onboard after she'd finished her research.

Miguel drew up short, realizing he'd started to assume that she would. What if she didn't? What if she left to pursue her career or simply because—like he had so many times before—she felt it was time to move on?

It was too soon for promises. But he officially made it his goal to persuade her to stay from that moment forward. He wasn't ready to let her go and he doubted he would be any time soon.

He took his time plucking the tool from its holder so that he could school his expression. Tonight was about her. This moment they shared. Nothing more.

Before he could ask for another pick, she spoke up. "I liked what you did before."

Was that a blush spreading across her cheeks?

"You mean when I spanked you?" he clarified, though he already knew that's what she meant. Her pebbled nipples and parted lips didn't lie. Especially not when coupled with the slumberous gaze she shot him. He knew it well after the nights they'd spent together lately.

It had nothing to do with being sleepy and everything to do with being horny.

"Yes." She lifted her chin as if he'd think less of her for that. "I want something like that."

"Good girl." He smiled, knowing exactly the right thing. Within seconds, he had his favorite leather slapper in his hand along with the fur and the clamps. Quite an assortment.

Sabine was ready for this.

So was he.

Miguel strode to her, inspired when she didn't flinch from his rapid approach. Topping a woman as strong as her would be a highlight of his sexual experience. He set his implements on a small shelf on the post at the head of the fuck net. Then he spun to face Sabine.

He couldn't resist sampling her lips before lifting her, settling her onto the wide mesh made of silk ropes. He rocked her a bit, letting her get the feel for the motion of her new resting place. When she sighed, he pounced.

It only took him a few seconds to shackle her wrists to fur-lined cuffs. The restraints were attached to a bar fastened in the center to the post near her head. Then he did the same to her ankles, binding them to the matching bar on the pole by her feet. Spread wide before him, she was utterly at his mercy.

To prove it to them both, he bunched her panties in his fists.

"Not these, they're my favorite," she protested an instant before he ripped them from her as he had several other pairs lately. When would she learn it was better to go without around him?

"He'll buy you a dozen pair to replace them, sweetheart." Tosin laughed, though his humor was mixed with a solid dose of appreciation. From where he sat, he had a perfect view of her pussy. Could he see the arousal glistening between her legs?

Miguel bet he could.

Too bad he wouldn't get to smell it, or taste it, like Miguel would.

Though he'd like to drag out this encounter, making it last the whole night—or an entire lifetime, for that matter—he knew Sabine would only have so much in her this first time. Already her pulse fluttered and her cheeks burned with desire. It would wear her out to be left in suspense too long.

So he picked up the pace.

Miguel pinched open the nipple clamps. He loosened them slightly before setting them in place. Both at once. Then he let go gradually, increasing the pressure around her nipples until they decorated Sabine's spectacular tits better than a fistful of diamonds ever could.

She arched into the sensation, setting herself in motion again.

When the gentle swaying lulled her, Miguel moved forward. He took the flogger and dangled it above her, letting the falls dance over her in the barest of brushes. Along her collarbones and the upper swells of her breasts, he drew swirls that grew and grew until he covered most of her upper body.

He dipped toward her ribs, grinning wickedly when the soft flogger tickled her and she jerked.

"You can't escape, *lindeza*."

She whimpered. The sound stiffened his cock impossibly. Soon he would give in to the need for contact on his aching shaft. Once he did, he wouldn't be able to stop himself from fucking her madly. So he employed every scrap of patience he possessed.

When Sabine had relaxed, used to the sensual slide of the fur over her skin, he flicked his wrist just so. The ends whipped against her belly, making her yelp and twitch. The motion made the clamps on her breasts sway. Each reaction fed another and soon she was squirming, practically begging him to take her further.

So he did.

Miguel leaned down to kiss her and whisper praise in her ear. "You're doing so well, Sabine. You were made to be mine, weren't you?"

She hummed.

He thought so, too.

So he covered her with the second layer of the fuck net. She jerked as the ropes fell on her face and front. Before she could figure out what he was doing, he took hold of the rope sandwich she was the juicy meat of and flipped her over.

The rotating hardware did its job. Both the bars her arms and legs were attached to and the double layer of netting spun like a propeller. Now she lay face down instead of face up, her spectacular ass on display, bared for whatever he chose to do to it. A spanking tonight. Fucking some other time.

Miguel moved the unneeded top layer of the net out of the way for the moment.

He figured it was time to suit up. It wouldn't be long before the need to fuck her overwhelmed his good sense. Better to be prepared. But first...

His clothes hit the floor in record time, leaving him standing naked before Sabine and Tosin, too, though his friend was fixated on the gorgeous girl between them.

He took his cock in hand, wondering if it had ever been this painfully erect before in his life, and inched toward Sabine. He put one hand on her jaw and, using his thumb in the corner of her mouth, opened her lips so that he could guide himself inside the steaming paradise.

She sucked without having to be told, treating him to the variety of amazing tricks she'd mastered over the past several weeks. Having a repeat lover did have its benefits, he'd realized.

Miguel fisted his hands in her hair and held her still as he carefully thrust into her eager mouth.

When it was pull out or come down her throat, he retreated.

His teeth ground together as his body called him every sort of awful name it knew. It needed to come. In her. As soon as possible.

Tosin must have been able to tell he was wavering on the edge of his control. He held up a fancy glass dish that held a few dozen rubbers. "You want a condom?"

"Yes," Miguel answered at the same time that Sabine shouted, "No!"

"What's that?" he asked.

"I don't want you to wear one." She shook her head, about the only part of her she could move.

"I won't ever put you at risk." He held his hand out and caught the foil packet Tosin tossed him despite her protests. "Not in this or anything else."

"I'm saying stop to this. Please. You promised you would. It doesn't feel right in here." Some of her calm eroded as she struggled to find the words to convince him though lust slowed the functioning of her brain cells. "I'm on birth control. And clean. Tell me you are too and let's not put anything between us anymore."

He blinked. "You trust me that much?"

"I wouldn't have let you stick me to Spider-Man's porno web here if I didn't, would I?"

Tosin tried to disguise his bark of laughter.

Any other time, speaking to Miguel like that in the clubroom would earn her some extra swats with his slapper. Hell, it still might today. Except that deep down, he was glad. Overflowing with joy that she matched him here as well as elsewhere. He'd never been so relieved in his life.

Miguel cupped her cheek, letting his thumb caress her cheek in a gentle arc. "Okay, *lindeza*. If that's what you want, you're going to feel me in you. Bare. I'll fill you with my come. Sear you with my release. Show you just how much it turns me on to see you like this."

"Yes." She lifted her ass as best she could. "Fuck me. Please."

"Aren't you forgetting something?" He took the slapper from the shelf and let her feel the cool leather on her ass for just a moment before he gave her the first swat.

If it had slipped her mind, she remembered now.

Sabine gasped. Then her ass rose again. So he repeated the gesture.

He wasn't counting his strokes, didn't need to because he could clearly sense the shift in her. At first, she indulged him, playing a sexy game that turned her on too, if the increasing sweetness of her scent told the truth.

She quickly moved beyond that stage and settled in, letting the repeated stinging blossom into something more meaningful than a mere form of entertainment, or a cheap thrill. The moment he'd put her over his shoulder in the laboratory, he knew this was what she needed.

No longer was he going to let her keep her most intense reactions bottled inside.

If venting was what she needed, he'd provide a safe outlet. One that would allow her to manage her stress. In a safe environment, he'd help her drain the poison from her system and replace it with rapture. A few more strokes and she'd be there.

A sniffle came from her.

Though his palms ached to rub her ass, soothe the inflammation, he knew that's not what *she* needed. But Sabine was stubborn and he wasn't sure she was ready for the pain it might take to set her free.

One more. And then another.

A sob escaped Sabine. Never once did she ask him to stop and he was reluctant to insult her by doing so now.

"Miguel," Tosin warned.

"Not yet," he replied. "She's nearly there."

"Or it's almost too much." His friend spoke up, addressing Sabine directly. "Isn't it?"

She didn't respond, lost in her own headspace.

Miguel took his friend's advice into consideration. It was, after all, why he'd given the man a front row seat to this show, the most important scene of Miguel's life so far.

His fingers shook as they cupped Sabine's chin, tilting her face toward him while he leaned down so that he could study her glassy eyes from a fraction of an inch away. The fire he saw, still banked deep within them, along with unbearable agony gave him the courage to take them both where he knew they needed to go.

She had to let the sadness and anger bleed from her soul so that she could channel her energy into something productive again.

He could perform that operation for her.

Sabine hovered right there, on the edge of breaking. He had the skill and the power to take her where she needed to go without pushing too hard. He hoped.

"One more." Miguel nuzzled her temple before placing a tender kiss there. "Let go, Sabine. Give me everything inside you. I can handle it."

He brought the slapper down again, hard, at the base of her cheeks.

The shockwave of pain seemed to rip through her this time. She cried out.

Huge, heaving sobs worked through her.

Miguel dropped the slapper on the floor. He tugged the top net down, flipped her again, then straddled the fuck net, which flexed to accommodate his stance. The contraption could easily hold both of their full weights. Face to face, he wrapped her in his heat and put as much of his skin as he could into contact with hers. He was sure she hadn't let herself exorcise these demons since Heinrich had died. Maybe not even since her parents had been forced to leave her behind.

Right then he promised himself he wouldn't abandon her.

Not ever.

If she walked first, that would be one thing. But he'd never let her go if he didn't have to.

As he soothed her, her shudders began to transform. It took a while, but eventually she was calling out, ready for him to soothe her in another, more primal, fashion. "Miguel?"

"I'm here, *lindeza.*"

"I need—"

"My cock?"

"You!" she cried in response. "I need *you.*"

He wondered if the subtle difference in her phrasing had been intentional. Either way, he wasn't about to deny her. He couldn't bear to be outside her a single moment longer.

Miguel nodded. "In that case..."

Without further hesitation he took himself in hand and aimed the head of his cock between her legs, then drilled forward. The shock of being so empty and then suddenly so full—filled with him—seemed to steal Sabine's breath.

It was like their lives.

One moment they'd been alone.

And then they'd met.

Ever since, it'd been like this. Complete, bursting with passion and laughter and pleasure. Even during some of the darkest times she'd experienced. That she could open herself to him, allow him to connect with her despite the darkness, made him work harder to deserve her affection.

That was a gift he never would have been bold enough to ask for. Or even to dare wish for.

Miguel began to move, withdrawing completely before plunging balls-deep within her.

Sabine's gaze winged from his face to Tosin's hand, which flew along the length of his cock as he perched on his seat as if it were a throne and he a king watching his servants perform for his delight. Then she'd glance back at the intersection of their bodies. She was so busy observing that she had started to lift out of the trance-like state he'd worked so hard to put her in.

That would not do. It was more important for her to feel and be honest with herself about her emotions in the moment. Yet he couldn't bring himself to stop fucking her long enough to fix the problem.

"Tosin," he grunted.

"Yeah?" His friend seemed startled when addressed. His steady jerking hitched.

"Blindfold my beautiful pet."

She shook her head violently, so he put his hand carefully around her neck, keeping her still. All the while he drove into her, addicted to the feel of her body trying to pull him in farther. When she could, she explained, "I like to see you. Him."

"Not this time," Miguel refused, knowing better than her what she needed at the moment. "Feel instead. Feel me. More important, feel what's coming from within you. Go ahead, close your eyes."

She did.

Tosin was there to wrap a scrap of black silk around her face to keep her from disobeying even as the ecstasy he gave her mounted. Her pussy began to hug him tighter, sucking him deeper into her body.

"*Lindeza*, you've never been more stunning to me than you are right now," he promised as he plowed into her, his feet still planted on the ground giving him enough leverage to shake the fuck net violently. Hell, their exchange felt momentous enough to rock the entire ship. "The only thing that will make you more gorgeous is your release. I can't wait to see you come for me. On me."

"Miguel!" she screamed. "Please!"

As he'd expected, the lack of sight had turned her concentration inward, magnifying her own feelings.

"That's so good." He couldn't wait to reward her. "Go ahead. Come for me."

Sabine threatened to smother his cock in velvety warmth. Her body simultaneously drew him in and nearly squeezed him out. Oh no, he wasn't going anywhere.

Miguel fucked deeper. Harder.

He embedded himself as far inside her as he could get while she quaked and came.

And when she relaxed the slightest bit, he pumped into her mercilessly, only then freeing his restraint on his own pent up desire. His balls drew tight to his body and he swore he shot so hard he might have broken something.

As he pumped jet after jet of come into her depths, she cried out again, her climax rejuvenating as he flooded her pussy.

Far in the background of his awareness, he heard Tosin finding his own relief.

How could he watch Sabine unravel like that and not be affected?

Miguel didn't blame his friend in the least.

For a while, he added his weight to the fuck net, sprawled on top of Sabine, crushing her at least a little. She didn't seem to mind though, as she moaned softly on occasion. Her pussy massaged him with periodic aftershocks that extended their bliss. A particularly strong one rolled through her when he unfastened the clamps on her breasts before sucking each nipple lightly, soothing it.

When he could manage to lift his head, he kissed her as gently and sweetly as he knew how.

She deserved his reverence.

Tranquil in the aftermath of their tempestuous emotions and the outlet he'd provided, it jolted him when she gasped a few minutes later.

"Miguel!" she shrieked. "Miguel, it's like I'm blind!"

"It's only silk, *lindeza*." He shushed her with feather-light kisses as he worked quickly to untie the knot. While he did that, Tosin rushed to her and unfastened her restraints, freeing her almost instantly. "You're fine, I promise. I'm right here."

"I know." She stilled then. "I'm not afraid."

"Then what's wrong?" he wondered as he slipped the blindfold over her hair, marveling at the contrast of her nearly platinum waves against the midnight silk. Other women might consider it unruly or in need of a cut. He liked that she left it natural, untamed, and slightly uneven. When the wind blew through it on deck, she reminded him of a cross between a gypsy sailor and a super sexy pirate. Especially when he took in the sea glass necklace of his, wrapped around her throat.

"The darkness." She blinked furiously as she returned to her senses. She tried to sit up, so he helped her into position, hanging onto her so she couldn't tumble out of the net while he looked to Tosin for help. Had his orgasm addled his brains or was she not making any sense?

His friend only shrugged.

"It's the darkness, Miguel. It blinds you." Sabine squirmed until he lifted her and set her on her feet. She began to pace, freaking him out just a little. He'd unlocked something within her. It was his job as a dominant to help her work through it, but he'd never seen something like this before.

Didn't know how to support her other than to assure her he would take care of her and give her anything she needed. "We don't have to do that again, *lindeza*. I'm sorry if I upset you."

Had he judged everything wrong?

"No! It was perfect. Exactly right." She waved her hands at him, making her breasts bounce as she turned to him with the most brilliant smile he'd ever seen. "Don't you understand?"

"Not a clue here, honey," Tosin answered for him as he cleaned up the massive load he'd shot across his chest and abs. "Can you break it down for us non-geniuses in the room?"

"Heinrich said we had to blind ourselves or we might never look at the answer in a way that allowed us to see it." She practically buzzed with excitement.

"So you think..." He started to see where she was coming from.

"We're going night diving, Miguel." Sabine's enormous smile dazzled him with its brilliance.

"I'll get the UV torches and see how much bottom time Archer has left today." Tosin already headed for the door.

"You should probably put some clothes on!" Miguel shouted after him. "Safety first—wouldn't want an eel to bite that thing off, would you?"

Tosin jogged back into the clubroom and hopped into his trunks. "Good looking out, man."

"That's what friends are for." He clapped Tosin on the back, hoping the other man knew how grateful he was for his participation that evening. If nothing else, he'd have someone to relive the night with, someone who could vouch for the intensity of the experience when he began to doubt it could have been as incredible as he remembered.

If Sabine left him, at least he'd have that memory. Forever.

"Anytime," Tosin muttered, too quietly for Sabine to hear. "No, seriously. *Anytime.* Lucky bastard."

ELEVEN

Sabine's heart raced as they skimmed the moonlit waves toward the silhouette of Molokini. Other than the whir of the outboard engine on the rigid hull inflatable tender and the slap of waves against its side, there were no sounds. Even the army of nesting seabirds that made the scrap of land their sanctuary had hunkered down for the night.

"Are you sure you're up for this?" Miguel asked. "You've already had a crazy day. Going under at night can be challenging, especially if you've never done it before."

Honestly, she was scared shitless.

But if she had trusted the man to take her on the intimate journey he had earlier, holding her life in his hands wasn't much more of a stretch. The things he'd done to her—not the physical ones, but the emotional ones—caused her to shiver despite the balmy overnight temperature.

Miguel drew her closer to his side and rubbed her arm, transfusing his heat and confidence into her. The three men onboard looked between each other, silently communicating.

"Tosin and I are more than happy to do this dive for you," Archer offered. "You two can chill up here and man the boat while we collect samples. Tomorrow night, when you're better prepared, we can dive in two teams."

"No, no." Sabine waved them off despite the temptation. Following in Heinrich's footsteps, or flipper kicks, had become an obsession. She had to see this through.

They slowed as they approached a mooring ball and Tosin began to tie the boat off.

"If at any time you want to call the dive, just give me the thumbs-up signal and we'll make a controlled ascent immediately," Miguel promised. "I know this area super well now. I promise you I can get us back to the boat from anywhere within the crater."

"Which site are we at?" She tried to orient herself against the islet. Everything looked different at night. Further apart.

"This is Middle Reef," Tosin told her. "It bottoms out between fifty and sixty feet, so you don't have to worry about dropping too far or narcing yourself by accident. Not that Miguel would let that happen even if you could."

Sabine nodded. Nitrogen narcosis referred to disorientation suffered by divers breathing certain gases at high pressure. In less than ninety feet of water, the risk decreased drastically. The chemistry of the phenomenon fascinated her. That didn't mean she felt the need to experience it herself. Although it was easy to cure by rising until the pressure decreased and symptoms abated, once in an altered state of consciousness—confused and numb—it could be difficult to remember how to react properly.

Many unfortunate sufferers had mistaken up for down and only made the situation worse, or drifted off until they ran out of air. In the inky darkness below, it would be even more difficult to know which direction the surface was if you weren't alert enough to monitor your own bubbles for clues.

She shivered.

"If we sit around talking long enough, I'm going to chicken out." She clipped her buoyancy control vest into place and fastened the cummerbund so that her tanks were secure, then double-checked her fins and pulled on her mask.

"Don't do something you're not comfortable with." Miguel gave her one last out.

"Sometimes pushing your limits can be terrifying. It's also extraordinarily rewarding." She took his hand then, hoping he realized she'd enjoyed the hell out of the rush he'd given her earlier and wanted to go two for two tonight. "I need to do this."

"Then I'm with you. And I'm not letting go." He kept his word, holding her fingers tight as Archer and Tosin helped them get situated on the rounded sidewall of the tender. Tosin flicked on a torch that she would swear could be seen from space considering how it sliced through the darkness. He also pressed a plastic bubble on her tank, which began to glow so Miguel could spot her if they were separated, she guessed.

Thinking about that possibility didn't alleviate her anxiety any.

"I had an idea," Miguel said to her, just before they were set to go. "You know how Heinrich's message to you said we needed to look at things differently?"

She nodded.

"We sometimes dive with UV lights instead of these super bright full spectrum ones. It allows you to detect the florescence in coral polyps. It's really awesome-looking, but I never thought about the fact that it might let you see different things than you would with the standard torch," he explained.

"Can you see well enough to collect samples with the UV light?" she wondered.

"Definitely."

"Then let's try it." She held her lamp out to Tosin and he exchanged it for one of the UV variety. Miguel's too. "If nothing else, it'll be pretty, right?"

"Nowhere near as beautiful as you, *lindeza*." Miguel snuck in a quick kiss then put his regulator in his mouth. She followed his lead.

On his count of three, they did a backward roll. Tumbling through the water, she panicked. Her breaths came in and out faster, filling her vision with a riot of bubbles.

Miguel's firm squeeze on her fingers reminded her that she wasn't alone.

She calmed her respiration and opened her eyes, which had been squeezed shut.

Staring at her from less than a foot away, Miguel used his thumb and forefinger to make a circle while his other three fingers were extended. The universal signal for okay.

She flashed it back.

With him, she was.

He nodded then changed his gesture to a thumbs-down, indicating they should begin their descent. As she lay flat and aimed the ultraviolet beam of her light toward the reef, she gasped.

It wasn't dark or eerie as she had expected. The sea floor teemed with life. Typical daytime fish were nowhere to be seen, hiding from nocturnal predators while they rested. In their place, a cluster of ctenophores—some sort of comb jelly, she thought—drifted by like a fleet of mini UFOs. Lights twinkled from inside the organisms as they propelled themselves through the currents.

The hard corals she'd spent so much time staring at the past few weeks had also been altered. Instead of their calcium carbonate skeletons, which were typically the only visible part of the animal, the polyps themselves had emerged and the coral heads were unrecognizable. Animated, instead of rocklike. Their tentacles swayed in the surge and waved around as they caught zooplankton that drifted past. Neon colors reflected by the UV rippled in a mesmerizing light show caused by the undulating motion.

It was like visiting the same reef in an alternate universe. How had she never done this before?

They closed in on a mound of cauliflower coral. While Miguel carefully took a sample, she peered around, transfixed by their surroundings. Though she'd seen pictures of these phenomena before, witnessing it firsthand was something else entirely.

Sabine turned to Miguel, her eyes wide. He flashed her the okay hand signal, a question.

She nodded vigorously.

With his fingers and palm now flat in a blade, he held his arm out straight, indicating the direction to swim for their next collection. Again, she wanted to kick herself for taking time to enjoy the view before getting down to business. How could you not be awed by this scenery, though?

They worked as efficiently as possible. Given the other dives they'd done that day, they couldn't afford to stay down at sixty feet more than thirty minutes without requiring a decompression stop. The time flew by as quickly. Too soon, they were preparing to ascend.

Not before she'd spotted an octopus hunting and took a few moments to admire a free-swimming Javanese eel that was even longer than Miguel. With a reluctant sigh, she took one final look around.

Which was when she thought she saw the flicker of a white beam of light, brighter than the UV variety she and Miguel carried. She shook the metal cylinder hanging from her BC to get her divemaster's attention. He whipped his head around. But when she tried to point to what she'd seen, it had vanished.

She shrugged and shook her head.

Maybe it had only been the shimmering of another of these wondrous night dwellers.

Miguel tapped his dive computer, reminding her of their deadline, then ascended slowly along the mooring line she hadn't even noticed until they were within an arm's length of the cord. They went up it until they hovered fifteen feet below the surface. After a ninety-second safety stop, they were back on the surface.

Archer and Tosin reached down to lift her into the boat.

Due to the nitrogen load they'd taken on during their regular daily dives, they had even less bottom time available. Especially since they were picking up Miguel's divemaster slack, though they'd never once complained.

"What'd you see down there?" Miguel asked when he'd joined her in the boat.

"I'm not sure. Maybe just a funny reflection. For a second, I thought it was another dive light. A white one. But since the guys are already up here, I guess it wasn't that." She shrugged as she began to break down her gear while Archer got them underway, returning to the *Divemaster* with some more work for her to do.

"We used UV lights, too," Tosin said. "Not full spectrum."

The guys exchanged another one of those infamous stares, probably saying she was clearly nuts, so she changed the subject. "How many samples did we get? I hope I can process them all before tomorrow night so we know what to concentrate on next...if we don't already have the winner."

She grinned at that. They had to be closing in on Heinrich's secret.

"*Lindeza*, you need to sleep first." Miguel didn't seem like he was going to listen to her arguments about how she could power through with the help of a gallon or so of black coffee. It might be hard for him to take her seriously when a huge yawn escaped her at the reminder.

Even harder would have been for her to persuade him in any fashion when she was unconscious, which she was by the time they arrived back at the ship. The ups and downs of the day had sapped her energy.

It was a good thing she rested before tackling her next round of experiments, because none of them panned out. On the bright side, she got to experience the gorgeous nightly display over and over with Miguel by her side. It never grew old, though she had to keep reminding herself that it would be better if they had achieved their goal even if it meant the end of her quality time with her favorite divemaster.

Nearly two weeks after her first night dive, Sabine stumbled from her laboratory and plopped onto the dive platform, dangling her legs behind the *Divemaster* as she watched the waves roll by endlessly.

Her renewed optimism had suffered the same fate as her original bout of worthless enthusiasm following more than a dozen fruitless collecting expeditions. Everyone was feeling the strain of their pointless trips.

They'd all agreed to take a night off and regroup.

A month into her research, she wasn't a single step closer to figuring out exactly what Heinrich had uncovered. If she didn't stumble across it soon, she'd have to admit it wasn't here to find. Then pick a different approach. She'd already inconvenienced Archer, Tosin, and *especially* Miguel long enough.

It would be nearly impossible to find someone who'd fund continuing research with this mammoth failure under her belt, even if she could figure out where to look next. Maybe another Indo-Pacific location that had been on Heinrich's route. Hell, she might have to return to Germany to regroup. Sabine would see if she could salvage anything from Heinrich's home computer or the rubble of his laboratory.

The odds of that tactic being productive were even worse than those of the Molokini Crater divulging its secrets to her at this point.

Worse, it would mean saying goodbye to Miguel.

How many blows could she take before they crushed her?

✬ TWELVE ✬

Miguel finished tucking the last of the items for their excursion into his backpack and zipped it as quietly as possible. Sabine needed every minute of rest she could stockpile. The experiment, and the lack of results she desperately hoped for, weighed on her more and more.

When he'd fallen asleep with her in his arms the night before, he'd noticed her hipbones dug into him a bit. Using gentle caresses, he surveyed the rest of her and was convinced she'd gotten thinner during her stay. Consistently shorting herself on sleep had given her dark circles below her eyes that hadn't been there before, either.

This time he knew better than to let her reach her breaking point. She needed to step away for a quick break so she could stay positive. Clarity of mind was a job requirement she couldn't meet when she got too down on herself. Not even their clubroom sessions seemed to help her relax as much as they had at first.

Maybe because the more attached they grew to each other, the more troubling it was to consider what would happen if she didn't make progress soon.

Miguel had considered that as he beat the stuffing out of the punching bag in the ship's gym during his past few workouts. He had the bruised knuckles to show for it, too.

Fortunately, he had an idea about how to help her rejuvenate. One that involved less intensity and, hopefully, more fun than his previous methods. That's not to say they hadn't been enjoying some quality time in the clubroom. Because—oh, fuck—had they. Even there, she was his well-balanced counterpart.

It was just that he felt compelled to show her that great sex wasn't the *only* thing he cared about because he might have to make his case soon for why she shouldn't leave him. What if he couldn't persuade her to stay when the time came?

In the back of his mind, he thought about the out Archer had given him. One he'd never planned to take. Could he sell his share of the *Divemaster*? Would he if that was what it took to follow Sabine wherever she needed to go next?

Incredibly, he was starting to consider the possibility.

With everything ready, he couldn't delay waking her any longer. If he did, they'd miss the main event. Stalking to the side of the bed, he took a few precious moments to memorize what she looked like as she slept in his bed. Facedown, sprawled across most of the wide-open space, she'd burrowed into the super soft sheets wearing nothing but his necklace, which she'd never once taken off. Though she'd only found her place there a month ago and could be a total cover hog, he couldn't imagine what it would be like to climb into bed alone after sharing it with her.

He wouldn't.

If she wasn't there, he didn't want to be either.

Whoa.

Miguel drew a deep breath then knelt beside the bed. He shook her shoulder lightly, awed as always by the softness of her skin. "Good morning, *lindeza*."

He waited for her to smile at him slowly before he placed a kiss on her cheek.

"Am I late for the lab?" She closed her eyes for a moment as if psyching herself up, then pushed onto her elbows. He tried not to stare at her rack, or even to notice how amazing it was, in case he fell back into bed with her to wake her up properly. They didn't have time for that.

"Not exactly." He handed her a bra and underwear—practically a crime—along with a soft T-shirt and a pair of comfortable shorts. "Get dressed."

"Is something wrong?" She bit her lower lip.

Miguel hated that disaster came to her mind as the first motivation for his actions. "Nope. Everything's great. It's a field day. Or I guess, if you want to be more grown up about it, I'm taking you out on a date."

"Huh? You are?" She pushed fully upright, rubbed the last lingering bit of sleep from her eyes with her fists, then perked up, always down for an adventure.

Could she be any more adorable?

"Yep." He stole one more kiss then tweaked her nipple. "Hurry up. We don't want to miss our ride."

"Where are we going?" she wondered.

"You'll have to come with me to find out." He nudged her toward the edge of the mattress.

Sabine took the clothes, hopped from bed, and scampered to the bathroom still naked, giving him a great view of her ultra-spankable ass and long legs.

Damn, maybe he should have woken her up just a little earlier. He rubbed the growing bulge in his cargo shorts.

She'd taken care of business, brushed her teeth, and reappeared in a few minutes, fully dressed. He liked that about her. Sabine didn't bother wasting time primping, didn't need to because she was so damn gorgeous naturally.

He already had his backpack over his shoulder.

"Let's go!" She darted ahead of him out the door and down the hall. Her easy smiles and genuine enthusiasm made his hours of planning worth it.

"Up to the helipad," he told her when they neared the elevator.

"Ohh, fun." She clapped then poked the button for the appropriate deck.

Miguel couldn't help but laugh. He drew her to him and squeezed her tight. "It's so great to see you happy again."

She froze. Had he said exactly the wrong thing?

"Maybe we shouldn't go." She swallowed hard enough that he heard it. "The samples—"

"Can wait one day." He'd prepared this argument. "You need time off, a mini vacation, and when we get back you'll be twice as effective, making up any delay."

Miguel expected her to argue. She didn't.

She must have felt even worse than he'd realized. Shit.

The elevator dinged and opened onto the deck with the helipad. Waverly and the chopper stood by. He kissed Sabine's forehead then swung his backpack around so he wore it on his chest. She looked at him funny until he turned and crouched. "Piggyback ride?"

Whatever he could do to keep her smiling today, he would gladly do it.

"Woot!" She hopped on, wrapping her legs around him. The heat of her core against him had a million other dirty thoughts racing through his mind. She hugged his shoulders and laid her cheek against one of them.

As he jogged, he heard her say softly, "Thank you, Miguel."

"You can thank me properly later," he said with a wink as he reached the chopper and helped her inside.

"Noted." She blew him a kiss, then glanced around as if only now realizing it was still dark out. "I think I'm jacked up from our night dives. What time is it?"

"Four fucking thirty in the morning," Waverly grumbled. "Who takes someone on a date at the ass crack of dawn?"

Miguel laughed. "Sorry, babe. Tell Banks to give you a bonus for putting up with outlandish requests."

"It's not the request that's a pain, it's the owner," she mock-grumbled even as she smiled. "Happy to take you anywhere, anytime, you know that. Now hop in and let's get going."

He kissed her cheek then climbed inside, taking a seat next to Sabine on the triple-wide bench side of the passenger area across from two captain chairs that were extremely comfortable but far too separate from each other. The center seat had been folded down to make a table and an assortment of fruit, juices, croissants, and yogurt was laid out.

Sabine was digging in. This had definitely been a good idea.

He owed the kitchen staff a personal thanks when they returned, too. On the floor, he spotted another delivery from them that he'd need later. Perfect.

When they'd buckled in, Waverly lifted off so smoothly they didn't even have to hang on to their glasses. She had mad skills.

Licking pineapple juice from her fingers, Sabine peeked out the window. Miguel did the same. The view from up here never ceased to impress. He remembered when he'd first met their resident scientist. Could it really have only been a month ago? They'd made this trip in reverse and she'd asked about the Haleakala Observatory.

"Are we going to see the sunrise from the summit of Haleakala?" She practically bounced in her seat as she swung around to face him. "It's supposed to be amazing. Did you know Haleakala actually means 'House of the Sun'?"

"I didn't, no."

"Sorry, is my inner nerd showing?" She grimaced as she brushed her hair out of her eyes.

"Just a little." He finished the job for her then leaned in for a quick kiss. "No worries, I think she's cute."

More like Miguel loved this side of her. He wondered if he could convince her to wear thick-rimmed glasses and a plaid skirt for him in bed sometime.

He grinned as she rattled off facts to him and Waverly without stopping to draw a breath. "The summit is 10,023 feet above sea level. There's a plant you can find around the main parking area called a silversword that's endangered. People walk right by it and don't even realize how rare it is. The observatory on top of the mountain is run by the University of Hawaii Institute for Astronomy and it's regarded as one of the best in the world in part because it sits above the tropical inversion layer, so the view is crystal clear from there."

He had no idea what that meant, but he nodded anyway, feeling better and better about his itinerary for the day. They landed a few minutes later. He helped Sabine into the foul-weather jacket he'd brought for her, handed her the shoes she'd had to give up when onboard the *Divemaster*, then snagged the two-man sleeping bag he'd stowed along with the rest of his supplies.

Sabine asked Waverly if she wanted to join them for the sunrise. She declined, opting to stay with her helicopter instead.

Silently, Miguel thanked her. Not that he didn't love the woman, in a completely platonic sort of way, but he felt some indescribable urge to have Sabine to himself today. They spent so much time around others onboard the *Divemaster* that it was a rare treat.

He figured that was one reason his relationship with Sabine seemed so intense. They'd been together damn near every second of the past month. And yet he wanted more.

On a relatively level spot, he laid out the sleeping bag and a thermos of Sabine's favorite hot tea then climbed in beside her, drawing her onto his lap. She cuddled up to him, curling into his embrace.

For a while, they sat there in silence, observing the stars.

She was right—they did look unbelievable from up here. If he lifted his hand, he might be able to pluck one from the sky for her. Gradually, the dots were joined by hints of color that illuminated the clouds, which were actually below his and Sabine's perch. The sky looked like the ocean on calm mornings when fog blanketed the surface.

Golden rays gilded the wisps, which began to be offset by a background of salmon and burnt oranges. Finally, the sun peeked above the horizon, setting the vibrant colors to shame. And when the magic faded, leaving behind a bright, beautiful day, Sabine cheered.

He caught her as she turned to him and kissed her, savoring the flavor of tropical fruit mingled with her lips.

Miguel made love to her mouth as thoroughly as a public park would permit. The entire time, he stared into her eyes, which gazed right back at him, never shying away from the bond that shone brighter than that epic sunrise had.

"I think I'm ready to go home now," she whispered.

It thrilled him that she had called the *Divemaster* home. Nearly as much as it affected him to realize she was equally eager to get him in bed as he was to have her there.

"Are you sure?" He kissed the tip of her nose. "Because it turns out I know people who fund a shit-ton of grants. Including ones to the Institute of Astronomy."

As of two days ago, anyway. *Thank you, Banks.*

Sabine's eyes went wide. "Seriously?"

"Yup." He nodded. "Out of respect for their patrons, they've arranged for us to take a quick peek around the facilities. You know, unless you would rather split. I'm not opposed to taking you back to bed if you prefer."

Well, okay, it wasn't an either or proposition. He'd do that later. There was no way she'd pass up this chance.

Sabine squirmed from the sleeping bag and yanked on his hand. "Come on!"

He didn't release her fingers during the trek to the observatory or the admittedly interesting tour they were taken on by one of the leading researchers. Sabine asked tons of technical questions, but Miguel zoned out, spending his time wondering about what might be out there in space and if he could ever find a place, a home, a group of friends, and a lover that made him as content as he was at the moment.

When he decided the answer was a resounding no, he knew it was official.

He'd fallen for Sabine.

Lost in thought, he almost didn't hear the latest man they were being introduced to ask Sabine about Heinrich. The slight uptick in her tone and the way she stepped closer to Miguel alerted him to the situation.

He put his arm around her waist, cursing the probably well-meaning fuckface for reminding her of things Miguel couldn't fix for her, not even with the influence of several billion of Archer's dollars.

"So what are you doing in the area?" Professor Bookworm asked her. "Working on a new project? Or maybe something of his he hadn't finished before he passed away?"

The question seemed a little too casual and way too insensitive for Miguel's liking. "Sorry, I didn't catch your name. Who are you again?"

The guy shrugged. "I'm Brad Post. Just a grad assistant around here."

"It's been nice talking to you, Brad. But if you'll excuse us, we've got somewhere else to be." Yeah, like anywhere people weren't asking too many questions about something Heinrich had been trying to keep under wraps or topics that hurt his woman to discuss.

Sabine nodded. "Thank you for the tour, Dr. Pickering."

They exchanged handshakes before Miguel and Sabine retraced their steps to the helicopter.

"You okay?" he asked Sabine.

"Fine." She smiled, though some of the shine had dulled. "Lots of people know he was my mentor. Especially in academic circles—everyone knows everyone."

"Then you're up for more fun?" He could salvage the rest of the day, he figured.

"I'm not sure how you can top this." She rose onto her tiptoes and kissed him sweetly. "Honestly, Miguel. This is the nicest thing someone's ever done for me. You know, other than the whole *Divemaster* thing. But this is...personal."

"Yeah, it damn well is." He kissed her this time, lingering for a while. Their next activity wouldn't be very comfortable with a boner, though, so he reined himself in before he could get carried away.

"So what now?" Resilient and tough as ever, Sabine perked up again.

He strode to the cargo hold of the helicopter and withdrew two bikes along with helmets and other protective gear.

Waverly met them around back and held out the picnic basket he'd spotted earlier. "Are you going to be able to balance that on your handlebars?"

He laughed. "Don't insult me. Of course. I can even ride with no hands."

Sabine shook her head. "Have you ever seen what the road down from here looks like? It's no joke. Hands the whole way, please. I need you in one piece for the things I have planned for tonight."

"I like the sound of that." He gave in to the disapproving stares of two kickass women. "I bet I can fit this stuff in my backpack. Will that make you feel better?

"Yes," they answered together.

So he stuffed as much as possible in there then hefted it onto his shoulders.

"I'm going to fly down to the Kula Botanical Garden. They've got a spot for me to land. Take your time and call me if your plans change." Waverly hugged Sabine then waved. "Be careful!"

"It's been a while since I've actually ridden a bike." Sabine made a funny face as she climbed on.

"The good news is it's entirely downhill. All you have to do is glide." He watched her as she took off in front of him, mentally rating this portion of the day with five solid gold stars when he realized her ass would be on display for him to perv over the whole way down the mountain. That was more likely than a picnic basket to make him wreck.

She may not have had a lot of practice, but in customary Sabine style, that didn't keep her from going for it wholeheartedly. He loved that about her. Always willing to try new things, or check something out, she never shied away from new experiences.

He hoped they could have lots of those together.

Wind stung his cheeks as they picked up speed.

Sabine proved to be quite the daredevil, taking the hairpin switchbacks in the mountain road far faster than he was comfortable with. It was a long way down on the other side of the guardrails, when there were guardrails. Maybe he shouldn't have unleashed her.

Watching her hair whip around her and hearing her exclamations float over the stark beauty of the cinder desert surrounding them, he fed off of her elation.

Together they whooped and hollered to each other, pointing out highlights as they wormed their way toward the park where Waverly waited with their ride home. Lush tropical trees and flowers soon replaced the barren landscape of the summit.

Another of Hawaii's many ecosystems engulfed them in greens so vivid they made him think of the variety of blues that made up the ocean. Underwater would always be his favorite place, the pinnacle of nature to him. This wasn't too shabby, though.

When they coasted into the parking lot at the botanical garden, Sabine turned toward him—face flushed, eyes bright. He helped her climb off her bike and steady herself before leading her along a path to the spot he'd picked for lunch.

A half-mile down the trail, he heard the rush of water. A few more turns through the jungle and an enormous waterfall loomed above them. Moss clung to the rocks on either side of the long, ribbony stream, which poured over the edge of the cliff hundreds of feet in the air.

"It's gorgeous." Sabine paused, staring up at the feature in awe.

"I *still* haven't seen anything that comes close to you, *lindeza*. Never will." Miguel took her in his arms, simply hugging her tight. He buried his nose in her hair and breathed deep of the scent of clean mountain air blended with her.

While she wandered around the clearing snapping photos, including a bunch of selfies of them laughing and goofing off together, he spread out their blanket and unpacked the gourmet feast. For the first time since they'd met, they enjoyed normal people stuff together.

Okay, normal people stuff, if you were extraordinarily lucky and privileged, too.

He refused to feel guilty about the perks he could provide his companion after working hard and building his life from nothing. Because he knew that even if he was still dirt poor, it wouldn't matter.

They only needed each other.

Sabine smiled up at him. Her fingers played with his hands. Stuffed, and in need of a power nap, he grinned back. "You ready to head home?"

"Will that lead to your dick in my pussy sometime soon?" She surprised him with her directness, as always.

He laughed. "Definitely."

"After the best blowjob of your life, of course, for being such an amazing—" She hesitated, as if unsure of what to call him, until finishing with, "lover."

Except it sounded like more of a question by the time she got to the end of her sentence.

He wondered what he'd prefer her to say.

Boyfriend? Nah.

Partner? Maybe.

Soul mate? That's what it felt like to him.

For the first time, he understood guys who introduced a woman as their wife and the pride that accompanied their declaration—equal parts possession, ego boost since they'd chosen you in return, and honor.

Maybe someday...

"Am I doing it wrong or something?" She tipped her head.

"Huh?"

"My attempt at seduction. I thought you'd be sprinting for the chopper at the promise of a BJ. I mean, I did say the *best* BJ ever, didn't I? Not one of those sloppy, half-assed, get it wet so you can put it in faster kind. I mean like the unreciprocated, lay back and enjoy—"

If she didn't stop talking, he was going to yank down his shorts right there.

So he lunged to his feet, snagged the backpack, then grabbed Sabine, too.

She laughed as he ran, carrying her, the entire length of the trail.

After he boosted her into their waiting ride, Miguel spoke quietly to Waverly, who had already loaded their bikes and moved on to her pre-flight checks. "When you radio in to Captain Alex with our flight details, can you please ask him to check out Brad Post, grad student at UoH. He's probably just some socially awkward bookworm, but he was poking around, asking Sabine a lot of questions about her work this morning. It's been bugging me ever since. Maybe we should add some security to her lab, too. Cameras, extra locks, stuff like that."

Of all people, Waverly would understand. Shit could turn ugly in an instant.

"Sure, Miguel." She put her hand on his forearm and squeezed. "Things are going to turn out okay."

"I know." He really did believe that.

After all, he didn't plan to let anything happen to Sabine. He'd waited a lifetime for the perfect woman to spend the rest of his life with. Now that he'd found her, he didn't intend to lose her.

✧ THIRTEEN ✧

Sabine couldn't wait for Waverly to whisk them back to the *Divemaster*. Maybe Miguel would take her to the clubroom and help her work off some of this naughty energy he'd had her stockpiling all damn day in his sexy, generous, romantic presence. If he didn't, she'd probably tackle him the moment they got back to their cabin.

Their cabin.

When had she started thinking of his space as her home?

She wasn't sure, but somewhere along the line she had. There was nowhere else she felt more comfortable, and not only because of the lavish amenities. Truthfully, as long as Miguel's arms were around her, holding her close to the steady thump of his heart, she'd make do.

Sabine glanced at Miguel and found him staring back at her with the same red-hot lust burning in his gaze. That would never get old.

"Hey, Waverly!" he called up to their badass lady pilot.

"Yeah?"

"Remember that time I helped you make Archie's underwater sex fantasy come true?"

He did what? Sabine wondered exactly how that worked and if they could try it sometime. She forgot to ask him, though, when he kept talking.

"How about you pay me back now?" He winked at Waverly while his hand wandered up Sabine's thigh, beneath the hem of her skirt.

"What'd you have in mind?" Waverly joked, "Kind of hard to have a threesome when I'm doing the flying. Besides, Archer would kill you."

"Very funny." Miguel chuckled. "I want you to roll up that partition and take a few laps around the island. I'll knock when we're ready to go home."

"We have an intercom, you know?" She grinned. "Pretend to be the worldly multi-millionaire you are, Miguel. Or at least act as if you're civilized."

"What fun would that be? Besides, we all know I'm asking for privacy because I'm going to fuck my date until she can hardly walk. Nothing refined about that, is there?" He poked around on the control panel by his seat, finding the button for the partition himself. "Toodles, Waverly."

The dainty finger wave he gave his best friend's girlfriend was so utterly ridiculous that both women burst out laughing.

Sabine's humor faded fast when he turned on her with his blue laser stare. "Strip."

"Like burlesque strip or like set-the-world-record-for-getting-naked strip? I'm not very coordinated, but I could give the sexy variety a whirl if you've got some music…" It wasn't nervousness, exactly, that had her rambling. More like anticipation and the desire to be perfect for him. As wonderful as he was for her without trying.

"Ditch your clothes. Now." Though brusque, his gravelly command didn't alarm her. She'd been teasing him for hours. A man—or a woman for that matter—could only stand so much sweet torture in a single day.

"Oh. Right." Sabine toed off her sneakers and socks, wriggled out of her shorts and panties, then whipped her shirt and bra over her head. The necklace he'd given her stayed, as always. Without it she would feel naked in ways she'd never anticipated before. It comforted her, reminding her of his presence in her life. She understood the importance of talismans to some cultures much more after wearing his.

It carried an enchantment for her that she didn't ever want to go without again.

He seemed to wholly approve of her obsession with his gift.

"That's better." He admired her, bared completely to him. And she didn't mean only her nudity.

Miguel saw her clearly. He understood her moods, boosted her up when she was low, took charge when she longed to be free of responsibility for a little while, and never left her unsatisfied when she craved him. Like she did now.

"On your knees at my feet." He took her hand and tugged, helping her sink to the plush carpeting as he spread his thighs wide.

Sabine looked up at him, waiting for his direction.

"Undress me," he ordered.

She started with his sneakers, untying them and slipping them from his feet. It was unusual to see him wearing shoes of any kind since they weren't allowed on the precious decks of the *Divemaster*. When she peeled off his socks, revealing his tanned toes, she felt like she was uncovering the man she'd gotten to know so well.

Her hands trailed up his legs, the thick dark hair on them tickling her palms.

When she reached his shorts, skimming her fingers over the front of them, she intentionally goaded him before undoing the fly so that his already hard cock could spring free. His massive erection was framed by the canvas as it rested on his abdomen.

The resolve she'd had to go slow and steady flew out the window then.

Hell, she could climb into his lap and sink over his shaft in a matter of seconds if she hadn't promised him a world-class sucking.

Sabine rushed, shoving his shirt up before tugging it over his head and flinging it somewhere behind her. Then she yanked on his shorts.

He laughed as he lifted his fine ass from the seat so she could slip the last of his clothes from his body. "In a hurry?"

"Uh huh." She nodded, licking her lips.

"Tell me again about how you're going to give me the best blowjob of my life." He speared his fingers into her hair and brought her face close to his groin. Not close enough for her to taste him yet, though.

"Why don't you let me show you instead?" She peered up at him through the veil of her lashes as she asked for permission to suck his dick.

When he didn't respond right away, she begged, "Please. I want to taste you. Feel your heat and hardness on my tongue. And when you come, I want to know it's for me, because I've made you feel even a tiny bit as good as you've made me feel. Today especially. But since the moment I met you, really."

"Every day I spend with you is a happy one, *lindeza*." He brushed his thumb over her parted lips, dipping it inside for a split second, long enough for her to flick her tongue over the tip. "But go ahead. Suck my cock. Make today one for the record books."

She rocked forward, swallowing his length in a single long glide, not stopping until she had all of him wrapped in the heat and softness of her mouth. He prodded into her throat. Good thing she didn't have much of a gag reflex, because he had enough length and girth to be a serious choking hazard.

Either would have made his cock impressive.

Together, they made him God's gift to her pussy.

Sabine shivered as she began to suck on him, hoping later he might show her again how well they fit despite his decidedly above average endowment. She bobbed over him, paying special attention to the sensitive spot beneath his crown before sinking lower once more.

His fingers clenched in her hair and on her shoulder. Soon, he began to pump upward as she sank over him. The veins along his shaft grew more defined as his sac tightened in her palm.

"Sabine!" he called out for her as he reached the limits of his restraint. She didn't bother to slack off. Instead, she fluttered her tongue across the underside of his shaft and sucked harder on his tip at the apex of each stroke.

It was then that she felt the first gush of liquid coat her tongue, a precursor to his actual orgasm.

With one final plunge, she took him deep and swallowed around him.

Miguel roared as he came. His body arched, coiled as tightly as a loaded spear gun, before bursting into motion. His abs flexed as he emptied his balls down her throat, making her gulp to keep up with the pulses of his come.

Part of her pouted, just a little. He wouldn't leave her hanging. But even his spectacular pussy-eating or the dexterity of his fingers—or both of those things together, for that matter—couldn't get her off as well as the pounding of his cock within her.

"Don't stop sucking." He tapped her cheek when she slowed, preparing to let him slide from between her lips.

Her gaze snapped to his.

"Keep going and you'll have me hard again in a few minutes." He grinned wickedly then. "You didn't think I was going to pass up the opportunity to fuck you in a helicopter, did you?"

She shook her head, doing something that apparently felt great to his dick in the process. Whatever hint of firmness he'd lost after his orgasm began to return. The fat tip of his cock bumped against her palate. Damn, how did he do that? And how many times in a row could she make him come?

Sabine planned a naughty test for another day. Right now, she had to have him buried within her as quickly as possible. She hollowed her cheeks and increased the pressure on his shaft.

He groaned and thrust upward, nearly making her choke.

Redoubling her efforts, Sabine cupped his balls in her palm and rolled them lightly. A soft touch there never failed to arouse him. Today was no exception.

"Yes," he hissed. "Suck."

She did, bringing him back to full erection before long.

When her jaw had begun to ache, he lifted her to the seat and pushed her to her back. He crushed his mouth over hers, making her forget about any mild discomfort with swipes of his tongue and the brush of his lips.

While she ate at him, he fed her pussy his cock.

He pressed against her opening, working to penetrate as he always had to at first. But when he poked through the rings of muscle and spread them around his shaft, her body accommodated him. He hunched his back so that he could suck on her nipples as he began to turn the tables, raining rapture on her.

Because he'd already come, taken the edge off, he was able to pump into her relentlessly. Sabine couldn't resist that much direct stimulation. She felt her orgasm coalescing, barely out of reach.

Miguel clenched his ass tighter with every stroke, rubbing her clit with the root of his cock. It didn't take long before she was clawing at his back, whether to slow him down or egg him on, she couldn't say.

It didn't matter. He worked her as he pleased, which turned out to be exactly how she needed it. Hard and steady, with evenly spaced thrusts that her body began to anticipate.

One or two more strokes and she'd be past the point of no return.

Of course he knew that, too.

"Come, *lindeza*." He kissed her then, swallowing her cries of completion. And only when she'd finally quit spasming around him did she realize he hadn't stopped fucking. "Do it again."

"I can't—"

"You will." He wouldn't accept any other outcome.

So she settled in and focused on the muted friction of his cock, which glided through the evidence of her arousal more easily now that he'd inspired her body to unleash one of the strongest waves of ecstasy she'd ever experienced. He never once paused as he kissed her, bringing her back to full arousal much more quickly than she would have thought possible.

When she was with him, moving against him to steal more pleasure from his body, he smiled.

Then he pulled out, though only long enough to roll her over.

He lifted her hips and helped her get into position so that one knee was on the seat while her other foot planted itself on the floor. Ass up, face pressed to the supple leather, she gasped when he reentered her from behind, then sank even deeper than before.

She was certain no one had ever been so far inside her. The thought alone spurred another orgasm. A violent one that only left her hungry for more right away. "Miguel!"

"Damn, Sabine," he panted as he blanketed her back and bit her shoulder. "That was amazing. I wanted better access to your clit, but I guess I didn't need it that time."

Still he fucked her, slow and steady as she caught her breath.

"Not when you hit right...there." She moaned when he tapped the spot inside her again. "Oh God. That's so good. So *deep*."

"Going deep is my specialty," he growled.

"Miguel," she gasped. "Seriously, I think you're so far in me you might poke out my mouth soon."

He laughed at that, but didn't stop fucking. To have a man who could appreciate humor in bed without losing his hard-on or feeling threatened was a bonus. Sabine grinned against the seat. At least until he got serious real quick, adding the stroke of his thumb across her clit to the rock of his pelvis.

She didn't stand a chance at resisting when he played her like that.

He knew all her secrets by now.

Somehow, that didn't scare her as much as it should. In fact, it amplified the pleasure he bestowed with his fluid movements and the unrelenting drive of his cock within her.

"When you go over this time, I'm coming with you," he promised. "Almost there?"

The thought of him painting her with his release, marking her—even if it was inside, where no one else could see—was almost enough on its own to trigger her climax. "Yes."

"Good girl." He lifted his chest upright far enough to expose her ass a bit. She knew what he was about to do, but it didn't make it any less enjoyable when his palm connected with her cheek.

It only took three solid swats before she shattered.

Sabine muffled her scream against the seat as she unraveled.

The pulses of Miguel's hot come splattering against her over-sensitized tissue triggered wave after wave of spasms. Only when she was sure he'd flooded her pussy did he release his grip around her waist and withdraw his softening cock.

He held her in place with one palm at the base of her spine while he reached for his shirt and did his best to clean the trickles of semen that escaped to ice her thighs.

Sabine sighed, feeling like she might deflate or melt into a puddle on the spot.

"I didn't hurt you, did I?" he asked, serious for a moment.

"No, I like it when you go deep." Too bad he didn't realize just how far within her he'd tunneled. He'd wormed his way straight into her heart. Denying it any longer would be foolish.

In silence, they got dressed as best they could. Miguel stuffed his messy shirt in his backpack and finger-combed her hair into some semblance of order. The entire time, he kept staring into her eyes, as if he could see her soul. As deep as it was possible to get inside a human, she supposed.

"*Lindeza*, I lo—"

She sure wished the bolt of inspiration that had struck her then had waited a measly half-second longer. Because her imagination was trying to convince her that he had been about to drop the L-bomb when she interrupted with a shriek.

"Might want to take it easy, Miguel." Waverly's snark came over the intercom before she said, "Seriously, though. Everything all right back there? I thought you were finished. We don't have enough gas left for too many more rounds like that."

Miguel dropped the partition even as he stared at Sabine as though she might have lost her mind.

"Sorry!" She slapped her hand over her mouth. "It's just that you inspired a thought..."

"If it has to do with his cock or some freaky sex shit he was pulling on you, I don't want to hear about it." Waverly kept her eyes on the horizon as she aimed them toward the *Divemaster* and the rest of their friends.

"Maybe I had it wrong again." Sabine gestured with her hands, wishing they could read her mind. "What if the darkness Heinrich referred to wasn't caused by night at all."

"Depth?" Miguel's stare snapped to hers.

"His letter said something about digging deeper." She squinted as she pictured the email in her mind. "'Until you change the way you look at things—blind yourself to what you think you know and dig a little deeper—you might never see it.'"

"Hmm." Miguel tapped his chin. "There aren't that many parts of the crater interior that are very deep. Certainly none enough to cause perpetual darkness. But..."

"What is it?" Sabine turned in her seat to face him, clasping his hands in hers. "Nothing is too out there—he was telling me to think outside the box."

"What if we think outside the crater instead?" Miguel peered at the sea. He pointed to Molokini. "See how the water changes color on the backside, shifting from turquoise to navy?"

"Yes," she and Waverly said in unison.

"It's deep over there. The far side of the islet drops straight down to at least three hundred and fifty feet. With strong currents. Advanced divers drop in there. Their boats take off to the opposite end of the island and pick them up after they drift along the entire length." He looked at her then, his pupils dilating.

"What?"

"The other reason people avoid it—or seek it out—is because it's in constant shadow."

Sabine felt the familiar rush of hope. This time she was too afraid to embrace it fully.

"And if you go a bit farther out, off the shelf, the bottom falls away rapidly in the Alalakeiki Channel to twice that easily," he explained.

"That's deep enough to be around the bottom of the disphotic zone or maybe even to the top of the aphotic zone." She tapped her chin as she considered the possibilities.

"What does that mean?" Waverly asked as she began their descent to the *Divemaster*.

"It's very close to the limit light from the surface can reach. Worth a try to investigate, but way too deep for us to dive and collect samples from if there are even any deep sea corals down there," Miguel answered for her.

Sabine nodded. "I know this is kind of crazy...but you don't happen to have a submarine lying around in your stash of billionaire toys, do you?"

Waverly jumped in to help. "With Archer's money and my connections in the Navy, I bet we can scrounge up a DSV to borrow. That's a Deep Submergence Vehicle for you non-military acronym types. And you know, by *we*...I mean *Banks*. He can sweet-talk anyone. Besides, he's becoming a pro at writing donation checks."

Miguel laughed. "He's going to love this."

∾ FOURTEEN ∾

Sabine stood on the launch deck of the *Divemaster* less than a week later, blown away by what true wealth could do. What if everyone who'd somehow amassed a personal fortune used theirs for the benefit of others, like Archer did?

To secure use of a DSV from Woods Hole Oceanographic Institution on her own would have taken her years of grant writing, which would have required support from top quality research papers with far more promising results as initial proof than she currently had. Even if by some miracle she could have made it that far, it might have taken another couple of years to assemble a qualified team and book their field time, which would have been extremely limited.

Probably less than the length of time she'd already spent on the *Divemaster*.

Which meant they might have failed, walked away from whatever was waiting for them below the surface. And after so much time had passed—five years minimum—maybe whatever it was Heinrich had found would have moved on or disappeared forever.

This had to work. She would never have a better opportunity than this.

Miguel stood shoulder to shoulder with her as someone from the DSV's permanent crew trained them on how to pilot the personal submarine. "Honestly, it's unbelievably simple. You just use the joystick. If you've ever played videogames, you're probably set."

"Dibs on driving," Miguel said to her.

"Fine with me." She figured she'd be too busy gawking at their surroundings to be of much use in that department.

"I'll also have redundant controls," the sub crewman told them. "I can handle things from the surface if you aren't comfortable once you're down there. I'll also be backup in case something breaks on your dashboard. This is a shallow mission for this kind of vehicle. A walk in the park compared to some of the places we've visited, like the Mariana Trench. I'll essentially be able to see everything you see and can even operate the collection arms and the slurp gun, which will suck up specimens without harming them. So if you prefer, I can take over and you can just sit back and enjoy the ride."

They both nodded at that, glad for the support.

"I can't believe we're really going to do this," Sabine murmured to Miguel.

"I know. It's going to be one of the top ten most amazing things I've ever done in my life." Leaning in closer he whispered, "Right up there with fucking you."

Sabine rolled her eyes.

"Do that again and I'll have you over my knee in the clubroom later. I'm not joking." He kissed her temple, then returned his attention to the researcher. "So when can we be ready to go?"

"Frankly, anytime." He shrugged. "We've checked the launch area and conditions are ideal today. Calm and clear. You don't have to worry about racing the daylight since you're going deep anyway."

"I don't want to wait." Sabine had a nagging sense that they were running out of time.

"Let's give the rest of the crew a one-hour warning." Miguel asked, "Will that work?"

Sabine and the DSV handler both nodded.

Fifty-nine minutes later, Captain Alex had brought the ship into position. Banks, Tosin, Waverly, and Archer were on the sidelines of the launch deck lending moral support. Sabine had come to think of them not only as Miguel's friends, but as her own also.

Their guests lined the rails on the decks above, curious about the unusual addition to today's agenda. With so many eyes on her, Sabine felt the pressure building.

Rather than stand there and let it ramp up her apprehension, she wandered over toward Tosin and patted his back. "It's killing you not to get to play with it, isn't it?"

"I think if you need to make another trip under, you should rotate your assistants for fresh eyes." He'd been trying for days to weasel into a mission.

"Fair enough." She smiled up at him. "But you have to tell Miguel."

"Tell me what?" He joined them, having finished the last of his briefings with the ship's staff.

"I'm getting a turn in that thing one way or another." Tosin grinned. "Don't make me resort to joyriding in the middle of the night. You know I will."

Banks closed his eyes and shook his head. "I have no desire to deal with that much paperwork."

Sabine found herself laughing, completely at ease within seconds. More each day, she felt she belonged here. With them. What happened in the next couple of hours would likely change her life forever, one way or another.

She hoped it ended up for the better.

"Dr. Reynolds, we're set!" the DSV crew lead called to her.

Banks stepped forward first, hugging each of them. Waverly, Archer, and even Tosin followed suit. He crushed her in his embrace. "Have a safe trip."

"Thank you." Her throat tightened, making anything else she might have said impossible to get out.

Hand in hand, she and Miguel approached the DSV, which looked like a giant glass bubble with canary-yellow legs, almost cartoony in its odd proportions. They climbed in, Miguel first to give him more room, then her. When the hatch was closed and locked behind them, she jumped.

"Things are starting to feel pretty damn real, huh?" Miguel looked at her, reading her reaction.

"Yeah." She hoped he knew she counted their growing connection in that agreement.

They strapped in to the bucket seats and waited for the crane to lift them over the edge. Miguel held her hand as the countdown commenced over the radio.

"Three...two..."

And then they were freefalling a dozen or so feet into the ocean, where they landed with a sploosh worthy of a blue whale doing a belly flop.

Sabine cheered even though her stomach had executed some Olympic-level flips in the process. Miguel hooted right along with her as bubbles skated in front of the submarine's viewing window.

She had come to accept that it would be like this for them. Even in the midst of one of the most important expeditions of her career, he was there with her. A part of it, fully engaged. And if he was there, that meant they were going to enjoy each other and the time they spent together while they could.

It didn't mean she cared less about her work.

It meant she cared more about him.

"I take it from that reaction that you're both fine after entry?" the DSV's crewleader asked.

"Yes!" Sabine shouted, somewhat breathless from the rush.

"Beginning descent," he droned, taking things much more seriously than they were. She was glad someone responsible was watching their backs. In truth, there wasn't much for them to do except hang on and peer out the window, looking for who-knew-what.

They'd agreed to start their quest at the site called Edge of the World since the notch in the back wall of Molokini was well known for casting shadows on itself; that meant it existed in perpetual darkness. From there they would comb the wall. If they still hadn't found anything, they'd zigzag out to the trench.

With a maximum bottom time of ten hours, they started checking off squares on the search grid. For the most part, there was a lot of not much to be seen.

Humpback whales were common in this part of the ocean, though not typical at this time of year. Sabine couldn't imagine staring through their bubble into the giant eye of a creature that size. Especially not one as intelligent as a whale. That would be a treat in itself.

A few bluefin trevallys buzzed past on the hunt for smaller, unsuspecting fish. They also spotted a giant barracuda and a couple of white-tipped reef sharks in the distance. But none of the corals here were different than the ones they'd already studied.

They took their time, collecting a half-dozen samples just to be sure before moving deeper.

As the light continued to fade, Sabine started to lose faith.

There weren't any deep-sea corals known to live in this area. They were going to look anyway.

The DSV followed the crack in the cliff deeper, deeper, deeper.

Back on the *Divemaster*, Tosin barked out their depth in hundreds of feet. They kept ticking away. Thinking of the weight of the entire ocean pressing in around them caused her breath to come in short blasts.

"It's okay." Miguel squeezed her hand. "You heard the expert. This thing is designed to go way deeper than this."

She nodded. "It just seems so...desolate down here. I know it's not. There are squid and microorganisms, and who knows what else. Compared to where we've been diving for the past month, though, it's like night and day."

"And even this is probably teeming with life compared to some of the vast expanses of uncharted territory in some places of the world. Sometimes I get the feeling people think the entire ocean is like the parts they see right offshore. Maybe if more of them realized the density of wildlife is actually disproportionally dispersed, they would think twice about taking so much from the sea unsustainably."

Sabine completely agreed.

"We're nearing the bottom," Miguel said, partially for their friends back on the *Divemaster*, as he read the radar screen. It had taken them more than four hours to get there. Not because they couldn't have gone faster if they'd taken a direct route, but because they'd been working along the whole cliff face, determined not to miss a thing.

"Are my eyes catching reflections from the instruments on the viewing window again or do you see..." She squinted, trying to make sense of the faint bluish glow coming from below them.

It got more intense by the second.

"It's not you." Miguel sat forward, peering beneath the DSV as best he could.

She flipped through the various camera feeds on the display embedded in the dashboard until she found the one she was looking for. And when she did, Sabine could only stare in shock.

"What *is* that?" she whispered.

Miguel replied, "My best guess would be some sort of bioluminescent algae that uses an internal chemical reaction to create light. It seems to be concentrated on those rocks over there."

He guided the research vessel closer to the phenomenon. Over the radio, people back on the *Divemaster*—researchers and boat staff alike—were losing their minds. Gasps and shouts, even some clapping, were clearly audible over the speakers.

As they approached, Sabine detected a shimmer in the water and the DSV's sensors noted an increase in temperature.

"There's a good-sized hydrothermal vent down here." Miguel came to the same conclusion she did at precisely the same time.

And still Sabine sat there, unblinking, unmoving. She didn't make a peep.

"Why aren't you freaking out right now? Jumping up and down or screaming?" he asked. "Something."

"Because I'm scared." She tried not to let him see the tears that began to stream down her cheeks. Of course he noticed, and wiped them away. He focused on her while she kept looking at the flickering lights that danced before them.

"Of what?" He rested his non-driving hand on her thigh.

"If this isn't what Heinrich was working on, I can't imagine what the hell it might have been." After a month of false hope and disappointment, she wasn't sure she could believe again or survive another disappointment.

Miguel was silent for a moment as they both stared, in awe of the bizarre environment almost no one else had ever witnessed. Except maybe Heinrich. Fairly certain he'd somehow been in precisely this spot, she felt closer to his memory. At times like these she was reminded how little humanity understood about the place they called home. She hoped they could figure out the critical stuff before they ruined it.

Gears whirred and the teams above began using remote operations to gently collect their samples. While they worked, she started scribbling observations in her journal.

She noted that the edges of the glowing algae bed didn't seem quite as vibrant as the rest. Die off seemed to have shrunk the mass of algae by as much as a third recently enough that she could tell where it had once reached. With rising ocean temperatures, increasing pollution, and the introduction of radioactivity from the Fukushima nuclear disaster not *too* far from here on an oceanic scale, who knew what kind of undiscovered organisms were on the verge of extinction?

If this one turned out to be some miracle cure for one of the most prevalent diseases on their planet, could they harvest enough to start growing it in a lab? What if the rest of this colony disappeared before they could figure how to maintain the conditions it needed to thrive?

To have discovered a solution to the cancer crisis only to have it slip away...that would be a catastrophe.

Sort of like if you'd fallen completely in love with a man then had to give him up.

Miguel sat still, letting her process her thoughts as if he felt as reverent as she did in this moment. After a few minutes, the machines beneath them fell quiet.

They had what they'd come for.

Finally, she turned toward Miguel. He deserved her honesty. "I'm also terrified that this might be the thing we've been searching for. If it is...then what? Where does that leave us?"

He shushed her. "We'll figure it out."

What did that even mean?

How could she be involved in the years of research and development it would take to turn a raw material into a viable drug without either leaving Miguel or forcing him to abandon his own fulfilling life's work?

Neither of them would be happy if they sacrificed their careers for the other.

"Come here." He released her harness and tugged until she'd landed in his lap. It was a tight squeeze, but manageable.

Miguel put his arms around her then kissed her. "For now, let's celebrate the incredible things we've seen together already. Who gets a chance like this?"

"To discover something groundbreaking?" she clarified.

Is this what Jonas Salk had felt like when he cured polio? Or Louis Pasteur when he'd developed a vaccine for rabies? To think that someday people might remember Heinrich—or maybe even her and Miguel—like one of those pioneers blew her mind.

"No, *lindeza*. The chance to have sex in a sub." He grinned. "If Tosin thought he was jealous before, wait until that sucker finds out we joined the mile deep club."

⌁ FIFTEEN ⌁

Sabine filled their tiny space with peals of her laughter. While Miguel loved the sound of it, he hadn't been kidding in the slightest. From the pad in front of him, he peeled off a sticky note and put it over the lens of the interior cabin camera.

"What are you doing?" Sabine asked, her eyes growing even wider than they'd been when she'd spotted the glow of the blue algae.

"I told you. I'm about to fuck you in a sub. Going deep has never sounded so good." He winked. "So hike up that skirt and let's see just how flexible you are. There's not a lot of room to spare here but I think we can get the job done."

Before she could protest, Miguel tapped the transmit button on the radio and said, "Surface control, we're having a minor glitch. Could you take the wheel for a minute?"

"Yeah, I see we just lost a camera, too. All other systems are green light, though. I've got you covered. Don't panic." The operator's cool, professional tone only made what they were about to do more illicit and a little risky.

If his cock hadn't already been hard, it would have pumped up in a hurry with that added edge of rebelliousness.

He thought he might have to persuade Sabine, but he should have known better. She'd already started squeezing around instruments to orient herself properly in his lap, willing and eager to join him on yet another adventure. Hopefully, he could make it good for her.

"Sorry, we don't have more than a couple minutes at most." He unzipped his shorts and took out his cock.

Sabine kissed him as she put one knee on either side of his thighs, careful not to squash his balls in the process of contorting herself into a position that would allow her to ride him. Miguel put two fingers up, letting her suck on them to get them nice and wet.

When he shoved the crotch of her panties aside and rubbed them against her pussy, he found he hadn't needed to. She was already slick.

"Damn, *lindeza.*" He kissed her neck alongside his necklace, which was conveniently at mouth level.

"Yeah. I guess playing explorer turns me on. Who knew?" She let her head fall back so that he could lick and nip the sensitive spot below her ear. The motion turned her hair into golden streamers, making his hands itch to twist it up and use it to tug her onto his waiting shaft.

So he did.

Unlike the long, drawn-out lovemaking they'd indulged in most nights, this was something different. Fast and hard. Kind of desperate. It was everything he felt at the moment, knowing her time with him might be drawing quickly to a close.

Sabine guided his cock, angling it so that she could take as much as possible given their cramped quarters. She fit him to her opening then dropped, burying him several inches deep in a single thrust. She cried out, and not entirely in pleasure.

"Slow down." He held onto her waist, keeping her from impaling herself farther.

She shoved at him, bearing down and taking him bit by bit. "No. It's fine. Kind of hurts, but I like it."

He rewarded her honesty with a flex of his ass and abs, driving upward even as she sank some more. Sabine gasped. Her hands landed on his shoulders, clinging to him as she began to raise and lower herself, screwing him deeper within her pussy with every swing of her hips.

Having her on top, setting her free to use him to bring herself pleasure, had its perks. He settled back and enjoyed the view: Sabine, the rarely seen landscape, and the glimmering illumination provided by the algae decorating the rocks along the seabed.

It was almost otherworldly, this experience.

Miguel let his head rest against the seat and Sabine took advantage, leaning forward to kiss him. He let her have anything she wanted from him. Everything she could take.

She rode him hard enough that the sub rocked slightly. He found the motion comforting, arousing even. On the open seas or under them, with her was where he'd always like to be.

When her pussy began to tighten around him, he knew this moment couldn't last forever.

"Rub your clit," he rasped. "I'm not coming without you."

Watching her manipulate herself while using his cock to get off was one of the hottest things he'd ever seen. He clenched his jaw and waited for the telltale clamp of her muscles and the soft mewling sounds she made as she got close to orgasm.

He could listen to that on constant repeat.

"That's right, *lindeza*," Miguel urged her, thrusting upward with short jabs as her own motions became jerky and erratic. "Concentrate on the pleasure. Feel me inside you."

Sabine's eyes flew open then. She stared right into his as she surrendered to the passion they generated together. He crushed his lips over hers as she moaned and came, slathering his cock with her release.

His body reacted in turn, feeding off of her ecstasy.

Come launched from his balls in several long, violent blasts that relieved the ache in his groin, but made him more aware of the one in his heart.

It wouldn't matter what end of the earth he searched—how high the mountains he climbed or how deep the oceans he scanned—he'd never find another woman like Sabine.

No one else could do this to him.

Miguel kissed her softly, smiling as she recovered enough to lift off of him and resituate herself on her side of the DSV. He checked his watch. It wasn't often he was proud of getting the job done in less than two minutes.

This was one of them.

Hey, a great fuck was a great fuck, no matter how long it took. He held his hand up to Sabine and she returned his high five. After zipping up, he leaned forward and pressed the radio transmit button. "Hello? Can you hear us?"

"Loud and clear," Captain Alex answered.

"Sorry, must have had some technical difficulties there for a few minutes. We've got what we need and are beginning our ascent now."

The captain coughed to cover what sounded like a chuckle. "That might be easier to believe if Sabine's ass hadn't been planted on the transmitter while you were nailing her, kid. Sounded like a helluva lot of fun, though. Now get back here before something really does break and we have to haul you out."

Miguel burst out laughing. He wasn't about to apologize. Anyone else would have done the same thing in his place. Sabine, even with her cheeks now flaming, was gorgeous and supremely fuckable.

"Thanks for the Sub Fucking 101 advice. See you on the surface." This time Miguel was careful to take his hand completely away from the radio when he spoke privately to Sabine. "Sorry about that."

She shrugged, surprisingly okay with being busted. "I guess the past month has made me realize that doing your job well and having fun are in no way mutually exclusive."

"Very true. I've always loved being a divemaster. I'd do it for free if I had to." Miguel practically *had* done it for free for years. Living simply hadn't bothered him in the least.

"You were meant for this. You belong here." She smiled sadly then looked out their giant bubble window.

He didn't like the sound of that. "I'm starting to think that I belong wherever you are."

"Don't, Miguel." She shook her head. "We haven't made any promises to each other for a reason."

"I guess." He hated it, but she was right about that.

That didn't mean he didn't wish they could. Or wish that they were in a position where things would work out if they did.

"This would be a pretty baller way to propose to someone, though." He tossed it out there casually, as if he wasn't pissed that he didn't have a ring in his pocket to give Sabine right then. Maybe if he had, he would've been able to talk her into staying before the realities waiting for them back on the surface crashed over them with the destructive force of a tsunami.

Hopefully it wouldn't wipe out the progress they'd made or the bond they'd formed so far.

He didn't place very good odds on that when she didn't respond at all.

They spent the rest of the return journey holding hands, but in silence.

~ SIXTEEN ~

Sabine stood in her makeshift laboratory, which had never been this crowded before. Besides herself, Miguel, Tosin, Archer, Waverly, Banks, and Captain Alex, a couple people from WHOI packed like sardines into the space. Plus, her laptop was open. Marta's head floated on the screen as she joined them remotely.

No pressure.

She'd worked in a few of the top facilities in the world, but nothing would ever replace this nook of the *Divemaster* as her favorite place to work. So she had mixed emotions about what she was hoping for as she watched seconds ticking by on her stopwatch.

"This is as bad as waiting on a damn pregnancy test," Waverly muttered from beside her. "Staring at that indicator trying to convince yourself you see lines, or don't see lines, depending. I'll stick to flying, thanks."

Sabine laughed and turned to her friend. "At least I didn't pee on myself. Well, I haven't yet anyway. We'll see when these results—"

DING!

That simple sound nearly stopped Sabine's heart. She froze. Everyone stared at her.

"Go ahead, *lindeza*." Miguel nudged her toward the sample.

She prepped the slide and took it to the microscope. Before she looked through it, she scanned the room. Banks flashed her a thumbs-up. Optimism. Hope. Unwavering support. They radiated positivity and encouragement.

Marta especially. If she could be strong enough to do this, Sabine had to live up to that standard. She drew a deep breath then put her face against the eyepiece. It took a second to bring the specimen into focus.

When she did...

Sabine thought she might pass out. She gripped the countertop as if it were the only thing holding her upright then looked again. And a third time, just to be sure.

If she hadn't prepared the sample herself, she wouldn't have believed what she saw.

Not only had the cancerous cells been destroyed, but the healthy tissue appeared completely intact, something modern medicine hadn't been able to master after decades of research. Until now.

No. Until a few months ago, when Heinrich had seen this very same thing. She was sure of it.

Sabine couldn't hold her emotions in check another moment. She lost it. Completely. Though she wasn't normally the kind of person to burst into tears, she did it for the second time that day.

She cried so hard she couldn't breathe.

Miguel raced to her side and held her tight. "It's okay, Sabine. We'll try again. There are more samples to test."

"No—" She couldn't get more out than that.

"I'll search every ocean on Earth with you if that's what it takes. We'll do this. Together." He held her tighter, breaking her heart more with every amazingly kind word he spoke. Because she knew she wouldn't be able to commit to him in the face of what she'd just seen.

"Miguel, stop," she begged.

As if he was thinking of their time in the clubroom like she was, he didn't say another word. Instead, he peered down at her, waiting.

"It worked."

"What's happening?" Marta asked from the laptop. "Is Sabine okay?"

"Are you serious?" Either Sabine was shaking hard enough to move them both or Miguel was trembling along with her.

She nodded. "It's...incredible."

Miguel put his hands around her ribs, his thumbs below her breasts, and lifted her high above his head. He spun her around and around, then shouted, "You did it!"

When he put her down, everyone surged forward, encapsulating them both in one giant group hug. Through the ruckus, she heard Marta thanking some nameless entity in German.

"*I* didn't do it. Heinrich did." Sabine would be diligent about making sure any credit for the discovery was correctly attributed to him.

"Don't short yourself. You didn't have to pursue this. You could have quit after the string of failures. But you didn't." Miguel took her shoulders in his hands then and stared directly into her eyes so that she couldn't dismiss what he was saying. "I'm honored to be able to say that the woman I love did something so impressive. Something that will improve millions of lives. I'm proud of you, Sabine."

"Wait, what did you say?" She blinked up at him.

"That I'm in awe of your accomplishments? How could you possibly doubt that?" he wondered.

"I don't." Her eyes were filling with tears yet again. After this she'd get her shit together, she swore.

Tosin helped out. "She's talking about the part where you admitted that you love her. Although, it's not exactly a secret, is it? We figured that out a while ago."

Archer and Waverly were beaming at them and Banks nodded softly to himself, as if he wholly approved of Miguel's choice.

"Me too." Miguel kept dropping weights on Sabine—good and bad, good and bad—balancing the scales between elation and heartbreak. "From the moment I spotted her trudging through the airport, on her way to do what was right despite her broken heart, I knew on some level that I wanted a person like that in my life."

"I appreciate how much you've given me during this time. How you kept me going even on the toughest days." She hugged him tight.

"So what do we do now?" He asked the question she'd been dreading since they'd seen the blue shimmer in the deep. "It seems like we need to make some kind of announcement. Call CNN. Something like that. Right?"

"No!" Marta shouted at the same time Banks did, as if they were parents scolding a child playing too close to a busy road.

Sabine cringed. "I'm not sure that's wise. Heinrich kept this a secret—even mostly from me since he didn't trust communications to be secure—for a reason. He was the smartest person I've ever met. That explosion in his lab was no accident. I'm sure of it now. What we have here is practically priceless. I think we need to protect ourselves before making any public disclosures."

"I think that's best." Marta backed Sabine up, a hint of fear in her declaration.

"Then considering how late it already is here, and that it's the middle of the night in most of the rest of the country, maybe we should go celebrate then figure out our next steps in the morning." Archer stirred everyone up when he announced, "Champagne is on the way!"

A few hours later, after indulging in one glass more than it took to make her dizzy, Sabine craved the quiet, softly lit interior of the cabin she shared with Miguel.

"Ready to head to bed?" he asked.

"Mmm." She practically purred.

"Not like that." He laughed and kissed the tip of her nose. "I think you've had a little too much to drink."

Sabine pouted.

"Besides, I hope you don't mind but I kind of want to enjoy some quiet time with you."

Before you leave me.

He didn't say that last part. They both knew it was hanging there in the air between them anyway.

"Let's go." Sabine took his hand. She gladly accepted hugs, kisses, and cheers from each of the remaining people in her laboratory as the party dissolved along with the exit of the guest of honor. After she'd made her rounds, they strolled to their quarters, stripped at the door, and practically fell into bed.

After a slightly awkward silence, Miguel blurted, "What if I come with you?"

"Huh?" Sabine sat up, crossing her legs.

"You're going to need to file patents, do clinical trials, give lectures, and whatever other junk I don't even know about. You'll need a real lab and a home base that's not always moving or in some remote, unreachable place. But the only thing I need is you."

She tried to respond a few times and couldn't find the right way to say what she was thinking. "I'm not sure that you belong in my world, Miguel."

He jerked as if she'd slapped him. "The fuck I don't. I might not have ever made it to college, but I've learned all about you. Enough to know we fit together. In the morning, I'll show you just how well. I'll make it impossible for you to deny."

"It's not always about sex, Miguel." She tried to explain what she'd truly meant. "Of course, I don't disagree. That's the best I've ever had. Ever will have, I'm sure. And while I have no doubt you could fit in where I'm from, *this* is where you belong. With Archer and Tosin, diving all the time."

"I think I should get to decide that for myself," he insisted.

"Except that I've already thought about this a million different ways, Miguel." She tensed, her buzz rapidly disappearing. "I can't be your everything. I can't replace your beloved ocean. And when you're unhappy, locked with me in the glaring lights of a lab instead of the warm rays of the sun, you'll start to resent me from taking you away from your first love. I won't do that to you, Miguel."

"What you're doing by leaving me behind is worse," he snapped. Already proving her point. This wasn't how she wanted things between them to be. It was better to remember the perfect times they'd shared already than to ruin those memories with a bitter breakup.

Sabine hung her head, defeated.

"Hey, I'm sorry." Miguel put his hand on her shoulder and rubbed his thumb back and forth across the bare skin there. "I'm certain I don't want to spend whatever time we have together right now arguing."

She raised her hand across her body to her shoulder and squeezed his fingers. "Me either."

"So come here and let me hold you. We can worry about the rest tomorrow, after we've slept on things and have clear heads." He pulled her backward, so she didn't fight, tumbling to the bed they'd shared for a while now.

It was one of the very few times they didn't fool around before calling it a night. Cuddling with Miguel, listening to his breathing slow down and even out, relaxed her even if it filled her with profound grief. Because she could already clearly see her path, and it led far away from here, from him, and from the *Divemaster*.

From everything she'd come to love.

∽ SEVENTEEN ∽

Sabine tossed and turned. Despite Miguel's heat and hardness beside her, she couldn't quiet her mind long enough to drift off. She'd even found out that he snored, if lightly. Every other night she'd spent by his side she'd been well and truly unconscious—exhausted from the physical demands of diving and the mental burden of stress. Plus she'd been under the influence of a solid afterglow, which made a phenomenal biochemical sleep aid.

After what felt like an hour or two of torturing herself—the thing she wanted most within arm's reach and still totally unattainable—she swung her legs over the side of the mattress and sighed.

For a while longer, she watched Miguel sleep. Even unconscious he was one hell of a man—built, handsome, and surprisingly trusting given his upbringing. She thought of all the times he'd called her beautiful and figured he had that one wrong. *He* was the gorgeous one—inside and out—though he probably wouldn't appreciate her assessment if she shared it with him.

She kissed her fingers then pressed them lightly to his lips before rising.

His discarded *Got Air?* T-shirt draped over the desk chair. She lifted it to her nose and breathed in his scent, maybe crossing the line into creepy stalker territory, but she didn't give a shit. She might not have the chance to do weird stuff like that soon.

Sabine tugged his shirt on. It came nearly to her knees despite her being taller than average. She hugged herself, then slipped from the room with one final glance over her shoulder.

She murmured, "I love you, too, Miguel."

Then shut the door as quietly as possible.

Wandering along the hallway while most everyone else dreamed, Sabine trailed her fingertips over the shiny exotic woods and took time to really observe each of the art pieces in the crannies she'd strode past daily. Suddenly she had the desire to slow down and soak it all in.

Say goodbye.

Eventually, Sabine found herself reclining on one of the dive bay benches. She could see hints of Miguel everywhere. The neatly wrapped hoses he coiled just so. His wetsuit hanging up to dry outside his locker. The heart Tosin had drawn around her and Miguel's names on the whiteboard they used to record their dive plans for the day.

Would she be erased from the *Divemaster* as easily as her name could be wiped from that surface? Would Miguel start fresh with some new guest as soon as she had moved on?

Sabine slapped her hand on her thigh then continued her slow-motion tour, stepping into her laboratory. She flicked on the lights and came face to face with a man dressed entirely in black.

"Holy shit!" She recoiled, grasping her chest. By the time her synapses began firing enough to scream for her to make a run for it, it was too late.

The intruder wrapped one arm around her upper chest and put his hand over her mouth. "I thought you would never get up. Saved me a trip inside, though—thanks."

Sabine didn't have any formal training in self-defense. She had never been in the military like Waverly. But she had learned to fend for herself at an early age. More importantly, she had already been in the kind of mood that made her appreciate someone to punish.

Raw anger seeped from her every pore. She snarled and gnashed her teeth, biting the bastard's hand, hard. At the same time, she thrashed. Flailing elbows and knees and heels might not have been artfully aimed. They were, however, fueled by some of the most brutal emotions she'd ever experienced.

One of her wild stabs connected with something soft and hopefully really sensitive. Her attacker doubled over, letting her go. Sabine dashed through the door.

And was met with three more guys as sinister looking as the first.

Fuck.

She drew in a huge breath, ready to scream at the top of her lungs for help when one of the intruders stepped forward and jabbed a needle in her neck, directly into some major blood vessel. It was hard to say which because the world grew wobbly and unfocused almost immediately.

Sounds distorted, and she dropped to the deck boards.

The men were professional enough to get right to business, ignoring her for the most part. They began to trash the laboratory as she tried to orient herself and crawl to stop them from causing any irreparable damage to her equipment or her test result cultures.

Sabine wished she could do anything to delay them. From her spot on the ground she could see the security cameras Banks had installed overhead after they'd returned from their date day on Maui. Who was watching? Would someone be coming to save her even if it was too late for her samples?

She tried again to shout. Or stand. Or...do anything but slump uselessly on the floor.

It was pointless. Her arms and legs weren't cooperating with her brain's scrambled directives. And her disorientation only worsened by the second.

Glass shattered, computers were smashed, and when they'd done their worst, they lit the entire thing on fire. The initial whoosh of the flames singed her brows, filling her nose with the acrid smell of burning hair.

"Time to go," one of the men said as he hauled her up by her hair.

"What the fuck is going on here?" a familiar voice roared a moment before Tosin charged into view.

No! Sabine screamed, though only in her mind. Her mouth had stopped working.

Though he was a total badass, he couldn't possibly fend off the men now crawling over the dive bay like a pile of bristleworms. When he realized how serious these guys were, and that some shouting and bright lights weren't about to chase them off, he swung around to a supply cabinet. When he withdrew his hands he held an air horn in one and a multi-shot flare gun in the other.

He'd done a hell of a lot better than her in the thinking on his feet department.

Her vision blurred further. Still, she managed to get the gist of his attack when the air horn rent the night. Hopefully it would also draw more help. When the disposable can was empty, he threw it at one of the guys he was fighting off. The attacker stumbled, but kept coming.

Next, Tosin leveled the signal gun at one of the men charging him and fired. *BANG! BANGBANG!*

That took care of a few guys. More took their places.

Right about then the fire alarms began to wail. The suppression system that kicked in wouldn't do her laboratory any good. Everything was already ruined.

But things only got worse when Miguel charged into the fray.

If Tosin had thought on his feet, using the tools around him, Miguel operated on pure testosterone and fury. He pummeled his opponents with his fists in a sequence of altercations that had her head spinning even more.

Sabine got as far as her knees, trying to reach him, when someone kicked her in the ribs, putting her down and out once more. He got right in her face and screamed, "Tell us where the stuff is! We've looked all over this damn place for months. Where the fuck is it?"

She couldn't have answered if she wanted to. Her tongue was a brick in her mouth.

"I think you gave her too much of that shit," the man snarled, then picked her up. "We'll have to take her with us if we want answers."

Oh fuck no.

Blackness encroached on Sabine's vision. She fought, but nothing happened. Except that they toted her to the dive platform and tossed her onto a waiting speedboat below.

From her new position she couldn't see Miguel. She sure as shit heard him, though, as he fought his way to her. With one last effort, she managed to groan and lurch toward him.

"Knock his ass out and take him too," someone said. "That's her boyfriend. He'll be useful for making her talk."

It didn't take long before Miguel had been overpowered, completely outnumbered.

When he hit the bottom of the boat beside her, blood trickling down his face, his eyes open, she freaked the fuck out. Was he dead? Had they killed him because of her?

She could never forgive herself for that.

Sabine slumped slightly in his direction, ecstatic that her jarring motion roused him if only enough for him to groan and prove that he was alive.

Men leapt onto the boat, surrounding them.

From the *Divemaster*, Sabine thought she heard Captain Alex shouting orders. Soon it was impossible to tell over the noise the engine made when the bad guys opened up the throttle and drove them through the night to some unknown hellhole.

⚮ EIGHTEEN ⚮

Miguel paced the brig of whatever pirate ship he'd been stashed on. He only got in a couple steps before he had to turn around, but sitting there doing nothing had been driving him insane. Especially when he could see Sabine, crumpled on the floor of the cell across the hall, but couldn't reach her. She hadn't responded to any of his shouts either.

Please, let her be alive.

From the time he burst into the dive bay and was greeted by flames, things had been kind of a blur, but he thought he'd seen her watching him as he took out as many of the intruders on the *Divemaster* as he could. Unfortunately it hadn't been enough, and by the time he came to, in this damn prison cell, he had no idea what had happened past then, or what those bastards had done to Sabine.

The only thing giving him hope at the moment was that she was far more valuable alive, given her knowledge of Heinrich's operations and the methodology he used for his experiments. Then again...why had they burned her lab?

He didn't have to wait long to find out.

Some surprisingly normal-looking dude in a crisp shirt and well-tailored slacks approached their cells. He smiled at Miguel then barked orders to two of the hired muscles that followed a few steps behind. "Wake her up. We don't have much time. Those bastards on the megayacht are going to have the authorities here soon. It has to be done before they arrive."

Miguel could only imagine that their lives were about to go from bad to worse, but he still thanked every power in the universe that Sabine was still alive.

One of the goons opened her cell then reached inside. He kicked her.

Miguel roared and slammed his shoulder into the barred door of his cage. He knew it wouldn't do any good, but he couldn't overrule the primal part of his brain from insisting that he act on her behalf. They would pay for that.

When Sabine grunted and tried to fight back, though sleepily, a flare of pride rose in Miguel. Even under the influence of potent drugs, she was a fighter. They might still have a chance at escaping if they kept calm. A slim chance…

"This one could be some fun. Can we have her when you're done with her?" the guard taunted, staring at Miguel as he asked the boss.

"I may keep her for myself," he answered, also trying to read Miguel's expression.

He made it simple for them by flashing his middle fingers.

If they gave him a chance, he'd do a lot more than that.

Before things could deteriorate even further, Sabine came alert enough to cry out for him. "Miguel!"

"I'm here, *lindeza*. Stay calm."

She whipped her head toward him then groaned, clutching her skull between her hands. Even with her eyes scrunched closed in pain, she thought of him first. "Are you okay, Miguel?"

"I am now that you're awake," he tried to take his own advice and stay calm for her.

"How sweet." The man in charge gave a fake *awww*. Then he commanded his goon, "Get her up."

The guy grabbed for Sabine, latching on to her necklace. He snatched it in his meaty fist then yanked, choking her until the strands snapped.

"No!" Sabine fought like the wildcat she was then, landing a bunch of slaps and scratches before the guard subdued her, flinging her to the floor with a sickening *thud*.

"That's enough!" the well-dressed man shouted.

"Who are you? Why are you doing this?" Sabine asked as she got to her feet.

"Don't worry about that." He smiled. "Just worry about making your life something other than a living hell. You can do that by telling me where exactly you found the blue algae."

"Fuck you." Sabine spit at him.

Miguel winced even before the guard now inside her cell backhanded her. He rattled his cage door, bruising his fists as he pounded on the steel.

"Let's try this another way." The man jerked his chin toward Miguel and the second brute unlocked his door. Though he tried to rush the man, it didn't matter. There was nowhere for him to go and the guy was prepared. Soon they were both inside.

Miguel lunged at him. Still sluggish from whatever had given him the giant knot on the back of his head, he couldn't grab the guy before he landed a few solid punches that might have permanently changed the shape of Miguel's jaw.

Worse, the dude shook his fist then shoved it beneath his jacket and drew a gun. He pointed the thing straight between Miguel's eyes. Livid or not, he wasn't stupid. He stopped fighting and raised his hands, palms facing out in the universal sign for surrender.

"Would you like to reconsider your answer?" the slick guy asked Sabine.

"What are you going to do if I tell you?" she asked. "Steal it?"

"I guess you could say that." He didn't really answer her.

Miguel narrowed his eyes. What was this guy's angle?

"Don't tell them where it is, Sabine." He crossed his arms. "One life isn't worth it. Not mine."

The lackey in her cage pulled a matching gun to the one held by the guy in his cell and then they were equally threatened.

"Yours might not be." The guy in charge smirked. "But how about hers then?"

"Sabine, no!" Miguel didn't give a fuck about his own personal safety. If he witnessed her death, they might as well shoot him, too.

"Tell me where to find it," the man swiveled toward Sabine and repeated himself. "I have your laptop and your notes from the lab. I'm sure I can find the answer eventually. Help me get there faster, and I'll let your boyfriend go."

"Don't believe him!" Miguel knew how that would end.

The guy aiming his gun between Miguel's eyes didn't take kindly to that. He whacked Miguel in the temple with his gun, making him see stars again as his brain rattled around in his already bruised head.

"I can't watch you die over this, Miguel. Not you, too." Sabine fisted her hands. "He's got everything already. I don't care about glory. Let him publish my work and patent a cancer-fighting drug then sell it for premium prices only the ultra-elite can afford."

She winced at her own worst-case scenario before continuing, "Patents only last so long. It'll be available to the masses within a decade. And you'll be alive to see it."

"Don't," he warned her, until the man in her cage took a step closer and put the barrel of his gun directly against Sabine's head.

"That's really how you want today to end? With her impressive brains splattered across the wall?" the slick man asked. "That can be arranged. But it isn't necessary."

Miguel withered. Despite his instincts, he couldn't take the chance. "Forgive me, Sabine."

She stared, frozen, when he said, "The algae is at the base of Edge of the World. Seven-hundred and twenty-four feet underwater." Then he rattled off the coordinates he knew he'd never forget.

"We're in range still," the goon announced.

"Fire the missiles. Bombard the entire area. Then send the unmanned sub to confirm with photos. I want every last trace of it destroyed," the boss snarled. "If we fuck up this time, it'll be us that ends up swimming with the fishes."

"What?" Sabine looked back and forth between them as if trying to decide if this was some cosmic joke. "You're going to do *what*?"

"Your idea wasn't a bad one." The guy grinned. "However, my plans are much simpler than that. We're here to eliminate the algae and keep you from publishing anything about its existence."

"No!" Sabine shrieked. "Why? Why would you do that?"

"Because the clients I represent have fortunes invested in cancer treatment. Hospitals, equipment, expert doctors, and chemotherapy drugs that do a perfectly fine job of making buckets of money. If there's a cure...all that goes out the window." He frowned. "You're not going to eradicate the source of their income. Ruin their lives. They won't let that happen. You should have learned *that* from your mentor."

"That's ridiculous! What about all the lives it will save?"

She should have saved her breath, Miguel thought. Someone, or *someones*, as evil as this, who were driven by greed and selfishness, would never listen to reason. All the lives in the universe weren't nearly as important as their own financial security.

It didn't matter to them what the body count was so long as they could enjoy their spoils. He'd worked for clients like them sometimes as a divemaster.

Disgusting.

Sabine broke then. She pleaded. Told them she'd help them design other drugs to replace their cash flow. Promised to work for free in exchange for their reconsideration.

Instead, a rumble shook the entire boat.

Everyone froze, in shock or anticipation.

Then one of the goons grinned and relayed the message he'd received through his headset. "It's gone."

Time slowed to a crawl. A million things happened at once.

Sabine screamed. She launched herself at the man in her cage.

At the same time, the guy in Miguel's cell smirked. His trigger finger twitched.

Miguel braced himself.

A gunshot followed.

But not the one that would end his life. The man threatening him, however, wasn't so lucky.

He fell, dead before he hit the floor.

Soldiers, US Navy SEALs, stormed the brig. They captured the boss and as many of his accomplices as they could. Others, they killed. It was over in a matter of seconds.

Miguel rushed across the gap between their cells to Sabine. He cradled her in his arms, trying to quiet her hysterical wails. When he couldn't, he lifted her into his arms and headed for the exit, ignoring the shouts of the soldiers around them, but not before pausing to pluck her ruined necklace from the floor and tucking it into his pocket.

NINETEEN

Back on the *Divemaster*, Sabine sat in a stupor as they were debriefed by a combination of military personnel and her friends. Miguel hadn't left her side for an instant and Tosin had taken a seat on her other side, bracketing her.

"As a decorated pilot, Waverly had some pull when it came to the Navy. Captain Alex had even more. Together they reached out to high-ranking sources and explained the nature of the situation. Though Sabine and Miguel's lives were personally important to us, the recovery of the cancer cure prototype was certainly deserving of government intervention, so we focused on that in our plea for help," Archer explained.

"I appreciate everything you did," she mumbled.

"I wish they'd gotten there ten minutes sooner." He sighed, scrubbing his temples.

Just then the door opened and one of the WHOI staff who was still onboard entered the room. "I'm sorry to confirm that the algae bed is gone. Utterly destroyed. There's nothing left in a quarter mile radius of the site."

Sabine couldn't sit still a moment longer. She rocketed to her feet, frantic to search for any hint of the algae still alive.

"Where are you going, *lindeza*?" Miguel asked. He sounded surprised that even now she couldn't find it in her to quit.

"The lab. Or what's left of it. Maybe there's some residue on my equipment." Refusing to accept the truth, she ran to the dive platform and ducked under the crime scene tape keeping guests out of the fire-damaged area.

She had only one goal—to salvage some scrap of the prototype cure she'd whipped up yesterday and hope she could synthesize it in the lab. Make some artificial version with the same properties. Something. Anything. Even if it wasn't as potent as the original, natural substance, it could still be revolutionary in the fight against cancer.

Sabine stumbled when she saw the extent of the damage. Half-delirious, she staggered toward the ruins of her laboratory.

"Wait!" Miguel called after her. But she didn't.

She pawed through the debris, looking for a test tube, a Petri dish, *anything* that might have even a dot of algae on it. After a few minutes, and several new cuts, fresh blood was all she had to show for her efforts. Just like Heinrich's lab in Germany, her workspace had been leveled.

Now she knew why.

Sabine cursed. Not again. It couldn't all be for nothing.

"Hey, shhh." Miguel refused to back down this time. He bundled her in his arms and physically removed her from the wreckage. "The ocean is a huge place. We will find more. There could be other spots just like it along the channel somewhere. We didn't even look at a fraction of the seabed there."

In her heart, Sabine knew they could look forever. It wouldn't matter because it wasn't there to find. On the verge of losing her mind, she didn't see Banks approaching at first. He called softly to her, getting her attention when he waved her and Miguel over discreetly.

"Come with me, please. I need to show you something." He didn't wait for a response, striding from the room before any of the law enforcement officials could bog him down with requests or start asking too many questions.

They followed him to his office on the bridge of the ship in silence.

Captain Alex stood outside the door, feet spread, arms crossed, and a gun strapped openly to a holster around his waist.

Sabine looked at Miguel. He shrugged, unable to answer the questions assaulting her, but his spine straightened and he tugged her closer. If the captain felt there could still be danger, she trusted the guy. So did Miguel, apparently.

Neither of them could survive another threat like the one they'd lived through. She would never forget the moment she thought she would lose him, and how narrowly they had escaped even more tragedy today.

Banks turned to them and spoke in a whisper that had them huddling close. "When I set up the laboratory, I used the best practice standards of the American Chemical Society, which recommends daily backups."

"You've got copies of my files?" Sabine showed some interest at that, a tiny spark of her former self. "That's great, Banks. But that's not the most important thing. The algae. Without it...all I have is documentation for something that once existed and is now extinct."

She thought she might get sick admitting it.

"The protocols included duplication of files, notes, and office materials. It also specified proper storage of samples in redundant refrigeration units on separate power supplies in case of outages that could spoil entire research projects."

He changed their lives, and the world, with that one admission.

"You're saying you have a tiny bit of the algae preserved?" Sabine looked like a sea otter popping its head out of the water and glancing around, perking right up. "It's scary to work with such a limited resource, running tests and trying to figure out how to culture something we could accidentally annihilate in the process, but if we're careful... Please, tell me you did that."

"I did." He swallowed hard. "But it didn't turn out quite like I thought."

Fuck, how many ups and downs could they go through before they finally gave up? Sabine didn't know if she could handle another blow.

"You're scaring her, Banks." Captain Alex shook his head. "Get to the point."

Banks pointed to the edge of his door. That's when she noticed the faint blue light pulsing around it. "Is that—?"

Sabine rushed forward and flung open the door.

Algae covered every surface in a dripping blue goop.

"Apparently it doesn't mind being out of the water." Captain Alex chuckled. "It busted right through that wine chiller he hides his personal stash in and took over the place."

Globs plopped from the ceiling onto piles forming on the already coated floor.

"If this wasn't the most beautiful thing I have ever seen," Sabine whispered as if in a sacred temple, "it would be totally gross."

Captain Alex and Banks laughed.

Sabine whooped then launched herself at Banks. She kissed him with a giant, noisy smack, full on the lips. "We owe you everything. The *world* owes you."

"Hey, I guarded the door." Captain Alex tapped his toe, as if he could possibly be upset.

Sabine grinned, then treated their captain to the same effusive treatment before flying into Miguel's open arms for a decidedly steamier kiss.

Then, with one lingering glance at their miracle, they closed the door tight.

⌒ TWENTY ⌒

Miguel didn't bother talking to Sabine as they headed to his cabin. There wasn't much to say, nothing to compete with how he felt right then. He lifted her hand to his lips and kissed it a dozen times, though. When they closed the door behind them, safe inside their refuge, she whispered, "In the morning, I have to go. Waverly is coming for me as soon as the private jet is ready to take off."

He nodded once. "I know. However long it takes, I'll be here when you're ready to come back."

Nothing had changed since she'd argued that this was his place.

In his heart, he believed she'd been right. Except that without her, it wouldn't be the same.

From his pocket, he withdrew the broken necklace she'd worn during her stay. He grabbed the small tool kit he used for working on his gear from one of his shelves then plopped into the desk chair to repair it as best he could. In order to reattach the part that had been torn, directly in the center, he used some monofilament he had in his tackle box then drilled a small hole in an unusual shell he'd pocketed on one of their collection dives.

When he'd finished, the shell looked like it had always been there. It dangled from the line that now hung down off the main strand of the necklace and would land somewhere at the top of her cleavage.

He stood, surprised to find her nude, sitting on the edge of the bed behind him, watching.

Miguel smiled as he approached, holding out his gift. She pulled her hair off to the side then lifted her chin, giving him full access to her graceful neck.

"This belongs to you." He fastened the homemade jewelry, hoping it might remind her of him during the long months ahead. "Same as I do."

"I wish I had something to give you in return." She frowned until he kissed the downward curve of her lips.

"All I want is you." He stripped off the shirt and shorts he'd donned in a matter of moments when the fire alarms had roused him earlier. Naked, he leaned down and into her, taking her to her back on their bed.

"You already have that, Miguel." She kissed him tenderly then paused, staring up at him as she promised, "I love you."

His heart seemed to do a backward roll right there in his chest.

"Thank you." She hadn't had to give him that reassurance. In some ways it made things messier, but he was so glad she had. "I love you too, *lindeza*."

He covered her completely then, hoping to impress himself on every inch of her. He entwined their fingers and brought her hands up beside her head before kissing her endlessly. Or for as long as he dared, knowing their time could run out any moment now.

His body moved over hers, reveling in the caress of her skin over his, even as he tried to imprint himself on her. Without taking his hands from her, he glided across her until his cock aligned with her opening.

It took longer than if he'd let go of her to guide himself inside, but he didn't want to do that until he had to. So he used his hips to work himself into her bit by bit. It seemed only fair since she'd done something similar to him, taking up residence in his heart during her time onboard.

Sabine gasped, her mouth opening as she concentrated on the pleasure he imparted.

He took advantage, kissing her, rubbing his lips over hers softly before licking along just the tip of her tongue. The barest of contacts set them both on fire.

Though he tried to drag out their lovemaking for hours, the sense of urgency built fairly quickly. Desperation began to seep from him and it manifested in the driving thrusts of his cock through her clenching rings of muscle.

Sabine's legs shifted, hugging him tight as she prepared to shatter.

And when they came, they came together.

Her pussy milked every drop of come from his balls, holding as much of him as he could give deep within her. Completely empty, he crashed to the mattress and drew her on top of his heaving chest. He wrapped his arms around her and didn't let her go.

Until he had to.

A while later, a knock on the door startled them both. Miguel called out, "Yes?"

"It's time," Waverly answered, reminding him of a guard calling a prisoner to execution. He had to keep reminding himself that this was the opportunity of a lifetime for her and one that would end suffering for millions of people.

A broken heart meant nothing compared to that.

Two broken hearts even.

He kissed Sabine one last time, until the sheen in her pretty eyes receded some. "Ready?"

"No." She stood and dressed then grabbed her purse, not bothering to pack her suitcase. Having her things there would be a comfort to him even if it was an illusion. "But I'm going anyway."

Miguel nodded. "You've got this."

They marched to the helicopter together, as if they were walking the plank.

He was surprised to see not one, but three other choppers circling the *Divemaster* when they got there.

"Uncle Sam is committed to providing security for the trip and in the undisclosed location where they're setting up Sabine's temporary laboratory. She's going to be fine, Miguel," Waverly promised.

He nodded, but it didn't feel *fine*.

Not when her palm was sweaty against his, though her fingers felt like ice.

Brave and glorious, she stood beneath the wash of the propellers, her hair rioting around her. His sea glass and shell necklace made her look like some ocean goddess.

Miguel couldn't possibly have loved her more. He told her so in between kisses, taking one more and one more until there were no one mores left.

Tosin, Archer, Banks, and Captain Alex stood at the edge of the helipad, waving as Sabine climbed into the helicopter. She turned just before shutting the door and said, "I love you, Miguel."

"I love you, too. Until next time..." He lifted his hand to wave. It had been impossible to say goodbye.

"As soon as I can, even if that's years." She winced then blew him and the rest of their little gang kisses before disappearing inside.

He stood on the deck and watched the flock of helicopters as they raced for the shores of Maui and the private jet that would at least ensure her comfort until she got wherever they were taking her.

And then she was gone.

⟋ TWENTY-ONE ⟍

Miguel sat at the long outdoor dining table, pushing food around his plate without any intention of eating the rest of it. Nothing seemed appetizing. Hell, even diving didn't sound very good right now. Maybe Tosin wouldn't mind guiding Miguel's group today.

It took a while, but he finally realized that his friends had stopped talking. They exchanged worried glances over his head. He pretended not to notice. After all, what could he say? That he was fine?

Everyone onboard knew that was a lie.

Tosin broke their silence. "Dude, when are you going to quit moping and go after Sabine?"

"You want me to leave?" It pissed him off after what he'd given up to stay.

"Of course we don't," Banks jumped in then. "But it's clear that being here without her isn't good for you anymore."

Archer and Waverly held hands as they studied him. He hated the pity in their stares. Waverly tried to smooth things over. "I know how you feel. It was hell being apart from Archer. I did it for ten years. Don't recommend it, either. To be perfectly honest, the first few were miserable and the ache never entirely went away. I regret how much time we wasted. None of us want that for you."

"We'll be here when you're ready to come home. *With* Sabine," Archer promised.

"Won't you need another partner? Someone to fill my spot?" He cleared his throat then spoke one of his worst fears aloud. "It could take *years*. Will I have to sell my share in the *Divemaster* so you can keep going without me?"

Now he was glad he hadn't eaten much—otherwise he'd probably be hanging over the railing like a landlubber who hadn't gotten his sea legs yet. Still, they were right. If that's what it took, he'd do it.

Living without Sabine wasn't living at all.

She'd been gone for a month and though they tried to talk every day, the truth was that she was busy with incredibly important things. Given her schedule and the crazy time differences between them, it was tough. He felt like he was losing touch with her.

It'd been three days since she'd even answered his emails.

Maybe she hadn't had nearly as much trouble forgetting about him as he'd had moving on without her. *Shit.*

"Don't be a dumbass." Tosin shoved him. "No one is letting you cash out. You'll come back. Eventually."

Why didn't that do much to make Miguel feel better? Probably because his friend didn't seem hundred-percent confident even as he said it.

He nodded, then tossed his balled up napkin onto his plate. "Okay."

It was time to find his woman, wherever she might be in the world right now.

That turned out to be a far easier task than he'd imagined. When he stood, he noticed a sleek powerboat racing directly toward the *Divemaster*, which was now anchored off the coast of Kauai.

Banks pulled out his cell phone and had someone— probably Captain Alex—on the other line instantly. "Are we expecting visitors?"

They'd gotten jumpy after first Waverly's trouble and then the attack on Sabine. Having people board the *Divemaster* had been an enormous violation, one none of them would forget anytime soon.

"Ah, thank you." Banks was grinning now.

"Who is it?" Archer asked.

But Miguel didn't need to hear the answer. A woman waved from the boat, golden curls flying everywhere. Sabine! She'd come back to him.

He charged across the deck and down the stairs to the landing area, sprinting by the time he made it to the gangway.

Sabine seemed equally ready to be back in his arms. She didn't bother to wait until the boat had finished docking before flying over the edge at him. He smothered her in a bear hug as he carried her onto the boat and deposited her in the midst of their friends.

After stealing several kisses, he said, "I guess I see why you haven't been responding to my messages."

"Sorry, I wanted to surprise you. But there were delays and my luggage got lost and...ugh, you know how it goes when traveling halfway around the world."

"Why wouldn't you have called for the private jet?" Banks asked.

She blinked a few times. "I guess I'm still not quite used to the way you all roll."

"Well, you'd better get used to it." Miguel crushed her to him. "Because I'm not letting go of you again. How long can you stay? I'm going with you when you have to leave."

"What if I want to stay forever?" she asked, making his heart start to pound in his chest.

"Can you do that?" he wondered. "Without jeopardizing the drug development or giving up on your career, I mean? Of course you're welcome for as long as you like."

She kissed him again, as if she needed to reassure herself they were truly together again.

He knew the feeling.

"Maybe?" She shrugged. "It'll take some creativity to make it work, and some traveling, but I was miserable without you, Miguel."

Sabine blushed, as if uncomfortable with admitting it.

"You couldn't have been any more pathetic than this guy." Tosin slapped Miguel on the back.

"I don't know about that." She toyed with his necklace. "Even if I have to make some serious sacrifices, this is where I want to be."

Miguel wrapped her up in his arms again, afraid he might be dreaming about this as he had so many times in the past several weeks.

Banks waited until they had settled down a little before asking, "Where do you stand with everything? If you let me know where you are and what needs to be done still, I'm more than happy to help you in any way. I'm sure if we work together, we can arrange anything you need."

Sabine smiled and crossed to Banks, hugging him as well. "I missed you, too, Banks."

He ruffled her hair as if she were a little girl.

"Well, I'm happy to say they put our patent through on a rush due to the unusual circumstances and whatever you did to motivate them. Once I had it in hand, the very first thing I did was publicly post every scrap of research I had. I plastered every open source science database on the Internet with pictures, descriptions, chemical compounds, trial results. Everything. I figured that's where both Heinrich and I went wrong. Trying to keep it under wraps was pointless. This way, no one can try to steal it or say it doesn't exist or whatever." She winced. "The drug companies that had been fighting over me and the right to produce any future drug that comes of my work are pretty pissed about it, but I don't give a fuck. I'm not taking the chance of anything being lost. That information belongs to the world, not people looking to make a buck. Besides, if it's all out there, there's no reason for people to hunt me anymore, right? They know everything I know. Or at least that's how I figured it."

Archer held out his fist for her to bump. Of course he would approve. It wasn't so dissimilar to what he was trying to do with his inheritance. In fact...

His best friend made the suggestion Miguel had just nearly proposed.

"Look, no pressure or anything, but why not work for the Banks Foundation? We'll pay you ten times whatever the next competitive offer is." Archer waved away her protests. "My only stipulation would be that someday, when the drug is ready, you let us give it away. I want this cure to be available to everyone, everywhere."

Sabine sagged, as if she'd been too afraid to hope for such a blessing. "That's what I was hoping for. It's what Heinrich would have wanted, too, though he might not have had the choice. To fund his research, he would have had to sell rights to a private firm."

"Or maybe the Banks Foundation would have found him— and you—anyway." Banks shrugged. "Life is kind of funny like that sometimes."

Miguel couldn't keep his hands off Sabine. Not because he wanted to fuck her so bad his dick might fall off soon— though he did—but because he couldn't believe everything could go from shit to sugar so fast.

"So I'll start making some arrangements." Banks never seemed to grow tired of providing for them. It truly seemed to make him happy to give them whatever they needed. "I'll start with refitting a section of the lower deck for a proper laboratory. Give me a list later of what improvements you'll require."

"Honestly..." Sabine smiled then. "The algae is remarkably easy to work with. Kind of like the penicillin of the sea. I thought it over on my flights here and I can't imagine anything we couldn't easily get for the ship. Some space, some time, some funding...I've got this."

"What about human trials?" Archer asked. "I realize that could be a while yet, but if we enhance our medical bay, could we do them at sea? Expand the Divemaster Project. I mean, who's more deserving of a vacation than people willing to put their lives on the line for the advancement of science, while hopefully finding a cure for themselves?"

"Wow." She blinked. "I hadn't thought of that yet, but...yes, I don't see why not."

Miguel couldn't believe how amazing she was. He was willing to support her however necessary to guarantee her success. Both for her, and for everyone who would benefit from her work. "And when you need to travel, I'll go with you."

"I would love that." She bit her lip. "There's something else I kind of had you in mind for..."

Tosin cracked up. "Oh, can I guess? Can I guess?"

"Not that." Sabine blushed. "Well, okay, yes...that. But something else."

"How can I help?" he asked.

"As long as I live, I'll never get the feeling of them obliterating that algae bed from my mind." She shuddered.

Miguel drew her close to him and held her tight. "Me either."

"So I think we should start algae farms. Wherever we happen to travel to. It's easy to grow, as Banks found out for us, but I think we should do some research into how to manage it responsibly, without introducing a foreign species to the natural environments. Somehow, though, we need to create contained grow houses or something to give as much redundancy as possible to the supply."

"I'd love to take that on." He started dreaming up systems they could build and implement. Underwater harvest stations that he could service on deep-water technical dives that would challenge him over and over. "Sign me up."

"Perfect! So...about those trips I might have to take on occasion..." Sabine lit up.

"Yeah, you have one planned already?" he asked.

"Nothing concrete." She shook her head as if in disbelief. "But I've been told that if this pans out, I should expect to attend the award ceremonies for the Nobel Prize in Chemistry in a year or two with a speech, prepared to accept since they don't allow posthumous nominations. They said I could talk about Heinrich as much as I wanted, though."

"Whoa." Even Tosin didn't have a smart ass remark for that.

"Yeah." She held her hands out, palms up. "I hope no one will mind if I name the drug after him."

"That's a lovely idea." Banks squeezed her shoulder. "I'm sure Marta will appreciate the gesture. Maybe she'll come check out our operations sometime. And she certainly wouldn't miss such an important day in your life. If it comes to pass, and I have faith it will, I'd volunteer to be her date to the ceremony."

"Subtle, Banks. Reaaal subtle," Tosin teased.

They all laughed. Sabine included. "Hey, leave him alone. I sincerely hope everyone I love finds as much happiness as I have with Miguel. Banks and Tosin, you especially."

"Are you thinking what I'm thinking," Waverly asked Sabine.

"Definitely." They grinned at Tosin. "We should team up to do some matchmaking for our final single divemaster."

"Oh no. *No.*" He waved them off. "I'm perfectly fine living this bachelor life over here. Don't start slinging your relationship cooties on me."

"You don't know what you're missing," Archer promised.

"But when you realize it, we'll gladly say I told you." Miguel punched Tosin's biceps then spun to Sabine. He'd had enough talking for one afternoon.

Now it was time to welcome her home the right way.

He threw her over his shoulder as he had the first time he'd taken her to the clubroom, then marched below deck to make some more memories. The first of many in their new life together.

JAYNE RYLON

NEW YORK TIMES BESTSELLING AUTHOR

GOING HARD

DIVEMASTERS #3

"Jayne can melt the words off your ereader!"
~Guilty Pleasures Reviews

DEDICATION

For everyone who wishes they could travel more.

∽ ONE ∽

Tosin Ellis braced himself against the railing on the uppermost deck of the *Divemaster* megayacht. He tipped his face toward the breeze then drew fresh island air into his lungs until they threatened to pop. He loved the salty tang of the ocean, always would. Yet something about that first scent of earth after weeks surrounded by the sea overpowered his senses. Ripe with flowers and vegetation and rich dirt, it smelled like coming home.

In fact, after a long passage—like the nearly four thousand miles they'd just finished cruising from Midway Island, west of Hawaii, to the Cook Islands, in the BFE neighborhood of the South Pacific—his nose told them land was near before they spotted it on the horizon.

Well, his nose and Captain Alex's trusty GPS, along with the rest of the technology onboard. The bridge of the ship looked like it could easily transport them to Mars and back. Crossing a remote stretch of ocean...*pfft*. No problem.

An approaching boat carrying a welcoming committee drew his attention away from the green lump of Rarotonga on the horizon. The sense of rightness that accompanied the first indications of an approaching shoreline reminded him that although he spent a large portion of his life below the waves, guiding SCUBA divers through a marine paradise, he hadn't yet grown gills or evolved into a merman.

His new life goal.

Hey, he had to dream up something even wilder and crazier to aspire to than "multimillionaire", since Archer Banks had already helped him check that off his bucket list. He shook his head then rubbed his thumbs over the polished wood beneath them. The idea that he co-owned the *Divemaster*, a nearly three hundred foot luxury vessel, along with his two best friends still didn't seem quite real.

It had been about a year since Archer had inherited his father's billions and transformed himself, Tosin, and Miguel from perpetual beach bums into benevolent cruisers who invited deserving people on all-expenses-paid vacations of a lifetime. Together, they made sure their visitors had a great experience while they explored whatever corner of the world the ship happened to occupy at that moment. Maybe someday Tosin would accept that he wasn't dreaming.

He figured he could live and work here forever without growing sick of it. Something he'd never been able to say about a place or a job before.

Right then, though, he had visions of one thing he was lacking: a juicy cheeseburger.

The *Divemaster* had ridiculous amounts of storage compared to a typical yacht, but after the lavish meals the staff had prepared during their voyage, even she had grown light. It took a lot to feed the crew, the owners, and their guests for so long. Especially to their chef's standards.

Gone were the days of munching a granola bar or a banana for breakfast on his way to some backwoods dive shop. No, the kitchen staff insisted that everyone involved in the Divemaster Project ate well. And he wasn't complaining.

Tosin had enjoyed many delicious fresh fish dinners in a row. Some of which he'd contributed to himself through the bounty of his late afternoon deep sea fishing sessions. Still, he couldn't wait to sink his teeth into a hunk of low-grade, greasy ground beef.

If he was lucky, maybe he'd also find some female company to liven up a shared meal. Someone adventurous, willing to join him for a late-night private party in the ship's naughtily appointed clubroom afterward, would be even better.

Tosin observed as Captain Alex coordinated with the local harbormaster to position them as close as safely possible to the island before dropping anchor in a spot that wouldn't damage the reef encircling the volcanic island.

They didn't have facilities to accommodate a ship as large as the *Divemaster* within the ring of coral that formed a protective barrier between the open ocean and the beachside villages of Rarotonga. So they'd anchor out here and take tenders into Avatiu Harbour.

He should probably figure out where he'd stowed his flip-flops last time he'd come onboard, and scrounge around for a shirt. Maybe even one with buttons. Most of the time—when he wasn't suited up in dive gear—he roamed around in only his swim trunks. Or less.

It felt weird to wear actual clothes anymore. Still, he'd attempt to look halfway civilized when they stumbled onto these foreign shores, trying to find their land legs again.

Despite their inflated bank accounts, Tosin, Miguel, and Archer couldn't claim to have gotten much more sophisticated than they'd been when they roamed the globe, hopping from place to place whenever the whim arose and they could afford plane tickets to the next destination. Not so different from what they still did, except now they took their very fancy house with them when they moved.

Enjoying the perks of their newfound fortune, and sharing joy with as many other people as possible, held far more value to them than appearances.

With that said, his two best friends had somehow managed to snag a pair of the hottest, toughest, smartest women he'd ever met. More miraculously, it had nothing to do with their wealth. Their constant kissy faces, shared intimacy, and genuine affection were starting to make Tosin think he might have to change his greatest ambition from becoming Aquaman into something slightly more...*domestic.*

Otherwise he'd end up kicking it with Captain Alex and Banks—the manager of the Divemaster Project and the larger Banks Foundation, which consisted of the rest of Archer's charitable holdings—when he'd reached the confirmed bachelor stage in another decade or so. Not a terrible club to join if it came to that, he thought. Those two were pretty badass dudes.

Worse things could happen.

He should know, since trouble had accompanied their influx of cash. They'd pulled together to survive some hairy situations. Hopefully the crazy shit—you know, like murders, kidnappings, heists, and the rest of that ridiculous stuff—was behind them so they could simply relax from now on.

Out here, surrounded by a whole lot of not much for miles and miles and miles, Tosin was looking forward to some good old-fashioned sunning himself on the beach, dancing and drinking the night away, and maybe a hook up or two minus any drama.

Plus diving. Always diving.

The Cook Islands had some unique features he couldn't wait to investigate, starting with the lagoon between the shore and the barrier reef. It was like one giant aquatic playground. The cerulean water he could now see clearly contrasted with the darker midnight of the deeper ocean beating against the coral. It couldn't be more than ten feet deep in most places. It would be warm and teeming with sea life.

His version of paradise, for sure.

Overhead, the *whop whop whop* of a sleek helicopter taking off from the other side of the ship quickly faded as the transport zipped toward the verdant mountain that rose above the palm-dotted shore. He wished he'd planned ahead enough to grab a ride with Waverly, Archer's girlfriend, who would be flying the staff over to start their provisioning runs.

Less than a minute later, Archer trotted toward Tosin as if his thoughts had summoned the guy. Miguel trailed behind, joining them on the deck as the ship settled into its anchorage and the shore tenders were prepared. Time to go.

"You heading into town?" Archer asked as he chucked a white linen shirt and Tosin's shoes at his head.

He caught them with hardly any effort then nodded as he put them on. "It's probably too much to hope they have a Five Guys, huh?"

It certainly didn't look like a commercial sort of place from where he was standing. Large buildings or shopping malls didn't exist here. Hell, they'd be lucky to find a supermarket. He didn't truly mind, but he was serious about scoring some food.

Miguel snorted. He rubbed his flat stomach. "Yeah, but I could hit up a restaurant. You in?"

He looked to Archer, who cleared his throat before asking, "Could we make a pit stop first? While Waverly is busy helping the crew restock in the chopper, I thought we could check out the Punanga Nui Market. I hear they have a couple world renowned artists who sell their stuff there."

"Who'd you hear that from?" Tosin narrowed his eyes as his friend didn't quite meet his gaze. The Cooks were remote. Hardly anyone they knew had come here before and it certainly wasn't something he could ever remember talking about with travelers they'd run into along the way.

"Google," Archer admitted below his breath.

"You were looking up art galleries? Since when are you into that, Archie?" Miguel wondered.

Sure, the guy was technically a billionaire. He lived frugally, megayacht aside. They appreciated the beauty of nature above all else. The female form especially. Tosin would bet Archer couldn't name any more fine artists than he could. Van Gogh, Picasso, Michelangelo, the basics.

"I thought *Waverly* might be into it. I—uh, want to surprise her. If something catches my eye, I mean. I'll know it when I see it." Archer turned away then motioned for them to hurry. "You coming or not? Let's go."

Tosin looked over at Miguel, who shrugged then said, "I've got nothing to do for a while anyway. Sabine is taking advantage of the better internet connectivity here to transmit her test results and hold a few videoconferences.

Besides, we'll probably stumble across someplace to eat along the way."

"Sounds good." Tosin strode side by side with his friend as they both studied Archer, who hustled to the tenders as if he needed to reserve a spot on his own damn boats.

What was up with that?

✧ TWO ✧

Tosin and Miguel continued to tease Archer about his unusual desire to shop as they skipped across some pretty gnarly waves. The island grew as they approached. The peak at its center loomed overhead. Blanketed with thick foliage, the craggy core of Rarotonga was obviously uninhabitable, which pushed its relatively small population of thirteen thousand people out into a ring around its edges.

Everything seemed supersaturated in the tropical sunlight. The bright sapphire of the water and the emerald of the trees were soon outdone by the scarlet birds fluttering around neon pink and yellow flowers they spotted as they tied up to the town dock. Used to the astounding hues of the underwater world, Tosin thought this might be one of the few places on Earth that could come close to mimicking its splendor. It was almost like when his sunglasses got smudgy and he cleaned them. Suddenly everything around him was crisp and clear and hyper-detailed.

"The market isn't far." Archer ignored their snickers and took off, marching down the street in the direction he'd pointed.

Miguel and Tosin exchanged a quizzical glance then followed at a stroll, taking more time to appreciate the landscape than their friend had. They traveled the length of the small town in only a few minutes before a cluster of tents, carts, and tables came into view.

Tosin sniffed the air as the scent of something sweet and coconut-y reached his nose. Miguel hummed and checked out a street vendor, buying a crispy stick of fried dough covered in what looked like cinnamon sugar. That would do for starters.

Tosin reached over and snagged the end of it, breaking it in half. "Thanks."

"Asshole," Miguel grumbled, though he laughed. "It's not like I wouldn't have shared it with you anyway."

"I know. But that was more fun." Tosin grinned as he chomped down on the treat. Flavor exploded in his mouth, making him eye Miguel's half enviously.

"Oh no. Go get your own if you want more." Miguel snarfed his portion in a couple of large bites, probably to make sure Tosin didn't steal any more of it. Wise move.

Up ahead, Archer turned back, glowering when he realized they'd been distracted by junk food. Not that that should come as a surprise to him. He waved them closer then ducked under a pretty purple and gold awning that held a very tidy array of jewelry.

Tosin peeled his gaze from ornate gardenia head wreaths, endless souvenirs, and the wooden Tangaroa carvings with giant dicks as he stepped inside just ahead of Miguel. He glanced up. When he saw the woman managing the stall, he nearly crashed into a display of long necklaces made of zillions of tiny pupu shells.

Only Miguel's fist at the back of his shirt helped steer him clear of disaster. His friend whispered, "Settle down, buddy, or you'll never have a shot. Better wipe those crumbs off your face, too."

Not the first impression Tosin would have liked to make.

He stepped fully into her booth, swiped his hand over his mouth to rid it of any stray sugar crystals or drool, then nudged his sunglasses lower on the bridge of his nose so that he could study the woman without heavy tint obscuring any of her beauty.

A white frangipani flower adorned her chestnut hair, which brushed the top of her perfect ass. A modified sarong—signs in other stalls they'd passed had called them pareu—wrapped her slender frame in a vibrant scarlet fabric with bold lime green leaf patterns.

Her rich skin tone reminded him of the oiled teak that dominated the interior of the *Divemaster*. It made his fingers itch to touch her. The exotic features of her striking face held an Asian flair made even more beautiful by her Māori ancestry. Lush lips and a bold nose kept her from appearing too delicate. He'd give her a solid seventeen on a scale from one to ten.

Despite her striking appearance, it was her smile that nearly burned out his retinas. Warm and welcoming, as pristine as the environment surrounding them, she could easily have been some Oceania goddess.

Immediately, he knew what he wanted to take home. Her. *Damn.*

"Good afternoon. Can I help you?" She hadn't even noticed Tosin, her greeting aimed at Archer instead. That bastard.

Tosin attempted to focus by peering into the jewelry boxes propped on the tables around him instead of at her gorgeous face. Wow. It really was awesome. Everything he looked at called to him. Reminded him of the ocean and the wondrous things he admired beneath the surface. Carved shells, pearls of all hues, coral—she'd used a variety of nature's beauty to make her art.

"Are you Kahori Akama?" Archer asked.

Kahori. Tosin practiced saying her name a few times in his mind and decided he liked the way it sounded. Having an unusual name himself, he always appreciated someone else's.

How did Archer know of her? And why the fuck had he been holding out?

"I am." She held out a skilled hand—since it had presumably created the assortment of remarkable adornments surrounding them—to Archer.

Tosin didn't bother tamping down his jealousy when his supposed friend made contact with her.

"Nice to meet you. My name is Archer. I read the feature article about you in Australia's *Style Magazine*. It said you have a shop here on the island that showcases your more upscale creations," he explained to the pretty jeweler. "Is it open right now? I'm hoping I can take a look at some of your higher end pieces. I—uh—have my eye out for something special to give my girlfriend."

Tosin's head snapped to the side then as he finally pried his stare from Kahori. He met Miguel's knowing gaze. Things were starting to make sense.

Could Archer be looking for a *ring* for Waverly?

Miguel was grinning back at him. He must be thinking the same thing.

Kahori ignored their antics and dealt directly with Archer. "No, sorry. We're a small family-run business. My main operation is located on a smaller island north of here, Aituataki. It's where I grew up. I do have a gallery here, since Rarotonga draws the most tourists. But on market days we close up since my cousin and I are the only two clerks and we're both needed out here."

She gestured to the guy beside her that Tosin hadn't even noticed while his vision tunneled on her. The man was glaring at him. Probably because Tosin was scoping out the guy's family member as if she were the juicy cheeseburger he'd been hoping to devour earlier.

"I understand." Archer smiled.

Tosin could tell he was disappointed despite his graciousness. Sure, he could come back some other day, but he spent nearly all his time with Waverly and had taken a hard line approach against lying, even innocently, ever since a few misunderstandings and omissions had nearly wrecked the most important relationships in his life. Including his friendship with Tosin and Miguel. It wouldn't be easy for him to break away unnoticed in order to surprise her with his purchase.

"We'll keep Waverly busy if you want to sneak out and buy her a present another time." Tosin knocked his fist into

Archer's shoulder. "What are friends for? I can't be responsible for how I distract her, though."

Archer practically snarled at that.

Kahori laughed then shook her head, setting the petals in her hair fluttering. "No need for violence, boys. The shop is just a block away. I'd be happy to take you over there for a quick look. You don't mind, do you, Hemi?"

She glanced over at her cousin, who did indeed seem put out. Or maybe he was just protective. Tosin could respect that. One gorgeous woman, three foreign men who looked like...well, them. Lots of expensive merchandise that they probably didn't seem able to afford. Yeah, he'd be bristling, too.

"I'll walk her home safe and sound when we're finished," Tosin promised.

"The islands aren't like that." Kahori rolled her eyes as if overwhelmed by too much testosterone. She patted her cousin on the shoulder. "This isn't some big city. It's fine. I'll be right back. I'll even bring you a beer."

The man nodded grudgingly at that. As they left the stall, he drew out his cell phone and spoke quietly to someone on the other end. Tosin figured they'd be supervised by Rarotongan natives the entire way.

He didn't mind.

But he did settle his sunglasses back into place so that it was less obvious that he was admiring the view from a few steps behind Kahori. She led Archer, Miguel, and Tosin as they proceeded down the street to her boutique.

Double damn.

⌒ THREE ⌒

Kahori acted as if she couldn't feel the tall blond foreigner watching her. The weight of his stare held a lot of impact, though. It bummed her out that she couldn't study him as intently as he seemed to be doing to her while she led him and his friends to her store.

It had been a long time since she'd been singed by the spark of attraction like the one he'd ignited when he'd stepped into her stall at the market. And it had been effortless on his part. The man hadn't spoken a single word to her. His impressively cut body and that self-depreciating smirk he'd flashed when he'd nearly trampled her display had been enough to do the trick. Her carefully practiced cool reserve had gone up in flames like deadwood smothered in lava.

Hopefully he couldn't tell how attracted she was to him on sight.

The easy friendship he shared with his almost-as-sexy companions, along with his unusual accent, had sealed the deal. She may not even have officially met the guy yet, but she already wished she could have bumped into him under different circumstances. In a different time. Before she'd vowed not to entangle herself in affairs that could only scar her further.

Which was precisely why she should continue pretending to ignore him. He could be dangerous to her and the walls she'd built to keep herself safe within them.

By the time she'd finished her self-lecture, she'd crossed the narrow road and drew her key from her clutch. Key. Singular. She didn't own a car and there was no need for locks on her home. If Rarotonga was tiny and remote, Aitutaki was ten times so. Everyone knew everyone. No one would dare steal from another resident. Heck, they were almost certainly related.

She opened the door and ushered the three men inside, shivering slightly when the blond man brushed up against her on his way inside. The doorway was no match for his broad shoulders. If she paused to savor the smell of him, sandalwood and spice, no one could blame her, right?

Shaking her head to clear the visions of what he might look like beneath that thin shirt from her mind, she focused on business. She couldn't let the opportunity for a sale slip through her fingers. It had been more than nine months since her last disastrous trip overseas and her savings were taking a hit. If she could put off leaving the security of her islands a while longer, she'd be grateful.

Kahori took a mental inventory, then asked, "So, what exactly is it you had in mind?"

"I'm looking for an engagement ring." Archer confirmed her suspicions.

The article he'd mentioned had highlighted her previous wedding sets. Unfortunately for him, that also meant she'd sold out of most of what she'd made. Though she'd recently completed a few new pieces, she hadn't brought them over to the store from her workshop yet. Mostly because they were more extravagant than what she typically sold here and had been hoping for an online buyer. Figured.

"I knew it!" The man with the South American accent whooped then high-fived Archer. The blond added a congratulatory slap on his back that would have rattled a normal person. Archer only beamed.

Kahori couldn't help herself. She grinned at his obvious devotion to his partner and the support his buddies gave him over his decision to commit himself to her. A wide network of friends her own age was something she missed out on growing up in the sparsely populated region. There had only been a couple dozen children around her age. Most of those had moved away in search of work on one of the surrounding islands or a higher standard of living and the modern amenities their homeland couldn't provide.

For a while, she'd thought that would be her fate, too.

Until she realized she couldn't cut it in the big, bad world.

Living in paradise had tons of benefits, and a few drawbacks she had learned to deal with. So she settled for vicariously enjoying her visitors' bond instead. When the guys had settled down, she opened the case that held her handmade rings. Most featured the very best pearls harvested from black-lipped oysters that she could source. The luster, orient, shape, color, size, and surface were each of the highest caliber. Thick layers of nacre provided plenty of aragonite crystals to reflect the light.

Considering the Cook Islands were the second largest source of black pearls, some of which she'd been lucky enough to collect herself, she had a decent selection even after she'd burned through a bunch.

Archer and his friends—she'd heard him call the dark-haired guy Miguel and the blond Tosin—leaned in, their heads nearly cracking together as they tried to fit their well-muscled bodies in the compact space. They complimented her designs. Their praise seemed genuine as they pointed out features they liked.

Warmth flooded her when Tosin peeked up at her and said, "I don't know shit about this, but everything I see is amazing. We're divemasters. This one here reminds me of a wave."

Which was exactly what she'd intended with the shell swirled in gold. Bonus, now she could imagine him in a skin-tight wetsuit, gliding beneath the surface of the ocean, one of her favorite pastimes.

Archer hummed. "They're all fantastic. Seriously. But..."

"It has to fit your girlfriend's personality." Kahori wasn't placating him. Especially for something as important as an engagement ring, it had to be just right. "Tell me about her."

"Waverly is unique. Strong. A helicopter pilot who served in the US Navy for almost a decade. She doesn't take shit from anyone and she's survived a lot of things that would have crushed other people." Archer's eyes went kind of glassy as he sang the praises of the woman he wanted to spend forever with. "She's brave, feminine, and…"

"Sexy as hell," Miguel added with a wink.

Kahori giggled, wishing she were half as awesome as Waverly. Especially the brave part. "She sounds fiery and bold. Special."

Archer nodded. "She is."

Kahori had the perfect thing. Except… "I'd like to show you something. Unfortunately, it's not here in the shop today. It's back in my workshop on Aitutaki. I only fly out here once a week for the market and I've never had someone come in looking for anything quite like this, so I've never brought it here. It's on my website, though. I can show you pictures."

"Sure, let me take a look." Archer smiled. "We're actually heading up that way in a few days, after we restock and refuel. Miguel and his girlfriend Sabine have a proposition for the island council regarding a business they'd like to establish in the area."

Kahori didn't burst their bubble by letting them know how reluctant some of the natives could be when it came to working with outsiders. They'd see themselves when they visited. Aitutaki made Rarotonga look like a bustling metropolis. What could they possible want with an area so secluded?

Not her problem at the moment.

"I should probably warn you." Kahori hesitated, scared of offending him but also afraid of springing the bad news on him too late, which could lead to an awkward conversation. "It's my most expensive piece."

"That's okay. I'd like to see it." Archer didn't hold her cautioning him against her.

"Great, let me bring it up on my laptop." She scooted around the counter and browsed to the ring's listing while the guys roamed the shop.

Miguel tapped the glass over a set of chandelier earrings dotted with baroque black pearls she favored for their unusual shapes and oil slick colors. "When you're done with Archer, I'll take these. They'll go great with Sabine's necklace."

Archer hummed. "Good eye."

"Just saying, I'm hoping to reserve the clubroom later. So time your gift wisely if you're hoping for a special thank you from her," Tosin mumbled to his friend.

Kahori had no idea what that meant. From his smoky tone and the flare of his friend's eyes, she could guess it was something scandalous, though. What would it be like to have a man like that worship her?

She shivered.

Meanwhile, Tosin paused and inspected the matching set of bracelets she'd tucked into the far corner of her display. Though they were for sale, she'd semi-consciously sabotaged them by hiding them behind other items. Kahori had been tempted to keep them for herself. But after her last trip abroad, she'd given up on the dream of finding someone to wear them with her and put them for sale. They were her favorite things she'd made, though by far not the most elegant or the priciest.

No, for that, she had to come back to Archer.

"Here it is." She spun the laptop around so he could see the screen. "It's a size five as is. I can adjust it as needed."

The man stood there, his mouth slightly open, and stared.

He blinked.

Didn't say a word.

Archer must hate it. She'd been so sure, though. Based on his description, it fit.

"What do you think, Tosin?" Archer asked, his voice kind of wispy and odd.

Except Tosin couldn't have an opinion. He hadn't so much as glanced at the computer or her crowning achievement. When Kahori flicked her gaze in his direction to assess his reaction, she realized he had removed his sunglasses and was staring at her again with the palest steel blue eyes she'd ever seen. "Stunning."

She blushed when Miguel snorted softly behind his hand. Then he peered over Archer's shoulder and whistled. "Wow. Now *that's* a ring."

Tosin did look then. He whipped his gaze to the picture then back at her in a dramatic double-take. His eyes grew wide as he scanned the purple-hued black pearl surrounded by a circle of alternating pear-shaped diamonds and fire opals, set in a lotus pattern around it. The fine band split into a Y on either side of the center. Perched on top, the embellishments appeared to hover over the finger of the wearer.

"You seriously made that?" he asked Kahori.

"I did." Pride bubbled up in her at the appreciation and awe he projected with his slightly tipped head and squinted eyes, as if he couldn't quite believe her capable of a feat that marvelous. To be frank, she'd blown herself away with this ring.

"What are you waiting for?" Miguel elbowed Archer.

The man raked his fingers through his short hair then scrubbed them over the stubble shadowing his cheeks and strong jaw. Then he asked his friends, "Am I doing the right thing?"

"By proposing? Hell yeah. Waverly is the woman for you," Miguel reassured him.

"No, I'm certain about that. Never have been more positive about anything in my life. But...the ring..."

Kahori understood his concerns. It was an unconventional selection. Not in the least bit traditional. Though she guessed his soon-to-be fiancée would approve, she only had the few scraps he'd shared with her about the woman to go on.

"Would you maybe just block your ears for a second? I think what I'm about to say might sound rude." Archer grimaced at her then turned to Miguel and Tosin. "Do you think Waverly will be into this instead of some honking rock? I could buy her a big ass diamond. I like this a million times better. It reminds me of something a mermaid queen would wear. But we're all about the ocean. Maybe she's not as into it…"

"Archie, quit worrying." Tosin put his hand on his friend's shoulder and squeezed. "Waverly is into *you*. That's the only thing she gives a fuck about. This ring is the bomb and she's going to freak out when you give it to her because, for some reason, she really loves you. Dumbass."

Kahori sighed behind the counter, her eyes going soft and melty at his passionate speech. If the men's friendship made her jealous, the fantasy of a soulmate like that…

Whew.

She fanned herself a few times while the guys talked amongst themselves.

"How are you going to pop the question by the way?" Miguel asked. "It's got to be something elaborate. A huge gesture, right? Something she'll never forget."

"I haven't thought that far ahead." Archer groaned. "Can't I just give it to her in bed after amazing sex and tell her how much I want to spend every night just like that?"

"No." Miguel and Tosin both caught her by surprise when they objected in unison.

"That doesn't sound half bad to me." She clapped her fingers over her mouth when she realized she'd spoken her thought out loud.

Tosin met her gaze and they chuckled together. The heat in his stare rivaled the sun beating down on the shop in its intensity. She wondered what it would be like to look into his eyes as he made love to her.

Whoa. No point in torturing herself with visions of something that would never happen.

"I'll worry about that later." Archer looked again at the picture of the ring, running the cursor over it as if he could stroke it through the screen. "How much is it?"

"Uh…" Kahori winced. "Remember, I told you—"

"I'm not surprised." Archer smiled. "Hit me."

She wrung her fingers, recalculating the cost of her materials. It was clear this ring had been destined for these people. It would make her happy for them to leave the Cook Islands with it. But she also liked to eat and pay her bills.

Finding a middle ground, she gave Archer a discount without him knowing. "Fifteen thousand."

He didn't so much as flinch.

"Is that a fair price?" Archer asked her point blank.

She nibbled her lip before nodding.

"You're sure?" he asked again. "Look, I'm not even going to try to haggle with you. I don't know what I'm doing except appreciating something this beautiful. So I'm trusting you here. It's spectacular, and I think my girlfriend will love it. That's my only concern. If you tell me it's worth fifteen grand, I believe you."

"You're getting one hell of a deal," Kahori promised. "It's the best piece I've ever made. Easily worth what I've quoted you even if you smelted it and sold it for its components."

She grimaced then, pained to consider such a fate.

"Then why'd you hesitate?" Tosin asked. Nothing in his tone was accusatory. He seemed genuinely curious.

"Everything is relative, I suppose." She smiled softly then gave them a sliver of the truth. "You're here, the ring is here—well, nearby—and you're saving me a trip to Australia, New Zealand, China, or one of the bigger markets to find a buyer. I used to travel more often when I was establishing my brand. I just...prefer not to do that anymore if I don't have to. Now that my work is out in the world, gaining recognition, high-end buyers have been coming to me. Searching me out in person like you have or working with me remotely through my website on custom designs."

"Hang on..." Tosin interrupted her rambling as he realized where she was going. "You're saying you quoted Archer less than you would otherwise because you don't have travel expenses and time invested in unloading it?"

"Exactly." Kahori beamed. He blinked, as if her smile dazzled him far more than the jewels surrounding them did. "In one of those locations, the price would have been double."

Miguel slapped Archer on the back. "You'd better pony up. Don't want Waverly to think you cheaped out on her."

Kahori laughed.

Until she figured out that they weren't joking.

Archer held his card out to her in a flash. "Charge me for the full thirty-thousand, please."

She gawked, her stare winging between the three men as if they were about to spring some kind of trap.

Tosin intervened. "Trust me. He can afford it. Go ahead, *Kahori*."

The sound of her name rolling off his lips in his European accent was the best bonus she'd ever received. She hoped he couldn't see her pebbling nipples given the way she'd tied her pareu that morning, mimicking a strapless sundress.

"You're sure?" she asked Archer one final time.

"Absolutely." He waved toward the register. "Hurry before someone else comes along and swipes it out from under me."

Not likely. This single sale would be her biggest ever. It would cover her modest living expenses for several years. He was handing her what amounted to a fortune for some of her neighbors, who still practiced—and enjoyed—subsistence living. Though she was starting to get the feeling it was a drop in the bucket to these guys.

When the transaction was complete and Archer laid the pen next to his fresh signature on the receipt, she reached out and shook his hand. "Thank you so much. What size would you like the ring to be when you pick it up next week?"

Archer laughed. "I tried to get a few stealth measurements off other ones she has. I was going to go with a five anyway. Banks, a friend of ours, keeps rambling about fate lately. I'm starting to believe that old bastard might be on to something."

If that was true, did it mean she was destined to exist in solitude?

Was that what she'd learned on her disastrous voyage away from home? That she didn't belong anywhere else but here? Alone?

Kahori refused to let those shadows darken her mood. Not today, bad memories. Not today.

Before she could derail her own happiness, Miguel reminded her about the earrings he wanted as well. She wrapped them in pretty paper and a box, thinking about how on any other day it would have been a major sale. While she did that, Tosin pointed to the bracelets he'd noticed before.

"I can't be left out. How much for the masculine version of the leather, coral, and shell bracelet? This one, way in the back." He lifted his chin at his friends. "Unlike these guys, I'm single. Selfish, too. I want some of your work for myself."

"Oh." Kahori paused, trying to find a tactful way to decline. "I'd prefer not to separate the his-and-her set. They're carved from the same components. See how they fit together? It's actually my favorite thing I've ever made, though obviously not the finest."

Archer had clearly snagged that object for himself.

Kahori opened the back of the case and laid the bracelets beside each other. Tosin watched carefully as the organic curves tucked into each other and made a single shape when connected, sort of like a best friend charm girls gave each other.

"You're right. They belong together." He smiled at her, close enough as they leaned over the counter together that she could detect the flecks of silver mixed into his irises. Tosin inspired all sorts of ideas for creations in her mind. She wished she had a sketchbook right then. "I'll take them both, please."

Kahori trailed her finger over the familiar length of the bracelets in a loving goodbye before she packaged them as well. The day was easily the best in the history of her shop. And she had these three guys to thank for it.

When she handed Tosin the package, their fingers brushed. She sucked in her breath and tried not to drop the bag when he curled his hand around hers.

Tosin repaid her unintentional compliment. "I'm not going to lie. I expected to be bored out of my mind when Archie dragged us out shopping this afternoon. But you've made the experience extremely enjoyable."

"Thank you." She tried not to stammer when hit with the full blast of his charm. "I'm just doing what I love. Making unique, wearable art out of the beautiful things around me."

Way to sound like a commercial, Kahori.

"And doing it well. Since you seem to be a fan of uniqueness, and I'm willing to bet you've never met a person named Tosin before, maybe you should let me buy you dinner to celebrate today's success?" He rubbed his thumb lightly over her knuckles.

She laughed, wishing she could say yes. Desperate to keep from doing something foolish, she latched onto the obvious excuse. "Sorry, I really have to get back to the market. Hemi is probably losing his mind by now. He hates using the register app on his smartphone. Or technology in general, really. Or talking to strangers. And the daily commuter flight to Aitutatki leaves right after we pack up."

"Too bad." He released her hand by degrees, letting their fingers glide over each other almost reluctantly as he let her go.

Kahori sighed, deflating a little as the absence of the contact left her feeling hollow.

Instead of leaving it at that, Tosin tried once more, flattering her with his persistence. "Well then, how about when we pick up the ring in Aitutaki?"

"I'll think about it." She smiled softly then turned away to hand Archer her contact information.

When they'd made tentative plans for his pick up and exchanged thank-yous, she leaned against the doorframe. Free to stare, she greedily eyed Tosin until he disappeared around a corner, admiring the way he moved—sure and smooth. As much as she would like to learn more about the handsome stranger, she knew there was no way she'd accept his invitation.

Hopefully he'd forget all about it, and her, by the time he visited her hometown.

She should have realized he wouldn't.

"Dude, from the amount of pacing and primping you've been doing this morning, I'd almost think you were the one picking up an engagement ring today," Miguel grumbled at Tosin. "Sit your ass down. You're making me jumpy."

Archer, on the other hand, relaxed on a lounger beside Banks. The older guy patted Archer's shoulder and smiled. "I've waited a long time to see your ring on Waverly's finger. You did well, kid."

"Guys, she hasn't said yes yet." Archer did seem to tense then. Not only because he was peering around to make sure his girlfriend didn't hear their conversation and blow his cover, either.

Miguel, Tosin, and Banks only cracked up.

"What's so funny?" Captain Alex asked as he joined them on the deck.

"Archie's worried Waverly might turn down his proposal." Banks shook his head ruefully.

"Don't be an idiot, boss." Captain Alex laughed too. "That woman loves you more than I love this ship. And that's a hell of a lot." Then he turned to Miguel and said, "So...are you really going to let him show you up like that?"

"What do you mean?" the divemaster asked, crossing his arms. They were competitive if nothing else.

"He wants to know when you're going to man up and commit to Sabine." Tosin enjoyed turning the tables on his friend. Take that, asshole.

Miguel blinked. "I—uh—I mean, you know, I already *am* committed. At least I have a girlfriend, unlike you. It's just that this doesn't seem like a good time. She's completely engrossed in her study and has so many other more important things going on right now. Or at least that's what I figured. Am I messing this all up again?"

Now the guys laughed at him. It was fun to see him squirm.

Except Banks let him off the hook. "You know what's best for the pair of you. It's clear that you love her. Don't rush if you're not ready. Either of you. Plus, Marta will be visiting soon—"

"Don't you know the exact number of hours until she touches down with the next batch of guests?" Tosin teased. No one was exempt from their ribbing around here. Banks had shown definite interest in Miguel's girlfriend's quasi-mom. At this point it was clear the woman was visiting to see *two* people, not just one.

"One hundred and twenty seven," Banks confirmed with a wink. "Anyway, since she's the closest thing to family Sabine has left, I'd recommend you do the gentlemanly thing and speak to her about it first while she's onboard if you think it's something you might pursue down the road."

"If you let Marta out of your cabin, you mean?" Captain Alex joked this time.

"Precisely." Banks flashed a sinful grin that proved beneath his proper exterior he had a wicked streak at least as wide as any of the divemasters'.

Poor Marta wasn't going to know what hit her. Or maybe she already had a clue since she and Banks had been videochatting—or exchanging emails when the connection speed didn't permit screen-to-screen conversations—pretty much every night for the past six months or so.

Miguel swallowed hard. "I'll talk to Kahori about sketching something up while we're there. I don't have to give it to Sabine until the time is right. *Right*?"

Captain Alex slapped him on the back. "Smarter every day. Anyway, I came out here to tell you lazy fools we'll be anchored and ready to go ashore in about ten minutes. I'd better see to that."

Tosin could make out Maunga Pu, the highest point on Aitutaki, barely four hundred feet above sea level. They really were close. If it wouldn't have taken him longer to swim than to wait for Captain Alex to park the *Divemaster*, he would have gladly launched himself over the rail and torpedoed toward the crystalline beaches along the shore.

It had only been a few days since his run in with Kahori, but he hadn't been able to think of much else beside her smile. And the things he'd like to do to her to guarantee he'd see more of it. Of her in general.

In addition to their appointment with her, the guys had a busy day planned. They'd set up a meeting with the village council in Aruntanga, the main town on the island, to pitch a grow dome for the medicinal algae Sabine and Miguel had discovered, which gave every indication it would be the central component in a cure for cancer that could eliminate deaths from the disease in their lifetime.

The Banks Foundation would fund the initiative and provide jobs along with income to any residents willing to work on the project. They could drastically improve the entire economy of the Cook Islands if the residents would allow it. Tourism, offshore banking, pearls, and fish exports lumped together couldn't do as much for them as involvement in the biomedical industry could.

To help prove they had only the best of intentions, they'd also arranged to sponsor an "island night", which Tosin understood was the Cook Islands' equivalent of a Hawaiian luau. There was only one woman on the entire island he would beg to accompany him to the celebration of local culture, complete with traditional music, dancing, and a literal boatload of food.

He would gladly beg if it came to that.

The first thing he'd done when they'd gotten back to the *Divemaster* after their shopping trip earlier in the week was steal the magazine Archer had discovered Kahori in. Tosin may or may not have clipped out the story and stashed it in his nightstand drawer after reading it a dozen times.

The interview about her commitment to her art and her connection to nature's beauty had only made him want to find out more about her. They had a lot in common. A passion for ocean conservation, for one. Diving, for another.

Kahori had named SCUBA as her favorite recreational activity.

Only really fantastic sex surpassed diving in Tosin's estimation.

He would happily enjoy some of both with her. If she'd only give him a shot. The *Divemaster* could be in the area for a while if the village council gave them the green light. He was looking forward to spending as much of that time as possible with Kahori.

Would she be down with that?

It seemed like at least as long as it had taken them to cross the Pacific, but was really probably less than an hour, before Tosin strode toward Kahori's main workshop, located in her house. He tried not to crush the bouquet he'd bought from a vendor at the dock as he kept up with Archer's absurd pace.

"You two are killing me," Miguel laughed, not at all winded but highly amused at their eagerness.

Neither Tosin nor Archer gave a shit. They were men on missions.

Archer consulted the crude map someone had drawn for him. There were no street names or house numbers to reference. They'd followed more basic directions, turning at the yellow cottage then following the cracked stone pathway for about a quarter of a mile when a stucco bungalow with a thatched palm roof came into view. Sea glass and shells dangled from ribbons, making the entire porch sparkle. They also acted as a privacy screen that still allowed some light to pass through. Between the strands, Tosin spied an underwater mural, which covered the back wall of the outdoor space, setting him immediately at ease.

He didn't need a GPS to know this was where Kahori lived and worked.

Two men sat on a bench beside the front door as if guarding the home. From them?

Tosin tried to put them at ease when he recognized the younger of the pair. "Hey there, Hemi. How's it going?"

The guy only grunted in response. An older, tanner, grumpier version of the dude crossed his arms over a massive chest that did his Pacific Islander ancestors proud. Legit tribal tattoos covered a portion of his face in an inked mask. More designs covered his right shoulder and half of his torso. Intricately carved bone earrings pierced his lobes. Fierce and proud, he looked like he could rip someone in half with his bare hands if he chose.

"We're here to pick up a ring from Kahori." Archer tried to be civil, too.

"Ms. Akama, *my daughter*, will be with you soon. You're early."

Tosin noticed the man didn't offer them his name or a seat for that matter. Though he did glare at the flowers Tosin now attempted to shield behind his body. Miguel disguised his chuckle with a cough.

A solid five awkward minutes passed before Kahori appeared at the door. "Pāpā, when they get here, show them to my studio?"

Tosin cleared his throat and she jumped a little. "Oh! I'm so sorry. I didn't realize you were here. I hope you weren't waiting long."

"Not at all." Miguel shrugged, as if they'd spent the time with her relatives in engaging conversation instead of a staring match.

"Nice to meet you, Mr. Akama." Tosin figured it couldn't hurt to be nice. Maybe later his kindness would ensure he'd simply receive a stern lecture for ogling the man's daughter instead of the ass-kicking he probably deserved for the things he'd like to do with her.

Definitely *not* dad-approved activities.

"Sorry. He's not used to outsiders." Kahori winced at the term, probably the most polite way of putting it she could. "Okay, that's not quite true. My uncle owns the resort on the lagoon. *Pāpā* chooses to keep to himself and the people he grew up with instead of expanding his horizons."

"No one knows better than me that you can't dictate how your family acts." Archer attempted to put her at ease. "Don't sweat it."

Maybe things here were going to be more difficult for Sabine and her scientific crew than they'd anticipated. If too many of the residents felt like Kahori's dad, they might not be setting up shop here after all.

Miguel poked Tosin between the shoulders, hard.

When Tosin snapped out of his thoughts, he realized Kahori was staring at him and the flowers he clutched. "Hello again. These are for you."

He held them out to her and watched her eyes grow wide, as if no one had ever given her a bouquet before.

"They're beautiful. Thank you." She treated him to her full-on smile as she accepted them then spun to put them in one of the pretty glass jars that decorated the her windowsill before filling it with water.

Kahori leaned in and drew a deep breath, savoring their fragrance before lifting her gaze to his. When Miguel shuffled in the corner, the spell broke. She set the flowers down then wiped her hands on her pareu, which was tied in a halter-style today.

The vibrant colors and conforming fabric highlighted her killer body.

"Sorry. My studio is this way. Come. I can't wait for you to see the ring in person." She spoke to Archer then, as if ashamed for taking a moment for herself before conducting business. Maybe tonight, at the festival, she'd be more relaxed.

Tosin could stand to wait a little longer to have her to himself.

She was interested, he could tell. The rest he could figure out.

Soon any thoughts beside praise for her craftsmanship flew out of his brain. He studied her workspace—along with the jewelry in progress on every flat surface—before taking a look at Waverly's ring.

Holy hell. Miguel was screwed. Tosin couldn't imagine the guy coming up with something equally impressive for Sabine, though several of Kahori's other creations also blew him away.

"Thank you again." Archer practically groveled at her feet as they collected the box and prepared to leave. "I can't wait to introduce you to Waverly tonight. It's going to be hard to pretend like we don't already know you, though. I hate lying. Especially to her."

"I think it's okay in these circumstances," Kahori laughed. "Though now that you mention it, I hope I don't spoil the surprise either."

"So you're coming then?" Tosin double-checked. "I had hoped I might get to share a meal with you after all. Or maybe you could be my tutor on the cultural program for the evening."

And maybe after that, he could teach her a little about how he rolled too.

"Of course. Practically the entire island will be there. At least to grab a bite to eat, if not to socialize. Fewer than two-thousand people live on Aitutaki," she told them.

"Then it's a date?" he asked.

Right about the time her father ambled into the room. He huffed, then growled, "Kahori should focus on business tonight. The pearl traders will all be in from their posts. It's a good time to make deals."

"One night off won't hurt, *Pāpā*." Kahori softened her father's rough edges. "Besides, I already told Tuiara that I would perform. So you'll get to see me doing some of our traditional dances."

Tosin didn't care if her dad was right there and the size of a refrigerator. He nearly did a jig himself.

Night made.

His time in other South Pacific countries made him pretty damn sure this was going to involve a lot of hip shaking and bared skin. Count him in. "I'll make sure to sit in the front row then."

Her father took a step toward him.

Miguel intervened to keep Tosin's teeth firmly attached to his skull. "We'll stop interrupting you now so that you can enjoy tonight, then. If you have some availability in the next couple of days, maybe I could come back to discuss commissioning another ring from you. One for *my* girlfriend this time."

Kahori's father backed off a little at the promise of more profits. The three divemasters drifted out to the porch, leaving him to smolder in peace in her workshop. She glanced over her shoulder to make sure he hadn't followed.

"Thanks again for the flowers. See you tonight," Kahori said quietly to Tosin before rushing to close the gap between them. She went onto her tiptoes, braced her hands on his shoulders, and kissed his cheek before spinning away fast enough that he couldn't capitalize on the moment to forge a deeper connection. Her pareu flapped around her shapely thighs as she disappeared into her studio.

"*Pāpā*, I can't believe you were so rude," he heard her hiss. "They're good customers. And...just...good people."

"No *papa'a* is good enough for you. If you're finally interested in having a boyfriend, there are a half dozen local boys who are interested in the position," her father snapped in response without even trying to disguise his objection from the men outside. "Now, where are the boxes for today's shipment? If they're ready, I'll deliver them to the airport for you."

Tosin made sure they were well away from her cottage and out of sight of any prying eyes before he high-fived his friends. It may not have gone as smoothly as he'd hoped, but he was making progress.

Tonight was going to be epic.

FIVE

Kahori could have kicked herself for giving in to her impulse earlier. Kissing Tosin had been reckless. Especially with her disapproving father in the room next door. She hadn't wanted Tosin to believe her as intolerant and impolite as her family, though. Especially not when he'd been so freaking nice to her. And—okay, she admitted it—when everything about him turned her on.

Maybe indulging her lust with him would be the safest sort of affair.

After all, it wouldn't be long before he was waving *bon voyage* from the ridiculous yacht she'd heard he'd cruised up on with his friends. Given the way they'd dropped money without hesitation in her shop, she was beginning to wonder exactly who they were and what they were up to around these parts. They didn't seem like simple tourists.

Hopefully tonight she could find out more.

It couldn't hurt to get to know Tosin a little, could it?

Kahori took extra time lining her eyes and applying a stain made of crushed flowers and berries to her lips. She wove some of the blossoms Tosin had brought her into the length of her hair then shrugged into her traditional outfit. Every girl had a coconut bra or two in their closet, didn't they? If not, they should, because this one made her rack look pretty impressive.

She smiled into the mirror, humming as she tied her *kikau* around her waist. Over the grass skirt she fastened her most elaborate *titi*, which hugged her hips. The combination of feathers, shells, and dried fronds stood out from her midsection like a ballerina's tutu. It would accentuate the swing of her body to the beat of the drums. She'd made the costume herself, collecting only the most striking materials from the island around her until she was satisfied.

To her, the outfit was as much of a masterpiece as the ring she'd sold Archer.

Could Tosin be more appreciative of the unfamiliar than her own family? She hoped so.

Kahori didn't know how to make herself any more appealing than this. It had to be enough. Because although she hadn't intended to tangle herself up with him, the simple kiss she'd ambushed him with before hadn't quenched her desire for a taste of him.

She stared at herself in the mirror then adorned herself with wooden bracelets, pearl necklaces, and feather earrings from her collections until she was weighed down with a relative fortune in gorgeous things.

This was her turf. Tonight would be different than the last time she'd surrendered to curiosity about her sexual urges.

And if it ended badly, then at least her father would have the satisfaction of being right.

Kahori glanced at the clock, though she could already hear the sounds of drummers warming up on their *pates*. She had to hurry. Without bothering with shoes she'd only kick off when it came time to dance, or walk along the beach in the moonlight afterward, she set off down the dirt road that wound from her house to the village's gathering place, where island nights and other formal celebrations were held.

After she'd trekked nearly half the distance to town, she realized she'd forgotten the *poi*—weighted balls on chains wrapped in a slow-burning fuse—she needed for the *ura rama* fire dance. Cursing under her breath, praying she didn't ruin the effort she'd taken on her appearance, she trotted back toward home.

When she approached, it surprised her to see a glow coming from her studio. Had she forgotten to turn off the lights in her haste?

Get yourself together, Kahori!

She ripped herself over her forgetfulness and the way she'd absolutely lost her mind over a handsome man, who probably wouldn't turn out to be half as exciting or as good in bed as she had built him up in her mind to be.

Kahori charged inside, ready to grab her torches, and heard rummaging in the other room.

Someone was there!

"Hello?" she called.

"Kahori?" Hemi answered.

"Hey, did you need something? I'm late." She scooped up her torches, slipped the leather loops on their handles over her hands, and stuck her head in the other room.

"There were some packages that needed to go out this afternoon," Hemi reminded her.

"Oh, sorry. *Pāpā* took those to the airport office for me earlier. All except the one I haven't quite finished yet. I thought he would have mentioned it." Kahori hoped Hemi hadn't spent too long looking for them. "You coming?"

"Maybe later." He shrugged. "You look great, though."

"Thanks." She sighed in relief.

"That guy doesn't deserve one of our best." He shook his head as he mumbled then shut off the light, leaving with her, though they went in separate directions once they reached the street.

"Careful, Hemi, or you'll turn into my *Pāpā* soon." She rolled her eyes as she called over her shoulder to him. He shot her a vulgar gesture.

Kahori only laughed, then took off again, this time trotting as the rhythm of the drums rent the sultry evening air, calling her onward. She ran toward the savage pounding in time to the beat until she wasn't sure if the crashing of the sea on the barrier reef—the strongest force she'd ever experienced before—or the raging anticipation within her held greater power.

She was about to find out.

Please, let me be ready for the storm I am about to unleash.

Punctuality wasn't Tosin's strongpoint. Yet he'd dragged his friends to the island night celebration sickeningly early. He'd parked himself on a blanket right in the absolute center of the front row and refused to budge in case someone swiped his place. Delicious aromas wafting out of the *umukai*—an oven dug in the earth, filled with basalt rocks to hold in heat for slow roasting—as villagers unwrapped banana leaves from a feast of suckling pigs. Even those mouth-watering smells couldn't persuade him to abandon his spot.

Though it was making him hungry as hell.

"Waverly, if you love me you'll go grab me a snack to hold me over until after the performances." He flashed her his best imitation of baby seal eyes. "Please. I'm dying."

"Fine. Only because I think it's cute that you have such a crush on the girl who made Sabine's amazing earrings." She eyed the jewelry dangling from their friend's ears longingly, then patted his knee. "And because it smells so damn good I need to check it out for myself anyway."

Archer didn't need any prodding. He followed Waverly, and his stomach, toward the buffet that was being set up. Not before he flashed them a discreet yet enthusiastic thumbs-up. Tosin knew it was because his girlfriend had appreciated Kahori's artistry.

There was no doubt Waverly was going to adore the ring Archer had selected for her nearly as much as she loved the man himself.

That left Tosin wedged between Banks, who stretched out on his back, staring at the twilight sky, on one side of him and Sabine, who sat on Miguel's lap, on the other. "For the record, I do not have a *crush* on Kahori."

No, the things he had in mind had far less to do with puppy love and a whole lot more to do with very adult appetites.

"Probably for the best," Miguel said with a smirk. "Because if you did, you'd have to compete with every other dude between the ages of eighteen and sixty on this island for her attention."

Tosin followed his friend's gaze to the woman in question. She approached at a trot that set all his instant favorite parts of her body jiggling enticingly. Even Banks hummed. "That's her?"

"Yup." Tosin tried not to pant.

Worse, he clamped his mouth shut to keep from extolling her other virtues. Like how she'd been super insightful when helping Archer find the perfect ring. Or how she'd been honest and fair in setting her price despite Archer's disclaimer. Or how she'd advocated for the use of clean energy with logical strategies in her magazine interview. Or how she excelled at both creative and business pursuits, building her brand from the ground up while earning the appreciation of thousands of art connoisseurs around the world.

And yeah, she was gorgeous and inherently sensual on top of all those other things.

It wasn't often that Tosin's dick and his brain both appreciated the same woman. Major red alert.

"If it wasn't for my obsession with Marta, I might give you a run for your money, kid." Banks grinned when Tosin glared at him.

Sabine laughed. "Aren't you supposed to be the role model around here?"

"Maybe this old dog is learning some of the young dogs' tricks instead." Banks waggled his brows then went back to admiring the last lingering pastel clouds left in the wake of what had been a spectacular sunset.

Tosin would have gone to speak to Kahori, except a woman in a similar—though less extravagant—traditional costume whisked her away. Waverly and Archer made it back and fed him a few scraps of delectable pork and grilled papaya. Just like Kahori's peck this afternoon, the tender meat only made him crave a bigger bite.

Before he could sneak another helping, the drummers assembled in a semi-circle. They stayed within the bamboo poles lying in the sand, which delineated the "stage" for tonight's performances.

People crowded together as they settled down and gave their full attention to the collection of men who began to play as one. The primal thundering of their fists and tapered sticks on hollowed out logs and sharkskin drumheads mesmerized Tosin along with the rest of the audience.

As the last of the sunlight faded, dozens of tiki torches were lit. Flames flickered, casting dancing shadows onto the beach. The soft slap of gentle waves accompanied the music made by dozens of hands acting in unison. If he closed his eyes, Tosin could imagine this place and similar humans entertaining themselves the same way a thousand years ago.

Even still, in all the time in between then and now, he was sure a woman as captivating as Kahori had never existed. She confirmed his theory when the drummers parted and admitted her into their midst. Singing layered on top of the percussion as she began to sway from side to side. She kicked off the show solo, clearly its star. Her arms and hips moved sinuously in an unhurried style that appeared similar to hulas he'd seen in Hawaii, though fiercer and extraordinarily sensual. Tosin overheard one of the local women tell Banks the dance was called the *hura*.

It didn't take long before Tosin had to crumple up a corner of the blanket he sat on to cover his lap, though it might take the entire quilt to camouflage the effect she had on him. Fortunately, he got a bit of a reprieve as the song ended and an ensemble of about a dozen men took her place.

Their power and precision awed him, but it didn't tug at his soul like Kahori had. They performed a fast-paced drum dance, shaking the dried grass tied around their calves furiously with moves that reminded him of exotic birds. Crouched, feet together, they flapped their knees apart then closed triple time to the beat while their arms sliced through the air. Percussive claps and shouts punctuated their actions. Shark-teeth necklaces stood out stark white against their bronzed skin.

They were badass and would definitely have given him pause if he were a rival tribe leader. A group of men so in sync and in shape would be tough to beat on the battlefield.

When he thought he'd seen it all, women began to join them as the men made way. He scanned the troupe for any hint of Kahori.

She wasn't there. Tosin would know in an instant if she was. Still, there was a hell of a lot of bare midriff, soft skin, and undulating abdomens to keep him interested in the change of crew. These women could shake it. Seriously.

As impressive as the guys had been, the women were even more so. Grace tempered the fury of their movements, which were coupled with a walloping helping of seduction.

The instant the music changed, Tosin leaned forward. As he had hoped, Kahori rejoined the dancers. This time two men approached, one from each side of her. Both carried torches. Her features stood out in the harsh lighting, making her appear otherworldly. Strong and worthy of devotion from mere mortals. Sign him the hell up.

As if the image she projected wasn't enough to keep him engrossed, she locked her stare on his before offering him a coy smile.

Tosin gazed into her eyes until something sparked by her side, startling him. It was only then he realized what had happened. The men had lit the contraptions dangling from chains cuffed to her wrists. Now she wielded two actual fireballs.

What the fuck?

Though the sight of her in paraphernalia that reminded him of bondage gear took his fantasies straight to the next level, he wasn't sure it was wise. What if she got burned?

Instead, it was him that began to smolder. If her previous dance had been sensual, this one was a frenzy of passion. The drumming escalated until her hips damn near shook the feathers off the belt that hugged her low around her waist, right where he'd like to lay a trail of open-mouthed kisses.

He hadn't known humans were capable of movement like that.

Twerking had nothing on the *ura rama*.

And all the while, she swung the fireballs in elaborate swirls to the beat. As the song progressed, her tricks got more and more daring. Dangerous.

Tosin's pounding heart threatened to burst as she swung the *poi* behind her back, over her head, and even between her legs. Right where he wanted to be. He imagined fucking to this insane tempo, being driven on by the primordial pulse that matched his crescendoing lust.

Kahori had him lunging half out of his cross-legged position when she appeared to lose her grip on those whirling flames. Instead of crashing into her or the crowd, they landed at her feet in just the right place to ignite a ring of oil he hadn't noticed earlier. She danced on, cocooned in an inferno, dropping into a crouch while still working her hips.

Every man in the place must have imagined what a woman with that kind of muscle memory would be capable of during sex. She could ride him to hell and back, he was sure.

Tosin was ready and willing to let her burn him up all night long.

With one final flourish, the flame extinguished, the drums halted at a dead stop, and the entire beach was plunged into dark silence that rang in his ears. Only the paths of light from Kahori's whirling fireworks, which were probably etched permanently into his eyeballs, remained like the light trail from a sparkler.

Tosin struggled to catch his breath, maybe drawing air into his lungs for the first time in twenty minutes. Beside him Miguel groaned, "Daaaaammmmmnnnnn."

Then applause rang out from everywhere around them. Tosin clapped loudest.

When it died down and the torches around the buffet were lit, the divemasters and their little gang sat speechless despite the line rapidly forming under the food tent.

Sabine gawked at Miguel. "I should smack you for that reaction… But daaaaammmmmmnnnnnnn is right."

Waverly leaned over to ask her, "Do you think Kahori could teach us to do some half-assed version of that?"

Archer and Miguel wore matching grins when Sabine said, "I don't know, but I think we should ask for a lesson."

"I second that motion," Archer said while staring at his girlfriend, as if picturing her in Kahori's place.

Tosin didn't have to make any mental substitutions. He'd never forget what he'd seen tonight. It would be hard to when the woman who'd played the goddess on the stage before him raced around to rejoin them. He tried not to be disappointed when he realized the bottom half of her ornate traditional costume had been swapped for another *pareu*, this time wrapped around her waist and knotted off center at one hip. It was lovely. But he hoped someday he could convince her to give him a private showing of her moves in her full regalia. At least she'd kept the coconut bra.

"That was incredible," Banks said as Archer introduced him.

Waiting for Kahori to thank each of his friends for their lavish praise nearly killed Tosin. But when she worked down the line and finally stood in front of him, he couldn't find the words to tell her how much of an impact her performance had made on him.

"Wow," he breathed as she looked up at him expectantly. "Is there anything you suck at?"

She tipped her head back and laughed, drawing appreciative stares from every man within hearing range. "Plenty of things."

"Yeah, like what?" He couldn't help himself. He reached out and encircled her wrist with his fingers, rubbing the light marks left by her fiery apparatus. If only they were rope marks instead...

"For starters, I wish I'd given you a better kiss earlier." She bit her lip as soon as the confession escaped, as if she hadn't meant to say it aloud.

"I'll give you a do-over." He leaned in, his mouth parting of its own accord.

"Come eat, Kahori," her dad shouted at her. "You must be hungry."

They sprang apart as if busted doing a hell of a lot more than flirting.

After the initial shock wore off, she amazed Tosin by smiling—slow and wide—then holding out her hand to him. "He has no idea how famished I am."

Tosin licked his lips. "Same here."

⌣ **SEVEN** ⌣

Endorphins released by dancing had clearly made Kahori high.

It was the only reason she could come up with to explain the outrageous remarks she'd made to Tosin. No matter how many times she chastised herself, reminded herself of the dangers, he teased out her inner sex kitten. Hell, she hadn't even known she *had* an inner sex kitten before him.

Stupidly, she kept on indulging the riskiest and most vulnerable aspects of her personality. Yet she couldn't help but want to meet that part of her she'd never before unleashed.

Though Tosin had acted like a perfect gentleman while they ate, praising the cooks as he devoured his meal, all she could see was the way he followed local customs by sucking the rich juices off his fingers one-by-one in compliment and the lingering hunger in his eyes, which food alone couldn't satisfy.

Despite the undercurrents, she found him remarkably easy to talk to. Him *and* his friends. Female companions who were more interested in their careers than immediately

410

raising families were rare in Aitutaki. It was refreshing to have people to talk to who could understand her ambitions.

Knowing that one day, hopefully, Waverly would wear a ring Kahori'd made as a symbol of the woman's partnership with Archer felt rewarding. Kahori had put so much into that piece, it thrilled her to know it had found a worthy home. The evening topped her list of favorite festivals. Memories she'd already made would last long after they'd sailed away again.

For including her in his inner circle, she intended to thank Tosin properly. Plus, make sure she never forgot the way he made her feel simply by being nearby. If his attention alone could make butterflies riot in her belly, what would his passion do?

Melt her completely.

Gathering every scrap of courage she could muster, Kahori drew a deep breath and asked, "Would you like to take a walk? There's a spot not too far from here I'd love to show you."

He stood so fast he drew the attention of several of the village elders, including her father.

Damn!

Banks came to their rescue. "Miguel, Sabine, I think we'd better talk to the council about the algae grow operation before it gets too much later, don't you think? I wouldn't want any of them to leave before they can hear us out, and maybe take a vote."

Genius. Pure, utter, legendary genius.

Tosin murmured, "Thank you."

Before anyone could stop them, Kahori grabbed his hand then half-dragged him toward the lagoon so they could enjoy the view as they walked along its shore. It was easily Aitutaki's best feature. Land only accounted for about six and a half square miles of the atoll. It was comprised of the main mass and fourteen other uninhabited islets—little more than blobs of sand and palms, really—called *motus* around the perimeter. One of those held her uncle's private resort, complete with overwater cabanas and a single spectacular honeymooners' suite. The remaining fifteen or so square miles within the barrier reef consisted of placid, crystal clear water rife with sea creatures.

She didn't have to tug much before Tosin got the idea. They ran over the soft, warm sand with their fingers laced together. By the time they'd reached the placid surface of the trapped sea, a fit of giggles had assaulted them both.

It may not have been a daring escape, but they'd evaded her father's grasp.

Tosin drew her close to his side, his fingers running along the length of one of her necklaces, then murmured, "You know, I've been all over the world. Still, I've never seen a place full of as much beauty as this one."

She might have thought he meant the turquoise water, or the sugary beaches, or the pristine environment, or even the postcard-esque line of palm trees along the deserted stretch of tropical paradise if he hadn't been staring into her eyes.

When he slouched, angling his face toward hers, she shook her head. "Not here."

Sure enough, when she glanced over her shoulder, Hemi and his father, Kimo, monitored her interactions with the *papa'a* from their spots around the council's table.

Tosin nodded, then followed her silently, wandering into the shallows as if he loved the silky feel of the saltwater against his skin as much as she did. Beyond him, on the northwest side of the main island, she could see the impressive boat she knew he'd come from. It was a beautiful one the likes of which they didn't see often around here.

"So you're really a divemaster on that cruise ship?" She'd heard the whispers of the other women backstage tonight, many of them hoping to convince him to guide them on a midnight adventure. During dinner, he'd let Sabine and Waverly talk about themselves and what they did onboard, without insisting on bragging about his own accomplishments. His humble silence had impressed her more than if he'd boasted, but it left her wondering more about him.

"Sort of." Even in the starlight she could see his throat flex as he swallowed. "It's complicated. It didn't used to be.

Archer, Miguel, and I traveled all over the world. Diving for a living, visiting new places, and partying with pretty women. That was kind of our thing for a decade."

"It's not anymore?" she wondered.

"Well, you see, Archer sort of inherited six or seven billion dollars. But who's counting?" Tosin laughed, though his humor seemed tinged with disbelief. "He put most of it in a trust for charity stuff. Banks runs—"

"Wait. Banks. Archer. As in Archer Quartermaine. Founder of the Banks Foundation. *That* Banks?" Kahori stopped dead in her tracks. Why hadn't she put it together before now?

Because they seemed so damn normal, and the name on the card he'd given her hadn't been Quartermaine. That's why.

"Uh oh." Tosin grimaced. "I hadn't expected you'd have heard of us. Can we forget I said all that and go back to where we were before?"

"No." She shook her head. "I can't erase my memory like that. But it doesn't really change how I think of you. We are who we are. You're still the guy who brought me flowers. And the guy who nearly crashed into my booth when he first saw me. A divemaster on a really sweet ship. The rest...eh. Not as important."

"Did I mention that I don't just work there? Archer sort of gave Miguel and me each a one-third share in the Divemaster Project, including the boat itself."

"That must make you..."

Tosin nodded. "Rich. I guess. If I ever planned to sell, which I don't. It's everything I've ever dreamed of. A life where I do what I love forever and help make other people happy along the way. I'm the luckiest bastard ever. Doubly so because I'm here, spending this time with you."

Well, that whole "who you are isn't important" thing might not be true after all.

Okay...it was a Big Fat Lie.

Because now she realized clinging to this man for more than tonight would be utterly impossible.

When she didn't reply to that, he tried to lighten the mood some.

Tosin shook his head ruefully, "So you noticed my graceful entrance that day, huh?"

She appreciated the effort. There'd be time to mourn what she could never keep later, when she'd lost it. Right now, she should enjoy.

"I took it as a compliment." She squeezed his hand as she spotted the shadow of her landmark rock up ahead. "Why don't we see if I can show you something that will live up to the incredible sights you must have seen so far on your journey around the world, huh?"

"I'm sure you can, Kahori." He kissed her knuckles then followed her into the crevice between two giant slabs of basalt. It was narrow enough that they had to go single file, at least for a while.

"Are you sure we don't need some sort of lantern?" Tosin asked, sounding unsure after they'd shuffled a couple dozen feet into the cave entrance. "Sharks, eels, sting rays, whatever...underwater stuff never freaks me out. But I'm man enough to admit that if a bat swoops down in my face, you're going to have to give me mouth-to-mouth after I faint."

"Doesn't sound so bad to me." She patted his hand. "Just a little bit farther."

By the time they'd rounded the last bend in the tunnel she knew by heart, a faint light had already began to pulse around them.

"Is that my eyes?" he asked, rubbing his free hand over them.

"Nope. Glowworms."

"Seriously?" Tosin walked a little faster. "I hear water, too. The tide is out right now so that should be okay, right?"

"Yep." It thrilled her that he was so in touch with nature, a quality she could appreciate. "It's safe for a couple more hours. This entire passageway floods at high tide, though."

"Holy shit, wait until I tell Miguel and Archer about this." His enthusiasm energized her further.

But when they passed through the stone archway into the main cavern, his excitement turned to astonishment.

Kahori didn't blame him. It was fairly large, big enough to fit several cottages inside. Stalactites and stalagmites speared throughout like snaggleteeth. Illuminated by the glowworms on the ceiling, they took on hues from navy to teal. On the backside of the cave a waterfall tumbled gently from the ceiling, causing rings that extended out into the otherwise mirror-like surface of the subterranean pool. A stream ran out the other side to rejoin the ocean beyond. Not many living people knew about her secret place—potentially only her and Tosin—but the walls were covered with prehistoric paintings that bonded her to her ancestors, rooting her to a place she hadn't always felt secure in.

Especially after her mother had run off with a tourist when Kahori was a toddler. She supposed she couldn't blame her father for mistrusting Tosin, given the way he'd been betrayed by the love of his life. Kahori was all he had left. Another reason nothing serious could come of her time with Tosin.

Instead, she vowed to enjoy each minute he was there and interested in her to the fullest.

"Is it okay to swim here?" he asked her in a hushed, reverent whisper.

Kahori nodded then began to strip off her clothes. Why hedge? She didn't get the feeling that Tosin would object to nudity. She was about to find out if her impression was correct.

"Fuck yes. You're gorgeous, Kahori." His accent made her name sound special as he ditched his shirt and then his shorts. Bare beneath, he definitely didn't have any qualms about displaying his body to her. Or probably the world.

And why should he? His near-perfect form made her wish she was a sculptor instead of a jeweler. She'd pay particular attention to the distinct lines than ran from his hips to his groin and those that separated his washboard abs. And of course to his impressive cock.

"So are you."

"Show me where it's safe." He held out his hand to her, not afraid to let her lead. She imagined he was used to doing this for his own clients, but he didn't flinch when she navigated the craggy floor.

Kahori took him to the water's edge and beyond. Until her toes no longer touched bottom. She floated on her back, kicking lazily toward the waterfall as she observed the twinkling overhead.

Joining her, Tosin swam alongside her. Quiet for a while, he broke the silence to read her thoughts. "They look like constellations."

"I love looking at the stars," she admitted. "Especially here—they're so bright. When I was traveling to cities, it always made me sad to realize how little those people can see of the world and what's around us. Our people used the stars to find their way across oceans, but there…I was lost."

"Maybe you just needed a better guide." Tosin couldn't possibly know how true that statement was. Thankfully, it seemed like he was about to show her the way.

✦ EIGHT ✦

few moments later, they reached the far side of the cavern. When it became shallow enough, Tosin stood and tugged Kahori to him. She didn't resist, wrapping her legs around his hips. His hands fit perfectly over her ass, holding her close as he captured her mouth.

He covered her lips with his then, swallowing her soft moan as he kissed her thoroughly enough to curl her toes where they treaded through the water.

Kahori savored her first true kiss, from this man or any other. Her prior interactions hadn't been this affectionate, or as intimate. A sad but true statement on her lack of love life. Instead of dwelling on it, she snatched the opportunity she had now to indulge all the whimsical and romantic fantasies she'd entertained throughout the years.

With the cave sparkling around them and him filling her with equally glittery feelings, she lost herself in their exchange. Making out with him, she lost all sense of time or place. All she knew was the brush of their mouths, and tongues, against each other.

Tosin never let her slip, though eventually he did stride forward until she could perch on one of the stones that had been worn smooth by millennia of erosion.

Before Kahori had grown accustomed to the pure bliss he imparted with his lips and teeth, along with the rub of their torsos against each other, he'd moved on to the curve of her neck. A sharp nip followed by the wet heat of his lick caused her to cry out and cling to his shoulders in an attempt at grounding herself against the onslaught of pleasure.

"Easy," he crooned before wandering lower still to cup her breasts. He weighed and plumped them in his hands, accustoming her to his touch, before taking the tight tip of one into his mouth and flicking his tongue over it. Only when he'd damn near driven her mad with lust did he begin to suck on it, igniting her as easily as the sparks had kindled her *poi* earlier.

Cool water splashed across her skin, helping salve the blistering heat his touch left behind.

And still it shocked her, just how much more pleasurable it was when he kissed a meandering path across her stomach to her mound. The first contact of his mouth on her pussy had her spine arching impossibly. The position only granted him better access to her core.

She spread her legs without bothering to fight him, herself, or the inevitable course of events.

With a groan, he accepted her unspoken invitation. Tosin buried his face in her folds and devoured her slickness. He used his tongue to work her open then inserted one of his long fingers into her body. She clamped down on it, hugging it tight within her.

It felt better than anything she'd ever done to herself, and nothing at all like the pain she'd experienced the last time she'd let a man near her when she was this defenseless.

The bliss Tosin imparted left no room to think about her regrets.

Kahori concentrated on the waves of rapture washing over her along with the stream of the waterfall, which caressed her every place Tosin couldn't reach while otherwise occupied.

It didn't take long before her shouts threatened to crumble the rock walls. Unexpectedly, a strong orgasm hit her. She shuddered and quaked in his arms. His name echoed off the stone and filled the space with proof of her ecstasy.

He chuckled against her body, the amusement sending shockwaves through her sensitized flesh. The softest of tugs on her clit rejuvenated her pleasure, astounding her even as it thrilled her.

Tosin wrecked her. He brought her up and over the peak into climax time and time again until she was utterly boneless and gasping for air. "Mercy."

He lifted his head, smiling as he gathered her in his arms and lowered her into the warm, soothing water so he could place an almost chaste kiss on the corner of her gaping mouth. "Sorry, I got a little carried away. You taste so fucking sweet, and sound even better. It felt amazing when you came on my hand, too. I could never get enough of that. But I'd like to try."

His frank speech set off aftershocks that rattled her to her bones. What was she doing? She was so out of her league with him. Too late, she realized that she might have swum too far out to sea to make it back to shore.

A rookie mistake. One she might not survive.

This had been foolish. And she would pay the price.

Because now that she knew what she was missing, she would never be happy with life the way it had been. Not ever again. She'd destroyed her own haven as surely as the strongest typhoon slamming into the island could have.

The best she could hope for was to make it worth it.

It would help to know she hadn't only taken from him, but had given a part of herself as well.

"Will you show me how to please you?" she asked.

"Pretty much the same way as you do it with any other guy. Mouth on cock. Can't go wrong with that recipe." Tosin chuckled as he released her. He planted one hand behind him on the rock she'd so recently occupied then leapt so that he ended up seated there at the perfect height for her attentions. Water sluiced off of him in rivulets that drew her eyes steadily downward. To his—*wow*.

She floated closer until she could wrap one arm around his waist. Her other hand reached for his thick shaft, hovering a fraction of an inch away. Her fingers shook with her desire to do this well.

"Show me?" she repeated, hoping he wouldn't sense how artless she truly was.

No such luck. "Kahori..."

She refused to meet his probing stare, instead studying his erection close up.

"Look at me." He cupped her chin and pressed upward with gentle yet steady pressure until she did as he asked. "You're not a virgin, are you?"

"Not exactly," she hedged.

"It's really a yes or no sort of thing, isn't it?" His eyes were wider now, his pupils darker and growing. Did her lack of experience make him angry? Or was he getting even more turned on by the prospect of her near innocence? "Tell me what you mean before we go any further."

When she didn't answer right away, he softened the harsh rasp of his voice. His placid veneer in no way diminished his authority. It reassured her that he had everything under control. That he wouldn't rush her or take for the sake of taking.

Unlike before...

"I don't want to hurt you, Kahori. Or frighten you. Tell me what I need to know to take care of you properly. That's all I care about." He brushed the pad of his thumb across her lower lip.

Without thinking, she opened her mouth and took it inside for a moment. The entire time she toyed with it she imagined what it would feel like to do something similar with his cock, which was much, *much* bigger than the digit she rolled her tongue across.

"Don't distract me," he grumbled as he withdrew. "Talk to me."

She gave him the general idea. "There's no one on the island I'm interested in building a life with. No one I could have something casual with either. That's not how things work here. An affair would become political. Families would be involved. Before I'd even figured out if I could stand to share a house with a man, we'd be married. Just...no. There's no opportunity for fun without strings. So when I went on one of my trips, I did some research and found a club."

"What kind of club, sweetheart?" Tosin seemed still and calm, but she could sense a storm brewing within him.

"A sex club. It didn't mean anything, and it wasn't what I'd had in mind. I—" She shook her head. "I did it, but it didn't count for much besides going through the motions. I don't want to talk about it now. Don't want to ruin tonight with the ghosts of my poor decisions. So, please. I need some help making sure I'm doing this right, okay?"

His nostrils flared and his cheeks flushed in response to her entreaty. She'd definitely struck some kind of chord with him. She only wished she knew what it was. "I'll give you anything you need tonight, I swear. Come here."

He reached down and grabbed her beneath her arms, hoisting her up until he could crush his mouth over hers. The kiss he gave her then was ten times as potent as the ones before. His desperation transmitted something deeper, more genuine. It matched hers.

Ultimately he lowered her with a sigh, then reclined on one straight-locked arm that he braced behind him on the rock. "Start by running your fingers along my dick and balls. Lightly. Explore. See how they feel in your hands. Then against your tongue."

When his words alone threatened to shake her apart again, she stared up at him.

"Go ahead." He took her hand in his then placed it around his shaft and stroked himself some using her fingers for his gratification. Encouragement, yes. Force, no.

He let go, allowing her to proceed at her own pace, so very different from the last time she'd been this bold.

Kahori wondered at the blend of steel and softness against her hand. Even more so, she admired his restraint. Not once did he rush her as she took her time learning every inch of him and how her caresses affected him.

Each time he groaned, or cursed, or hissed, her smile widened. By the time a pearly drop of precome beaded on the very tip of his hard-on, she felt rather pleased with herself.

Tosin clearly agreed. He sank his fingers into her hair and nudged her nearer. "If you want to, you can taste me."

If she could have purred, she might have when she considered the possibility of returning the pleasure he'd gifted to her with his talented mouth. She parted her lips then surged upward until his cock was level with her face.

Kahori reached her tongue out, tentatively at first, and flicked it against him. She swiped the fluid from him and tested it out. Not bad. Even better was the hitch in his breathing, which grew heavier by the second. She could do that to him.

It revealed a power she hadn't known she possessed.

The feeling reminded her of the rush she experienced when dancing, except multiplied a thousand times. She was the focus of his rapt attention. The means to his ecstasy.

Tired of tiptoeing around, she opened her mouth wide and attempted to swallow him whole, like she'd seen women in porn do to their partners. Unfortunately, she choked.

"Not so fast. You don't have to do that to make it feel incredible." He lifted her and held her steady, keeping her from floundering while she recovered. "The most sensitive part is here."

Tosin took his cock in his fist and tapped the underside against her lips. She stuck out her tongue and swiped it just below the ridge of the head. He gasped.

So she did it again and again.

And when he let her have more of him, she settled for suckling on just the fat tip of his hardening cock, surprised when she realized he hadn't even been fully erect earlier. Damn.

Kahori took her time, testing different places and alternating sucking, licking, and massaging. She found that when she bobbed over his cockhead while swirling her tongue along the underside of his shaft, he began to tense.

The addition of her hand cupping his balls, rolling them as she marveled at the unique texture of his skin there, seemed to ramp up his pleasure. When she found something he liked, she did it more, harder and faster until her fun drove him to the edge of his self-control.

"I'm close, Kahori." She didn't consider the fact that he was also warning her that she was about to have a mouthful of his come until he froze, then bucked beneath her.

Tosin growled, making her wish she had a hand free to rub her clit while he pumped his release down her throat. It turned her on to witness his surrender to rapture. She drank him down, relieved to have pleased him, thrilled to have enjoyed it herself, honored to have some sliver of him to carry with her when they went their separate ways.

Kahori still sucked softly when he nudged her shoulders, urging her back.

As she withdrew, he slipped from between her lips. Except...

"Did I do it right?" she asked, peeking up at him from beneath her lashes.

"Hell yeah." He could hardly catch his breath enough to pant those two words she needed to believe so desperately. But—

"Then why are you still hard?" she wondered, embarrassed by her ignorance. "Is that...uh...normal?"

Tosin cracked up. "I have a feeling that with you it would be. Yeah."

"So you want me to do it again? Over and over, like you did to me?" Kahori licked her lips. She'd loved having him in her mouth and wouldn't mind practicing her newfound techniques to drive him wild. It was fun. Exhilarating. Empowering.

"I have a better idea." He slid into the water beside her then wrapped her in a tight hug before kissing her forehead lightly. The length of his shaft nudged her pussy.

If she angled her hips...

"Whoa. Hang on a second." Tosin cursed.

"Hmm? Why?"

"Condoms. They're in the pocket of my shorts." He shoved off the boulder and swam for the opposite side of the pool as if he were attempting to qualify for the Olympics, or being stalked by a shark. The drag caused by his substantial erection didn't seem to slow him down either.

Kahori grinned as she gave chase. She couldn't wait to sink her teeth into him.

His fine ass, which reflected the glowworms dotting the ceiling, seemed like a good enough place to start. By the time she had reached the edge of the water, he was returning with a foil packet in hand. He ripped it open then sheathed himself quickly and efficiently. Virginal he was not.

Kahori had a moment of doubt.

What did this mean to him? To her? Was she doing the right thing this time?

It was nearly impossible to think when every instinct screamed for her to fuck him while she could. That ferocious side of herself frightened her a little.

So when he sank over her in the shallows and began to lavish praise and charm on her in between tender kisses, a seed of guilt began to grow. Her passion began to fade and logic crept into the void it left behind.

"I'm glad we have tonight," she said as she tried to reassure herself that it was okay to savor what she could even if it was only a drop in the ocean of what she wanted.

"One night like this could never be enough," Tosin whispered. "I'm going to want a hell of a lot more of your sweetness. Don't you realize this is only the beginning? Ah, Kahori. Maybe I'll take you with me."

He groaned at the painful reminder that their time was limited. Or might even have already run out.

Just like that, she felt as if her blazing *poi* had smashed into her, scorched her, and raised painful blisters over her entire body. Especially in the vicinity of her heart.

What was she doing? She could never abandon her homeland or her *pāpā* like her mother had. It would kill him.

Despite her desires, she could never be so selfish.

Tosin made her spirit soar even as he shattered her illusions. Because she didn't have anything else to give this moment. Nothing more could come of their illicit interlude. And if she was teasing him by indulging their desires temporarily when she had no intention of pursuing their attraction after the first light of dawn, then she was only using him as others had done to her.

That kind of behavior she would not tolerate from herself.

"I—I can't." She shoved his shoulders, rolling him off of her, then staggered to her feet, leaving him crashed on the ground with empty arms and a monster erection. Add mortification to her agony. "I have to go. I'm sorry. I've made a mistake. A big one. I can't do this. I'm leaving before I make it worse."

"Kahori, wait. I'm an idiot for assuming you wanted more, too. I wasn't thinking. I'll take anything you want to give me and be grateful for it. I didn't mean that like it sounded." He grimaced when she kept backing away toward her clothes. "Hang on. If you're going, at least let me walk you home."

"That's not a good idea." She shook her head. Her father would take one look at them and know what she had done. How she'd betrayed him. Not only by fooling around with an outsider, but by considering what it might be like to leave this place behind. To be greedy enough to want to spend endless nights in Tosin's bed, damn the consequences.

Maybe she was her mother's daughter after all.

Kahori flung her *pareu* around her, cinching it closed with a well-practiced twist.

Though Tosin attempted to catch her, he didn't know the path as well as her and the darkness between the glowworm cavern and the sea meant he had to inch his way forward while his vision adjusted.

When she heard him cursing violently behind her, she winced. Sounded like he'd stubbed a toe. Hopefully he hadn't broken his whole damn foot.

Add another black mark to her tally. She'd repaid him poorly for the pleasure he'd given her.

Staying would only make it worse for them both.

Once on the beach, Kahori cut inland. Tosin would never be able to track her through the thick jungle on the shortcut she sometimes took to her house.

Unfortunately, the other men who'd been lying in wait—searching for her around the rocks where their sandy footprints had vanished—would have no similar troubles.

~ NINE ~

Kahori ran. The underbrush became thin green switches that whipped her cheeks, her arms, and the uncovered upper swells of her breasts. She didn't feel the sting. At least not until her tears dripped salt into the open wounds.

How could a night that had held so much potential turn into another mess?

Was she making everything worse?

She slowed from her dash to a jog and finally to a stagger, until the uncertainty and pain overcame her. Bracing her palms on her knees, she bent in half, trying to catch her breath and think clearly. Should she go back to Tosin? Beg him to forgive her waffling and confusion? At least explain what had set her off?

For a normally levelheaded person, being frightened and erratic—out of control in the face of her conflicted emotions—didn't sit well with her. Her cowardice disgusted her. Drawing herself up tall, Kahori glanced over her shoulder toward the beach.

Tosin bellowed her name. If he wasn't careful he'd draw attention from the island night guests, which was the very last thing she needed. Every nosy neighbor and town gossip would hear of their tiff, then speculate about what had caused it. Shit, had he even bothered to pull on his shorts before charging after her?

If not, she'd have a lot of explaining to do.

She had to turn around, if only to calm him so that he didn't shout the whole place to the ground or tear the jungle apart searching for her. She got the feeling he wasn't the type of man to give up easily.

Kahori took a single step in that direction before jumbled movement in the leaves surrounding her caught her attention. It wasn't breezy. The disturbance grew too big to have been caused by a bird or even a wild boar. Someone was out there.

"Tosin?" she called softly even as the hairs on her nape stood up.

Her luck had run out this evening. It wasn't her almost-lover. Instead, four men wearing black hoods and dark clothing emerged from the dense foliage. They stalked nearer, closing in around her like a casting net about to scoop up a school of fish.

"Who are you?" She stumbled backward, tripping over a vine before righting herself. Something told her that if she fell now, she wouldn't be getting back up.

"You know, don't you, Kahori?"

Hell, no. She didn't and she didn't want to either. So she attempted to flee through one of the gaps before it was too late.

For one glorious moment, she thought she'd slipped out of their grasp. Until her hair pulled taut and wrenched her backward. One of them must have grabbed a fistful as she darted past.

Kahori's instinctive scream pierced the night. "Help!"

This time it was terror, not pleasure, that echoed across the island.

Sleeping animals roused and charged deeper into the cover of darkness. She wished she could fly away as easily from the crushing impact of someone tackling her. The crack of her temple striking a log or a rock or something at least as dense as her skull ricocheted through her head. Her vision doubled before slowing refocusing.

"Where is he?" the man on top of her, pinning her to the dirt, snarled. His hot, stinky breath and aggression reminded her of the things she'd been trying to forget this evening.

"Get the fuck off me!" She lashed out—kicking, scratching, attempting to bite. Anything possible to inflict pain before he could.

Too late.

The man backhanded her, driving her teeth into her lips. An iron tang burst across her taste buds.

"You bastard! HELP!" she screamed again, projecting as loudly as she could manage.

This time she prayed Pāpā, Hemi, Uncle Kimo—or anyone else for that matter—could hear her after all. Let the entire village come running. She no longer gave a shit who saw. They had zero tolerance for violence. This would not go unpunished.

Hopefully she would be alive to see justice served.

"Now you've done it. We don't have much time. Someone's going to hear you squawking. So tell me...where is he? And where's the good stuff? You can't fool us with our own tricks, *yariman*."

"Who? Tosin? What?" That rock must have rattled her brains. Nothing her attacker said made sense.

"Play dumb if you like. We'll get what we're owed however we can. Let this be a lesson about what happens when you cheat us." One of the other guys kicked her in the ribs, knocking the wind out of her. She couldn't have asked more questions or raised a ruckus if she'd wanted to. "Tell him next time we won't stop here. Next time we'll take you and sell you to anyone willing to pay for your pussy until you work off his debt."

If that threat was supposed to subdue Kahori, they had miscalculated.

Instead, she redoubled her efforts to get loose. They might not have been very effective at warding off his blows, but at least they may have slowed the pummeling of his fists or impaired his aim.

Who would do this to her? Why?

Because she'd shown interest in Tosin? Because they wanted what she'd nearly given him?

Pure insanity. The sexy divemaster didn't deserve the wrath of small-minded losers, who apparently hated him on sight. Or because he'd taken something they considered *theirs*. Kahori had known there were still some extremely strong traditions on her island home. But this... She never would have expected this.

Another instant her faith in her fellow humans shattered.

This time cut deeper.

Her own people had turned on her. Or had they? Why didn't she recognize the voice of her attacker? Surely she knew everyone on Aitutaki.

It was impossible to think when they took turns waling on her now.

Kahori screeched and tried to crawl away, which only presented the perfect opening for them to drag her back by her hair again. As she lurched to the side, she felt the fine strings of her coconut bra snap. Someone grabbed her bared breast with bruising force.

Her thrashing weakened as horror bogged down her reaction time.

Hyperventilation didn't help either. Lightheadedness mixed with agony and despair.

She cowered on the ground, flinching from the fist that flew toward her face.

~ TEN ~

Tosin had barely stumbled out of the cave and onto the beach, his foot throbbing worse than it had that time a sea urchin had used it as a pin cushion, when he heard Kahori scream.

It wasn't a sound of anger or frustration.

No, it was fear.

Terror with pain mixed in.

Fuck! Had she fallen? Hurt herself in the darkness worse than he had? "Kahori!"

The following silence nearly frightened him more. Then another cry rang out, this one more urgent. It came from within the jungle. How the hell would he find her in there?

Glancing down, he tapped the face of his watch, a dive model complete with compass. He was an expert at navigating with it. Sometimes the divemasters tested themselves. One of them would keep his eyes closed as his partners hauled him to a random spot on the reef to see if he could find his way home. Tosin had never lost that little game yet.

Tosin took off after her.

He might not know where he was headed, but he could damn sure make it out again once he'd reclaimed Kahori. There was no doubt in his mind that he would. He wasn't letting her go that easily. And he sure as shit wasn't going to let her suffer out there, alone, because the thought of burying himself in her pretty pussy over and over had caused him to lose his motherfucking mind and say stupid stuff.

Tosin had spooked her bad.

Ironically enough, he seemed to have done the damage with words most of his other playmates would have killed to hear him speak. He tried to think about how he would fix things when he found her to distract from the anxiety her escalating shouts caused in him.

He needed to stay steady, keeping track of his landmarks and compass readings, in order to find her then bring her out again safely. Losing his calm and charging toward her might get him there faster, but then they'd be stuck. And it sounded like she might need immediate medical attention.

Tosin wiped sweat off his brow as he grew closer. Except maybe someone had beat him to her? He could swear he heard the rumbling of a masculine voice up ahead.

"You bastard! HELP!" Kahori begged.

Then nothing could stop him. It hadn't been a simple tumble that had downed her. Someone was mauling her! A person? Who the hell was out here hunting her?

Tosin took one final reading off his compass then crashed through every bit of foliage in the direct path between it and the struggle he could now hear clearly. A worthless motherfucker threatened her, spouting a bunch of nonsense, and then more rustling and grunts followed.

Was that Kahori fighting so viciously?

Pride and panic swirled together as he burst into the tiny clearing where she was being abused then launched himself at her assailant.

"Kahori!" Tosin roared her name like a war cry as he flew across the open area and intercepted one hell of a punch. It didn't do much more than inconvenience him as it drove into his side, but it could have smashed the delicate bones in her cheeks or caused irreparable damage to her more delicate parts, like her eyes or her brain.

Fury the likes of which he'd never experienced before surged within him. He kicked the fucker directly in the chest, throbbing foot be damned. The impact knocked the asshole back at least ten feet from Kahori, onto his ass. He must not have been as stupid as he was evil because he took one look at Tosin's unholy fury and took off, scrambling into the dense foliage. His cronies followed right behind.

Tosin looked between their retreating forms and Kahori, who sprawled in the dirt. She spit out a mouthful of blood then covered her bared breasts with one arm before attempting to stand.

"Catch them," she ordered.

He might have tried if she hadn't collapsed to the ground again, disoriented and wounded.

With a final lingering glare in the direction the men had disappeared, Tosin cursed viciously. He ignored her command. Instead, he rushed to her side and gathered her into his arms. "Fuck them. I'm not leaving you."

He didn't waste time with stupid questions like "Are you okay?" when she clearly was *not* okay.

Tosin cradled her as carefully as he could, somewhat alarmed that she didn't object and instead burrowed her face into the crook of his neck while she trembled in his grip. He glanced at the compass on his wrist then began to work backward.

He still had a ways to go when familiar voices called to him. Archer yelled, "Tosin!"

"Over here," he shouted in return, still angling for the shore.

"What the fuck, man?" Miguel asked when they practically collided with him.

Apparently he hadn't been the only one who'd heard Kahori's screams.

"I've got her. Someone jumped her. They ran away, heading northeast." He turned down the volume when Archer, Miguel, and Banks came into view. "Where's Waverly?"

"Standing by at the chopper with Sabine," Archer replied. She'd spent the afternoon giving kids rides and admiring the aerial view. They'd never expected they'd need her services for an evacuation tonight. "She'll be ready to take off the moment you get there."

Banks crooned to Kahori while the guys made their plans. He inspected her for obvious injuries as he tried to calm her. "Poor girl, look what they did to you. Tosin's going to get you fixed up, okay?"

She nodded then clung to him tighter, as if the twitch of movement was enough to cause her more suffering. They had to get the fuck out of here.

"Will you guys find her father for me? Let him know what's happening. See if anyone can figure out where those guys went and who they are, why they did this to her. I'm not waiting around in case they come back. I'm taking Kahori to the doctor on the *Divemaster*. Then I'm locking her in my cabin where she'll be safe." Tosin had already started walking.

Though he trod carefully, each step jarred Kahori enough to elicit groans from between her split lips. She stirred, seeming like she might object, so he added, "Convince him to come to the ship with you guys. She's going to need him by her side."

"Thank you," Kahori managed to croak. It seemed to sap the last of her energy. The next time her eyelids drooped, they didn't reopen.

So he gave up trying to be gentle and sprinted for the makeshift helipad.

~⊃ ELEVEN ⊂~

Kahori gasped as she came to. Something tickled her nose and the back of her throat. She coughed and flailed as her brain stem flashed warning signals throughout her body.

"Calm down. There's no need to be frightened." A warm female voice soothed some of her panic. "Those were smelling salts. Strong stuff, I know."

Kahori blinked, trying to focus on the people surrounding her in a well-lit room that smelled slightly of lemony disinfectant. She attempted to sit up. A hand rested on her shoulder, keeping her in place. Though she wanted to swat it away, her arms felt heavy and sluggish.

"It's just me," Tosin said. "I'm not trapping you here. I just don't want you to fall off this gurney and injure yourself more."

"Where am I?" She tried to remember what had happened after she left him in the glowworm cavern. Had she hit her head on an outcropping of rock as she fled like an idiot from the pleasure he'd tried to give her?

It certainly throbbed like a bitch.

"I brought you to the *Divemaster* so Dr. Kleveno could evaluate you." He ran his fingers lightly through her hair, thankfully avoiding the side that ached. "It doesn't look like anything's broken. Some of those bruises and scrapes are pretty nasty, though."

Bruises and scrapes? "What happened?"

"You don't remember?" the doctor asked, sounding slightly more concerned. "You might have a mild concussion."

As the woman prodded and poked Kahori, testing her reflexes and the dilation of her pupils with a penlight that stabbed her eyeballs as if it were an ice pick, bits and pieces began to return to her. By the time she remembered everything, her fists had bunched and she shoved past Tosin's restraint to sit upright.

"Those bastards!" She turned to Tosin, regretting the jerk of her head when the room wobbled a bit. "Please tell me you caught them."

He grimaced then shook his head. Negative. "Archer, Miguel, and Banks stayed behind to give it a go and fill in your dad. They're going to bring him here when they're finished with the hunt."

The fact that they weren't back already meant they probably hadn't been any more successful in rounding up her attackers than Tosin had. Damn!

Mostly she wanted to understand *why* they'd done it.

A light knock sounded at the door. Tosin plucked her *pareu* from a plastic chair next to the hospital bed and flapped it to fling off most of the dirt and sticks. The blood would never come out. Besides, it had ripped in a couple spots. It had been her favorite. Ah well. Could be worse.

Kahori lifted her arms so he could wrap it loosely around her like a giant bath towel. It would do for the moment.

Then Tosin went to the door and opened it a crack. Even here he didn't seem to be taking any chances with her security. Despite the evening's trauma, she felt protected and sheltered. Immune to the fear that would probably grip her while dreaming for a while.

"It's our captain," Tosin said over his shoulder.

"Let him in." Kahori shrugged. It seemed silly to make them talk through a gap in the door when she was decent and he might have information she'd like to hear firsthand.

"You're sure?" Tosin asked. She nodded.

When he admitted the man, who was probably around Banks' age, she smiled. Or at least she tried to. When her lips stung, she thought she might have reopened one of the cuts there. Dr. Kleveno was quick to daub some petroleum jelly on the area to keep it pliable. Kahori lifted her finger to the tender site, shocked by how puffy it was. Hey, maybe it gave her a sexy pout, she thought, trying to make the most of an awful situation. It was that or break down, and she didn't want to go that route. It would only make her pounding headache worse.

The new arrival studied her intently as he approached. "Captain Alex," he said in an efficient, staccato greeting that seemed as no-nonsense as the man himself. Fine silver lines in his otherwise dark hair and well-trimmed beard granted him an air of authority appropriate for the person ultimately responsible for the entire *Divemaster*. He was a little taller than average and sturdily built. He wouldn't be easy to push over in any sense of the phrase.

Kahori knew men like Archer, Miguel, Tosin, and Banks wouldn't entrust the ship and their own lives to just anyone. Dr. Kleveno stared at the captain as if he were a legend in his own right. Though she was easily ten—or even fifteen—years younger than the captain, Dr. Kleveno seemed awfully interested in him. She pushed her purple glasses up her freckled nose with her index finger. Possibly so she could see him better.

Trying not to grin, Kahori peeked at Tosin. He was glancing between the two crew members with interest. Meddling matchmakers on Aitutaki would have hooked those two up in a second.

When the captain held out his hand to Kahori, she shook it. He held her in a surprisingly gentle grip. She figured her torn nails and bruised knuckles had something to do with his overabundance of caution. Either that or she looked like the kind of woman who required a delicate touch.

Compared to Waverly, Sabine, and Dr. Kleveno, Kahori wasn't sure she stacked up to the strong females he was used to, though she planned to change his mind. "Nice to meet you, though I wish it were under different circumstances."

"I have a feeling we would have been introduced to each other soon enough no matter what." He looked pointedly at Tosin, who had parked himself at her side like a guard dog. Then Captain Alex asked, "If it's not too upsetting, can you tell me anything you remember that might help identify the people who hurt you? Either of you, really. The guys radioed in. They could use direction."

"When I ran up, I heard one of the guys threatening her. They were interrogating her." Tosin punched his fist into his opposite palm. "I couldn't quite hear it all. More of their tone than the specifics, really."

Her memory was still sort of foggy, but his nugget of information jogged her recollection. "They kept asking me where *he* was. Where the *good stuff* was, too. They also called me some kind of insult when I couldn't figure out who or what they meant. It sounded like *yariman*, which isn't a Māori word or one in any of the Cook Islands dialects that I know."

Captain Alex tensed, his face turning purple. He didn't look at her when he explained, "It's Japanese for slut." When Tosin shot him a bewildered look, the guy shrugged. "I was stationed in Okinawa for nearly four years during my time in the Navy."

Kahori shuddered. "I guess that makes sense. Tosin's right. They did threaten me. They said something about getting what they were owed, even if it meant...uh...selling me."

There really wasn't a more polite way to say that they'd planned to whore her out to rapists, was there?

Tosin growled. He breathed hard, reacting more strongly than she would have imagined to that bit of news.

"I'm sure they were only bluffing." She patted his forearm. "Trying to scare me."

Which had worked, by the way. Though she didn't intend to highlight her cowardice for them.

"Have you had dealings with any Japanese buyers lately?" Captain Alex asked her.

"Thanks to modern technology, I do ship all over the world. We send out orders once a week. I don't remember there being any to Japan in the past month or so, though. Nothing major for certain." She shrugged halfheartedly. "It has to be some sort of mix-up."

"That's a hell of a swing and a miss if so." Tosin wrapped his arm around her and scooted her closed to his side. "Regardless, no one's getting near you again. I swear it."

Kahori leaned against Tosin, closing her eyes. All she really wanted was to lie down somewhere dark and comfortable until her *pāpā* arrived, hopefully with some explanations.

"Can I take her to my cabin now? Is it okay for her to sleep?" Tosin asked Dr. Kleveno, who nodded.

She spoke directly to Kahori when she said, "Unless you'd prefer to stay in here. We have rooms set up for the people en route to participate in Sabine's trials."

"Thank you." She appreciated the out ,though it wasn't necessary. "I'd rather go with him."

"I don't blame you." Dr. Kleveno grinned. "I would too if I were you. The offer stands if you change your mind. There's room and I can keep an eye on you. Otherwise, I'll come check on you in a few hours and bring your next dose of painkillers."

Then she turned to Tosin. "Don't let her get out of bed unless it's to use the bathroom."

"I can do that." He nodded, taking his caretaker duties very seriously.

When Kahori would have hopped down, Tosin scooped her into his arms instead. Captain Alex opened the door so they could pass. "I hope you're feeling better soon. It pains me to admit it, at the risk of overinflating their egos, but these kids have excellent taste in women. You're going to fit right in here."

Kahori winced. She wouldn't be onboard long enough to become integrated into their gang. Why did that thought upset her? The captain's compliments meant a lot in any case. "Thank you."

She tried to stay alert as Tosin carried her through the ship. It was gorgeous. Beyond anything she could have imagined even after the luxurious hotel stays she'd splurged on every once in a while for her business trips.

"I can't believe that Archer—all of you—have pockets deep enough to own all this, and yet he chose to buy Waverly a ring from my shop. Now I get why he asked you about whether he was doing the right thing by not opting for a more traditional stone." She sighed. "He could always give her my ring for her birthday or Christmas or something and pick up a mega-diamond worthy of a billionaire's wife."

"Believe it or not, he's not like that. Waverly isn't either." Tosin laughed. "None of us are. I hope it doesn't disappoint you that I might technically be rich, but I'm still a poor slob at heart. That ring is perfect for her. You'll see when he gives it to her."

Kahori winced. "Yeah. You'll have to videotape his proposal if you can. I'd love to see it." Because surely they'd be long gone before he popped the question.

In fact, after today, maybe they'd be departing sooner than scheduled. She wouldn't blame them for leaving this mess in their rearview mirror. If megayachts even had rearview mirrors.

Staying silent, the craftsman in her settled for observing the fine woodwork and blown glass waves that enhanced the interior of the space as they made their way to the other side of the ship where the owners' quarters were. Right about the time she suspected Tosin had walked halfway back to Aitutaki, he stopped in front of his door and keyed in a code.

Unlike Dr. Kleveno, he didn't ask her where she wanted to sleep. Which was fine by her.

If she was being honest, she couldn't stomach the thought of being alone when she drifted off. Didn't care to wake up by herself in an unfamiliar place, either.

He set her on her feet long enough to slip the *pareu* from around her and toss it into a wad in the corner of his enormous quarters. She didn't blame him. It horrified her that she might stain something in his gleaming, pristine personal space. The linens on the enormous bed were the same steel blue as his eyes. Drawings of fish and sea creatures hung in shiny metal frames, and the modern shelving around the desk held an assortment of orchids and nanogardens.

It immediately felt like a place she could be comfortable.

Ridiculously so.

Though he kept the blackout curtains closed for now—*thank you*—she'd bet there was a spectacular view out the wall-to-wall windows opposite the bed. Tosin peeled back the thick comforter and helped her settle creakily in the plush nest. Though not in too much pain, she felt like a hundred year old elder.

It didn't surprise her when he tugged his shirt over his head, then tucked his thumbs in his waistband and shoved his shorts down with a single slick movement. In the dim light, she couldn't see as much of his spectacular body as she wished she could.

Tosin took his fancy watch off and placed it neatly on the nightstand. She was surprised to see the bracelet he'd bought from her shop lying next to it.

He picked it up and ran his fingers across the intricate carvings she'd slaved over for an inordinate period of time considering the set wasn't a big-ticket item. Then he sat on the edge of the mattress and held it out to her, along with his wrist. "Can you put it on me?"

She flexed her fingers a few times and found them less stiff than they'd been before. Dr. Kleveno must have slipped her some anti-inflammatories. "Sure."

It took her a couple of tries but she managed to fit the black pearl knotted on the end through the leather loop that held it closed. He smiled as he looked at her work adorning him. "I like having this reminder of you on me. I'm not planning on taking this off any time soon."

If Kahori had been a bolder woman, she might have asked for him to put the matching one on her. But she was afraid he might misinterpret that as some kind of commitment, when really she was thinking about a memento of their liaison that she could take out and sigh over after he'd left her behind.

"Mind if I snuggle with you while you rest?" He grinned. "Don't tell the guys, but it's right at the top of my list of favorite bedroom activities."

Kahori snorted then patted the bed beside her. "Yeah, right."

He laughed, but he did seem content as he cradled her against his chest. The lulling thump of his heartbeat helped her settle down. At least until she looked at where her fingers rested on his rib and realized he hadn't escaped their earlier fiasco unscathed. A huge bruise marked the spot that had intercepted that final punch.

If he hadn't shown up right then…

Kahori leaned over and placed a light kiss over the damaged area. "I'm sorry."

"That is in no way your fault." His tone turned icy. "I won't let you blame yourself for something some fuckface did."

"I shouldn't have run from you. Will you let me explain?" She couldn't believe she was offering this part of her—so personal, something that shamed her. But he deserved to understand. It was all she could offer despite everything she wished she could give him.

"Don't feel you have to. But I *am* curious." He rubbed her shoulders lightly, relaxing her further.

His unconditional acceptance made it easier to begin her confession.

∽ TWELVE ∾

Tosin concentrated on lying still and keeping his respiration measured. He didn't want to frighten Kahori away again, especially not when she was putting so much faith in him. Trust was something he sensed didn't come easily for her, for some reason he hoped he was about to discover.

If they were going to play again, harder next time, he had to be sure she would enjoy the same brand of loving he did. He couldn't deny his dominant streak, though he could definitely tailor how it manifested to suit her needs. The way she'd deferred to him, begging for instruction in the glowworm cavern, made him positive she could enjoy his hardwired sexual preferences as much as he did. Even if she didn't understand the various nuances of what a power exchange could entail...yet.

It didn't have to be something artificial with a lot of rules of engagement or anything too extreme. He'd love to educate her about the wide variety of pleasures available for her to sample.

Their easy companionship convinced him they would be great partners in and out of bed. But he had to find an approach to intimacy that would work for them both. Challenge accepted.

To do that, he had to understand her first. Her fears, her hopes, her triggers, her limits—each critical variable in the equation. So he kept quiet and studied her, greedily absorbing every crumb of information she fed him about the woman he was quickly becoming obsessed with.

Okay, fine, he'd been completely infatuated with Kahori since the first moment he'd laid eyes on her.

"I guess it started when my mom left us." She drew a deep, shaky breath, wincing slightly when the inhalation put pressure on her ribs. "I was still a toddler. I hardly remember her, to be honest. But I clearly recall how miserable Pāpā was after she had gone. He's always loved Aitutaki. Not only the place, but also the way of living. Truly enjoying each day instead of slaving away in an office, paid to perform a meaningless, repetitive task. He spends time on the water fishing for dinner, on walks through the jungle picking fruit. He soaks up the sun as he repairs our house. Pāpā is resourceful, making things we need out of what we have. So I guess when my mother left, it wasn't only that she abandoned us both and piled a heap of extra responsibilities on him, but she rejected his dying way of life, jabbing another knife in its back."

Tosin could see how that would hurt. What if he'd fallen for a woman who loved living in one place, maybe in a giant city far from the ocean? How could he choose between the person he loved and the only existence that could keep him happy?

He thought about it some more, wondering what might have happened if his grandparents had lived longer. Of course he would have relished every moment he got to spend with them. One day, though, would he have resented being held captive in a place he'd been born in but didn't love as much as others?

As shitty of a grandson as it made him, the answer was probably yes. Then again, they had always encouraged him to follow his heart. They wouldn't have guilted him into staying or anything like that. Still… he thought he understood where she was heading with this.

"So when your business started taking off, you hung around, sacrificing some potential to keep from trampling your dad's heart all over again, right?" Tosin could see how it would be a tough call. There wasn't any clear right answer.

"Yeah." Kahori sighed as if she'd never admitted it out loud before. "I would love to see more of the world than our little island, even though I do think this is probably as close to paradise as I could ever find. But I've felt like I had to tamp down those desires so that I didn't turn out like my mother. Every time I went on one of my selling trips, Pāpā would hug me so tight at the airport that I'm sure he thought I wouldn't come back. Twenty years after my mother split, he's still traumatized. As far as I know, he's never been with anyone else before or since. Who could walk away from their child and husband—one who loved her to his core—like that?"

"Hey, no judgment here." He cleared his throat, then said, "My mom's a hooker."

Kahori giggled. "Come on, I was being serious."

"So was I." He let that truth-bomb explode all over them.

"Wow." She hugged him. "I'm sorry. I shouldn't have assumed…"

"It's fine." He kissed her forehead. "I grew up in the wetlands just north of Amsterdam. She's a legit sex worker over there. I hear she's pretty good at her job. My mom never really wanted a kid. So she kept doing her thing and sent money to my grandparents, who raised me. We lived simply but had all the essentials. Unfortunately, my Opa had a massive brain aneurism and dropped dead while out in his garden one sunny afternoon. Not a bad way to check out, I guess. Oma didn't last too long after he'd passed. By the time I was fifteen, I was on my own. If I'd gone to my mother for help, I'm sure she would have done the right thing. But I figured a decade and a half of being bogged down financing another person's existence was enough punishment for a mistake or a fluke of biology, whatever I had been."

"No wonder you're so confident. You've always done things for yourself." She nuzzled his chest. "I admire that about you."

"Actually..." Tosin shook his head as he stared up at the ceiling. "I don't feel that way at all. It took me about two years of backpacking, wandering aimlessly with no home, no family, no purpose except to survive each day—and definitely no money—before I ran into Miguel and Archer. They became my family. Until them, I was pretty much a vagabond."

Tosin cleared his throat. Here came his biggest admission of all. "There were so many factors I had absolutely no control over that when it came to women and sex..."

"You like to be in charge," she simplified.

"I *need* it." He tried not to get turned on discussing this with her, considering her state. But imagining her peering up at him as she'd followed his directions earlier—sucking his cock so well, with enthusiasm if not skill—threatened to unleash another tsunami of desire within him. "The rush brings me satisfaction, yes. But the gift of a woman's surrender grounds me. Satisfying us both makes me sure that no matter what else happens, I have that part of my life in hand."

Kahori nodded slowly. She also squirmed against him, and he didn't think pain was responsible for her fidgeting this time.

"So that's why I'm curious." He hesitated until she looked at him. "Did you run from me because you liked the idea of sailing away with me, or did you run because you were afraid of the part of you that needs to submit?"

She took time to truly consider before whispering, "Both."

"Tell me more about the sex club you went to," he prompted.

"Ugh." She burrowed her face into his collarbone, hiding from him. "It was pretty much awful. Embarrassing and in no way enjoyable. It wasn't like the subtle way you took the lead before, which felt natural and honest to me."

Well, shit. That was going to make it a lot harder for him to admit he loved that sort of formal environment with established BDSM parameters. So much that he, Archer, and Miguel had their own private clubroom just down the hall. He would tell her, though, when she was ready to hear it and he was sure she wouldn't bolt again. If she stuck around that long.

First he had to know what he was up against.

"Did someone hurt you there?" He should have stopped devouring her in the cavern to have this discussion then, but he'd been too greedy and he'd paid the price for his avarice. Worse, so had Kahori. If he had done things the right way, maybe she never would have fled.

Instead, they'd be blissed out, probably lying on his blanket on the beach or enjoying the pineapple desserts back at island night.

The possibility that someone had raped her terrified him. He wasn't sure if he could overcome the deep scarring that such a violation could have left on her or if he was qualified to give her the support she would need if she had. He'd try his best, but maybe it wouldn't be enough.

She was quick to put him at ease, maybe underplaying things a little. "No. Nothing like that. It just was so contrived. There was no emotion. Completely opposite of what I felt with you tonight."

Kahori blushed as she admitted that, so he rewarded her with a careful kiss on her damaged lips. That tiny peck alone had him craving more. He stared into her eyes, scanning for any signs of discomfort, as he lingered there.

She practically purred and sank deeper into his sheltering embrace.

Perfect.

When they broke apart, she seemed stronger. She continued, "I convinced myself that if I was going to lose my V-card, it had to be then. I wasn't ready, but I wasn't going to have an opportunity again for who knew how long, so I picked someone who seemed decent enough to get the job done. Except when I realized the physical act alone wasn't going to satisfy my curiosity, I felt like I couldn't turn back. The guy—I didn't even know his name—held up his end of the bargain. He did as I asked and seemed to really get off on popping my cherry."

"Kahori, don't justify how he acted. He didn't do right by you." Tosin could see how she might think he had, though, if she'd never had a caring partner before. "Any man or woman has a responsibility to care for his or her partner. That shouldn't change just because you were at a club. I've fucked plenty of women casually. That doesn't mean I didn't take care of them, or honor their gift. Hell, I even think I gave them all the best parts of myself for that moment. That guy you were with should have seen it in your eyes, that you weren't really into it anymore. As the more experienced person, he should have cut you loose. He didn't. Selfish bastard."

"It would have been impossible for him to see my expression." She closed her eyes then, keeping Tosin from reading clues about her statement in them. He didn't care for that.

"What do you mean by that?" He noted the pounding of her pulse and the clenching of her hands as proof enough. If he could have kicked this guy's ass, he would gladly have done it. That loser *had* hurt her, even if she couldn't express the injury or admit it to herself.

"He put me on some kind of bench on all fours, with my ass in the air, then fucked me from behind." She winced then. "He said it would be less painful that way."

"That bastard lied to you." Tosin imagined how much deeper he could penetrate a lover in that position. He'd bet the guy hadn't been gentle either. He'd probably gotten off on impaling her on the first stroke, knowing no one had ever been deep in her pussy before.

Tosin had thought he'd reached a record level of anger earlier that night when he'd seen Kahori take a physical beating at the hands of a stranger. If he had, he shattered it again with a new high...or new low, depending on how you looked at it.

If he'd seen someone damaging Kahori that way, so much worse, he wouldn't have been able to stop himself from ripping their cock off with his bare hands to keep them from ever betraying a woman's trust so thoroughly again.

Tosin didn't bother asking if the fucker had at least taken time to get her off. It was clear he wasn't capable of that and she probably wouldn't have been able to climax after such rough treatment, even if he'd tried to take her there.

Then Kahori finished her story in a rush, as if expelling the last of the poison from a sea snake bite. "When he finished, he didn't even say goodbye. He walked away and left me there, wondering what the hell had just happened and how I could have been stupid enough to have thought this was what I wanted. A couple of strangers saw and helped me clean up the blood and get dressed."

"Wait." Tosin clenched his jaw. "He fucked you in a public space? Left you to fend for yourself after?"

"Yes. I'm kind of glad about that, actually, because those strangers were so kind. They tried to tell me not everyone there was like the guy I fucked. That if I came back they'd make it better. They drove me to my hotel, made sure I was okay. But I knew I'd never do it again. Despite what I thought, that kind of organized, artificial relationship isn't for me."

Tosin knew he'd have to respect her boundaries. Though she hadn't had a fair introduction to the kind of activities he sometimes indulged in, it would likely be a hard stop for her. And he would have to accept that if he wanted to spend more time with her. Show her how good sex could be with the right partner.

And he desperately wanted that. He'd never longed for something as badly as that in his life.

So he'd make sure she never knew that side of him or had a chance to mistakenly believe that he could be as callous as the person she'd had the misfortune to entrust with her virginity.

He'd make sure that the next time was the only time that counted.

Tosin held himself above her, careful not to apply pressure to any of her sore spots. He dropped his head and kissed Kahori, giving her a glimpse at how he'd be different from the only other man who'd been inside her. He'd ply her with anticipation, not fear. And hopefully, when their affair came to an end, he'd leave her with fond memories instead of regrets.

Fine cracks developed in his heart when he realized that it wouldn't be fair for him to talk about whisking her away from Aitutaki again. He wouldn't put her in that position—choosing between him and her father. Hell, they had a private jet. He could visit often. Or maybe even take a break from the *Divemaster* until they could figure something out.

Those were problems for another time.

For now, he only cared about taking away her pain and replacing it with something much sweeter. She sighed and touched his back, keeping him close to her. Hesitant at first, her inquisitive caresses turned into true embraces when he used his mouth and tongue to communicate just how much he enjoyed her touches.

One of her hands wandered from his shoulders to the dip of his waist. It crept lower, toward his ass. Meanwhile, he was careful to keep his pelvis far enough away that she couldn't feel how aroused he was by the strides they'd made, and her tentative affection.

Before he could get carried away, a knock came at the door and Archer called, "Can we come in?"

✑ THIRTEEN ✑

Kahori struggled to sit up, so Tosin rolled off her then lifted her shoulders, propping pillows behind them while she clutched the sheet to her chest. What was Pāpā going to have to say about seeing Tosin in bed with her and their clothes nowhere to be found?

This could be interesting.

Before she could bum a T-shirt off Tosin, he called, "Come in."

Except after Archer, Miguel, Waverly, Sabine, Banks, and Captain Alex piled into the room, making good use of the comfortable couch and pair of chairs in the seating area to the side of the bed.

"Pāpā?" Kahori asked.

Archer winced. "I'm sorry, we couldn't find him."

Kahori froze beside Tosin. Her breathing hitched and tears she hadn't shed for herself turned her eyes glassy. Had someone attacked him too? What was going on?

"Hey, hey. I'm sure there's an explanation. Maybe he's looking for you still?" Tosin didn't sound very sure as he attempted to reassure her.

It did seem pretty damn suspicious that he'd disappeared as soon as his daughter had been attacked. Kahori refused to believe that he'd somehow been involved. He would never do anything to put her in jeopardy.

"He was at the island night dinner," Tosin said to Archer. "Where the hell did he go?"

Miguel answered this time. "I was sitting right next to him arguing for the grow dome when we heard a faint scream. He shouted for Kahori, then took off sprinting toward her house. Most everyone else went in the other direction, heading for either the beach or the jungle. I know I did. So...no one's quite sure what happened to him after that."

Kahori didn't speak. Her vision blurred as flashbacks of the attack took center stage. "*Where is he? Where's the good stuff?* That's what they asked me. He couldn't mean Pāpā, could he?"

No one had answers for her. Unwilling to badmouth a man they'd never met, they let her make her own decisions on that front.

She looked up at Tosin then. He must have seen her fear in her eyes.

"Trust your gut, Kahori. Just because your mother cut you, that doesn't mean your dad stabbed you in the back." He'd nailed it. There was fear for Pāpā's safety, of course, but also fear of betrayal.

After tonight, she no longer knew what to believe when it came to other people.

Except that she trusted Tosin. She put her hand in his.

When she looked up, she noticed Banks's pinched expression. Oh shit, there was more?

Tosin gathered Kahori and lifted her gently onto his lap. He made sure he enveloped her in his arms as if they could provide some insulation against the next wave of agony that was about to get unleashed on her.

Eventually she realized that everyone was standing there, sober and quiet. Very unlike their usual chaotic state.

"Oh no. What else?" Kahori clung to Tosin like a black-lipped oyster's byssus adhered to the reef.

"I don't know if it was your dad or somebody else, but by the time we got to your house looking for him..." Archer shook his head. "Someone trashed your place. It seemed like they were looking for something. They went through your drawers and cabinets. Trashed your workshop. Your clothes, your bed..."

"We get the point," Tosin snapped, shooting Archer a *shut the fuck up* stare when Kahori began to quiver in his grasp.

"None of this makes sense!" She put her face in her hands for a few moments before gathering herself, striving for resilience. That was the only thing that was going to help them get to the bottom of this mess. "There's nothing of value in my house except my jewelry components—pearls and loose gems. Everyone on the island knows those are in a safe because of my insurance policy. It's kind of a running joke. I honestly only got the damn thing to protect against fires and floods, not because anyone would steal from me."

"That's pretty much what your cousin and uncle are telling everyone, too." Miguel clenched his fist. "It seems they're more in favor of believing us outsiders caused tonight's trouble. Hemi asked the council to kick us off the island. They voted down the grow dome and said they don't want our money or our problems."

"Oh no!" Kahori gasped. "That's ridiculous. Maybe I need to go back and straighten things out." She attempted to scoot out of bed, lack of clothes be damned.

Tosin refused to let her leave. "No way. Tonight has been fucked up enough as it is. We're safe on the *Divemaster*. You need to take it easy at least overnight."

"He's right, Kahori." Waverly jumped in then. "You scared the shit out of me on the flight back here. This mess can wait until tomorrow."

"In the morning, we'd be happy to take you home," Archer offered.

Tosin growled a warning.

"I don't think it's wise for you to stay there, but we'll escort you while you look around and see what's up. Maybe you can spot something we didn't notice." Banks suggested a middle ground. "For now, I think you should try to rest. Dr. Kleveno said it will do you a world of good. That's what your *pāpā* would want you to do, too."

She couldn't argue with that.

Another knock came at the door then followed by Dr. Kleveno asking, "Why does it sound like half the crew is in here?"

Captain Alex rushed to let her in despite the fact that she was probably going to ream them out for keeping Kahori awake. As if she could sleep now without knowing where her father was and what might have happened to him.

"Still doing okay?" Dr. Kleveno asked as she whipped out that insanely bright flashlight again. When she rotated the end of the device to turn it on, the beam flashed across Sabine.

Kahori froze.

"Does that hurt?" Dr. Kleveno frowned. "If you're that sensitive to the beam from far away, you could have more damage than I suspected."

"Kahori?" Tosin asked her when she didn't respond right away.

She couldn't look away from Sabine. From there she couldn't be sure of what she'd seen. Maybe she *had* hit her head too hard. "Hey, can I see your earrings for a second?" She held her hand out to Sabine.

The other woman looked at her like Kahori definitely might have bonked the sense right out of her brain. She glanced at Miguel, who shrugged. Sabine slipped one from her ear, then tipped her head to start on the other.

"You can work later," Dr. Kleveno scolded Kahori. "I didn't mean for you to have so many visitors. It's best if you take it easy. Rest."

"Please. I need to see them." She shook her hand, palm up, curling her fingers toward her, completely ignoring the doctor's advice.

Sabine seemed unsure, but she passed over the earrings.

Immediately Kahori could tell something was off. "What did you do to these?"

"Nothing," the other woman swore. "I mean, I wore them today. That's it."

Kahori pointed to the jump rings that connected the pearls to the setting. "This isn't my work. These are sloppy. Look how the ends overlap and the circles are kind of squished out of shape. You're sure you didn't take them off and reattach them for some reason?"

"Why would she do that?" Banks asked.

"I have no idea." Kahori stared, looking from person to person, wondering exactly who she could trust. Her own eyes told her something was very wrong. Her new friends acted innocent. But if they hadn't tampered with her work, who had?

"Light." She waved for Dr. Kleveno to shine the torch directly on the earrings. Up close.

Kahori squinted at the overwhelming brightness. It was subtle but... "Something's not right with these. The luster is off."

Her heart rate tripled. She was an expert, someone who'd grown up around pearls and spent hours each day handling them, studying them, yet she could hardly tell. A common buyer would have no chance at spotting the inconsistencies here.

She pulled her lips back, grimacing at the sting, though it seemed to have lessened already. Kahori rubbed one of the pearls across her front tooth. It was gritty, as it should be. Fakes had a too-smooth surface compared to the natural nacre of a genuine pearl. At least poor fakes. To be sure...

"Sabine, do you have a microscope in your lab onboard?" Kahori wondered.

The other woman nodded.

"Would you mind terribly if I sacrificed one of these? I'll replace it." She was already shoving herself toward the edge of the bed. Besides, if what she suspected was true, they weren't worth anything anyway.

"Do whatever you need," Sabine said even as Dr. Kleveno and Tosin teamed up to keep Kahori in place.

"Hey, where do you think you're going?" he asked her, deep grooves marring his forehead.

"I need to see these under magnification." Kahori tried to tug free, but budging him was impossible. A rising tide of anxiety clawed up her insides. She tensed all over, causing her head to throb.

"No, what you *need* is to stay calm and still." Dr. Kleveno put her foot down. "You're not leaving this room."

"Hey, don't worry. I'll prep a slide for you." Sabine came nearer. She looked at the doctor, then Tosin, and lastly—when neither objected—to Kahori. "My microscope is digital. I'll email Tosin pictures. Will that work?"

"Yes, thank you." She relaxed against Tosin, just a little bit.

"Give me five minutes." Sabine reclaimed her earrings then left with Miguel on her heels.

The air seemed heavy. It made it hard to breathe. Kahori looked at Archer, who met her gaze directly. They had to be thinking the same thing. But it was impossible to tell him she was terrified the engagement ring he'd bought could have been tampered with too with Waverly standing right there.

So instead she plucked Tosin's hand from where it still cupped her upper arm. She drew it near and turned it over so that she could inspect the pearl clasp. She ran her thumb over the knot in the end of the leather. It wasn't as crisp as when she'd tied it.

Dread swamped her guts. "Light."

Dr. Kleveno shone the beam directly on the pearl. Kahori shoved Tosin's hand away before she could rip the bracelet from him and fling it against the wall. More of the same. What the hell was going on here?

Her panicked gaze flew to Archer.

He lifted his fingers at her in a subtle acknowledgement. "I'll be right back. Gotta take care of something quick."

Waverly asked, "Do you want me to come with you?"

He shook his head. "Stay in case they need you."

Kahori massaged the lump on the side of her head, which felt smaller but had started to ache and pulse as if it were dancing to the beat of the drums from earlier in the evening.

Dr. Kleveno took pill bottles from her purple satchel. Tosin held out a glass of water even as she shook a few capsules into her hand. "You'd better take these. We don't want to let your discomfort spiral out of control or it will be harder to manage and take longer to recover from."

Kahori was pretty damn sure her *discomfort* levels were about to shoot through the roof. Her father was missing. She'd gotten beat up. Her illicit liaison had ended in disaster. And now she suspected that she'd been unintentionally scamming innocent customers by selling them costume jewelry for top dollar.

Out of energy, she didn't argue, still trying to figure out how this could have happened and if it could be related to rest of the evening's events.

It had to be.

You can't fool us with our own tricks, they'd said.

When Tosin's phone bleeped, she couldn't seem to draw enough air into her lungs. He held it out to her, open to his email app. There were two messages from Sabine. The subjects were Sabine's Earrings and Waverly's Ring.

Oh God.

She selected the first message. It didn't take more than a glance at the close up to be sure. "They're junk. Not real."

"*What?*" Banks's eyebrows seemed like they were trying to join the hair on top of his head.

"The pearls in Sabine's earrings are manufactured. They're amazingly good fakes, but they're worthless. I'm so sorry." She clapped her hand over her mouth, trying not to look at Waverly.

Because if the earrings were phony, so was the clasp on Tosin's bracelet.

Kahori began to doubt everything she would have sworn to a minute ago.

The ring...

She'd handed it to Archer personally the other day after retrieving it from her safe. It had seemed exactly as she remembered. If it was phony too, she would never know how long she'd been unintentionally swindling her customers. Her business would be ruined along with her reputation.

It took her two tries to click the second email. When the microscope's enhanced image popped up, she sagged in relief.

The proper crystal structure—consistent yet disturbed periodically by natural imperfections not present in the manufactured version—was evident. It was real. She wasn't losing her mind.

"That one's good?" Tosin asked as he peeked over her shoulder.

She nodded. Then frowned. "The stuff from the Rarotonga shop is garbage. I need to talk to Hemi."

Even as she said it though, the room dimmed. It was too much. The day she'd had, complete with epic highs and lows. Her body couldn't take anymore. It started to shut down as if she was a nuclear reactor about to overheat.

"In the morning, Kahori." Tosin glanced at Dr. Kleveno, who nodded. "If you're up to it then, we'll take you over to the island to figure out what the hell is going on."

"Okay." She wished she could say more. As her medicine kicked in and numbness began to take away both her pain and her alertness, she tried again. "I'm sorry."

These people—and the rest of her clients, too—had no reason to believe she hadn't known what was happening beneath her nose. Hell, how hadn't she figured it out sooner?

There would be plenty of time for self-recrimination later.

With disgust, shame, and shock mixing into a super shot of misery, her mind could no longer function. From far away, she thought she heard Tosin encouraging her to relax by promising her everything would be okay.

She figured that was the only time since they'd met that he'd lied to her.

It seemed that was more than she could say for her own family.

Kahori went under."

∽ FOURTEEN ∾

Tosin kept his hand low on Kahori's back, not letting her out of his reach. Both to make sure she was steady on her feet and to remind himself that no one was actively threatening her.

She'd woken up bright and early, eaten a full breakfast, then refused to take any more painkillers, insisting she was sore but fine. He suspected she also intended to keep her mind fog-free so that they had no legitimate reasons to block her from assessing the damage at her house.

Her strategy had worked, though he'd had a hell of a time letting her leave the safety of the *Divemaster* without having a panic attack. They'd had enough near misses in the past year to put him on high alert. The rest of the crew, too.

So they were making a quick run, unannounced, over to her place. Then they'd have to figure out what came next based on anything they uncovered. The first batch of subjects in Sabine's trials were set to arrive in a few hours, along with Marta. Waverly would be shuttling them in, so she'd stayed behind also. The security on the ship had been beefed up in anticipation, but Captain Alex and Banks were both opposed to stretching their resources too thin.

Finally Tosin fully understood how hard it had been for Archer and Miguel when their women had been the ones threatened. Both guys shot him sympathetic looks as their tenders docked and they strode as quickly as possible toward Kahori's house.

"Hanging in there?" he asked her, wincing at their pace.

"Tosin, I promise I'm good." She flashed him a tight smile that called her a liar. More on the emotional side of things than the physical ones, he'd bet.

He squeezed her hand. "Keep in mind I give awesome piggyback rides, okay?"

"Will do." She smiled up at him, weak compared to her usually brilliant grin. Even that faded though when they reached her yard. Archer and Captain Alex went inside to scan the place while Banks, Miguel, and Tosin stayed on the porch with her.

"It's all clear," Archer announced when he returned. Then he winced. "Kahori, the place is a mess. Are you sure..."

"Yes." She put her hand on his chest and thanked him before pressing steadily until he backed out of her way.

Tosin loved that she wasn't a pushover. It would make her submission in bed worth even more to him than it already was.

To her credit, Kahori didn't flinch. She stepped over her ruined belongings, including the smashed jar and the flowers he'd given her yesterday, which were now dead. Ignoring her personal space, she made a beeline to her workshop and to the cabinet in the far back corner. When she opened the door, revealing her safe, she gasped. The door was covered with massive scrapes and dents that had obviously been caused by unsuccessful attempts to break into the locked box. Or a velociraptor.

"I'm guessing it didn't look like that yesterday?" Banks asked.

She shook her head then spun the dial until she'd entered the combination. Tosin never left her side. He rubbed her back as she yanked on the handle.

Inside, neat trays held pearls in graduated sizes. One rack was loaded up with glimmering jewels and precious metals. As if she didn't care that her inventory was still intact, she stayed tense. He realized why when she plucked a pearl at random then took it to her workbench and scoured the floor in search of her loupe.

When she had it in hand, she turned on some powerful gooseneck lamps and examined the pearl carefully. "It's real."

"Should we pack up the safe contents then?" Archer asked. "The *Divemaster* has secure facilities onboard for just this sort of thing. We installed them after we discovered a sunken treasure then sort of had part of it stolen temporarily."

Kahori gawked at him for a moment. Then she shrugged and laughed. "Sure, why not? I didn't realize you had experience in this sort of thing."

"Unfortunately," Miguel grumbled.

She paused then, growing much more serious. "I guess I'm lucky you all happened to come along when you did. I don't know what I would do right now if it wasn't for you. Thank you."

"We're happy to help." Tosin leaned in and kissed her cheek. "Now, is there anything else you want to check out or need to pack up? I don't think it's smart to hang out here any longer than necessary."

Kahori swallowed then, glancing around as if there would be a note from her dad telling her he'd gone out on a long fishing voyage or something equally as innocent. No such luck.

Instead, she wandered over to the opposite corner of the room then began to dig beneath a pile of crumpled invoices that had been dumped out of her filing cabinet. Beneath it all, in a tiny woven palm basket, she withdrew a plain brown paper covered package. "I hadn't finished weighing this one and putting the postage on before Pāpā took the rest of the orders to the post office on One Foot Island for me."

"Does he usually handle your shipments?" Archer asked.

"No, Hemi does. He runs the store on Rarotonga, too." She closed her eyes. "I thought he was just being helpful as always. But something was strange about it. On the way to island night I forgot my fire poi, and when I came back, Hemi was in here searching for the packages. Pāpā hadn't mentioned his mail run to Hemi even though he knows Hemi always takes care of that. Looking back…"

For the first time she wavered. Tosin was right by her side to hold her steady.

"I feel like the world's worst daughter for even considering that he could have done this. But besides that, the men in the jungle asked me where 'he' was. The only person missing is Pāpā. Nothing else makes sense, does it?" She hiccupped.

"While I hope you're wrong, I'm glad you're keeping your eyes open." Tosin rubbed her upper arms, which were chilled despite the heat. "And if it turns out that he did this, then I think it's *him* that's earned the title of world's worst."

"For shits and giggles…" Miguel looked to Tosin, then Kahori. "I think you should open that. If they're real too, then maybe the switcheroo is happening on Rarotonga. Maybe it's Hemi we should be worried about."

Kahori looked ill. She plopped into her office chair as if the thought hadn't occurred to her. "They're my family. I can't believe we're even having this discussion. Besides, Hemi was at the island night the entire time last night, right?"

Banks nodded. "I was sitting right next to him when everything went to hell."

She turned the package over in her hands a few times before psyching herself up. When she grabbed a letter opener from a tipped earthen cup and went to slice the packing tape, she froze. "It's been tampered with. I can see two layers of tape already."

As if she still didn't want to believe, she practically stabbed the package then ripped it open. A pearl necklace poured into her hand. Kahori took one look at it and began to sob. She grasped the strand in each of her hands and yanked, snapping it in half.

Fake pearls rained on the floor among the rest of the rubble.

Tosin rushed to her and crouched by her feet. He hugged her, guiding her face to his shoulder as she cried.

"Pāpā! Pāpā, why?" She broke their hearts as she expelled her misery.

No one had an answer to that question except her father. And he was definitely missing. Either he'd realized they were on to him and he'd run, abandoning his daughter to madmen...or they'd gone after him too, and he hadn't been as lucky as Kahori.

When her bawling had slowed to weeping, Banks and the rest of the guys huddled around. "We really should get moving." Banks told them.

"But where?" Kahori asked. "You said it yourself, the ship has a lot going on right now. I won't endanger anyone else over my family's problems."

The guys winced. They'd like to argue, but the reality was they couldn't take chances anymore. They'd learned from past mistakes and wouldn't put anyone at risk.

"Look, we only need to buy a little time." Archer told her. "As soon as we're back to the *Divemaster*, Captain Alex and I will meet with the security team. Banks can have reinforcements flown in from New Zealand. It can probably be done in the next twenty-four hours. Where can we hide you until then?"

Tosin suggested, "How about the glowworm cavern? I'm staying with you. We can hide out there pretty comfortably for a while."

"I have a better idea." She wiped her eyes on the sleeve of the shirt she'd borrowed from Sabine. "Do you trust me?"

"Absolutely."

Kahori appreciated Tosin holding her hand for the entire boat trip over to the *motu* that housed her uncle Kimo's resort. Even that simple connection was enough to stabilize her. In the end, Archer and Miguel had decided to stay with them while Captain Alex and Banks returned to the ship to make the arrangements they'd agreed to.

Archer drove while Miguel searched the ocean around them with a pair of high-tech binoculars. Every minute or two he checked in with the head of their security detail back on the *Divemaster*.

They glided along outside the barrier reef, staying out of sight as much as possible before she directed Archer to duck through a slit in the coral on the backside of the *motu*. It was less than a minute before they had beached the rigid hull inflatable boat with its ridiculously overpowered engine then hauled it into the trees where it practically vanished from view.

The men walked in a triangle, keeping her at the center.

It felt so strange to be this cautious. To worry in a place that had only ever been peaceful before. The loss of that purity nearly shattered her again. Instead, she put her shoulders back and marched through the open-air lobby of Uncle Kimo's resort and into his office.

He stood as they entered, a spear gun in his hands. When he recognized her, he propped it in the corner then flew to her side. Tosin stepped in front of her, blocking her uncle from invading her space.

"Because I appreciate what you did for her, I won't hold that against you, *papa'a*. But I suggest you move now so I can see my niece." Kimo spoke softly. The *tā moko*—decorative scarring around his eyes and along his jaw—he wore gave his underlying threat some heft, too.

Still, Tosin didn't budge.

"It's okay." Kahori touched his arm softly. So he relented and let the man pass. When Kimo carefully enfolded her in his embrace, Tosin relaxed.

"I can't believe this is happening." Hearing the disbelief and pain in her gruff uncle's voice made Kahori feel better about how she'd broken down in her workshop.

"You're hurt. Ruru is missing." At the mention of his brother, Kimo let Kahori go then pounded his fist on his desk hard enough to rattle everything on it. "What the hell is going on?"

"We're not sure yet." Kahori glanced at Tosin. He shrugged, leaving it to her discretion to confide in Uncle Kimo or not. They had to start asking some questions to find the answers they needed. This was as good a place as any to start.

"But you have some clue?" Kimo narrowed his eyes.

Kahori told him about the fake pearls and how they suspected the brutes who'd chased her had been some sort of collection crew that her father may have attempted to double-cross.

"They'll be back." Kimo sagged against his desk. "You can't go home, Kahori."

"I know." She considered how he might take the news of the rest of their plan. In the end, she divulged everything. If she trusted her family and that ended up being the wrong call, she'd have to accept the consequences. But mistrusting even the people who'd loved her most seemed like a greater crime. "These guys are going to help me out. They've got more security coming in first thing in the morning. Until then, I was hoping Tosin and I could hide out in the honeymoon suite. Archer and Miguel will stay too, to guard the entrance."

Her uncle frowned at first. Thinking of his gorgeous niece and a foreigner in the same sentence as "honeymoon suite" probably didn't sit well, though as the island's resort owner he certainly had more exposure to visitors, which had softened his traditional views. Eventually, he relented. "You're right. It's the easiest spot to protect. Since there's only one way in…"

Kahori thought about the overwater cabana. It would be like a mini fort. No one could sneak up on them. "That's what I was thinking, too."

"Go ahead, Kahori. The longer we talk, the more likely it is someone might see you." He shooed her. When she turned around, Hemi stood—feet spread, thick arms crossed—blocking the doorway.

"You're letting them stay here?" He spat the question as if it were an accusation.

"She's family—of course. Your uncle Ruru would do the same for you if something happened to me." Kimo gestured for his son to move.

He didn't.

The three divemasters huddled around her like a living, breathing shield.

"See…here you are inviting them in when they probably killed Uncle Ruru and fed him to the sharks," Hemi snarled, viciously enough that spittle launched from his ruddy face.

"Right now you seem more violent, and far less civilized, than our guests." Uncle Kimo put Hemi in his place.

"*I* can take care of Kahori." Hemi bucked against his father's authority. "We don't need them."

"If Tosin goes, so do I," Kahori objected at the same time Tosin simply said, "No."

"I never expected you to be the sort to choose a *papa'a* over your own blood." Her cousin scanned her appraisingly. Then he shrugged. "Have it your way."

Then he retreated to the check-in desk, where he answered a ringing phone, speaking quietly into the receiver as if he hadn't been shouting moments earlier.

Kahori thanked her uncle then edged out the door toward the honeymoon suite.

"*Tamāhine,*" Uncle Kimo called for his niece. "Ignore my foolish son. He is hurting too. Don't lose hope. Your *pāpā* is coming back. He would never choose to leave you. Understood?"

"Yes, uncle." She wished the sickness in her gut didn't say otherwise.

∽ SIXTEEN ∾

Kahori waved Archer and Miguel inside when they hesitated on the threshold. She knew why.

Because the honeymoon suite was clearly a place designed for romance. The overwater cabana had multiple decks complete with loungers and even a splash pool. Inside, it was a whole new level of cozy. Entire walls were made of glass. Gauzy fabric billowed around a giant four-poster bed. Flowers overflowed vases around the room.

For nearly everyone who stayed here, it was a once-in-a-lifetime way to commemorate the happiest days of their life. A new start with their soul mate.

"You guys can keep watch from in here." Kahori smiled. "No reason to be uncomfortable. Besides, you'll be less visible if you stay inside."

Of course the three divemasters were already peering off the edge of the deck into the shallow water below. She didn't blame them. A gorgeous reef sat in about twenty feet of water, drawing a million colorful creatures.

Miguel elbowed Tosin. "You hear that? No nookie for you. We're your roomies for the night."

"Fuck you," Tosin grumbled.

Archer laughed at them both.

Kahori had other plans. She took Tosin's hand, loving how large and strong it felt cupping hers. Even better, she was excited that she might be able to do something amazing for him. Give him an experience that even his millions might not have bought him yet. "Don't worry, Tosin. You'll have the last laugh tonight."

"Ohh, a peep show?" Miguel asked. "I'll have to text Sabine and see if I'm allowed to watch."

"Not exactly." Kahori patted him on the shoulder. "Don't be too jealous, okay?"

That got the guys' attention. All three of them stared at her as she wandered toward what appeared to be a glass-topped table in the center of the room.

Kahori grabbed a handle hidden on the underside then lifted. The top pivoted open, revealing a hatch and a ladder going down.

Tosin's eyes grew wide as he rushed to her side and peered into the space below. Instead of ocean waves, a richly appointed room inside what was essentially a giant glass bubble awaited. "Is that for real? An underwater bedroom?"

"Why don't you check it out and see for yourself?" She smiled then waved him toward the space usually reserved for the resort's most extravagant customers.

He didn't hesitate another moment. Tosin clambered down the ladder so fast it might as well have been a fireman's pole. He ignored the high-end finishes of the unique bedroom to stare at the ocean surrounding them through the transparent walls of the suite. "It's like I can finally breathe underwater. Pretty much my biggest fantasy. Well, you know, other than the sex kind."

"I suppose that's true." She hopped to the ground, happy when her ribs and skull only protested the jarring maneuver a tiny bit. "Best of all, no one can sneak up on us down here. Hell, they're not likely to find us even if they raid the cabana."

From above, Miguel and Archer were cursing their best friend. Miguel tried to bribe his way inside. "Dude, I'll give you a million dollars if you switch places with us."

"Make it two million." Archer didn't sound like he was joking either.

"Sorry, boys, you'll have to try some other time. We're all booked up for tonight." Tosin waved cheekily at his partners. "Close the door—er, table—would you?"

"Have fun, lucky bastard," Miguel said then did as asked.

The second the sound from above was eliminated, the room seemed like a giant people bowl—you know, an aquarium where they were on display for the entertainment of the fish around them. Kahori had loved this room as a child. Hell, she still did now.

"I could stay here forever." Tosin wandered to an oversized window seat that was really more of a spacious divan. He stretched out on it then patted the space in front of him.

Kahori joined him. When she neared, he reached for her, wrapping his arm around her waist then drawing her down in front of him so that they were both lying on their sides, her head pillowed carefully on his biceps as they stared at the butterfly fish schooling beyond the glass.

"If everything wasn't so shitty outside right now, I'd say this was heaven. You, this place...I've got everything I need right here," he murmured close to her ear as he curled around her.

"I need a break, Tosin. Until tomorrow, can we leave everything but us and this beauty out there? Forget it exists?" She ran her fingers along the arm he'd tossed over her waist.

"That sounds like the best idea I've heard in a while." He kissed her cheek then acted like the only important thing in the world was them and their connection. He asked, "What's your favorite sea creature?"

Kahori was happy to play this game with him.

"Easy. *Pā'ua*. I think you call them giant clams." She pointed at one of the most beautiful examples she'd ever seen, nestled at the base of the reef about ten feet away from where they were laying. The enormous mollusk shell was impressive, but the mantle of neon blue and green photosynthetic material was easily the most unbelievable and stunning thing she'd ever seen in nature. It didn't look real. "That one is about four feet wide. It's lived here for at least seventy-five years. My grandfather wrote about it in his journal. It was one of the reasons Uncle Kimo chose this spot for the honeymoon suite."

"Good choice. They're awesome." He hugged her as tight as possible without causing her bruised skin any discomfort. "Unfortunately, they're also endangered."

Not so different than her these days.

No, she would not let those thoughts intrude.

For a very long time they simply enjoyed each other's company, pointing out the interesting things—like a manta ray, and a massive travally, and even a few black-tipped reef sharks—that wandered past their outpost. The constant swirl of color and life mesmerized them both.

As fascinating as the scenery was, Kahori eventually couldn't stand facing away from the one thing she most wanted to see. She rolled over in Tosin's arms so she could study his face. His eyes were even more striking since they reflected the turquoise water surrounding them. "You know, this isn't called the honeymoon suite for nothing. It would be a shame to pass up an opportunity like this…"

Tosin leaned in to kiss her. The brush of his lips was even gentler than it had been the first time he'd tasted her. So she knew he was holding back.

Though she understood his concern, she couldn't help but be kind of insulted that he didn't think her tough enough to handle him. "Lame, Tosin."

He barked out a laugh. "Sorry. I'm afraid I'll hurt you. Or frighten you. Why don't you let me hold you again tonight? I enjoyed the hell out of that last night and we didn't even have this view to entertain us."

"Not good enough." Kahori hoped he didn't call her on that whopper. She would be satisfied with his comforting embrace in this ultra-peaceful haven if that was all they could muster. But she knew they were capable of a lot more than that.

And if this was her one chance, she didn't want to waste it like she had during their time in the cave. If only she'd stayed, maybe none of this would have happened.

Maybe her father wouldn't be missing.

Maybe she wouldn't have been brutalized.

"You want me to make love to you?" he asked.

She nodded. "Please."

"I'm warning you, Kahori. If we have sex tonight...here, in this magical place, with my emotions so wild already, and it being essentially your first time—the first time that counts, as far as I'm concerned—well, I can't be responsible for what happens."

"They're just a few bruises, nothing major. You're not going to hurt me if you get carried away," she reassured him.

"That's not what I meant." He sighed then kissed her again, deeper this time. "If we do this, I'm going to fall in love with you. Hell, I'm halfway there already. Are you sure you want me following you around begging for your attention for the rest of your life?"

She laughed.

Except maybe he wasn't kidding.

"I haven't said those words to anyone since my grandparents passed away, Kahori. You're the first person who's made me even consider exposing myself to that kind of complication. I'm loyal, or stubborn—your call. Once my mind is made up, I'm not going to change it. So be sure that you really want me too—for more than a solid fuck—before you spread your legs for me."

How could he say something so nasty, so crude, yet make it seem so romantic?

She didn't understand, but that didn't keep her from swooning a little inside.

That was what she'd thought she was signing up for when she'd gone to that club.

"Count me in. I've waited forever for this moment, Tosin. Now I know I was waiting for you." Kahori pounced then, clasping his head in her hands, loving the brush of his short blond hair against her palms. She held him still as she advanced, then devoured him thoroughly.

Going Hard

Until he turned the tables on her.

Kahori obeyed the pressure of Tosin's hands, which guided her into a kneeling position, straddling his narrow waist. He smiled up at her as he grabbed the hem of her shirt then lifted it. She accommodated him by putting her arms up and hunching forward to allow the material to slide off.

Braless, her breasts were on display for him.

Coconut bras didn't go well beneath shirts, even if she'd been able to salvage the ruined one from the night before. Fortunately, or maybe unfortunately for Tosin, she was more pert than plump.

He didn't seem to mind.

His hands landed on her waist, his thumbs brushing low on her belly, making her squirm. Of course that only rubbed her pussy over the front of his shorts and the thick erection waiting beneath.

"Are you sure you're up for this?" he asked as he skimmed upward until he lightly traced the outline of the purple discoloration on her breast, an unpleasant reminder of the day before. He brushed his lips over the area as if he could kiss it and make it better.

Maybe he could.

It sure as hell felt fine when he did that.

"Yes." She let her eyes fall closed for a moment as he amused himself with her body. "I'll beg if you really want me to."

"I'm not opposed." The gravelly rasp his voice picked up then made her smile.

"Please Tosin, take me. Make me yours." She shrieked then giggled when he growled. His hands cradled her as he lifted her and rotated all at once.

Kahori wasn't entirely sure how he managed it without dumping both their asses on the floor, but next thing she knew she was gazing up at him as he rid her of her skirt and himself of his own clothes. While he did, he removed another condom from his pocket and rolled it down his hard-on.

Too bad—she would have enjoyed tasting him again.

She licked her lips.

"Don't worry, you're going to have me inside you soon." He dropped low over her to kiss her, then asked, "That's what you want, isn't it? Me fucking you, slow and deep?"

Uh huh. Yep. That sounded about right.

"Tell me, Kahori." He brushed the pad of his thumb over her mouth. "Invite me inside you."

"I want to feel you pressing into me, locking us together." She practically panted then. "Please Tosin, give me your cock."

"Oh fuck, you're a little too good at naughty talk." He strangled his cock then stroked a few times, as if he couldn't help touching himself because of her and her dirty desires. "But I think I can make you beg even more prettily next time."

She didn't understand what he meant until she realized he was sinking between her legs. Not hips to hips, though. No, he was shoving her legs wide to accommodate his shoulders.

"You should have known I wasn't going to dive right in without eating this pretty pussy again first." He licked her from the bottom of her slit to her clit.

Kahori didn't plan to argue. She arched her back and spread her legs farther open, giving him room to work.

"That's right." He hummed as his mouth settled over her pussy and began to reward her for being bold.

It was every bit as spectacular as the day before. Maybe more so because now she was certain that this was only the appetizer to a banquet. She planned to feast—on Tosin.

He'd made her come a few times, asking her again if she wanted his cock following each orgasm. When her begging didn't motivate him to fuck her, he started over again with his mouth.

So this time, when he wiped his lips on the back of his hand, smirked, then said, "How badly do you want my cock now?" Kahori writhed on the divan. She lunged for his erection, which bobbed just out of reach.

Then a stream of utter depravity she never would have believed herself capable of poured out of her. "I'll do anything to have you inside me. Please, Tosin, give me your cock. My pussy aches. Fill me up so that I never again feel empty or alone."

"That's better." He grinned, though it turned soft and affectionate pretty quickly.

"You do the same for me, you know. Make me feel fully engaged with life." He kissed her softly then, aligning their bodies. Finally, finally, he was going to show her what she'd been missing.

Kahori held her breath as if they truly swam beneath the surface of the ocean that surrounded them. Funny enough, she in no way felt like she was drowning when Tosin levered himself over her carefully. Instead, she felt more like she was flying, or could take off soon.

"I want to make up for everything that other guy did wrong with you," he murmured.

"You already have." She hugged him, hoping she never had to let go.

"You should know this is different for me, too." He kissed the tip of her nose. "I've gotten so used to emotion-free fast fucks I'm not sure I'm going to be any good at this kind of sex."

Could he seriously doubt that? "I'm going to go out on a limb and say you'll do just fine."

Tosin threw back his head and laughed. He pinched her nipple teasingly. "You're lucky I'm too horny to put you over my knee right now."

Was she? Kahori shivered. Because the thought of his hand on her bare ass turned her on even more. Something she never would have expected.

"If you look at me like that any longer while you're thinking about me turning that ass red, I might shoot before I get inside you." He growled, then nipped her neck. "Are you ready for me, Kahori? Ready to seal this deal?"

"Do it." She grabbed his hips, her fingers splaying across the upper swells of his tight ass.

When he advanced, the tip of his sheathed cock prodding the opening to her body, she was grateful for the time he'd taken to warm her up. He glided through the slick furrow of her pussy, coating himself in her natural lubrication.

Then he pressed down on his cock with two fingers, aiming himself properly as he began to sink inside her, penetrating every last barrier she'd erected to protect her heart from being stolen.

Unlike last time, there was no sting, no burn, no stabbing white-hot poker between her legs.

Instead, there was only pleasure.

Tosin worked himself within her clinging sheath so carefully she thought she might go crazy before she could come on his shaft. When he was finally fully seated, he kissed her, then asked, "Still good?"

"Amazing." She wrapped her legs around his waist and tried to draw him in tighter with her heels.

"You've got all of me," he promised her.

Kahori swallowed hard, overwhelmed by emotions. She touched his face lovingly with the tips of her fingers. And then he began to move.

Slowly at first. With liquid glides that caressed her from the inside. He rode her with measured strokes that inspired her to think of new and filthier ways to beg him to make her come. The persistent drilling of his cock and the stroking of his fat head near the entrance of her pussy eventually proved too much.

His careful probing turned to something less restrained. And when he cursed, then scooped his hands beneath her shoulders to brace her against the increasing tempo and pressure of his thrusts, she knew she'd gotten to him too.

Tosin hunched his back so he could suckle her nipple as he began to dig deep on every forward pass. He brought all of her most sensitive places to life. Of course her pussy and her breasts, plus everywhere they rubbed skin on skin. Even better, he began to restore her faith in men and in the benefits of a true physical and emotional connection with a sexual partner.

"You're almost there, aren't you?" He smiled as if nothing could make him happier than delivering bliss to her.

"Yes. So close." She rocked her head from side to side as her hips lifted, trying to bury him to the hilt within her.

Too late—he was already as deep as he could get.

Tosin picked up the pace again, this time pressing his body against her clit and swiveling his hips just a bit at the apex of each thrust. But it was when she opened her eyes and looked directly into his that she knew she had lost everything—her heart most of all—to him.

"That's right, let me have your first orgasm with a man. Squeeze my cock with that tight pussy. Show me how much better this is. How perfect."

Kahori had no idea how he could still talk. She opened her mouth, but all that came out was a scream right as her climax struck. Her pussy strangled Tosin's dick and he joined her, pumping his release into the condom keeping them just the tiniest bit separate.

Next time she'd convince him to remove the last of the barriers between them, though she wasn't sure it could feel any better than this without killing her in the process. Her heart galloped wildly, her pussy clenched, wringing his cock dry, and euphoria spread into every cell of her body.

Utterly content, she collapsed onto the divan, welcoming the weight of Tosin's equally drained body lying on top of her. They dozed then fucked then dozed some more. The entire night passed in a blur of passion and discovery she would never forget.

The next morning, soft blue light filtered through the shallow water and illuminated their hidey-hole. Kahori leaned her back against Tosin's chest. He had her wrapped in his arms and legs, utterly secure in his embrace. They didn't speak as they watched the ever-evolving aquatic landscape swirling around them.

After last night, what would happen now?

Part of her felt guilty for having the best night of her life while her father was missing. Another part swam in gratitude that Tosin had reminded her the world held as much beauty as pain. Kahori was terrified to leave this place knowing their bubble would burst and the peaceful intermission they'd crafted for themselves would end.

Starving, she couldn't stay down here much longer without going in search of breakfast. Tosin's stomach was growling too. Yet instead of acknowledging it, he only rubbed his cheek against the crown of her head and held her tighter against him.

Until something in her peripheral vision caught her attention.

"Is that—?" Kahori started to ask at the same time Tosin waved.

A second diver joined the first she'd spotted. They descended until they were level with the bed and Kahori and Tosin's very naked bodies.

"Oh my God!" Kahori dove under the comforter. "Miguel! Archer!"

Tosin cracked up, giving her ass a playful swat before ensuring she was covered. "You know, there are plenty of times we make the *Divemaster* clothes-optional. There's no need to hide if you don't want."

The divemasters waved from outside the glass enclosure. Miguel tugged a slate from a retractable cord on a carabiner attached to his buoyancy control device. He drew something quick then turned it around so she could read what he'd written.

Good morning! Did you miss us? Extra security is here, watching your door for us, was surrounded by hearts, flowers, and a big-ass smiley face.

"You know the only way to prank a prankster is to one-up them, right?" Tosin asked her as she snickered.

"Then I guess you'd better get over here and give them a show," Kahori responded as liquid heat filled her belly. Who would have thought the idea of being watched surrendering to Tosin would turn her on?

It did.

In the end, they had the last laugh...and a pair of orgasms to go with it.

When Kahori remembered where she was and opened her eyes, the men had disappeared. She didn't care. Only one man mattered. Then and always.

It would always be Tosin.

"I warned you last night, didn't I?" He gazed down at her as he disengaged himself from her body.

She blinked up at him.

"I love you, Kahori."

What he hadn't said then, or now, was that it wasn't only him who had been affected. She'd been trapped just as surely and it was impossible to regret it even if she couldn't take it back.

"I love you, too."

"Thank God." He groaned. "Now, can we please find something to eat before I'm reduced to gnawing on my own arm or something? I'm dying."

Kahori slapped his shoulder then laughed. "You did work up quite an appetite, didn't you?"

"Mmmhmm." He looked at her as if he might consider eating her again instead, then sighed. "You ready?"

"No, but at least I know you'll be with me." She put her hand in his.

"Always." Tosin took one last lingering look around the underwater room. "You think Archie will let me install a giant glass panel somewhere in the *Divemaster's* hull?"

"Doesn't hurt to ask, huh?" She would love to recreate the best experience of her life. "If he does, I want a do-over."

"Deal."

◠◡ EIGHTEEN ◠◡

With their enhanced security in place, Tosin, Kahori, Archer, and Miguel didn't dally before heading home to the *Divemaster*. Archer hated being away from the ship during such an important transition, and Miguel seemed half-excited, half-terrified to meet the woman who was as close to an in-law as he'd probably ever have.

He shouldn't have worried. Marta greeted them along with the rest of their friends when they charged up the gangway into their waiting, open arms. Relieved hugs were exchanged all around.

It felt nice to have them to return to when all that was left for Kahori on the island was a ruined home or becoming an obligation for her uncle to take care of. Before she could depress herself with thoughts like those, or worry about her *pāpā*, she'd been whisked off for a checkup by Dr. Kleveno.

Tosin had some dives to do with the family members of Sabine's trial patients, so Kahori found herself wandering, alone, after a while. When she stumbled on a lovely seating area beside the pool, she curled up in a lounger and took a nap since Tosin hadn't let her do much sleeping the night before.

Kahori yawned and stretched some time later. Soft voices drifted to her on the light breeze. She blinked and scrubbed her eyes seeing Marta and Sabine not far away. She was about to get up and join them when she realized their posture was slightly tense, so she listened before approaching.

Marta took Sabine's hand. "Do you think this is right? Especially so soon? It's only been six months since Heinrich left us. Would he be upset with me?"

"For loving someone else? A very decent, generous, and devoted person?" Sabine hugged Marta. "Never. He would have hated for you to be lonely."

"You know no one will ever replace him in my heart, right?" Marta asked.

"Of course," Sabine whispered. "I'm sure Banks understands that too. Remember, I lost my parents, but that didn't stop you and Heinrich from taking up the job where they left off. There's room enough to love an infinite number of people in our lifetimes. We should do that. You two taught me that."

Kahori didn't mean to eavesdrop. Neither did she want to shatter such a critical and dear moment between the two women. Unfortunately, their unconditional support and sage advice got to her. She sniffled.

Marta looked over and smiled. "Oh, hello, sleepyhead. Feeling better now?"

Kahori nodded. "I'm sorry to interrupt, I just..." She waved at her chair and then to them.

"Join us for a moment, would you?" Marta asked.

Kahori respected her elders, so of course she didn't decline. She slipped into an empty seat at the table where the women were sipping iced tea. They poured her a glass as well.

"I'm very sorry to hear about your father." Marta put her hand over Kahori's and squeezed.

Kahori couldn't speak, and not because of the giant gulp she'd taken of her drink in an attempt to swallow the fear that kept rising up within her.

"I know it's hard—we both do—losing someone so important in your life, whether in a tragedy or because you have to find your own way. But I think most parents would agree that they want their children to grow into the best versions of themselves. To venture beyond what was possible for themselves. I don't know you yet, honey. And I may never meet your father. But it was obvious to me after a moment or two, that you've found your future with Tosin. I'd think awfully hard before throwing that away. Sometimes you don't get a second chance."

Kahori agreed. *When* her *pāpā* came home, she would talk to him about Tosin and the changes she needed to make in her life to be happy regardless of how things turned out with the sexy divemaster.

"And that's all I'm going to say about that." Marta smiled then hugged Kahori.

The women moved on, discussing everything from jewelry to experiment results to favorite destinations. She'd never had these kinds of independent female role models growing up. But now that she saw how strong and career minded Waverly and Sabine were, and the way their guys supported them, Kahori had a new goal.

Restless as she considered how to broach the topic with Tosin, she excused herself from Marta and Sabine then wandered the ship. Every place she turned, there was something amazing she'd never seen before. And when she was nearly back to Tosin's room, where she planned to wait for him to finish his session—anytime now—she noticed Waverly and Archer slipping into that funny black door she'd wondered about on several occasions.

It didn't quite shut behind them, so she hurried to catch up.

"Hey, Archer. If you're back, does that mean Tosin is finished too?" She poked her head in the door, which she realized had been kept open by Waverly's bra lodged in the opening.

Things only got more bizarre from there.

The interior of the space looked nothing like the rest of the ship.

Dark leather chairs that looked almost like thrones faced an open area dotted with black-painted equipment. She recognized a St. Andrew's cross, a suspension harness, and—worst of all—a spanking bench like the one she'd been forced to bend over at the club on her disastrous outing.

Waverly and Archer were already pressed up against some contraption she couldn't make sense of as they tore at each others' remaining clothes.

Holy shit.

Kahori squeaked in surprise.

Both of them whipped around to look at her. Surprisingly, neither seemed very upset to see her there.

"Hey." Archer grinned. "Did you and Tosin have the clubroom booked? I'm not going to lie, I didn't bother to look at the schedule when Waverly propositioned me."

"Tosin? Clubroom?" she stammered.

"Uh oh." Waverly nabbed her shirt off the floor and flung it haphazardly over her nakedness.

"Fuck." Archer was already on the move. He hit an intercom on the wall and said, "Tosin. Clubroom. Right fucking now. Kahori is here."

"Don't let her leave until I get there," came the immediate reply.

Not... "Hey, what's a clubroom?"

Or... "Why would she be in there? I hate that kind of thing."

Or anything else that would alleviate the betrayal and fear bubbling up within her.

∽ NINETEEN ∾

Tosin didn't dally. Neither did he run.

More than ever before in his life, it was critical that he stay calm and handle the situation carefully. Prove to Kahori that not everyone who enjoyed structured playtime would disregard the needs of their submissive partner.

He had to believe that, deep down, she knew that already.

It was his job to unlock her emotions, and smother her fear, so that her brain could catch up with the rest of her.

When he reached the clubroom's onyx door, his hand hovered over the handle. He was surprised to see it trembling. It was too late now to pray that he hadn't gone about this all wrong.

Tosin drew in a deep breath, then opened the door.

"You liar!" Kahori ripped free of Archer's light restraint and flew at him, her fists pounding on his chest. "You're into the same things as that guy at the club. At least he didn't try to lure me in with pretty words and gentle sex before showing me what he really liked."

"I never deceived you, Kahori." He kept her from assaulting him by braceleting her wrists with his thumbs and forefingers. He didn't apply a lot of pressure. Didn't need to. She responded to him beautifully as always, completely in tune with his intentions.

"How can you say that? You listened to me confess about that club. How contrived it was, how unappealing to me. And yet this... You went to enormous lengths to have a place like this onboard so it must be important to you! Why waste your time on me or make me fall for you when you knew we're interested in two totally different things?" She railed at him and he let her get it all out before explaining what he'd been attempting to do. "Here I was, feeling guilty about fucking you when I can't leave my home, abandon my *pāpā*, and the whole time you were hiding...*this!*"

Archer shook his head—probably mentally labeling Tosin an idiot for that kind of supposed gaff—then snuck out the door with Waverly, shutting it gently behind him.

"You weren't ready for this." Arrogant, maybe. But it was the truth. "From what I've seen so far, you haven't yet accepted that you enjoy being topped by a responsible lover. You don't understand the subtleties of the relationship because of very valid fears. I was working on showing you the more subtle flavors first before I asked you to try something the equivalent of mainlining hot sauce."

"What the hell is that supposed to mean?" She propped her hands on her hips, practically daring him to enlighten her. So he did.

"Remember in the cave, when I instructed you how to blow me? Or in the underwater lodge, how hard you came on my cock when I commanded you to?" He would never forget it. "You like letting go. Giving me complete control. But you don't know me well enough to look beyond your history with a dumbass, reckless user who doesn't know how to treat a prized partner to realize that with someone else, it would be a different experience entirely."

Kahori had gone silent.

"A power exchange doesn't have to be this blatant. There are lots of shades to enjoy on the spectrum of BDSM. I was simply trying to figure out what colors would be our favorites together. But if you'd like to test my theory about which hues you'll come to love, I'm happy to try that out, too."

"Who are you?" She squinted, as if trying to detect some hidden marking on him that would have declared his alpha tendencies.

"The same man you claimed to love." He held his hand out to her. "We've hardly met. You can't think you know all of me yet. I'm certain I've only scratched your surface. But if you like, I'll introduce you to another side of me."

"Why do you keep speaking in riddles?" She wasn't saying no. She also wasn't leaving despite the clear path to the exit. He took that as a good sign, both that she was interested, and that she wasn't freaking out.

Deep down, she knew he would never hurt her. She trusted him enough to hear him out.

That had to be a good sign.

Tosin wanted nothing more than to reward her bravery and be the man she didn't even know she so desperately needed. He smiled at her, hoping she could see that enjoying what went on in this room didn't detract from the genuine devoted exchanges they'd had outside of it. "Sometimes sweet is sexy. But sometimes I like going hard. I think you'll like it a hell of a lot too if you give it a chance. You were interested enough to check it out on your own. But I think you might not have understood that any sex can be good sex with the right person or a disaster if you don't have a true partner."

Kahori wrung her hands in front of her. She took a tiny step closer to him.

So he held out his hand to her and asked, "Will you let me show you?"

"Will you stop if I realize it's honestly not for me?" Her eyes begged him so prettily as she asked, though she must already know the answer.

"Of course. Would you like a safe word?" He rubbed his palms up and down her arms, chasing away the goose bumps there as she proved yet again how spectacular she was and how strong their bond had grown in a matter of a few intense days. "If you say it, at any time, everything stops. I'll take you out of here and we don't ever have to mention it again. Believe it or not, with you, I don't *need* this. We have something harder to find. This is a means to an end, a shortcut where everyone understands the rules. What you and I were building was something more intricate, more subtle, and...well, just *more* in every way."

Kahori squeezed her eyes shut as she considered what he was offering. Then she opened them and stared directly at him as she nodded.

"Thank you for trusting me." He held his arms open and she flew into them. How hard could he push her? "Your safe word will be *glowworm.*"

She smiled softly at that, as he'd intended.

So he decided to trust his instincts, though the scheme swirling around his brain was either the best or worst idea he'd ever had. A smarter man would start slow and gradually introduce her to elements of his lifestyle. He leaned toward the ultimate test right off the bat. If she couldn't handle it, there was no sense in torturing them both with further outings to the clubroom.

"Help me, Tosin. What should I do? I don't like feeling clueless." She waited for him to take the reins. So he did.

"I'm only suggesting this because I think you're strong enough to handle it..." He hesitated. Once the words were out of his mouth, he wouldn't be able to reclaim them.

She looked up at him expectantly.

"Let me conduct a little experiment. I want to fuck you on that." He pointed to the spanking bench.

At first she recoiled. "How could you? I told you—"

He shushed her then, wishing they were far enough along in their explorations for him to have been able to gag her, blindfold her, prove his point without letting her work herself into a darker place first. If he did this right, he could mitigate those memories.

Replacing them with something decidedly not terrifying or horrible.

He hoped.

"Exactly, Kahori. What better way to show you how different I am and how much pleasure you can take from this place if you let go of the past?" He nuzzled her temple. "I know what I'm asking of you is difficult. Feel free to use your safe word, now or at any time. It won't change how I feel for you."

But this could destroy the budding love she had for him. Might have already done the damage like a late spring frost.

"May I see it first?" Kahori asked, a natural.

He led her to the apparatus and let her explore. Though she seemed wary at first, by the time she ran her hands over the custom-built frame and the deeply padded surface covered in the softest leather, she nodded.

"This seems much more comfortable than the one they had at the place I went to." She surprised him then with her bravery and daring. "Would you tie me to it? So that I don't freak out and fall?"

She couldn't know that bondage was his favorite aspect of BDSM.

It was just another way they were ultimately compatible.

"Of course." He kissed her gently. "But why stop there? I think I'll spank your perfect ass before we get to the good stuff." Kahori shuffled before him. He smirked. "Something wrong?"

She shook her head.

"Getting horny thinking of me having my way with you, and bringing you even more pleasure than last night while I do it?" He leaned in closer, whispering the suggestion so that she had to concentrate only on him and what he was doing to her.

Kahori nodded.

Tosin's hand flashed out, burying in her hair. She didn't flinch, not even when he fisted the strands then used them to tip her head back slightly. Instead, her lips parted and her cheeks flushed.

There was no doubt—she was made for this.

"I want to hear you answer me. Say, 'yes, sir,'" he commanded.

When the words rolled off her tongue, they were the sweetest thing he'd ever heard.

Tosin rewarded her appropriately. He kissed her until neither one of them could breathe. At the same time he unwound her fresh *pareu* from her body and dropped it to the floor. It was handy for quick disrobing. His new favorite garment. If she wasn't strutting around this place naked while they were at sea, he hoped she'd always wear one of those.

He froze. She'd never said she was coming with them. They hadn't discussed it since the disastrous end of their cave sex.

"Did I do something wrong?" she asked.

"No." Tosin rubbed the tip of his nose against hers. "You're perfect."

Refocusing, he lifted her onto the spanking bench then withdrew a set of silk ties from the drawer at the base. It didn't take long to have her secured to the equipment.

Kahori tested her bonds, unable to budge, never mind break free.

To be absolutely sure she wouldn't get carried away and injure herself later, he landed a single stinging swat on her ass.

She yelped and jerked but didn't budge. So he ran his finger down her crack then slipped a single finger into her pussy. It didn't surprise him in the least to find her soaked.

It did relieve him, though. He licked her slickness from his hand after he withdrew.

Perfect.

Though ordinarily he would take pride in teasing her for hours, today he planned to lean toward simple and to the point. The one where she couldn't deny how hard she came for him in these conditions. That was all he needed to show her today. The rest could follow later.

Tosin ran his hands all over her body, making sure there were no uncomfortable contact points, especially considering her lingering bruises. Another reason to keep things short and sweet.

He spoke to her the entire time he admired her body, assessed the right way to make his point. And when he was satisfied, he ripped off his bathing trunks then mounted the table and her.

His cock was painfully hard. It rested between her cheeks, making him long to claim her ass as well as her pussy. Some other time.

Tapping the head against her clit, he realized he'd nearly forgotten a condom.

Kahori groaned when he retrieved one from a fishbowl on a table nearby. "Tosin?"

"Yes?" He caressed the length of her back as he repositioned himself.

"When you come, will you..."

"Ask for anything you want, Kahori. I'm here to make your dreams come true." He kissed her shoulder blade as he notched his cock in her hungry pussy.

"Will you pull out and come on me instead of in that rubber?" She couldn't move much, but she squirmed within her confines. "I want to feel your passion for me."

"Fuck yes." He couldn't stop himself then from pressing into her, though he tried to go as slowly as his libido would allow. "See how much deeper it feels this way?"

"Mmmm..." She didn't object.

"You're okay, right?" He reached forward and cupped her neck in his palm, getting her attention. He should have put a mirror in front of her so he could monitor her expression. Based on her moan, this would work just fine for now, though.

"Yes, sir."

"Good girl." He beamed as he began to ride her, making sure to grind his pelvis into hers so that her clit stroked the ridge of the spanking bench just so.

Tosin withdrew his cock completely then reintroduced it to her, sliding deeper until his balls tucked tight against her ass. He did this repeatedly, fucking her with the entire length of his dick. It didn't take long before she was rocking back against him and calling out his name.

"What would you like, Kahori?" he asked, though he already knew the answer.

"I want to come. Then feel you coming on me. I want to know you feel this too," she admitted.

"I do." He leaned forward, blanketing her even as he began to drive into her body faster and harder. If he'd thought she was responsive the night before, it was nothing compared to the way she unraveled then.

Her pussy milked his cock, tugging on it even as she prepared to shatter.

When he realized she couldn't hold out a moment longer, he murmured, "Go ahead, come for me. Come on me, Kahori. Prove to us both that when we're together, that's all that matters. Feel how much better it is when you come like this. Give everything to me. And know that you have all of me in return."

Kahori screamed his name as she came. Spasms racked her for so long he thought she might pass out. Instead, she shouted, "Please, Tosin, now! I want to feel it!"

How could he resist an invitation like that?

He couldn't.

Tosin pulled out of her pussy, mourning the loss of juicy pressure on his shaft. Then he stripped off the condom. It only took a couple of powerful tugs before come rushed from his balls out the tip of his shaft. He painted Kahori with his release, making sure every last drop splashed onto her back and ass.

And when he'd emptied his balls, he used his trunks to dry her off before untying her and wrapping her in her *pareu*. She floated, not quite seeing anything clearly, it seemed. So he let her enjoy the high while he took care of business.

He'd already lifted her into his arms and looked down into her rosy face when she smiled up at him and tipped her face toward him for a kiss. He obliged her request.

"What did you think?" he asked softly. He knew how her body voted on the experience, but what about her mind?

"I think I want to do it again. Soon." She smiled sheepishly. "Can we do that?"

He laughed. "Give me ten minutes, then I'll be happy to show you around."

As it turned out, they didn't leave until Kahori's stomach growled and he realized he needed to take care of all her needs, not just the sexual ones.

Tosin threw on his shorts and wrapped her up again before carrying her toward his room. *Their* room. Whether she stayed or not, it would never belong to anyone else. "I love you, Kahori."

"I love you too, Tosin," she murmured groggily.

Of course, on the way to his quarters, they seemed to pass everyone else. What were they all doing in their cabins in the middle of the day anyway?

Waverly and Archer gave them a thumbs-up as they headed toward the lunch buffet. Sabine and Miguel teased him about the hickey Kahori had marked him with at some point. He didn't care. He wore the thing like a medal of honor.

And when Marta slipped out of Banks's room, she tossed Kahori a wink.

"I'm surprised the whole ship isn't rocking by now!" Tosin shouted with a laugh.

At that, Dr. Kleveno poked her head out of Captain Alex's room and said, "We're working on it. Now shut up and go away, would you, loudmouth?"

Kahori and Tosin cracked up as they fell into his bed and ordered room service. He didn't want to let her out of his sight even long enough to inhale a meal upstairs. He'd much rather eat her while they waited for the main course.

She had no objections.

TWENTY

A few days later Kahori paced the lobby of her uncle's resort. Even the gorgeous views of the overwater cabins and the lagoon beyond couldn't calm her any longer. Behind her Miguel and Sabine were signing the contracts that would establish one of the grow domes for their priceless cancer-fighting algae right here on Uncle Kimo's *motu*. After meeting the guys and seeing how they looked out for her, he'd changed his mind about getting involved in their project. And that was even before he'd seen Sabine's demonstration of how her developing formula destroyed cancer cells.

While it should have been a day of celebrations, shared prosperity, and pride that her often overlooked country could become such an important part of bettering the entire world, her father's absence was even more pronounced than it had been as she'd passed the time hoping for his return while on the *Divemaster*.

Steadying hands came to rest on her shoulders, keeping her from making another circuit of the open-air gathering place. Tosin asked, "How can I help?"

Those four simple words, so full of empathy and kindness, nearly had her bawling.

She spun around and plastered herself to him. Sheltering arms enfolded her in his warmth.

"Pāpā isn't coming back." She finally admitted it to herself. "Not ever. He's gone."

"Don't give up, Kahori." He squeezed her. "We're going to keep looking."

Shaking her head, she insisted, "He would never have left me. Not after my mother—"

Sniffling, she tried to hold herself together. Too late, she realized the conversation had ceased.

Miguel and Sabine were watching her worriedly, while Uncle Kimo joined her and Tosin.

"I want to say you're wrong." Uncle Kimo ran his knuckles over her cheek, collecting her tears. "But I feel the same. He would never have betrayed you. He's not involved in this scam. But I bet he figured out who was. He always was the smartest one in the family."

Kahori lost it at that. She sobbed, clinging to Tosin.

He rocked her, promising to help her search for answers, if not her father himself. Nothing could console her. Snot and tears leaked from her despite her best attempts to bottle it up inside again.

Kimo wandered to the reception desk where Hemi usually greeted their guests. He opened a drawer and rummaged toward the back, muttering about tissues. Instead, he froze, as if he'd laid his hand on a scorpion instead.

"What's wrong?" Banks asked.

Uncle Kimo's face twisted in disbelief as he withdrew a velvet pouch. One Kahori recognized from her workshop. When he looked inside, he cursed. Next, he took a wad of cash that would easily cover several years' worth of the resort's operations from the hiding spot, along with a passport. A plane ticket was jammed inside. When he flipped the book open to the photo page, he roared. "HEMI!"

"Yeah?" Her cousin—who might as well have been her brother—stuck his head around the corner as if the sound that had just ripped from his father's chest at the proof of his betrayal and imminent departure was something he heard all the time. The noise was one Kahori would never forget.

It echoed her own pain and terror.

"You?" Uncle Kimo's clay-colored skin shed its vibrancy. Ashen, he stared at his son. Then he threw the damning evidence at him. Pearls skittered across the floor, bouncing everywhere. "Tell me this is not what it looks like. No son of mine could be this rotten inside. He couldn't do this to another human being, never mind his own family. Hemi! Tell me!"

Kahori quivered in Tosin's hold, only staying upright thanks to his arms banded around her.

Instead, Hemi drew a long bone-handled knife from a sheath on his belt.

"I never meant for it to come to this." He stopped short of apologizing. "I only wanted to make enough extra money to get the hell off this island. Have a real life in a modern city. But...things got out of control. Once I'd earned what I needed, my partners wouldn't let me stop, let me go. I was still just as trapped as ever in this ass-end of the Earth. And now that I'm an hour from leaving, you won't stop me. No one will. I'm finally going to be free."

"You could have been honest!" Kimo's face gained all its color back and then some. He looked nearly burgundy as rage and disbelief brewed within him. "I would have helped you achieve your dreams. Here or elsewhere."

"Good. That's what I want from you now. Let me go. Let me leave." Hemi inched toward the exit.

"Where is my brother?" The frosty calm with which Uncle Kimo asked the question lodged in Kahori's throat terrified her. She didn't want to hear the answer she already knew in her heart.

Hemi didn't answer. He stared out at the ocean beyond the lagoon.

"What did you do?" Kimo stepped forward. Then again.

"*I* didn't do anything!" Hemi waved his hands in front of him as if he was completely innocent. "Uncle Ruru got too nosy, taking those packages to the airport. He noticed that I'd opened and resealed them all. Figured out that I'd swapped the pearls for fakes. Really amazing fakes. Stupid *papa'a* would never know the difference. Hell, even my partners didn't realize I'd started swapping out fakes for the 'real' stolen merch I was passing on to them for a little while. I guess they weren't quite as stupid as Kahori's other customers, though, since they showed up here. I'd almost gotten away. And now I will. Finally. Thanks for chasing them off for me, Tosin, so that I had time to finalize my travel plans and set up a place to go from here where no one will ever find me."

"Hemi," Uncle Kimo growled in warning. He looked as dangerous as their ancestors when fighting a rival tribe.

"When they went after Kahori, assuming she was in on the double-cross, I ran to her house. I wanted to clean up that one last package I couldn't find earlier in the evening and any other evidence. I didn't want them snapping my neck. You don't know them and what they're capable of."

"Yes, I do," Kahori whispered.

Her agony was enough to cut through the father and son's argument. They both looked at her, with various degrees of dismay and lament.

"I never meant for you to get hurt," Hemi swore. "Uncle Ruru either." He balked then. "But he came straight to Kahori's when he heard her scream. Thought she might be on her way there. Or maybe he followed me since he knew what I'd gotten tangled up in. Uncle Ruru came for me. Out of his mind. I told him I'd split the profits. He went crazy. Told me that if anything had happened to Kahori, I would pay. He charged me. It was reflex. Instinct."

He looked at the knife in his hand.

"What did you do, Hemi?" Uncle Kimo dropped to his knees.

"I only tried to defend myself." He swallowed hard. "I never meant to kill him."

Kimo threw his head back and unleashed a wail that Kahori felt straight to the core of her soul. She accompanied him with a scream of her own that made a ghastly duet. Her body thrashed in Tosin's hold, but he wasn't letting her out of his grip, away from the madness unfolding across the room.

"You're not going to let me go." Hemi wasn't asking.

His father snarled, then sealed their fates. "No. You're going to confess to the council and accept your punishment."

"I can't do that." Hemi shook his head.

Archer, Miguel, and Banks rose, stalking closer to Hemi.

They were nowhere close enough to stop him from charging, knife raised, toward his own father.

Uncle Kimo closed his eyes for the barest of moments then swiped his arm out, beneath his desk. When he raised it again, his spear gun pointed straight at Hemi's black heart.

He didn't stop.

Kimo pulled the trigger, launching a harpoon through the chest of his only offspring. He'd always prided himself on clean, quick kills when he provided for his family from the fruit of the island's life. This time was no different.

Hemi staggered one more step then fell, face-first, onto the floor, already gone.

Uncle Kimo knelt beside the corpse. He spoke in his native tongue, offering a prayer and a plea to the gods for *utu*.

"What is he doing?" Tosin whispered in her ear.

"Seeking balance." She sniffled. "He's asking for *mana* to restore our family's honor. Sort of like karma in other cultures. Trying to erase Hemi's sins and protect us from any lasting effects of them."

Tosin may not have understood or believed as the elders from her village did, but he respected her uncle's values and let the man do whatever it took to process his betrayal, grief, and loss.

Kahori wondered then what her father would think of Tosin standing strong beside her, propping her up on the hardest day of her life, and if Uncle Kimo's sacrifice would appease his spirit.

A single clap of thunder boomed out over the clear, sunny day. It rattled the windows and lasted for so long that everyone stood and examined the sky for a rogue cloud.

There were none.

"I love you too, Pāpā." Kahori kissed her fingers then held them to the sky. "Goodbye."

∽ TWENTY-ONE ∾

Kahori stood on the deck of the *Divemaster* a few days later. It had taken a while to wrap up the legalities surrounding her father's and Hemi's deaths to the satisfaction of both the Cook Islands Ministry of Justice and the tribal elders.

Tosin took her hand in his and kissed it softly before surprising her by reaching into his pocket and withdrawing something she recognized immediately. "I want you to wear this, and think of me."

He fastened the leather around her wrist before placing his palm flat against hers so that their complementary bracelets aligned perfectly for a moment, just as she had designed.

Never had she thought she would be the lucky person to share a bond—or the symbol of it—like this.

"Where will you be going?" she asked.

"I'm not sure." He shrugged as if he didn't care anymore either. "In fact, I was kind of thinking I might stay a while. There's a clause in my contract with Archer that says I can sell my share to him if I ever want out."

She couldn't keep silent then. "No! That would be such a waste!"

Tosin spun around, away from her. "I understand if you don't feel the same way I do…"

Kahori covered her mouth with her hand before reaching for him. With gentle pressure on his shoulder she attempted to turn him to face her again. "That's not how I meant it. It's just that I've already decided…if your offer from the glowworm cavern still stands…"

He whipped around to stare at her, seeming to hold his breath as he waited for her to finish her sentence.

"I'd like to come with you."

"Are you sure?" He rushed to close the gap between them then, nearly crushing her in a hug worthy of all eight of an octopus's arms.

She nodded. "Yeah. To be honest, I don't think I can ever call this place home again. There are too many bad memories. Pāpā—"

Her voice cracked. Tosin rocked her gently until she could continue.

"He was the reason I stayed as long as I did. I love it here, don't get me wrong, but it was holding back my career—and my ability to live my life to the fullest. With you, everything is possible. You've shown me that every day that we've spent together. There are so many things I regret not telling my *pāpā*. About how important he was to me and how I stayed because of him. I don't want to screw that up again. I love you, Tosin. I won't ever forget to show you how much."

"I promise I'll keep proving my love to you, too." He lifted her chin so he could stare into her eyes when he swore, "I'll make you so fucking happy that you never get homesick. And if you do, well, I do happen to have a private jet at my disposal. Just saying."

Kahori laughed. "Good to know."

Just then Banks and Marta wandered over wearing matching grins. "I didn't mean to eavesdrop, dear." Marta squirmed in between her and Tosin to hug her. "But did you say you're staying?"

Kahori nodded, tears welling in her eyes. How had she gotten lucky enough to find the man of her dreams and extend her family all at once when she needed them most?

Tosin squeezed her then teased Marta. "Why does that sound like you might be joining us for an extended visit yourself?"

"I guess there's something about this boat. It sucks you in and you can never leave." She beamed up at Banks. "Or maybe it's the abundance of sexy men onboard that tempt us women to become permanent cruisers."

"Arrrrgh, I can agree with that." Sabine did her best—really awful—pirate imitation as she joined them.

Miguel, Archer, Waverly, and Captain Alex came to see what all the fuss was about.

"Did I hear we've got ourselves a new permanent cruiser?" Captain Alex asked warmly. When Kahori nodded, he squished her in a one-armed hug.

"You know, now that Kimo signed on to add a grow dome to his *motu*, we'll probably be making Aitutaki part of our regular rounds." Miguel shared the good news. She wondered if he'd been keeping it in his back pocket in case he needed to persuade her not to break Tosin's heart.

As if she could do that without also crushing her own.

Kahori looked around at the smiling faces that surrounded her with love, companionship, friendship, inspiration, support, and parental-esque advice. As sunset began to light the sky on fire, she couldn't imagine a more perfect way to finish one phase of her life and welcome in another. "Thank you all for making this the easiest decision of my life. Despite everything that's happened, and how quickly things changed, I'm sure that this is where I belong. With you. I hope you don't mind if I say I love you all. I'll be forever grateful to Banks and Archer, and the rest of you, for making this special project a reality."

Archer ruffled her hair as if she was his beloved little sister.

And when he turned around, Kahori noticed a sheen in Waverly's eyes. Pride in her boyfriend overwhelmed her.

"She's right, Archer. Without you—without what you've built—we'd all still be lost."

He cleared his throat as if searching for the right thing to say and faced Waverly. "You know, I didn't have very much to do with it. Banks deserves credit for both the brainstorming and the hard work that made the Divemaster Project and the Banks Foundation realities. But I have to say that I'm happier now than I've ever been in my life before and with you—everyone, but especially you, Waverly—by my side, each and every day will only get better. That's why..."

Archer reached into his pocket as he dropped to one knee in front of his soul mate and the rest of their makeshift family. Everyone gasped when he flipped open the lid of the jewelry box Kahori knew so well and exposed her creation to the final rays of the tropical sun.

The ring came alive, diamonds and fire opals reflecting the light, which enhanced the luster of the magnificent—definitely genuine—black pearl nestled at its center.

It was the perfect thing, at the perfect time, for the perfect people.

Kahori was convinced.

This had been meant to be.

She leaned into Tosin as Archer said to Waverly, "...I'm begging you. Please, marry me."

The socialite turned badass military pilot squealed like a little girl then flung herself at her boyfriend. No, fiancé. He steadied her long enough to slip the ring on her finger.

It was a perfect match, and a perfect fit.

As everyone oohed and aahed over Kahori's handiwork, congratulations were passed all around.

"I have a feeling we may become wedding experts before too long." Captain Alex snorted. "I just have one question..."

"What?" Archer asked suspiciously.

"Can I be the flower girl?" Captain Alex propped one hand on his hip and flashed a silly smile.

Though they laughed at the time, none of the guys let him back out of his commitment down the road.

And he made the prettiest flower girl ever. All four times he filled the role before taking Dr. Kleveno for a walk down the aisle.

ABOUT THE AUTHOR

Jayne Rylon is a *New York Times* and *USA Today* bestselling author. She received the 2011 RomanticTimes Reviewers' Choice Award for Best Indie Erotic Romance.

Her stories used to begin as daydreams in seemingly endless business meetings, but now she is a full-time author, who employs the skills she learned from her straight-laced corporate existence in the business of writing. She lives in Ohio with two cats and her husband, the infamous Mr. Rylon.

When she can escape her purple office, Jayne loves to travel the world, SCUBA dive, take pictures, avoid speeding tickets in her beloved Sky and—of course—read.